Unfortunately, before she could say one word, Alberta noticed something odd about the life-size snowwoman. It was supposed to be standing next to the snowman, but instead it was starting to tilt to the other side.

The other odd thing was that she was bleeding.

A thin stream of blood was running down the left side of the snowwoman's body.

Alberta got up, but before she could move toward the tableau to investigate the scene further, the snowwoman fell onto her left shoulder and rolled onto her back. Bambi looked annoyed at being upstaged by an oversize Christmas decoration, but her attitude changed when the snowwoman's body cracked open at the seam to reveal what had been hidden inside . . .

Books by J. D. Griffo

MURDER ON MEMORY LAKE

MURDER IN TRANQUILITY PARK

MURDER AT ICICLE LODGE

MURDER AT VERONICA'S DINER

MURDER AT ST. WINIFRED'S ACADEMY

MURDER AT THE MISTLETOE BALL

Published by Kensington Publishing Corp.

J. D. GRIFFO

A Ferrara Family Mystery

MURDER AT THE MISTLETOE BALL

KENSINGTON
PUBLISHING CORP.

www.kensingtonbooks.com

KENSINGTON BOOKS are published by

Kensington Publishing Corp.
119 West 40th Street
New York, NY 10018

All Kensington titles, imprints, and distributed lines are available at special quantity discounts for bulk purchases for sales promotion, premiums, fund-raising, educational, or institutional use.

Special book excerpts or customized printings can also be created to fit specific needs. For details, write or phone the office of the Kensington Sales Manager: Attn.: Sales Department. Kensington Publishing Corp., 119 West 40th Street, New York, NY 10018. Phone: 1-800-221-2647.

The K logo is a trademark of Kensington Publishing Corp.

First Printing: November 2021
ISBN: 978-1-4967-3097-8

ISBN: 978-1-4967-3098-5 (ebook)

10 9 8 7 6 5 4 3 2 1

Printed in the United States of America

This book is dedicated to all the people who
make me feel 'cozy.'
Some of them are family, some of them are friends,
all of them are loved.

Special thanks to the entire Kensington team for
their continued support of my work. And to my
agent, Evan Marshall, for his guidance all these years
and for starting me on this journey in the first place.

PROLOGUE

Stai attento a ciò che desideri.

Christmas would have to wait.
Traditionally, the day after Thanksgiving was the start of the holiday season. Around the world it was known as Black Friday, the day most people started their Christmas shopping. It was also known as the day of the year most people began to deck their halls, trim their tree, and commit acts of goodwill toward man, woman, and child in the hopes of not ending up on Santa's naughty list. But not this year, at least not for the Ferraras. This year would be different, and it was all because of Alberta's daughter. That's right, Lisa Marie Scaglione Maldonado had officially ruined the holiday season.

Truth be told, it wasn't the first time Lisa Marie did something that upended the family dynamic. Her actions were legendary and long-lasting. After a long respite, it seemed that history was about to repeat itself.

Anyone who knew Alberta knew about her tumultuous relationship with her daughter. They knew that she and Lisa Marie had always squabbled, they had always fought, they had always answered simple questions by yelling accusations, they simply did not get along. The family feud started when Lisa Marie was a toddler and only grew worse as she got older. When she was married and had a family of her own, Lisa Marie decided to put an end to the endless war and, one morning, moved her entire family from New Jersey to Florida.

It was a radical decision, but it achieved the desired result: the fighting stopped. There were no more arguments, no more hurtful comments, no more apologies to never again speak to the other in such a vicious tone of voice, no more lies, no more insinuations, no more relationship. Not only did Lisa Marie sever all ties with her home state, she severed all ties with her mother. The war between parent and child was over, but could either side label themselves victorious?

For fourteen years there was silence between mother and daughter. No telephone calls, no e-mails, no texts, no conversation whatsoever. Lisa Marie had become a daughter to Alberta in name only. As a result, Alberta only had minimal contact with her grandchildren, Jinx and Sergio, until Jinx moved back to New Jersey after graduating college. They quickly made up for lost time, and Alberta and Jinx were almost inseparable now, although Alberta's relationship with Sergio remained cursory. Birthday cards, an occasional phone call, a random text, little more. Still, it was better than the nonexistent relationship she had with her daughter.

That, however, was about to change thanks to four little words.

I need your help.

That's all that was written inside the card Alberta received with dozens of others after she made her stage debut, alongside her sister Helen, in a community theatre production of *Arsenic and Old Lace.* While the other cards congratulated her on her performance, wished her continued success in her next theatrical endeavor, and rambled on about how stellar the show was, the simple four-word sentence made the most impact.

There was no signature and no return address on the envelope, but Alberta knew who the sender was thanks to Sister Catherine, a teacher at St. Ann's Elementary School. The nun was passionate about penmanship and taught all her students the art of cursive writing. She believed handwriting was not merely a form of communication, but a way to present a flow of ideas in the most elegant way possible.

Many of the things learned in childhood are not easily forgotten, which was why Lisa Marie's capital *I*s still looked like *J*s. When Alberta saw her daughter's handwriting for the first time in over a decade, she was overcome with joy. A feeling that quickly transformed into dread.

After all these years, Alberta's estranged daughter had finally reached out to her. It should be a cause for celebration. How many nights had Alberta lain awake in bed, hoping Lisa Marie would finally break the silence that had grown between them? How many times had she seen a mother and daughter walking hand in hand, or having a meal at a restaurant, and wished that she and Lisa Marie could share such a moment that was so casual it wouldn't warrant a memory? More than ten years of silence—and silent wishes—were about to come to an end. So why did

Alberta feel as if her world was about to be turned upside down? Yet again.

The first time was several years ago, when she unexpectedly inherited her Aunt Carmela's house on Memory Lake as well as Carmela's fortune, which no one knew she had. Everyone in the family considered Carmela to be a spinster aunt living with her brother and surviving month to month on her Social Security checks. They had no idea she had somehow amassed three million dollars and a Cape Cod cottage in Tranquility, New Jersey, overlooking the crystal-blue water of Memory Lake, all of which she bequeathed to Alberta, her sole heir.

The difference was that Alberta never wished to be given her aunt's fortune, but she did wish to be given another chance with her daughter. Now that her wish seemed to be granted, Alberta was forced to ask herself if this was a wish that she truly wanted fulfilled. The answer seemed simple—of course she did, of course she wanted a reconciliation—but when it came to Lisa Marie, nothing was ever simple.

When Alberta first received the card a few days ago, she had been sitting around her kitchen table with family and friends eating Entenmann's desserts, drinking Red Herrings, which was a cocktail her granddaughter Jinx invented, and chatting about the show that had just closed. They didn't even have the opportunity to discuss the Thanksgiving dinner Alberta was hosting because Vinny, the chief of police and Alberta's childhood friend, burst into the house and slammed a bag filled with fan letters onto the table.

A few minutes later Alberta was staring at a card with

blue hydrangeas on the cover, the very same kind that grew in her backyard, and then at her daughter's words. Her heart began to race, her breath caught in her throat, her cheeks flushed. Because everyone knew the history between Alberta and Lisa Marie, no one pressured Alberta for an answer; they merely stared at her with anxious faces. They knew this was an unprecedented surprise and they knew Alberta needed time to absorb the shock. Lola, however, didn't possess such social graces.

Alberta's beloved cat, long, lean, and all black except for a patch of white above her left eye, was hungry, and she couldn't understand why her mother was more interested in the thing she was holding than in filling up her empty food dish. Something had to be done to rectify this unacceptable situation.

Lola jumped onto the kitchen table and rolled onto her back in an attempt to capture Alberta's attention. When that maneuver didn't elicit a response, she let out a meow that could've been heard on the other side of Memory Lake. It worked. The sound startled Alberta back to reality and made her realize that the world would keep on spinning even if she sat still.

"*Stai attento a ciò che desideria,*" she said, more to herself than her company.

"Why do you have to be careful, Gram?" Jinx asked. "Isn't this exactly what you've wished for, to be reunited with my mother?"

Alberta felt her mouth smile and her head nod more out of reflex than honesty, and she knew Jinx was right— this was what she had wished for. However, she also knew, as Eve must've known in the back of her mind before she bit into that apple, not every wish that comes true has a happy ending. Her feelings at the moment were complicated.

"It is, lovey," Alberta replied. "I'm just thrown, that's all."

"That's completely understandable," Sloan said. "This is quite the surprise."

Alberta could hear the compassion and strength in her boyfriend's voice and was grateful to have a good man like Sloan McLelland in her life. She was thankful for her family as well and could feel their positive energy reaching out to support her. When Lola meowed even louder, Alberta was relieved to have a diversion. She took a can of cat food from the cupboard, opened it, and started to dole it out onto a plate as Lola curved in and out of Alberta's legs. Alberta placed the plate on the floor and watched Lola dig in.

Preparing Lola's food had been a slight reprieve, but when Alberta watched Lola eat, she thought once again of her daughter. Lola's patch of white fur reminded Alberta of the birthmark next to Lisa Marie's right eye. She had never made the connection before, but there it was, clear as day. Unlike her daughter's cryptic message.

"I can't imagine what Lisa Marie needs from me after all this time," Alberta said.

"There's an easy way to find out," Jinx said. "I'll call my mother."

Three voices combined as one to shout the same answer: "No."

Alberta didn't have to look around the room to know that Helen and Joyce's were the other two voices that joined in with hers. Without discussing it, Alberta knew that the two women understood what she was feeling, they understood the depth of pain and confusion she was currently experiencing. As much as Alberta loved her granddaughter, Jinx was still too young, and in many ways too naïve, to understand how a missive from a long-lost relative could ignite such turmoil.

"Why not?" Jinx asked. "I can ask my mother and we'll find out exactly why she sent you that card."

"Because your grandmother isn't ready to know that just yet," Joyce explained.

Jinx had grown very close to Alberta and her aunts these past few years, even though there was a substantial gap in their ages. Most of the time it served as a benefit, each teaching the other something new. Other times, like now, Jinx felt they spoke a different language.

"Gram's been waiting fourteen years for this to happen," Jinx said. "How can she not be ready?"

"There's really no way to prepare yourself for something like this," Alberta said.

"I know it won't be easy, Gram, but my mother made the first move, now it's your turn."

"That's exactly the problem."

As was often the case, Helen Ferrara's simple proclamation silenced the room. It was a combination of her gruff voice, her concise vocabulary, and her no-frills approach that made people listen to the subtext of what she said and not just her words. In four more words, Helen made everyone understand that as the mother—and particularly an Italian mother—Alberta felt that she should have been the one to reach out to her daughter in an attempt to repair the damage and destruction that had occurred between them, and not the other way around. Alberta was embarrassed that her daughter did what she should have done many years ago.

Although Sloan had no interest in controlling Alberta and never felt the need to assert his manhood by playing a traditional masculine role, he understood that this was one of those moments where he needed to swoop in and assert his authority to save the woman he loved from what was becoming an uncomfortable situation.

"I think it's time for everyone to go."

In response to Sloan's suggestion, the group muttered their agreement and started to leave the kitchen.

"I'm sorry, Gram. I thought this was what you wanted."

"It is, lovey," Alberta replied, grabbing Jinx's hand. "But sometimes when you finally get what you want . . . it's terrifying."

The one thing Jinx had learned while being in her grandmother's company was the importance of looking at the world through other people's eyes and not just myopically through your own. She thought her mother reaching out was a joyful miracle, but she understood her grandmother could feel differently. Jinx hugged Alberta tightly and kissed her on the cheek before leaving.

When it was just Sloan and Alberta, he sat in the chair next to hers and held her hand. She brought his hand up to her lips and kissed it. She held it there, and soon it was wet with her tears.

Now, several days later, nothing had changed. Alberta still hadn't worked up the courage to reach out to her daughter and she still didn't know why she needed her help. The only thing she did know was what her every instinct told her: This was going to be a Christmas no one would ever forget.

CHAPTER 1

La casa che giace costruita.

It felt like the North Pole.

Alberta was sitting in one of the Adirondack chairs in her backyard, facing Memory Lake, the quilt her mother made for her sister Helen when she left home to enter the convent wrapped around her. The design was an elaborate display of squares, triangles, and circles in a rainbow of colors and patterns, with an underside that was lined in light blue fleece. Elena Ferrara had stitched in a photo of the Blessed Mother, along with the words to the Hail Mary, so Helen would always feel connected to her religion. At some point over the years, the hand-made heirloom came into Alberta's possession. Her mother must have known she would need its comfort one day.

Elena knew that neither of her daughters needed a reminder to embrace their spirituality, but part of a mother's job was acting as a *rete di sicurezza*, a safety net, in case her child faltered. It was what Alberta was being asked to do now for her own daughter. Maybe it was because she had spent the past several years reinventing herself—becoming self-reliant, becoming someone's girlfriend, reintroducing herself to Jinx as her grandmother—but for whatever the reason, Alberta was suddenly having difficulty imagining herself in the role she'd played almost her entire adult life—that of the mother.

Half asleep, Lola squirmed in her lap, and Alberta rubbed the cat's soft black fur reassuringly. She looked at the card that she held in her other hand and wondered if it was a coincidence that the blue hydrangeas on the cover were the same as the ones that flourished in her backyard each spring, or if Lisa Marie intuitively knew that fact. Perhaps Jinx had mentioned it to her when she was describing Alberta's house to her mother and Lisa Marie thought it would personalize her plea for help.

"Ah *Madon*." Alberta sighed, shaking her head at her own stupidity. She knew her daughter had picked the card at random and didn't give any thought as to what was on the cover. Lisa Marie could not be described as sentimental.

Similarly, Alberta had not been old-world maternal. She loved her children unconditionally, but as a realist, Alberta recognized their flaws and weaknesses and didn't sugarcoat them with the delusion that her offspring were perfect. Just as she knew exactly who she was, Alberta knew exactly who her children were. And as painful as it was to admit it, both Lisa Marie and her younger brother, Rocco, took after their father.

After thirty-two hours of agonizing labor, Alberta finally gave birth to her daughter. Alberta was so exhausted and relieved to be on the other side of her first pregnancy that it took her a few moments to realize that her child hadn't yet made a sound. No wailing cries filled the delivery room, only silence.

Exhausted and drenched in sweat, Alberta searched for clues in the faces of the doctor and the nurses. Why wasn't her child screaming? Why wasn't the room bustling with activity? Weren't they supposed to be placing her baby in her arms?

Immediately, Alberta feared the worst and believed her child was stillborn. The child she carried for nine months, the child she had just pushed into the world would not be her child after all. Not in the real sense, not in the sense that mattered. Despair was only demolished when a loud scream erupted that filled the room with glorious sound. Lisa Marie was alive and well but had decided to take her time in announcing her arrival.

Her cries continued after the nurse placed her in Alberta's arms and didn't stop until twenty minutes later, when Sammy, fed up with listening to his daughter screaming, took Lisa Marie from Alberta's arms and was about to give his child to the nurse with the instructions "to do something to make it stop" when silence once again filled the room. Cradled in her father's arms, Lisa Marie stopped crying and within a few seconds was sleeping. Sammy was filled with pride, but Alberta felt betrayed. Lisa Marie was clearly her father's daughter.

Sammy Scaglione wasn't a bad father, not by any means, but he wasn't the best role model either. He had been dismissive, a bit of a drinker, and demeaning. But the worst of Sammy's traits that Lisa Marie inherited was his ability to lie with ease.

The first lie Alberta caught Lisa Marie telling occurred when her daughter was four years old. Alberta was home with the two kids and was suffering from a stomach flu. She placed Rocco, who was not yet a year old, on her bed and surrounded him with pillows as he took his nap so he wouldn't roll off while Alberta was in the bathroom. Earlier, Lisa Marie had been jumping on the bed, but Alberta yelled at her to stop because she might wake up Rocco or, worse, hurt him if she fell. Of course, while Alberta was out of the room, she heard a thump, and when she raced back into the bedroom, she saw Rocco was on the floor and Lisa Marie was sitting on the edge of the bed, watching television.

When Alberta admonished her daughter for disobeying her, Lisa Marie had looked away from the TV screen and directly into her mother's eyes. She didn't blink. Instead, she expertly and effortlessly lied to cover up her role in her brother's accident.

"I wasn't jumping," she had said. "Rocco rolled over and fell on the floor. I didn't pick him up because I heard you coming and didn't want to hurt him."

Alberta felt as if an unknown force was poking a finger in her back, telling her to watch out for this one. And, indeed, she had.

Over the years the lies had continued, and Alberta remembered an incident when Lisa Marie was eight years old. She sent her daughter to the corner grocery store to buy bread and milk as a way for Lisa Marie to gain independence and learn how to make her way in the world. When she returned, Alberta found candy in the pocket of her jacket.

"Lisa, did you buy candy at the store?" Alberta had asked.

When Lisa Marie turned to look at her mother, it was

with the same calm, irreproachable expression that had become her trademark.

"No," she replied. "Mr. Terranova gave it to me for being such a good girl, doing the shopping for my mother."

The next day, when Alberta was picking up some tomatoes and fresh basil, she thanked Mr. Terranova for being so kind to her daughter but asked him to please not make it a habit to give her candy because she had two cavities at her last dental visit. Mr. Terranova explained that he thought Lisa Marie was well-behaved, but he didn't give her candy as a reward. Alberta put an extra dollar in the March of Dimes collection can before she left.

One of Lisa Marie's more audacious lies took place while she was a junior at Immaculate Conception High School. At sixteen, Lisa Marie was not yet a woman, but she felt that if she didn't raise the hem of her school skirt as high as the Catholic church would allow, she would forever remain a child. Alberta vehemently disagreed and thought her daughter's skirt hem was perfect skimming her knee. Lisa Marie, on the other hand, felt that if her mother wouldn't allow her to change the length of her skirt, she'd change schools.

Unbeknownst to her parents, Lisa Marie made an appointment with the new principal of Hoboken High School. She explained that her family had just moved to New Jersey from Sicily and because her parents didn't speak any English, she had come to enroll herself in the school. If it wasn't for Rafaella DeFilippo, the principal's secretary and, luckily, Alberta's cousin's brother-in-law's wife, Lisa Marie would've been Hoboken High's newest student.

Resigned, Alberta gave Lisa Marie an impromptu

sewing lesson, and she went to Immaculate Conception the next day with her skirt two inches higher. She showed more leg to her envious classmates, but she showed her mother her true colors. Alberta could no longer dismiss Lisa Marie's lies as a phase or a natural part of childhood; she was forced to admit that her daughter was deceitful. She wasn't beyond saving—hardly—but from her vantage point, Alberta saw more bad than good in her daughter.

What made matters worse was that Sammy thought his little girl was an angel. No matter what Alberta and Lisa Marie were arguing about, whether it was unfinished homework or an unfulfilled promise, Sammy always took his daughter's side. She could do no wrong in his eyes and he felt Alberta was too strict, too old-fashioned, and the one who needed to bend. It created a rift in the family and brought out a not-so-pretty side of Alberta.

Sammy's comments directly confronted every one of Alberta's insecurities. His words reinforced her belief that she wasn't a good mother, that peace and happiness weren't attainable, that life was meant to be endured, not celebrated. She hated how strong the bond was between Sammy and Lisa Marie and, as a result, she hated herself for harboring such a hateful thought. A father and daughter should be close, but not at the sacrifice of the mother. Their relationship was built on the fact that they both disregarded Alberta, they both categorized her as the villain in the family. For a time, Alberta was more than willing to play that role.

Lisa Marie had rejected Alberta's maternal instincts, so Alberta tried other tactics to communicate with her daughter. She was sarcastic when she should have been compassionate, dismissive when she should have been interested, short-fused instead of patient. It was a poor strategy and only succeeded in pushing Alberta and Lisa Marie further away from each other.

Things got worse in Lisa Marie's senior year of high school, when she announced she wasn't going to college but was going to marry Tommy Maldonado. Both Alberta and Sammy were surprised by the announcement because they didn't think she and Tommy were that close, but after the shock of finding out that wedding bells would quickly follow the pomp and circumstance of graduation, Sammy accepted the idea. Tommy came from a good family, he had never been in trouble with the police, and he was going to be an electrician, which was a secure job that would allow him to provide for Lisa Marie. As far as Sammy was concerned, that was all a man had to do. Alberta, however, thought there was much more for a woman to do.

Alberta wanted her daughter to have the opportunities and options she never had. She instinctively knew that if Lisa Marie married Tommy, her daughter would have the same life that she had with Sammy. And she wanted so much more for her child.

"Why do you have to rush into marriage?" Alberta had asked. "You're not even out of high school."

"You got married right after high school," Lisa Marie replied.

"Not *right* after," Alberta corrected. "I worked at the Kleinfeld Insurance Agency."

"For like a month."

"*Six* months."

"And you said you hated every second of it. Look, Ma, just because you're unhappy in your marriage doesn't mean I'm going to be unhappy in mine."

"I'm not unhappy!"

"Bull! I don't know why you just don't divorce Daddy."

"*Dio mio*! Because when you get married it's for life, those are the vows you take."

"Trust me, Ma, the Catholic church isn't gonna crumble to the ground if you and Daddy call it quits. The Pope's not gonna lose any sleep over one more failed marriage."

"Our marriage isn't a failure!"

"It's a joke! I don't know if you ever loved each other, but you sure don't love each other now."

"*Basta!*" Alberta cried. "Watch your mouth when you talk to me!"

Lisa Marie stared right into her mother's eyes and smirked. "You might want to take your own advice."

Even though Lisa Marie had made her intention to marry Tommy the following spring imminently clear and even wore his engagement ring—which Alberta told Helen was only visible if it was viewed underneath a magnifying glass—Alberta hadn't given up hope that her daughter might choose an alternative path after she graduated from high school. With all good intentions but without her daughter's knowledge, Alberta applied to several colleges on Lisa Marie's behalf. When her daughter found out what she did, Alberta didn't receive Lisa Marie's blessing.

"You did what?" Lisa Marie screamed.

"I applied to a few schools for you, that's all," Alberta explained. "You make it sound as if I went behind your back."

"That's exactly what you did, Ma! I told you, I'm not going to college."

"But you got into Rutgers *and* Montclair State."

"No, I didn't, *you* did! Because you forged my name on the application!"

"And I wrote you a very good essay too, don't forget that."

"Trust me, Ma, I'm never going to forget that!"

Lisa Marie leafed through the papers that had come in the mail from Montclair State College. The acceptance letter, the course brochure, the financial aid packet. She stopped when she got to a copy of the essay that bore her name but not her thoughts.

"'*The main reason I want to attend Montclair State is because of my mother*,'" Lisa Marie said. With every word that she recited, she mocked Alberta. It was evident that the essay had nothing to do with Lisa Marie's desire for a higher education and everything to do with Alberta's desperation for her daughter to have the kind of life Alberta never could.

"'*She's instilled in me a sense of purpose and conviction so I could achieve more than she ever could. It's only because of her that I have the courage to reach my dreams.*'"

When Lisa Marie was finished, she threw the papers in her mother's face. Both women were furious. Lisa Marie because she felt her mother had betrayed her and Alberta because she felt her daughter was betraying herself.

"This isn't my dream, Ma, it's yours!" Lisa Marie yelled. "You want me to live the life you didn't have the guts to live!"

"What's wrong with a parent wanting their child to have a better life?"

"Nothing! But you don't get to decide what I do with my life!"

"I'm not trying to do that! I'm trying to show you that

you can do things other than get married and have children."

"Stop lying, Ma! We both know that you resent being a wife and mother and you wish to God every single day of your life that you had done something else with your life!"

Alberta wanted to disagree with her daughter, but she couldn't. They both knew that Lisa Marie was right.

After that incident, it was obvious by the way he acted that Sammy noticed the rift between his wife and daughter had deepened, but neither one told him the source of the tension. Alberta didn't confess because she was ashamed, and she assumed Lisa Marie kept quiet to use that piece of information against her at a future date. It was a thought that filled Alberta with even more shame.

Sitting underneath the quilt, Alberta shivered. November had been a colder-than-usual month and, according to the *Farmers' Almanac*, which Alberta still trusted more than the local weatherman, winter was going to come early. It prompted another memory, this one of the last Christmas before Lisa Marie got married.

As had become the norm, a harmless exchange of words turned into an argument. Lisa Marie and Alberta were decorating their tree, the same store-bought tree they'd been decorating since Lisa Marie was a toddler. That year, Lisa Marie only wanted to use silver and white decorations. She had seen the window display of a department store in New York and wanted to replicate the chic, elegant look in their own home. Alberta thought it sounded pretty but pointed out that if they adopted that color scheme, they wouldn't be able to use the gold star topper that Alberta's grandmother gave her for the first Christmas she was married.

"So what?" Lisa Marie replied. "The woman's dead, just like your marriage to Daddy."

Alberta looked into Lisa Marie's eyes, searching for regret, remorse, even hatred, but couldn't find anything. Her daughter believed what she said and didn't think there was anything wrong in saying it. She didn't consider what the words would mean to her mother; she didn't consider her mother at all.

Sammy was surprised that the tree that year was trimmed with only silver and white decorations, but he said he liked it better and didn't notice they also used a different topper. It was a white angel in a thick silver robe that Tommy had given to Lisa Marie. Alberta lied and said she thought it was very pretty. Lisa Marie lied and said she was sad it was going to be the last Christmas she'd celebrate at home. Sammy lied and said he was going to miss the constant bickering that would end after Lisa Marie left the house.

"*La casa che giace costruita*," Alberta had muttered to herself.

She held Lola up to her face and rubbed her cheek on her smooth fur.

"A house of lies," Alberta said. "That's what it was, Lola."

Another shiver gripped her spine. She wasn't cold; she was scared because she knew that some of those lies were on their way home.

CHAPTER 2

L'attesa è la parte più difficile.

Alberta knew she was in trouble when she saw two wise women enter her backyard bearing gifts. Helen and Joyce stood in front of Alberta, holding bags from the Tranquility Diner, and despite the emotional strain she was under, Alberta smiled because the women only traveled together when they had a mission, and they only brought food when they thought Alberta was too upset to cook. It lifted her spirits to see that the two women had joined forces on her behalf. It wasn't an everyday occurrence.

Alberta's sister and sister-in-law had grown much closer these past few years. Every once in a while, the friction that had outlined their relationship would bubble to the surface, but mainly the two women had learned to embrace their differences. And there were many.

As a former nun, Helen had taken a vow of poverty, while Joyce, a retired Wall Street investment banker, had made a fortune. Helen's wardrobe consisted primarily of calf-length dresses in various shades of gray like her hair, black shoes with sensible heels, and her black pocket-book, which she was never without, while Joyce's wardrobe took up a guest room in her house and contained designer couture from the last seven decades. Helen was diminutive, pale, and blunt, whereas Joyce was full-figured, African American, and polite. They were an odd pairing, but time and a little understanding on both their parts had brought them closer together. Their love for Alberta brought them to her backyard.

"What are you doing here so early?" Alberta asked, looking at her watch. "*Dio mio*! It's barely seven o'clock."

"You've been up all night, haven't you?" Helen asked.

"Maybe," Alberta replied.

"And you didn't have any dinner or breakfast," Joyce said.

"Maybe," Alberta repeated.

"I know you've been thrown a curve, Berta," Helen said. "But you still have to eat."

"What did you bring?" Alberta asked.

"French toast, sausage, a side of hash browns, a stack of silver dollar pancakes, and fresh blueberry croissants," Helen replied.

"Also too, Kwon may be from Korea, but he makes the most delicious Greek omelets," Joyce added. "Feta cheese and kalamata olives, it's my new favorite."

"I am a little hungry. I guess I could nibble," Alberta said. "But who's Kwon?"

"Kwon Lee, the new owner and chef of the Tranquility Diner," Joyce replied.

"Right, sorry," Alberta said. "My mind is elsewhere."

"Could we get elsewhere before the food gets cold?" Helen asked.

"Go inside, the door's unlocked," Alberta said, rising from her chair.

As Helen passed by Alberta, she said, "And don't think I haven't noticed you're snuggled underneath my quilt."

"Possession is nine tenths of the law, Helen," Alberta remarked.

"It's on loan, Berta!" Helen cried.

Once inside, Joyce and Helen hung up their coats on the hooks next to the door. Joyce's burnt orange cape in bright contrast to Helen's black parka. They transferred the contents of the bags to plates, and Helen poured them all coffee from the pot that was being kept warm in Alberta's Mr. Coffee machine. It was a vintage kitchen accessory, but one that Alberta couldn't live without.

Joyce cut up a sausage link and half an omelet and put it on a plate for Lola. She daintily ate her breakfast, while Alberta, who was hungrier than she realized, didn't come up for air until she finished three links of sausage, two pancakes, and a slice of French toast. Helen refilled their coffee cups and cut one of the blueberry croissants in thirds so they could all share. Helen and Joyce immediately started to eat the buttery pastry, but Alberta stared at hers for a moment, as if she had forgotten how to eat.

"What should I do?" Alberta asked.

Both women knew she was talking about Lisa Marie.

"The only thing you can do, Berta, is call her to find out why she needs your help," Helen said.

"How can I call her after all this time?" Alberta asked.

"Because she reached out to you," Joyce replied. "According to her note, she needs you to call her."

"I'm her mother, I should've called her years ago!"

"You tried and she only picked up once to tell you to stop calling her," Helen said. "We were there, remember? We know what happened."

"What happened was that I didn't try harder," Alberta said. "I should've flown down to Florida and forced her to come home."

"That would've been a stupid thing to do and you know it," Helen said.

"Helen's right, Berta," Joyce said. "Lisa Marie didn't leave in a huff; her departure was contemplated and planned. When she left you, she left for good."

"Ah *Madon*!" Alberta cried. "The two of you aren't making me feel better."

"Because you're playing the martyr and it doesn't suit you," Helen said. "Don't you remember what Gandhi said?"

"No, Helen, I don't," Alberta said sarcastically. "Why don't you remind me?"

"*Nessuno brami il martirio,*" Helen replied.

"Gandhi said that?" Alberta asked.

"Yes. He was the biggest martyr of them all, but he said no one should lust for martyrdom, so knock it off!" Helen cried.

"I'm not doing any such thing," Alberta protested.

"Berta, I know this has made you question your role as

a mother," Joyce said. "But your daughter was the one who packed up and left."

"She severed ties with the entire family," Helen said. "She wouldn't even see me when I took the girls at St. Dominick's to Disney World on their senior trip."

"She doesn't live anywhere near Disney World," Alberta said.

"I told her I would take a side trip on the way home, and do you know what your daughter said?" Helen asked. "She told me she didn't need one of her mother's spies checking in on her."

"*Dio mio*!" Alberta cried. "You never told me that."

"Because I don't like to talk bad about people!" Helen cried. "Now, were you the sweetest, most patient, understanding mother who ever lived? Of course you weren't. But Lisa Marie was hardly the nicest, most considerate, innocent child either. Back in her heyday, that kid of yours could've given Patty McCormack a run for her money."

"You're saying Lisa Marie was a *seme cattivo*?" Alberta asked.

"I think calling her a 'bad seed' might be a bit harsh," Joyce said. "But a woman who cuts off ties with her entire family isn't exactly Little Mary Sunshine."

"No child is perfect," Alberta said.

"And neither is any parent," Helen added. "I don't approve of the passive-aggressive way she's reached out to you now, but I also don't approve of your sulking and second-guessing yourself."

"I second that," Joyce said. "About the second-guessing."

"For whatever reason, your daughter has contacted you, and no matter how painful it might be, you have no choice but to accept her olive branch," Helen said.

"That's just it," Joyce replied. "Maybe Lisa Marie didn't reach out."

"I know Lisa Marie hasn't written to me in years, but I know my daughter's handwriting," Alberta said.

"There was no return address, and did you notice the postage mark?" Joyce asked.

"No," Alberta said. "What's so special about the postage mark?"

"The card came from Virginia, not Florida," Joyce replied.

"That doesn't make sense," Helen said.

"No, it doesn't," Alberta said. "I hate to say it, but now I'm starting to second-guess myself. Maybe it wasn't from Lisa Marie after all."

"There's only one way to find out, Berta," Helen said. "Give your daughter a call."

It took Alberta several hours to work up the courage. Finally, around eight o'clock, she sat on her living room couch, stared at the photos of her family and friends that hung on the opposite wall, and made sure that Lola was comfortable in her lap. She said a quick Hail Mary and crossed herself before punching ten numbers into her cell phone that she had never dialed before.

Her heart started to pound and somewhere in the back of her head she knew that she should try to control her breathing by inhaling deeply and exhaling slowly, but that information stayed buried, and in its place, panic rose to the forefront of her mind. In a matter of seconds, the many years of silence were about to come to an end and Alberta wasn't sure if she was ready to hear her daughter's voice after such a long time. Then a terrible thought entered her mind, a thought no mother should ever have to contemplate: Would she even recognize her daughter's voice? She shuddered. Yes, of course she'd recognize her daughter's voice; she knew the handwriting was Lisa Marie's, so she'd definitely know her voice. Wouldn't she?

The phone rang a third time and Alberta wondered what she would do when Lisa Marie picked up. Would she be filled with joy or would Alberta only hear the shouts and screams that used to fly out of Lisa Marie's mouth at the slightest provocation? Would Alberta find the strength to speak or just cry, knowing that she was making contact with her daughter after so many years? All those questions would go unanswered because when the ringing stopped Alberta didn't hear Lisa Marie's voice; she only heard an automated recording announcing that the person at this number wasn't able to take the call. It was as if Alberta had been punched in the stomach. When she heard the beep indicating it was her turn to talk, Alberta discovered that she was unable to speak and hung up.

Her entire body was tingling—from toe to head it felt as if an electric shock was reverberating underneath her skin. Alberta had looked into the face of fear, but there was no image staring back at her. One second her daughter was there and then she wasn't.

"Why did Lisa Marie ask for my help if she wasn't going to pick up her phone when I called?" Alberta asked the empty room.

Lola meowed in response and rolled on her back, expecting Alberta to rub her belly as she always did, but Lola didn't get her wish. Instead, Alberta redialed Lisa Marie's number, and this time when the call went to voice mail, she was no longer afraid, she was no longer nervous, she was simply a mother who wanted to speak to her daughter.

"Lisa Marie, this is your mother."

Alberta's voice was clear and strong.

"I got your card that you sent me . . . which was a very nice surprise."

Some of the bravado was beginning to slip away and doubt was creeping in.

"You said you needed my help, so I'm calling to offer you that . . . my help."

Then all Alberta's strength was gone; the only thing left was her longing to make contact and her fear that things were far worse than she'd initially imagined.

"Call me, Lisa Marie, anytime, just call me . . . so I can help you."

Luckily, Alberta had nothing more to say because the sob she was holding back erupted with such force that she couldn't speak. She couldn't breathe, she couldn't think, all she could do was cry. She cried for the lost years Lisa Marie was out of her life that she would never get back, she cried for giving in to the cowardice that kept her from reaching out to her daughter, and she cried because she intuitively knew that Lisa Marie was in danger. But how could she help her if she didn't pick up the phone?

She called a third time, and once again the call went to voice mail.

"*L'attesa è la parte più difficile*," Alberta whispered.

She was right—the waiting was the hardest part, after

she had waited fourteen years to hear her daughter's voice again. Instead of redialing, she called someone she knew would pick up immediately. Once again, she was wrong.

Usually when Alberta called her granddaughter, Jinx picked up within seconds. It didn't matter if she was at work, on a date with her boyfriend Freddy, or relaxing on the couch binging her favorite TV show, her grandmother's phone call or text always took precedence. Which was why Freddy found it so odd that Jinx was staring at her phone and not answering it.

"Dude, aren't you going to answer?" Freddy asked, looking at Jinx's phone to see who was calling. "It's your Gram."

"I can't," Jinx replied.

"Why not?"

"Because I'm afraid."

"Afraid of your Gram? That's ridiculous."

"Is it? After what I said the other night, she must hate me. I literally opened up a can of family worms and let them crawl all over the kitchen table while everybody watched. I made my grandmother feel like an idiot."

"You said what was on everyone's mind, and your grandmother respects your honesty. Plus, it wasn't a literal can of worms because that would've been gross even to me and I love to fish."

"I'm sure she thinks I'm taking my mother's side in their stupid feud."

Jinx wasn't crying, but her green eyes were starting to well up. She sat hunched over the couch, her long, wavy black hair falling on both sides of her face, cell phone hanging loosely in her hand, and she was staring off into the distance. Freddy put his arm around his girlfriend and pulled her close to him.

"Your grandmother isn't mad at you. All you did the other night was get caught up in the excitement of a potential mother-daughter reunion starring your mother and her mother, and you didn't stop to think that maybe your mother's out-of-the-blue shout-out brought up some not-so-pleasant memories for your mother's mother."

Jinx pulled away and smiled at Freddy. She was confused about why her mother suddenly reached out, she was nervous that her grandmother wasn't happy with her, but she was certain about how she felt about her boyfriend; she was in love. She loved everything about Freddy, from his floppy ears to his inability to stop calling her *dude* to his undying support of her and her family. If she couldn't trust him, she could trust no one.

She kissed him on the lips and pressed a button on her phone. Freddy kissed her cheek and got up from the couch. "I'll give you two some privacy."

As he closed the bedroom door, Alberta answered.

"Lovey, I need your help," Alberta blurted out.

"*My* help?" Jinx replied. "I thought you were mad at me."

"Why would I be mad at you?"

"The other night when I was, you know, kind of insensitive and told you to just call my mother."

"First of all, I could never be mad at you, and second of all, you were right, that's what I should've done from the start. But I did finally call your mother and it went straight to voice mail."

"The same thing happened to me."

"You called your mother too?"

"Several times after the card arrived, and she hasn't called me back either, or returned my texts."

"She probably knows why you're calling her and doesn't want to put you in the middle of whatever game she's playing."

Alberta rose from the couch so quickly she sent poor Lola scrambling to land on her feet. The cat scurried into the kitchen as Alberta began to pace the living room floor. She was beginning to understand exactly what was going on.

"That's it!" Alberta cried. "Why else would she send me a card? I mean, who does that? If she really needed my help, she would've called me like a normal person, but she doesn't need my help, she wants revenge!"

"My mother doesn't want revenge! And if she did, she would've done it a long time ago. I know it's been a while, but you must remember my mother is not a patient woman."

"Then what could it be? Why isn't she answering my call?"

Another thing Jinx had learned from her grandmother, as well as her aunts, was the importance of telling the truth, especially when it came to family. Relationships were only as strong as the foundations they were built on, and if lies and half-truths were part of the structural mix, the bonds would break. The only problem with telling the truth was that sometimes the other person had to hear things that could hurt them.

"She's probably not answering your call because she doesn't recognize your phone number. If you text her and identify yourself, I bet you she'll respond."

The truth of Jinx's words stung, but Alberta was grateful her granddaughter respected her enough to speak to her without caution. She was even more grateful to know Jinx hadn't acquired her mother's perfidious nature. But she was most grateful of all that Jinx stayed on the line with her while she sent a text to Lisa Marie, identifying herself, because when her daughter didn't immediately respond, Alberta started to panic.

"She has to know the text is from me, I'm her only mother!"

"Give it some time, Gram, maybe she's in the shower."

"Does your mother take showers at night?"

"Well, no, but maybe she changed her routine."

"No maybes . . . I'm sorry Jinx, but this doesn't make any sense."

"Yes, it does, Gram."

"Then why am I on the phone with you instead of your mother?"

"Because she must really be in trouble."

The words slowly sank in and Alberta was finally able to shake off her guilt, shame, and anger so the only thing that remained within her mind and her heart was the truth. Her daughter was in trouble and she needed her help.

"Meet me at the police station."

Less than fifteen minutes later, Alberta flung open the doors to the Tranquility Police Station to find Jinx and Vinny D'Angelo, the chief of police and her lifelong friend, waiting for her. Despite the late hour, activity buzzed all around her, but Alberta didn't see or hear anything; she was focused on the mission at hand.

"Vinny, I think Lisa's in serious trouble."

"I know, Jinx filled us in," Vinny replied.

"Then don't just stand there!" Alberta shouted. "Look for her!"

Vinny understood why Alberta was yelling and didn't take offense. His friend was frightened—and Sicilian after all—so he was going to do everything he could to calm her fears.

"Alfie, we're already on it," Vinny said. "The Eufala police are going to check on the house and get right back to me."

"Vinny is also checking the hospitals, Gram," Jinx said. "And . . ."

"I did a search for all the people killed in the last week in Florida," Vinny said, finishing the sentence Jinx couldn't.

Alberta kissed the gold crucifix around her neck and made the sign of the cross. She didn't want to know the results of the search, but she had to ask. "What did you find out?"

"Neither Lisa Marie nor Tommy Maldonado show up on hospital admittance forms or any S7 codes, which is the Florida code to report a death," Vinny said.

"Thank God!" Jinx cried.

When the tension in Alberta's face wasn't replaced with relief, Vinny knew something was wrong.

"What is it, Berta?" he asked.

"Try Sergio Maldonado," Alberta said. "My grandson."

"Oh my God, Gram!" Jinx cried. "I didn't even think about him."

"I'm sure he's fine, lovey, but he lives with your parents and, well, let's just make sure they're all safe."

Alberta gripped the edge of Vinny's desk so tightly it looked like her fingers might break. The three of them remained silent as they waited for the results of Vinny's new search. Around them, telephones rang, cops called out to one another, a radio was playing softly in the distance, but it was as if none of those sounds existed, nothing else mattered except the information they were waiting to receive.

When Vinny's cell phone pinged again it was as if an atom bomb went off in the room.

"Nothing!" Vinny yelled. "His name doesn't show up anywhere either."

"*Grazie Dio*!" Alberta exclaimed.

Jinx grabbed Alberta's hand and fought back tears. She knew that she should be elated, but something wasn't right. Her family might not be dead, they might not be in an emergency room waiting to be wheeled into surgery, but Jinx knew they were still in danger; she could feel it. Alberta squeezed Jinx's hand to give her granddaughter some reassurance even though she shared her fears. From the look on their faces, it was obvious they were still very concerned.

"Alfie, this is good news," Vinny said.

"Ah *Madonna mia*!" Alberta exclaimed. "This is *not* good news."

"What are you talking about?" Vinny asked. "We have confirmation that they're not dead or in the hospital."

"Which brings us right back to where we started," Alberta said. "We still have no idea where my daughter and her family are."

"Which means we have no idea what kind of trouble they're in," Jinx added.

Vinny stared at the two women he had grown so fond of these past few years. He took a deep breath and placed his hands on their shoulders.

"Then my team and I won't stop looking until we find them," Vinny said. "And on that you have my word."

Alberta knew Vinny's word was good, but she still had the feeling that whatever was happening to her daughter was very bad.

CHAPTER 3

Tanto va la gatta al lardo che ci lascia lo zampino.

The Christmas season would be nothing without hope. Hope for peace throughout the world. Hope for an end to mankind's suffering. Hope that Jinx could sneak into church without attracting Father Sal's attention. There was a better chance of the first two happening, because the third was at the mercy of the priest's trained eagle eye.

Standing in the middle of the altar at the top of the steps, Father Sal commanded the stage. He raised his arms to allow his Kelly green vestments to hang in their full glory from his sides. As he walked toward the marble column to his left, his robes rose a few inches off the ground, exposing his ruby red slippers, the gold buckle matching perfectly with the rings that adorned his fingers. His jet-black hair with its streaks of gray at the temple and his thick, black-framed retro glasses combined to give him the look of a slightly aging peacock. One who liked to command his flock.

On top of the column was a candelabra that held four candles, three purple and one pink. Elaborately, he lit a match and lit one of the purple candles because it was the first Sunday of Advent, one of the holiest days in the Catholic religion. The candle was lit for God's people and represented hope. For all of Sal's ostentatiousness, he completely believed in the sacraments of the church. He also believed in the public's desire to be led by a colorful personality.

"Before I let you go to celebrate the first week of Advent on this beautiful though brisk Sunday morning, remember to check out the St. Winifred's newsletter for all the details about the return of the Mistletoe Ball, which is guaranteed to be the must-see event this holiday," Father Sal said. "Oh, and anyone who can pull off an old-school Gucci teal and purple tracksuit with Adidas' hottest new canary yellow running shoe is welcome in my church any time."

He turned his back on the congregation, then quickly turned around again, making his vestments sway with the movement, and grinned. "Except next time, Jinx, try to make it here before my homily. That really is the best part."

Every head in the church turned to look at Jinx, who was sitting on the aisle in a back pew next to Alberta, Helen, and Joyce. Some made their disapproval known by tsk-tsking Jinx's tardiness, while the more fashion-friendly parishioners gave Jinx the thumbs-up. Alberta, however, was not amused.

"Lovey, you're late and you're wearing a tracksuit to mass," Alberta said.

"Betcha it came from Joyce's closet," Helen said.

"Indeed, it did," Joyce replied. "It's from the eighties and one hundred percent velour."

"You look cute, but you still shouldn't waltz into church two minutes before the end of mass," Alberta said.

"Sorry, Gram," Jinx said. "I went for my morning run but spent most of the time trying to reach my family. Not one of them has gotten back to me and it's making me scared and angry and I am officially starting to freak out!"

Father Sal stopped in the aisle when he got to their pew and raised his arms, once again giving breath to his vestments. He knew all the women very well and could tell from their expressions and the volume of their voices that they needed his guidance.

"Ladies, if you need a quiet place to chitchat," he said. "Follow me."

Father Sal led them to a small room in the back of the church known as the Mothers' Lounge. The soundproof room with its long bank of windows was built as a place where mothers with howling babies or rowdy toddlers could seek refuge and not disrupt the ecclesiastical proceedings. There were two monitors on shelves near the ceiling that piped in every word of the sermon. The room honored that old Christian dictate because its occupants were seen and not heard by the rest of the congregation.

When they were all in the room, Father Sal closed the door. But when he heard a sneeze, followed by a very loud sniffle, Sal realized there was an intruder in the room.

"God bless you, Katie," Sal said. "Now please leave?"

Katie Liakopoulos rubbed the sleeve of her altar girl's robe across her nose, causing the incense-filled thurible she was holding to sway in front of her. It filled the room with a musky scent not unlike what Jesus might have smelled when he took his first breath.

"You told us to follow you into the lounge," Katie said.

"My invitation was for ladies only," Sal replied.

"I'm a lady," Katie protested.

"That's debatable," Sal said. "Now be a good soldier and put the chalice and the other consecrated items back where they belong."

"Fine," Katie said, not pleased with being dismissed. However, as she closed the door behind her, she proved she was not only a disciple of Christ, but of Father Sal as well. Pointing to Jinx, she said, "She's got better footwear than you do, Father."

"It's hard to find good help these days," Sal said. "Now, what seems to be the matter? Are you still fretting over Lisa Marie's card?"

"No, we're fretting over Lisa Marie," Alberta said. "We've all tried calling and texting her."

"My father and my brother Sergio too," Jinx said. "But no one is getting back to us!"

"Is that unusual, Jinx?" Sal asked.

"Yes!" Jinx replied. "My mother's not a chatty Cathy like the rest of us, but she always responds pretty quickly when I text her, and if I leave a voice message she calls right back. My father's even faster."

"What about your brother?" Joyce asked.

"I never expect him to get back to me immediately," Jinx said. "But I told him it was urgent."

"Why don't you expect Sergio to return your call?" Alberta asked. "Aren't you two close?"

"We are, but he's twenty-three, Gram; he's always

running around somewhere or starting a new job or getting involved in a lame, get-rich-quick scheme," Jinx explained. "I'm used to him getting back to me on his own time."

Alberta reached into her coat pocket and clutched her rosary beads. She started to pray to the Blessed Mother asking for protection over her family and realized her family might be able to protect itself. Even those members of the family who hadn't always proven to be very helpful.

"Joyce, don't Anthony and Tommy still go fishing together?" Alberta asked.

"Anthony hasn't mentioned anything lately," Joyce replied. "And they really don't live near each other."

"Could you call him and find out?" Alberta asked. "Maybe they planned a family outing and they're somewhere without cell reception."

"I thought I was the only one who peddled a leap of faith," Father Sal said.

"I don't agree with you often, Sal, but I think you might be right about this one," Helen said.

"If you have a better idea, let's hear it," Alberta said. When her command was met by two pairs of shrugged shoulders, she added, "Joyce, call my brother."

Anthony Ferrara was the middle child, born in between Helen and Alberta. At a time when interracial marriages were greeted with contempt, he defied social conventions and married Joyce Perkins in a beautiful church ceremony. They lived in marital bliss until five years ago, when they realized they had grown apart and wanted to do different things with the remainder of their lives. Anthony moved to Clearwater, Florida, to live with his cousin Ralphie and Joyce took up permanent residence in their lake house in Tranquility. They both still loved each other and neither one of them wanted a divorce, but for now the situation suited them perfectly.

Joyce dialed her husband's number and put her phone on speaker so the rest of the group could hear their conversation.

"Hey, babe, what's going on?" Anthony said, sounding much more like a New Jerseyite than a Floridian.

"Have you spoken to Tommy lately?" Joyce asked.

"Not since our last fishing trip," Anthony replied. "Boy, that man wouldn't shut up, he scared all the fish away. I swear, he talks more than my sister."

"Which one?" Alberta and Helen both asked.

"Who's that?" Anthony asked.

"Your sisters," Joyce replied.

"Both of you!" Anthony yelled. "Why am I on speaker?"

"It's a long story, Ant," Joyce said. "Do me a favor and call Tommy and ask him to tell Lisa Marie to call Berta."

"That's never gonna happen," Anthony replied. "Berta and Lisa Marie disowned each other."

"We did not!" Alberta protested. "We had a fight."

"That's lasted fourteen years!" Anthony shouted. "Listen to me, Berta, the only way you're going to see your daughter is if you get on a plane and fly down here to Florida yourself."

"Thank you, Anthony. I can always count on you," Joyce said. She ended the call and addressed the group. "I'll get us tickets and we'll fly down this afternoon."

"If Muhammad won't come to the mountain," Father Sal said. "Then the mountain will take JetBlue to Muhammad."

"I have a better idea, visit Muhammad without ever leaving the mountain," Alberta said. "Jinx, is your mother friendly with any of her neighbors? We could just call them and maybe one of them will be able to tell us where they are."

Jinx hesitated. "My mother really isn't friendly with anyone."

"She's lived on the same block for over a decade; she has to have some friends," Helen said.

"Mrs. Passanante!" Jinx cried. "She lives across the street from them and she's the neighborhood watchdog. She literally knows the comings and goings of the entire block. My father can't stand her, but if anyone knows where they are, she would."

"Do you have her number?" Alberta asked.

"I should have it somewhere," Jinx said as she scrolled through the contacts on her phone. "Here it is! Under *f*."

"Why *f*?" Helen asked. "I thought you said her name was Passanante?"

"It's under *f* for *ficcanaso*," Jinx explained.

"The Italian word for nosy?" Sal questioned.

"I'm so happy you're making an effort to learn the language, lovey," Alberta said.

"Quiet, everybody, it's ringing!" Jinx shouted.

As Joyce did, Jinx put the call on speaker so everyone in the room could hear if the nosy neighbor lived up to her reputation.

"Jinx! How nice to hear from you!"

The voice on the other end of the phone was high-pitched, loud, and had the unmistakable accent of someone who had lived most of her life in Hudson County, New Jersey.

Since that was where most of the Ferraras grew up, they took it as a hopeful sign that Mrs. Passanante would be able to offer them some useful information on the Maldonados' whereabouts.

"How'd you know it was me?" Jinx asked.

"I have the phone numbers for all the next of kin on the block," Mrs. Passanante replied. "You know, just in case."

"That makes sense, I guess," Jinx replied.

"It most certainly does," Mrs. Passanante claimed. "Otherwise, it'll be a repeat of what happened over on McCrawley Drive. If I lived on that block, the Harrisons wouldn't have returned from their vacation to find a swimming pool where their basement used to be. I could've called a plumber and had them fix the water main break before there was any damage."

"The reason I'm calling, Mrs. Passanante, is because I hope you can help me," Jinx said.

"Please call me Providencia," she said. "All the relatives do."

"Okay, *Providencia*, the reason I'm calling . . ."

"Is to find out where your mother is," Providencia replied.

"Yes! How did you know?"

"Because people only call me when family goes AWOL."

"I've been trying to reach them, but I haven't had any luck, so I was wondering if you had any information."

"It's no surprise that you can't reach them, honey; they're gone."

"Gone!" Alberta exclaimed, fearing the worst. "What do you mean, *gone*?!"

"Who's that?" Providencia asked.

"That's my grandmother, Alberta Scaglione," Jinx explained.

"Oh . . . the *mother*," Providencia said.

Alberta did not like the tone of Providencia's voice. "What do you mean, the *mother*?"

"You're the reason Lisa Marie moved her family to Eufala in the first place," Providencia replied. "She wanted to get as far away from you as possible."

"My daughter told you that?"

"No, Lisa Marie's tight-lipped, but her husband, Tommy, *madon*! He talks more than a widow on the golf course at an over-fifty-five community," she said. "You know, because golfers are mostly men, and a widow is always chatting up the men, looking for her next husband."

"Hey, Providencia, tell us what you know right now or I'll come down there and make a widower out of your husband!"

"That must be Helen!" Providencia cried. "I've heard so many stories about you. I thought Tommy was exaggerating, but obviously he wasn't."

"I'm serious, Providencia. My Buick is full of gas and I just had the oil changed," Helen said. "It's ready for a road trip."

"It would be a waste of time," Providencia replied. "*Tanto va la gatta al lardo che ci lascia lo zampino.* Lisa Marie and Tommy packed up their Subaru and left town a week ago."

"Did they look like they were going on a trip or were they acting like they had to flee from the premises?" Sal asked.

"Who's that?" Providencia asked.

"This is Father Salvatore DeSoto, the parish priest at St. Winifred's of the Holy Well here in the idyllic lakeside community of Tranquility, New Jersey," Sal replied.

"That sounds fancy!" Providencia replied. "I didn't realize this call had been blessed."

"Mrs. Passanante, please!" Jinx cried. "Did they look like they were in trouble?"

"They didn't rush out in the middle of the night, if that's what you're asking," she said. "They took a few suitcases and Tommy's memory foam pillow, which he only takes on long trips."

"Was my brother with them?"

"No, I haven't seen Sergio for a while, but you know how it is with him," Providencia said.

"What do you mean by that?" Alberta asked.

"I'm sorry, I have to go," Providencia said. "There's some activity on the corner and the extension cord doesn't reach to that side of the house."

Before anyone could ask another question, the dial tone signifying the end of the call wailed through the lounge, like the cries of its more typical occupants.

"She was rude," Alberta said.

"And loud," Helen said.

"Also too, she has a landline?" Joyce added.

"What did she mean when she said that thing in Italian?" Jinx asked. "*Tanto* something."

"*Tanto va la gatta al lardo che ci lascia lo zampino,*" Alberta said, repeating the full phrase. "The literal translation means 'So much goes the cat to the lard that it leaves us a hand.'"

"Which in English makes no sense," Jinx remarked.

"No, but the figurative translation does," Father Sal said. "Someone who repeats the same misdeeds will eventually leave incriminating evidence behind."

"Mrs. Passanante thinks my mother committed some kind of crime?" Jinx asked.

"She's referring to her leaving home to move to Florida," Alberta said.

"And now leaving Florida for who knows where," Sal finished.

"But she didn't leave any evidence behind!" Jinx yelled.

Lisa Marie may not have left any clues when she and Tommy left for parts unknown, but Vinny, unfortunately, found something that might lead them down a much darker path.

"Vinny sent a text asking me to meet him at the police station," Alberta said.

"Why?" Jinx asked. "Did he find out something about my family?"

"I don't know, but he says I should come alone," Alberta replied.

"After all his talk about sharing information and not leaving anyone in the dark, he just wants to see you?" Jinx asked. "No way. I'm going with you."

"I rode shotgun with you, Berta," Helen said. "Plus, I have a feeling I should tag along."

"I'd join you, but I'm meeting Sloan and Sanjay at the Tranquility Arms for a Mistletoe Ball meeting," Joyce said, looking at her watch. "If I don't leave now, I'm going to be late."

Joyce ran out of the Mothers' Lounge, and when she opened the door, the din of the parishioners getting ready for the next mass infiltrated the room. It was time for the group to rejoin the outside world, Father Sal going back to his office to have an espresso topped with some anisette and the ladies going to pay what would turn out to be a surprise visit to Vinny.

When Alberta walked into Vinny's office followed by Jinx and Helen, Vinny's face turned gray. He looked fragile, which for a six foot four man with shoulders a football player would envy, was a difficult feat.

"Alfie," Vinny said. "I told you to come alone."

"Not on your life, Vinny," Jinx said. "Not after our agreement to share everything between us. If you have something to tell my grandmother, you can tell all of us."

Vinny stared at Jinx, and he looked like he wanted to cry. He took a deep breath and finally gained the strength to speak.

"We found a dead body at the Allamuchy State Park over in Stanhope," Vinny said. "Preliminary reports indicate that it matches Sergio's description."

CHAPTER 4

Una donna non è una donna finché non è una moglie.

The gravity of Vinny's words slowly descended upon the women, its weight crushing into their chests, making it difficult to breathe. Alberta latched on to the armrest of the chair next to her and managed to sit before her legs gave way underneath her. Helen grabbed Jinx by the elbow and guided her shaking body into the chair next to Alberta's. Sitting side by side, Alberta and Jinx's hands found each other and clasped as Helen stood behind them and found the rosary beads that she always carried in the pocket of her skirt, the ones given to her by the first Mother Superior she served under, Sister Mary Frances. She needed to borrow the nun's strength because she didn't have much of her own left.

"What do you mean, you found a dead body?" Alberta said.

Vinny moved from the side of his desk and knelt in

front of Alberta and Jinx. He put his hands on top of theirs and bowed his head. He was praying like the rest of them.

"There is no reason to believe that this man is Sergio," Vinny said.

"But it could be," Alberta replied.

Vinny looked at the woman he'd known since he was in grammar school. She had the same bright eyes she had when she was a teenager and used to babysit him and his younger sister, Frannie. He looked over at Jinx, the young woman who could drive him crazy with her stubbornness and impulsive personality, but who he had come to respect and admire. He wanted to lie to them and tell them that the search for their family could not possibly have a tragic ending. But he couldn't, so he told them the truth.

"Yes, it could be Sergio," Vinny said.

Alberta and Jinx fought back tears and tried to control their breathing, but Helen wanted to know why Vinny couldn't wait until he had definitive proof that the body was or wasn't Sergio before sharing the information with her family. Why put the grandmother and sister through such agony if the dead body belonged to another family?

"Sergio doesn't have a social media presence and I could only pull up his driver's license photo from when he was nineteen," Vinny explained. "That's why I asked Alfie to come alone."

"To identify my grandson's body," Alberta said.

"I was trying to cause as little pain as possible," Vinny said.

"You did the right thing," Alberta said.

Jinx understood that Vinny had wanted to spare her from worrying that the random dead body they found could be her brother, but she didn't understand why he didn't already know the identity of the corpse. Isn't that what the police did? Identify dead bodies?

"Can't you have someone send a photo of the victim?" Jinx asked.

"It's out of my jurisdiction, but Tambra is on her way to the crime scene and I've asked her to text me a photo when she arrives," Vinny explained. "I only found out about it because it came on the county blotter."

"How long will it take for Tambra to text you?" Helen asked.

"It should just be a few minutes," Vinny replied. He looked around the room helplessly and said, "Can I get you anything?"

You can get my mother, my father, and my brother, and bring them into this room to prove to me that they're all alive, Jinx thought. Out loud, she said, "No, thank you."

Alberta shook her head. She couldn't believe she might lose the grandson she hardly knew. How could that be possible? He was so young, so full of life. She almost laughed out loud at such a stupid thought. What a *stunod*! How many times had she seen young men and women struck down in the prime of their lives? She knew better. Death didn't care, it wasn't choosy; whatever it wanted, it took. Alberta couldn't believe that Death may have just taken her grandson.

Please don't let this poor boy be my Sergio, Alberta thought.

Immediately, she felt ashamed. If God granted her plea, it meant that some other woman's grandson had died. She remembered something Helen had once told her, something she never understood: Prayer can be complicated. She got it now.

The familiar ping of Vinny's cell phone reverberated

through his office, and the four of them remained frozen for a few seconds. Then Vinny leaned over his desk to grab his phone as Jinx and Alberta found the strength to stand. Helen stood behind them and they huddled together, waiting for Vinny to show them the photo that could change the whole trajectory of their search.

They couldn't tell from Vinny's expression if he recognized the man in the photo, but when he raised his cell phone in front of them, they all let out cries of relief.

"It isn't Sergio," Alberta announced.

They grimaced at the sight of a dead man sprawled out on the ground near the dumpster of a fast-food restaurant, his neck slightly swollen, burn marks at the corners of his mouth, but they were thrilled that they didn't recognize the dead man's face. They did, however, recognize the two men who burst into Vinny's office without even knocking.

"Sloan, what are you doing here?" Alberta asked.

"Same goes for you, Freddy," Jinx added.

"I texted them both and asked them to come down here," Vinny confessed. "Just in case you needed some emotional support."

"What do I look like?" Helen asked. "Tippi Hedren?"

"I thought you might need a little support too, Helen," Vinny said.

"You're a good man, Vinny D'Angelo," Alberta said. "And so are you, Sloan McLelland."

Alberta kissed Sloan on the lips and hugged him tightly. She knew she could lean on Sloan, but she had never noticed how strong his body was until now. She didn't want to be protected, and yet it was good to know her boyfriend was more than capable of taking care of her.

"Same goes for you, Freddy Frangelico," Jinx said.

Freddy rushed to Jinx's side, wrapped his long arms around her slender frame, and kissed her. She held on to him for a few moments and, like Alberta, was comforted to know she had found a man she could count on.

"I don't mean to be insensitive, but I guess this means the dead body isn't Sergio," Sloan said.

"Correct," Vinny replied. "For now, he's a John Doe who looks like he died of a drug overdose."

"That's terrible," Alberta said. "I didn't think there were many drugs in this area."

"Drugs are everywhere, Berta," Vinny said. "No neighborhood is immune. And neither is any family."

"I'm glad our family was spared," Freddy said.

"*Our* family?" Helen asked. "Don't count your chickens before they're hatched, sonny boy."

Their tears turned into laughter. Alberta hugged her sister tightly and hoped she knew how much she was loved. Alberta felt as if she had whiplash, first fearing her grandson was dead, then knowing her granddaughter was loved. It had been an emotional morning and it was about to get worse.

The door to Vinny's office burst open again without warning and this time it was Joyce who stood in the doorway. Her dark brown skin had lost some of its color and she looked like she had run a marathon.

"I found them!" Joyce screamed.

"Who?" Vinny asked.

"Lisa Marie and Tommy!"

"Where?" Alberta asked.

"The Tranquility Arms," Joyce replied. "I saw them while I was meeting with Sanjay."

"*Dio mio*!" Alberta cried. "This is a miracle!"

"How'd you know to find us here?" Helen asked.

"I turned on the Find My Friend app in all your phones," Joyce said. "None of you can make a move without me."

"Aunt Joyce, what did my mother say? Why hasn't she returned any of our calls?"

"I didn't speak with her," Joyce said. "They didn't even see me."

"But, dude, you said you saw them," Freddy replied.

"I'll explain it all on the drive over to the Arms," Joyce said.

"Guys, come with me and we'll meet them there," Vinny suggested.

The guys and girls split up, with the guys jumping into Vinny's police car, which, despite the seriousness of the situation, made both Sloan and Freddy feel like they were living out a childhood fantasy and going on a high-speed police chase, and the girls piling into Joyce's Mercedes. Despite the smooth handling of her car, Joyce had a bumpy ride fielding questions from her passengers.

"Tell us everything, Joyce," Alberta said as she sat in the front seat and fastened her seat belt. "How'd you wind up seeing Lisa Marie and Tommy at the Arms?"

"I was having a meeting with Sanjay and some other members of the Tranquility Business Association to discuss who should be awarded this year's Small Business Owner of the Year award," Joyce explained. "It's usually given at their annual conference, but this year they thought it would be exciting to announce the winner at the Mistletoe Ball."

Helen leaned in between Joyce and Alberta from the back seat. "Nobody cares about that, Joyce, get to the meaty part of the story!"

"As we were having our meeting, I saw Lisa Marie out of the corner of my eye check into one of the rooms and I almost passed out right there at the table," Joyce continued. "I thought I might have been hallucinating, so I asked Sanjay who was in room seven and he said it was a couple on their way to Canada."

"Did you go to room seven and confront my mother?" Jinx asked.

"No, because Sanjay told me the couple's name was Lana and Nicholas Goldschmidt," Joyce explained.

The revelation made Jinx groan, but it made Alberta and Helen gasp. It was proof that Alberta's daughter and son-in-law were in Tranquility.

"I can't believe Lisa Marie and Tommy are in town!" Alberta shrieked.

"They've been right under our noses the entire time," Helen added.

"No, they haven't," Jinx said. "It's some random couple named Lana and Nicholas Goldfarb."

"Goldschmidt," the three other women corrected.

"There's nothing random about that name," Alberta said. "Lana and Nicholas Goldschmidt are your Uncle Paolo's daughter and her husband."

"We have people named Goldschmidt living in our family tree?" Jinx asked, having never heard of the name before.

"It's a hardship, Jinxie, but we carry on," Helen said.

"It was a struggle, but Lana finally convinced her father to allow her to marry Nicholas, who didn't have an ounce of Italian blood in him and was the son of a German immigrant," Alberta said.

"The only reason Uncle Paolo allowed the marriage to take place was because Nicholas's father, Gunter, made the best Wiener schnitzel in Jersey and promised Paolo a free supply for a lifetime," Joyce added.

"The only reason he let his daughter marry the love of her life is because he got some free hot dogs?" Jinx asked.

"It's a veal cutlet," Helen corrected. "And you should know by now that this family is obsessed with food."

"This is a fascinating oral history of the Ferrara clan, but what does this have to do with my mother?" Jinx said as Joyce careened into the parking lot of the Tranquility Arms and pulled into a spot next to Vinny's police car. "Maybe Lana and Nicholas are in town for a visit."

Joyce and Alberta looked at each other with raised eyebrows, silently deliberating who would fill Jinx in on the more salacious part of their family's history. Because they were in a time crunch and Joyce was the one who had found the Goldschmidt imposters, Alberta felt it appropriate to let her sister-in-law get to share the juiciest part of the story. Helen had other ideas.

"Lana and Nicholas moved to Stuttgart back in the nineties in kind of a rush and they aren't allowed back in the States," Helen said.

"But it isn't entirely their fault," Alberta added as they all got out of the car and ran toward the men, who were standing at the entrance to the Arms.

"Nicholas had no idea the man he punched for making a pass at his wife was a Mafia kingpin," Joyce said. "Fredo was blond."

"When I see my mother I may kill her for keeping these stories from me," Jinx said.

"Speaking of your mother," Vinny said. "Follow me."

The entrance to the first-floor rooms at the Tranquility Arms were accessed from a wraparound porch. They all followed Vinny in single file as they worked their way to room seven. With the impatient group behind him, Vinny knocked on the door. When there was no response, he knocked again and said, "Open up! This is the police!"

"How can they open up? There's nobody inside!"

They all turned around to see the real Sanjay Achinapura, the owner and manager of the Tranquility Arms, standing behind them. The most compelling characteristic of the sixty-year-old man was that he was loud. Much louder than his skinny frame would lead an observer to believe.

"What do you mean, there's no one inside?" Joyce asked. "I saw Lisa Marie go in there less than a half hour ago."

"That wasn't Lisa Marie, it was Lana," Sanjay said.

"It was my daughter and her husband using fake names," Alberta replied. "Did they say where they were going?"

"They wanted to get on the road to reach Minneapolis before it got dark," Sanjay said.

"You told me they were here on a stopover on their way to Canada," Joyce said.

"Don't be mad at me, Miss Joyce!" Sanjay bellowed. "They must have changed their minds!"

Sanjay's second-most compelling characteristic was his undying love for Joyce. Despite the fact that he was married to Urja, who lived with their three children in Mumbai, he was constantly asking Joyce out on dates, and Joyce was constantly trying to keep him at arm's length. Now she needed to keep him talking.

"Why do they need to go to Minneapolis, Sanjay?" Joyce asked.

"The woman said they had to see the statue," Sanjay said.

"What statue?" Sloan asked.

"The one they built to look like Mary Tyler Moore from her TV show where she's throwing her hat in the air," Sanjay explained.

The women gasped so loudly it made the men jump. It was proof that Lisa Marie was deliberately trying to avoid seeing any of her family.

"That's a lie," Alberta said. "Lisa Marie hated Mary Tyler Moore."

"*That* must be a lie," Vinny said. "No one hated Mary Tyler Moore. She was universally beloved."

"She's right; my mother hated that show, specifically the women who starred in it," Jinx said. "She would comment all the time about how that Mary person destroyed the American family."

"That is insanity," Vinny said. "Mary Tyler Moore helped shape the modern American woman."

"She was a feminist icon, Vin, you're right," Joyce said. "But Lisa Marie did hate her guts."

"*Una donna non è una donna finché non è una moglie,*" Alberta said. "That's what she'd say all the time. 'A woman isn't a woman until she's a wife.' My daughter can be a bit old-fashioned."

"Joyce, you should've told me that you wanted me to keep that woman here," Sanjay said. "You know I'd do anything for you!"

"Thank you, Sanjay, but I figured if she had checked in here under fake names, she was trying to be incognito. I didn't want to confront her alone for fear that she'd run off," Joyce said. "Which is exactly what she did."

"Miss Joyce!" Sanjay cried. "If it's the last thing I do in my life, I will make this up to you."

He ran back to the lobby of the Arms, ashamed and upset. Joyce turned to face the rest of the group, distraught that she had let them down.

"I'm sorry I let them slip through my hands," Joyce said.

"It isn't your fault, Joyce," Alberta said. "But what I don't understand is why they're staying at a hotel when they could be staying with me."

The only one who looked confused was Alberta. The rest of the group understood that even though Lisa Marie had reached out to her mother for help after almost a decade and a half of silence, there was no way she would live under the same roof with her again, even if that stay was temporary. No one wanted to share this with Alberta, so they all went into action. They were all moving and talking so quickly, they couldn't believe Alberta didn't notice.

"I'll put an APB out on them," Vinny said.

"Remember, according to Mrs. Passanante, they're driving a Subaru," Jinx said.

"Vinny, why don't Jinx and I go back to the station with you and then use my car to drive around town?" Freddy said. "Maybe we'll spot them."

"I'll go with you too and get my car to head back to the library," Sloan said. "I have a quick meeting and then I'll come over by you, Berta."

"That's fine," Alberta said. "Joyce, could you drop me off at the police station? My car is there."

"Of course," Joyce replied. "I have another meeting at St. Winifred's Academy to discuss the student choir's role in the Mistletoe Ball, but I'll stop by later."

"Vinny, it goes without saying that the second you find them, you call me," Alberta said.

"Alfie, I'll bring them right to your doorstep," Vinny promised.

He wouldn't have to worry about keeping his promise because when Alberta walked into her kitchen, she saw Lisa Marie and Tommy sitting at her table. Lola was purring softly, nestled in Tommy's lap, and both he and Lisa Marie were smiling. Alberta's expression could not be described as joyful.

"What's wrong, Ma?" Lisa Marie asked. "You don't look so happy to see me."

CHAPTER 5

Dai nemici mi guardo io, dagli famiglia mi guardi Iddio!

Happy? Was Alberta happy to see her daughter after such a long absence? She pondered the question and couldn't immediately come up with an answer. She was greatly relieved to see Lisa Marie and Tommy alive and seemingly unharmed after thinking they could have been killed or racing toward the Canadian border to escape the country for some mysterious, but possibly felonious, reason. She was disappointed that her grandson, Sergio, wasn't also sitting around her kitchen table and she was confused as to why and how the couple were under her roof. But happy? It had been a long time since Alberta had been happy in connection with anything pertaining to Lisa Marie. She couldn't say that out loud and she could never say that to her own child, but she could use a tactic her child had regularly employed. She could lie.

"Of course I'm happy," Alberta said. "I'm also in shock."

Without taking off her coat, Alberta sat down in the chair closest to the door and placed her pocketbook carefully on the kitchen table. She held on to it, not out of necessity but security; she needed an anchor to something trustworthy to help guide her and keep her grounded as she entered unknown territory. She had imagined coming face-to-face with her daughter for many years, but she had never entertained this particular scenario. With no idea what to do or say, Alberta resorted to a familiar weapon in her tool kit: she accused.

"How did you break in?" Alberta asked.

"You left the door unlocked," Tommy replied.

"Which is kind of a dumb thing to do in your new profession, Ma," Lisa Marie added.

"My what?" Alberta said. "I don't work."

"I subscribe to *TUSH,* Ma," Lisa Marie said.

It took Alberta a second to realize her daughter was referring to *The Upper Sussex Herald,* the newspaper Jinx wrote for, by its less-flattering abbreviation.

"They prefer to call it *The Herald,*" Alberta corrected.

"Whatever," Lisa Marie replied. "I know that you're this detective now, and a pretty good one at that, which is why we're here."

"You need my help," Alberta said.

For the first time since Alberta's arrival, Lisa Marie and Tommy looked at each other. Their smiles faded and were replaced with the fear it seemed they had been trying to hide. It was the same fear Alberta had been feeling only seconds before she returned home.

"Yes, we do," Lisa Marie said.

Admitting the truth made some of Lisa Marie's bravado fade. It softened the hard exterior, so Alberta could get a glimpse of the woman her daughter had become. She was older, of course, and while physically she was the same, there were some significant changes.

Her long, unruly black hair had been cut to just above her shoulders, like Alberta's, and had either been professionally straightened or she spent every morning blowing it out. Alberta couldn't find a strand of gray, which meant her daughter had inherited her vanity and had her hair dyed regularly. She didn't know if Lisa Marie always parted her hair in the middle, but she liked it that way.

One noticeable change was her glasses. Before she left, she had needed to wear glasses, but only when she drove. It seemed that her vision had deteriorated over the years. The rectangular, tortoiseshell frames complemented her round face and brown eyes nicely, though they were unable to hide the small birthmark next to her right eyebrow.

There were a few more lines on her forehead and some crow's feet around her eyes, but her face looked completely natural, and it didn't look as if she was one of those women who used Botox and fillers to ward off the inevitable effects of aging. She had gained a few pounds, but because Alberta always thought she was too skinny, some extra weight was a good thing. At five foot four, Lisa Marie and Alberta were the same height, so she knew her daughter could carry more than the 105 pounds she was the last time she saw her.

When it came to aging, men got lucky, and her husband, Tommy, looked almost the same as he did when Alberta first met him. His sandy brown hair was still curly, but longer. On most men in their late forties, it would look silly, but Tommy still had his boyish looks, and the little-long-in-the-tooth, beach bum look worked on him. Alberta had not wanted her daughter to marry him, but she understood the appeal, at least physically. Just shy of six feet, Tommy had always had a lean, sinewy body and weighed less than 165 pounds when he got married. If he had gained five pounds since he exchanged his wedding vows, that was a lot.

Tommy and Lisa Marie looked exactly like what they were: high school sweethearts who had grown older together. Alberta had no idea how solid their marriage was, but she had to admit it had lasted longer than she originally expected. She also had to admit that it was wonderful to see them in the flesh again and not just in a dream. It didn't matter why they had returned, the important thing was that they did. True to her nature, however, Alberta was curious to know what kind of help her daughter thought only a mother could provide.

"You've kept me in suspense long enough," Alberta said. "Tell me, why do you need my help?"

"Because it seems that every other month there's an article about you solving some murder mystery," Lisa Marie replied. "And it isn't like you're getting special treatment because your granddaughter's the star reporter; you've earned every word of praise you've received."

"Mrs. Passanante calls you the Italian Miss Marple," Tommy said. "And she should know about old ladies who stick their noses in where they don't belong."

"Tommy!" Lisa Marie scolded. "That was actually a compliment, Ma."

Alberta knew she was an old lady, so her ego wasn't bruised. But she still didn't know why Lisa Marie specifically needed her. "Okay, I've solved a few crimes—with a lot of help, I might add—but I'm not a real detective, and if you're in trouble you should ask Vinny for help."

"No offense to Vinny and his department, but from everything I've read, those murders would still be cold cases if it wasn't for you," Lisa Marie said.

"Plus, this is a family matter," Tommy added. "We wanted to keep this in the family."

"Vinny's family," Alberta assured. "And we've discovered that things go much more smoothly if we work with the police instead of against them. Saves us all from a lot of agita."

"As long as you take the lead," Lisa Marie said.

Alberta remained seated and took off her coat, letting it hang over the back of her chair. She wasn't warm, but she needed a moment to think without making it appear as if she was thinking. It was obvious that she was not going to convince them to follow the proper protocol and let Vinny and his team of detectives do what they were paid to do. She almost laughed because what did she expect? That her rebel daughter, who had never met a rule she didn't like to break, would suddenly turn into a mild-mannered middle-aged woman who toed the line of social acceptability? The Lisa Marie sitting in front of her may have changed slightly, but she was still the Lisa Marie Alberta knew all too well. And if her daughter wanted her to spearhead an investigation, Alberta felt she owed her that.

"I may not have been there for you these past years, but you know I'll do whatever I can to help you, especially if this has something to do with our family," Alberta said. "What's the problem?"

Lisa Marie looked at Tommy and exhaled a deep

breath she had been holding before speaking. "Sergio is missing."

"My grandson?!"

"We have another Sergio in the family?" Lisa Marie asked rhetorically. "Of course it's your grandson."

"*Dio mio*," Alberta said, tugging on her gold crucifix. "How long has he been missing?"

"About a month," Tommy replied.

"He's been missing for a month and you're just looking for him now?" Alberta asked.

"I've been gone for fourteen years, Ma, when did you start looking for me?"

Alberta inhaled deeply and let the air slowly leave her body. Now that she knew why Lisa Marie needed her help, she understood that she was under a great deal of stress. Still, she couldn't completely ignore her daughter's comment.

"That isn't fair," she replied. "I've known exactly where you were all this time."

"I'm sorry, I didn't mean it," Lisa Marie said. "Well, I kind of did, but I don't want to get into all of that right now. We can sort out our issues later."

"Right now, we need your help in finding our son," Tommy said.

"You know I don't do this sleuthing on my own," Alberta said.

"Jinx has filled me in on all the details, and how this is some kind of crazy family hobby," Lisa Marie said. "How you solve these crimes without killing each other is beyond me. The important thing is that you get results."

"Yes, we do," Alberta said.

Although she was beaming with pride that her daughter finally needed her and had put aside their fractured history to be in the same room with her, the irony of the situation did not go unnoticed. But it did remain unspoken. After all these years the only reason Alberta's daughter had reached out to her was because her own child hadn't reached out to her. Instead of feeling in some way satisfied or even justified, Alberta was overcome with sadness. She knew what it was like to be on the other side of silence, and despite her volatile relationship with Lisa Marie, she didn't wish the feeling on her own daughter. It was time to break the cycle.

"I guess it's time I call in the troops," Alberta said. "Because the Ferrara Family Detective Agency has found its next case."

Tommy refreshed their coffee cups and cut up some mozzarella and tomatoes he found in the refrigerator. He sprinkled on some balsamic oil and placed them on plates as a snack while Alberta made a series of phone calls.

"Lovey, I need you to come here pronto," Alberta said.

She had put the phone on speaker, so when Jinx replied her voice filled the kitchen. "Freddy and I just spied a Subaru over near the trails where people go horseback riding," Jinx said. "I think it might be my parents."

"No, honey, it isn't them," Alberta said.

"You don't know that."

"Yes, I do," Alberta said. "Because I found your parents."

"You found them!" Jinx screamed. "Where are they?"

"In my kitchen."

"Why does everyone eventually find their way to your kitchen?"

"People know that's the best place to be."

"We're on our way," Jinx said. "And tell my parents that when I get there, I'm going to kill them myself!"

"We heard that!"

Alberta ended the call before Jinx could respond to her mother's outburst. It wasn't that she didn't want to hear any family squabbling; she just had lots of other calls to make.

"I found them, Vin," Alberta declared. "Well, two out of the three."

"Speak in full sentences, please," Vinny requested.

"Lisa Marie and Tommy are here at my house, so you can call off the APB," Alberta said. "But Sergio is still missing."

"What do you mean, *still* missing?"

"He hasn't been in contact with his parents for over a month."

There was a long silence on the other end of the phone. When Vinny finally spoke, he sounded very concerned. "I'm on my way over."

Next, Alberta called Helen, who was being driven home by Joyce. Once again she put the call on speaker and Helen did the same. "Lisa Marie and Tommy are safe and sound and having tomatoes and mozz in my kitchen."

"Thank God!" Joyce shouted. "That's wonderful news."

"You have a lot of explaining to do, Lisa Marie!" Helen shouted even louder. "You made us sick with worry."

"Sorry, Aunt Helen," Lisa Marie replied. "I'll make it up to you."

"How?" Helen asked.

"I'll write a nasty letter to that priest you can't stand," Lisa Marie said. "Father Sal."

"Oh, honey," Joyce said. "You've been away for a long time."

When Alberta started to dial another phone number, Lisa Marie threw the piece of mozzarella she was about to eat back on her plate.

"For God's sake, Ma, are you calling all of Tranquility to let them know I've returned?"

"No, just family, friends, and my boyfriend."

"Your boyfriend?"

"Yes, didn't Jinx tell you? I have a boyfriend."

"No, Jinx did not tell me that. You're too old to have a boyfriend."

"That's not what Sloan thinks."

"Sloan? What kind of a name is Sloan for a man?"

"It's a very nice name and you better be nice when you meet him."

"She'll be nice," Tommy said, interrupting their conversation.

"Don't answer for me," Lisa Marie said.

"Leese, I told you that if you two start yelling at each other like you used to, I'm outta here," Tommy said. "We came here to get your mother's help to find Sergio, not start another family war."

By the tight scowl that gripped Lisa Marie's face, Alberta could tell that her daughter didn't like the ultimatum her husband had just handed her. But in a surprise move, Lisa Marie suppressed her argumentative nature and agreed. "You're right," she replied. "I'll be nice to meet your boyfriend with the dumb name."

It wasn't perfect, but it was a start.

Within fifteen minutes the invited guests started to arrive and, one by one, Lisa Marie and Tommy had reunions with people they hadn't seen in quite some time.

Not all of those reunions started with hugs and kisses.

"Why didn't you answer any of my calls?!"

"I'm sorry, honey. We've been so focused on finding your brother that we let everything else slide by," Lisa Marie explained. "I knew that if we spoke, I'd give it away and only worry you."

"I am worried!" Jinx yelled. "What do you mean, you're trying to find Sergio? Where's my brother?"

"We don't know," Tommy said.

"What do you mean, you don't know?" Jinx asked. "How can you lose track of your own son?"

"We'll explain everything when the others get here," Tommy said. "In the meantime, why don't you introduce us to the guy standing behind you?"

"Is this the Freddy you can't shut up about?" Lisa Marie asked.

"One and the same," Freddy replied. He reached out to shake their hands and, being the good Italian boy he was, he shook Tommy's hand first. "Freddy Frangelico. It's nice to finally meet you both."

"Likewise," Tommy said.

"The jury's still out," Lisa Marie added.

"Ma!" Jinx cried. "Be nice!"

"Why the hell is everyone telling me to be nice?!" Lisa Marie cried.

"Looks like I just lost my title," Helen said, entering the kitchen. "There's a new Miss Congeniality in town."

"Aunt Helen," Lisa Marie said. "You definitely are a sight for sore eyes. And ears."

The women hugged and only stopped because Joyce literally pried them off each other. "Don't hog the hugs, Helen."

"Aunt Joyce," Lisa Marie said as she breathed in Joyce's perfume.

"What about me?" Tommy asked. "Am I not hug-worthy?"

"Be careful what you wish for, mister," Helen said.

Soon Tommy was embraced by not one but two Fer-raras as Helen and Joyce hugged him from either side.

"It's good to see you all again," Tommy said.

Alberta noticed that he was fighting back tears, but her daughter had remained stoic. She couldn't judge her; Alberta knew better than to do that because it had taken her years to allow the walls she had built around her heart to melt away. Hopefully the same would happen for her daughter. For now, however, Lisa Marie was all business.

"I've heard that the four of you have become pretty good amateur detectives," Lisa Marie announced.

"They might not have badges, but I don't know if you can call them amateurs any longer," Vinny said. "The same can't be said for Lana and Nicholas Goldschmidt."

"Sorry, Vinny," Lisa Marie said. "I wasn't sure we'd be welcomed with open arms."

"Then you, little girl, are not as smart as you used to be," Vinny said.

When Vinny embraced Lisa Marie, Alberta had to turn away and stare out the window because she didn't want her daughter to see her crying. Lisa Marie had come here for help in finding her son, not to have an emotional homecoming with her mother. When she saw Sloan and Father Sal walk past her kitchen window, she knew that God had answered her prayers. Sentimentality would have to take a back seat; there was about to be a show-down.

"Lisa Marie, Tommy," Alberta said. "This is Sloan."

"Please tell me your boyfriend's the one without the white collar," Tommy said.

"Alberta may be a mighty temptress," Father Sal said. "But as you can see from my wardrobe, I am otherwise engaged."

Smiling, Sloan extended his hand to Tommy, who graciously took it. "Very nice to meet you, Tommy."

Sloan turned to the unsmiling face of the woman standing next to Tommy. "So nice to meet you too, Lisa Marie."

He reached out to shake Lisa Marie's hand, but she kept her arms crossed in front of her chest. Her lips were pursed, her body tense, and her eyes glaring. Her disapproval of her mother's boyfriend was not subtle. After a few awkward seconds, Sloan dropped his arm to his side, but somehow managed to maintain his smile. Alberta couldn't think of anything to say that wouldn't call attention to the frosty situation, but luckily, her sister had no qualms stating the obvious.

"*Dai nemici mi guardo io, dagli famiglia mi guardi Iddio,*" Helen said.

Alberta thanked God again, this time for two blessings. First, she was grateful that Lisa Marie never really listened to her parents, which meant her knowledge of the Italian language was profoundly limited. And second, that no one asked Helen to translate. Her comment, an odd Italian proverb, essentially meant that a person could protect himself from his enemies but needed God's help to protect him from his family. Truer words had never been spoken in any language. Luckily, Alberta knew the one universal language that everyone understood: food.

"Why don't I fix us all something to eat?" Alberta suggested. "And then you can fill us in on all the details so we can find Sergio."

"That sounds great," Tommy said. "I'm starving."

"Good," Alberta said. "I'll put a lasagna in the oven."

"You don't still put those stupid hard-boiled eggs in there like Grandma used to, do you?" Lisa Marie asked.

Alberta swallowed hard and fought the urge to respond to her daughter the way she had responded to her countless times before. She knew if she did, however, she might lose the chance to help bring her grandson back home safely. It was partly because of situations like this that Alberta always maintained a well-stocked fridge.

"Make that my chicken parm," Alberta said.

Lisa Marie had won this round, but it was clear that the war was definitely not over.

CHAPTER 6

Per quanto le famiglie cambino, rimangono le stesse.

When the dishes were tucked away in the dishwasher and the only thing left on the table were two pitchers of Red Herrings, Jinx's creation, which was a mix of vodka, prosecco, cranberry juice, some orange juice, and a splash of tomato juice, it was time for Lisa Marie to tell the story of how she came to return to her mother's home. Everyone around the table appeared much more eager to hear the story than Lisa Marie appeared to want to tell it. But when Tommy gently placed his hand on his wife's back and nodded his encouragement, she found the strength.

"About six months ago we noticed Sergio had changed," Lisa Marie began. "He was far from perfect—I mean, who is, right? But he was a good kid. He followed the house rules, he respected both of us, he had never been in trouble with the police or even at school, but all of a sudden it was like we were living with a stranger.

"He started staying out overnight without telling us, he didn't call or text us during the day like he used to, he wouldn't go fishing with all the boys any longer, but the kicker was when he stopped working with Tommy," Lisa Marie said. "That's when I knew we had a problem."

"What line of work do you do, Tommy?" Sloan asked.

"I'm an electrician," he replied. "I have my own business."

"It's a good one too," Lisa Marie added. "Small, just Tommy, his friend Hector, and Sergio, until he up and quit."

"I was fine with Serge wanting to work somewhere else," Tommy said. "But I wasn't happy when he just didn't show up at a scheduled job one day. A family business is still a business."

"And it wasn't even because he didn't like being an electrician or working for his father," Lisa Marie said. "It was all because of a girl."

"Do not tell me Tricia is back in the picture," Jinx said.

"Dude, who's Tricia?" Freddy asked.

"Sergio's high school girlfriend who dumped him when she went to some fancy college out West," Lisa Marie said. "It took him forever to get over that one."

"Unfortunately, the new girl in his life is even worse," Tommy said.

"Does this girl have a name?" Alberta asked.

"Natalie Vespa," Lisa Marie seethed.

"Oh my God, she sounds like a snake," Jinx said.

"She is, but Sergio's head over heels in love with her," Tommy said.

"Lord knows why!" Lisa Marie exclaimed. "She's bossy, opinionated, disrespectful, and she dresses like a pole dancer, and not in a classy way like the one from *Flashdance*. Plus, she's got very expensive taste and makes Sergio pay for everything."

"My son is in love with a beautiful girl who's just using him," Tommy said. "Natalie's manipulative and condescending to Sergio, but when I tried to get him to see her for what she really is . . . he turned on me."

"Daddy, Sergio worships you!" Jinx cried.

"It didn't stop him from throwing a punch at me," Tommy said.

"He hit you?" Jinx asked.

"He tried," Tommy said. "Your old man is still pretty fast on his feet and I swerved out of the way."

"Sergio has a bit of a temper," Lisa Marie said. "Before Natalie came into the picture it was usually under control, but she brings out the worst in him."

"Let me guess," Sloan started. "The more you tried to tell Sergio that Natalie wasn't good enough for him, the further he pushed you both away."

Lisa Marie adjusted her glasses. Her right eyebrow raised in a perfect arch and she turned to face her mother. "Your boyfriend thinks he's a smarty-pants too?"

"He is," Alberta replied. "And he's right, isn't he?"

"That's exactly what happened," Tommy said. "I tried a different tactic and told Sergio that if Natalie's the one, then she's the one. The only thing that mattered to us was that he be happy."

"That sounds very reasonable," Alberta said.

"You sound surprised by that," Lisa Marie remarked. "You don't think Tommy can be reasonable?"

"Are you going to pounce on every word your mother

says?" Helen asked. "Or are you going to show some respect while you're sitting at her table?"

Somewhere outside a bird was chirping amid the snowfall and its resilient melody, faintly reminiscent of "The First Noel," could be heard in the otherwise silent room. Lisa Marie looked around the table, and while she was surrounded mainly by family, she was outnumbered. This was Alberta's turf and if she wanted her mother to help her find her son, she was going to have to play by these new rules.

"As you can imagine, I'm under a lot of stress," Lisa Marie said. "I'm sorry."

Before another Ferrara could make a comment that would sidetrack the conversation, Vinny reminded everyone that they had gathered for a very important reason. A person was missing and they needed to find out why. "What did Sergio do when you told him that?"

"He moved out," Tommy said.

"He never told me that he moved out," Jinx said.

"Why in the world would he move out?" Alberta asked. "He had a clean house, three meals a day, and he didn't have to pay rent."

"He went with Natalie to New York," Lisa Marie explained. "She got some new job and Sergio said he couldn't stand to be without her."

"Next thing we know, he's throwing some things in a bag, and out the door he goes," Tommy added.

"What does Natalie do for a living?" Joyce asked.

"I have no idea!" Lisa Marie yelled. "You could never get a straight answer out of that piece of trash! She always talked in circles, she contradicted herself, and then, when I pointed that out, Sergio would yell at me and tell me that I wasn't listening."

"He said he would call us when he got settled in New York, but he never did," Tommy said. "That was a little over a month ago."

"We thought eventually he'd come to his senses and move back home, but he won't even respond to our calls or texts," Lisa Marie said. "We don't even know if he made it to New York."

For the first time Lisa Marie choked up, but instead of allowing herself to cry in front of her family, she forced her emotions to retreat. Alberta fought every instinct in her body because all she wanted to do was wrap her arms around her daughter to comfort her, but she knew her daughter wasn't ready to accept her embrace. There was a question mark in Alberta's brain as well, and she wasn't sure how such a gesture would truly make her feel, which made it easier for her to remain seated and watch her daughter struggle.

Just as Tommy reached out his hand to place it over his wife's fist, she slammed it down on the table, startling everyone, especially Lola, who was trying to take a nap on the other side of Lisa Marie.

"No, I'm not going to let that Natalie Slimeball win," Lisa Marie spat. "I'm not going to let her make me lose control. I need all my strength to find my son."

"Let's take the first step," Vinny said. "Come down to the station with me to fill out missing person reports on Sergio and Natalie that we can give to the New York authorities."

They all started to get up and disperse, but before they could put on their coats Lisa Marie stopped them.

"I need to say something first," she began. "I know I screwed up. I should've called you, Ma, instead of sending that cryptic card, and I should've told you we were in town instead of hiding out at that hotel under fake names. I also should've answered your calls and texts. The truth is that I need my family, but . . . it's been a really long time and, honestly, I wasn't sure if you all still consider me a member of this family any longer."

Alberta spoke for the group in the family's native tongue. "*Per quanto le famiglie cambino, rimangono le stesse*," she said. "As much as families change, they still remain the same. And you, Lisa Marie, will *always* be a part of this family."

Alberta stared at her daughter, and it was almost as if the rest of the people in the room faded away and only the two of them remained. She saw Lisa Marie as a toddler, a teenager, the woman she was just before she left town, and as the woman standing before her now. All the women were different and yet all of them were the same.

Just as Alberta was going to reach out to grab Lisa Marie's hand as a way to assure her that her words weren't empty, but were born of truth, Vinny came between them.

"Follow me to the police station," Vinny said, standing up and passing a business card to Lisa Marie. "The address is on there if you get lost."

"Ma, why don't you come with us?" Lisa Marie suggested. "I'm sure you could get us there blindfolded."

"That I could," she replied. "Let's go."

It wasn't until Alberta was sitting in the back seat of Tommy's Subaru that she realized that driving with her estranged daughter and son-in-law might not be the best idea. She figured that was why Helen, Joyce, Sloan, and Jinx each asked her if she preferred to drive with them and they would drop her off at the police station. She thought everyone was being considerate and didn't realize they were trying to prevent Alberta from entering the wolf's den.

Just before she got into the car, Jinx whispered in her ear, "*In bocca al lupo.*" In conversation, the Italian expression meant *good luck*. The literal translation was something far less heartwarming: *Into the mouth of the wolf.* It was one of the first phrases Alberta had taught Jinx when she was a little girl, which had not pleased Lisa Marie. She hated the phrase because she felt it gave Jinx a false sense of security, that no matter how difficult and insurmountable the obstacles, all she needed to do was say *In bocca al lupo* and she'd somehow become impervious to disappointment and heartache. As they pulled away from the house, Alberta thought maybe Lisa Marie had been right all along and silently prayed that the phrase really did come equipped with supernatural powers.

The first five minutes of the drive were spent in silence, which gave Alberta a chance to daydream about when she was in the same position in Tommy's car as they drove to Atlantic City over twenty-seven years ago. Lisa Marie had been tired of being stuck in the house and she wanted to get out before she was stuck in the house permanently with a crying infant. After a few hours of playing the slots, Lisa Marie went into premature labor, their car wouldn't start, and they got caught in a torrential downpour, which was why Jinx was born on the floor of Harrah's casino a few minutes after midnight on the morning of Friday the 13th. They lost their money that day but came home with a treasure. Tommy always said Jinx was their good luck charm with the bad luck name.

It was only when they stopped at a red light that the silence became oppressive, which led to small talk. And small talk in a car among relatives who were the primary players in a family feud was like walking through a minefield blind and wearing clown shoes.

"What started all this amateur detective stuff anyway?" Lisa Marie asked. "I mean, you weren't very clever when Rocco and I were growing up. I bet you never knew he smoked cigarettes on the fire escape."

"He did what?!"

"Almost every night for over a year," Lisa Marie added.

"Ah *Madon*!" Alberta cried. "I thought he had that lingering cough from bronchitis."

"It was from smoking too many Camels unfiltered," Tommy explained.

"I hope he stopped," Alberta said.

"He did after Daddy found his stash," Lisa Marie admitted.

"Your father knew?" Alberta asked. "He never told me."

"Rocco begged him not to say anything," Lisa Marie said. "He knew you'd be disappointed."

A surge of pride raced through Alberta's body. She was upset that her son had been a closet smoker but delighted that he loved her enough that he didn't want to disappoint her. *I guess it's never too late to learn something new about your children,* Alberta thought. The same could be said about a parent.

"But seriously, Ma, when did you become so logical that you could search for clues and follow leads and finagle your way into places that the police don't even have access to?" Lisa Marie asked.

For a moment Alberta was stumped. No one had asked her this very obvious question before. She had no formal training as a detective, she had been curious about the world as a younger woman but hadn't acted upon her curiosity for decades, and she was hardly fearless. How did she become an amateur sleuth? The answer didn't surprise Lisa Marie nearly as much as it surprised Alberta.

"I've changed."

"You're telling me. You're more sure of yourself and not as, I don't know, frantic maybe," Lisa Marie stated. "You were always running around, fixing things, trying to run a perfect household, trying to cater to Daddy's every whim."

"I think what my wife is trying to say is that you're all grown-up," Tommy said as the light turned green.

"Stop joking, I'm serious," Lisa Marie said. "You're liberated, is that the right word? Independent."

"I think that's part of it," Alberta said. "Without your father to take care of or my children, I'm really only responsible for myself. And Lola, of course. *Dio mio*! Don't let her know I forgot about her; she'll never forgive me."

"I'm sure it helps being independent with all of Aunt Carmela's millions and her lake house," Lisa Marie said. "I still can't believe she left everything to you."

"Nobody was more shocked than I was," Alberta stated. "I'm still not sure why she singled me out and didn't spread it out among the entire family."

"Lord knows three million can spread pretty far," Lisa Marie said.

"You know I've been forbidden by the terms of the will to give any of that money away," Alberta said. "And the house can only be left to another family member after I die."

"I don't want your money, Ma," Lisa Marie said. "Well, not all of it."

Alberta started to laugh. Maybe her daughter had finally decided to stop lying and be more honest.

In Vinny's office, Alberta leaned against the console on the back wall because Lisa Marie and Tommy were sitting in the only two chairs in the room, giving Vinny the information needed to file a missing person report. They told him Sergio was five foot ten, one hundred and ninety-five pounds, had hair that was Tommy's sandy brown color but naturally wavy like Lisa Marie's, brown eyes, and had a tattoo of a Chinese symbol on his left shoulder blade—something Alberta had never known about—that allegedly meant *eternity*, but because none of them, Sergio included, could read Chinese, it was anyone's guess what it truly meant.

When they had answered all Vinny's questions about Sergio, he turned the focus from information gathering to suspect investigation. He wanted to know everything they could tell him about Natalie Vespa.

"She's a bitch," Lisa Marie stated.

"Yes, Leese, you've made it very clear how you feel about her," Vinny said. "I'm looking for more quantifiable data about the woman. Facts."

"I just gave you one," Lisa Marie replied.

"I need factual facts," Vinny said.

"Like what?" Tommy asked.

"Like, was Natalie married before?" Alberta asked.

Lisa Marie tried to swivel in her chair but was unsuccessful because she wasn't sitting in a swivel chair. Instead, she twisted her body to the left, so she could face her mother. "Why do you care if she was married?"

"To find out if she has a maiden name," Alberta explained. "It's necessary for when Vinny searches her name in the police database."

Lisa Marie looked at her mother suspiciously. She then looked at Vinny with the same expression. "Is that right?"

"As a matter of fact it is," Vinny said. "Was Natalie married?"

"We have no idea," Tommy replied.

"Is she originally from Florida or did she go to college there?" Alberta asked. "Or maybe her family moved there when she was a kid?"

"The girl hardly spoke to me the few times I was in her company," Lisa Marie said. "There's really very little I know about her."

"Same goes for me," Tommy said. "I tried to get details from Sergio, but whenever I asked a question, he clammed up."

"She doesn't have a social media presence either, which is odd for a girl her age," Alberta said as she scrolled through several different applications on her cell phone. "I checked the Facebook, Instagram, she doesn't Tweet or Snap, she's not even on LinkedIn, which is where most young people find employment these days."

Lisa Marie looked stunned, and Alberta couldn't help but relish that fact. The last time her daughter saw her, she was a housewife who barely knew how to flip her phone, and the only skills she had mastered were those that were appreciated in the kitchen. Alberta knew that the woman Lisa Marie was looking at was unrecognizable to her.

"Who are you?" Lisa Marie asked.

"Just a lady who's learned to use her brain to do more than recall her grandmother's recipes," Alberta said. "Do you have a photo of Natalie?"

"No," Tommy said. "But she's got a light complexion, stands about five foot five, she's thin, definitely someone who works out but not too much, probably more aerobics and not weight training, she has green eyes—no, they're more like hazel—dark blond hair—well, naturally blond with those dark highlights—and her hair is long and wavy; feathery, I guess you'd say, almost like the way Farrah Fawcett used to wear her hair on *Charlie's Angels*, remember?"

"I think you left out her shoe size," Lisa Marie said, her voice rich with sarcasm.

"If I had to guess, I'd say, seven, seven and a half tops," Tommy replied, either ignoring the tone of his wife's voice or so wrapped up in the memory of Natalie that he didn't notice it.

"I'm glad my husband has a photographic memory when it comes to describing the girl who has robbed us of our son!" Lisa Marie exclaimed.

This time there was no way around it; Tommy knew that his wife wasn't pleased with his performance. "I'm sorry, I'm only trying to help."

"And you did," Vinny said. "Thanks, Tommy."

"Do not thank him for having the image of that tramp seared into his brain!" Lisa Marie cried.

"It helped me narrow down my search," Vinny explained. "Believe it or not, I found three Natalie Vespas, but only one fits Tommy's description."

"What does it say about her, Vin?" Alberta asked.

"She was born in Emmaus, Pennsylvania, which isn't too far from here, but moved around a lot when she got older," Vinny conveyed. "She's worked in New York and Tampa."

"That isn't near Eufala," Lisa Marie said.

"But it gets her in the state," Vinny replied. "Is this your Natalie?"

Vinny turned his monitor around so they could see the photo of the woman he had been staring at, and they both confirmed that was Sergio's girlfriend. He pressed a button on his phone, and when Tambra picked up, he shouted instructions.

"Tambra, I'm e-mailing you a person of interest," Vinny said. "Run a check on her license plates, Social Security, the whole nine yards, and rush it."

"On it, Chief," Tambra said.

"Once we get the info on Natalie, we'll track her down and hopefully that'll lead us to Sergio," Vinny said.

"That might be harder than you think."

They all turned to see Sloan standing in the doorway, waving a piece of paper in his hand.

"What are you doing here?" Lisa Marie asked.

"I did a background check on Sergio at the library to see if anything out of the ordinary popped up," Sloan explained.

"We did the same thing, Sloan, but there were no red flags," Vinny said.

"Don't you think it's odd that he hasn't paid his cell phone bill for the past two months?" Sloan asked.

"That didn't come up in our search," Vinny admitted.

"How did you find out something that slipped through the cops' hands?" Lisa Marie asked.

"Sloan has picked up some *skills* working at the library," Alberta said.

"You're a librarian?" Lisa Marie asked. "I knew you were a smarty-pants."

"Sergio probably has a burner phone," Vinny said.

"That's what I was thinking," Sloan agreed. "Though I was hoping it wouldn't be true."

"Why?" Tommy asked. "What's bad about that?"

"If he's using a burner phone, Tommy," Alberta said, "it means he's serious about severing ties with the two of you."

The irony wasn't lost on Alberta, but she kept it to herself. This was no time to rub salt in anyone's wounds. Sergio was doing to Lisa Marie exactly what Lisa Marie had done to Alberta.

"There's no way to trace a burner phone?" Lisa Marie asked.

"No, there isn't," Sloan replied. "They're untraceable."

"Great!" Lisa Marie exclaimed. "What do we do now?"

"It's going to take a while before we get the info about Natalie," Vinny said. "Why don't you four take this time to go get, um, better acquainted?"

CHAPTER 7

Dipende sempre dalla famiglia.

The Tranquility Diner, like the town of Tranquility itself, had been possessed by the spirit of Christmas.

Although the restaurant was rechristened the Tranquility Diner after Kwon bought it from its previous owner, who fled town after being involved in a major scandal, it looked the same. The white, rectangular structure, with its long bank of windows, rounded edges, and red-and-baby-blue-striped roof still looked like a relic of midcentury Americana. The new name of the diner was still written out in vintage font, its *I*s dotted with starbursts. But now it had been given a Christmas makeover.

Santa and four of his eight reindeer were perched on the rooftop, captured in midflight, brightly lit Christmas trees flanked both ends of the diner, strings of lights outlined the windows, and a huge snowman was positioned at the front door to greet guests as they arrived. The snowman's hand was raised, and he was holding something green and leafy.

"What's Frosty got in his hand?" Lisa Marie asked.

"Mistletoe," Sloan replied.

"Looks like the diner's trying to play matchmaker," Tommy said.

"Looks like the Mistletoe Ball is taking over the town," Alberta declared.

When the two couples walked inside, they felt as if they had stepped onto the set of one of those Hallmark Christmas movies. Wreaths made out of garland hung from the walls, a huge, overly decorated Christmas tree stood in one corner, its angel topper bending slightly forward to avoid decapitation, and another set of lights, this kind of the blinking variety, framed the inside of the windows. Patti Page was singing about the magic of silver bells in the city, her voice smooth and comforting as it wafted from the speakers. Although their surroundings were completely artificial, the warm and cozy feelings they generated were genuine. Despite their reason for gathering, they couldn't help but smile. Alberta took it as a good omen that their lunch wouldn't be as awkward as she first imagined it would be.

Ten minutes later, as she sat in a booth next to Sloan and across from Lisa Marie and Tommy, the air between them thick and tense, she knew she had been duped. How could they make small talk when they were waiting for information about the woman who was responsible for luring Sergio away from his family? How could they fully embrace the Christmas spirit that was alive and kicking all around them when they wanted to turn back the clock to the day before Sergio ran off? Alberta racked her brain to find something to say that wouldn't sound frivolous or disrespectful or patronizing and came up empty. Luckily, Sloan wasn't as choosy.

"What have you two been up to for the past fourteen years?"

Alberta couldn't believe that Sloan, who possessed such wonderful social graces, could say something so ungraceful. Turned out to be the most appropriate thing for him to say.

The back of the booth they were sitting in was lined in teal vinyl, which cushioned Lisa Marie's head when she threw it back in a fit of laughter. Tommy looked at his wife with a bemused expression, but Alberta was in total shock. She couldn't recall the last time she saw her daughter laugh so hard.

"You might be a smarty-pants and way too thin for a man your age," Lisa Marie declared. "But I like you, Sloan. You're funny."

"Thank you, Lisa Marie, I like you too," Sloan said. "But I was being serious. What have you been doing since you left New Jersey?"

Lisa Marie busied herself by unfolding her paper napkin and placing it on her lap, smoothing it out several times before she spoke. "I don't want to bore you with a bunch of . . . boring details."

"*Sciocchezze*," Alberta said. "Don't be silly, we'd . . . *I* would really like to know what kind of life you made for yourself in Florida."

Alberta could tell from Lisa Marie's slightly puzzled expression that her daughter was trying to figure out if she was being sarcastic or serious—she could almost see the wheels turning in her head—but despite the long absence, Alberta still knew her daughter was a gambler at heart and couldn't miss the chance to call her mother's bluff.

"All right, then," Lisa Marie replied, giving her shoulders a little shrug. "Here goes."

She told her story with a detached air at first, sharing only perfunctory details and not embellishing them with tangential comments or anecdotes. Alberta learned that when they first moved to Eufala, they rented a two-bedroom in a garden apartment complex because the offer they put down on the house they wanted to buy fell through. For their first six months in Florida they lived barracks style, Lisa Marie and Jinx sharing one bedroom and Tommy and Sergio sharing the other.

"That must've been fun," Alberta said.

"It was," Lisa Marie replied, "for about two days."

She went on to explain that they finally closed on the house they currently lived in, but because it was at the top of their budget, several of the rooms were unfurnished for the first year. Instead of being embarrassed by their lack of furniture, they used the empty space to their advantage. Jinx turned one room into her private dance studio and Sergio and Tommy turned another into a game room, where they spent hours playing makeshift soccer games, boccie ball tournaments, and touch football.

"It was something that could've torn our family apart," Tommy said. "Instead, it brought us together."

"Until the kids got old enough to have their own cell phones, and then we never saw them again," Lisa Marie commented.

Then she thought about her comment.

"There I go, putting my foot in my mouth again," she said. "Making fun about not seeing my kids when I haven't seen my son in over a month. I'm the mother of the year."

Alberta wanted to do nothing more than reach out and hold her daughter's hand, but she was afraid. She didn't think she could handle it if Lisa Marie flinched or slapped her hand away. But she had to do something. She had to comfort her daughter in some small way. Then it came to her. If Sloan could break the ice by making a joke, why couldn't she?

"Then that makes me mother of the decade," Alberta said.

Once again, Lisa Marie's laughter filled the air and, oddly enough, timed perfectly with Barbra Streisand's energetic rendition of the classic song "Jingle Bells."

"I see Funny Pants has rubbed off on you, Ma," Lisa Marie said.

"Hey, I thought I was Smarty-Pants?" Sloan asked.

"You're both," Lisa Marie said. "You're funny and a smarty; put them together and that makes Farty Pants!"

This time when Lisa Marie cracked up, she wasn't alone; everyone at the table joined in, even Sybil, their waitress, when she served them their food. In fact, Sibyl laughed so hard that the bells on the reindeer ears she was wearing jangled louder than the ones accompanying Babs.

While they ate, Lisa Marie whipped through the highlights of their life. She explained that Tommy opened up his own electrician's business and, despite her protestations, called it Shocking Maldonado because it sounded like one of the punk rock bands Tommy loved growing up. Lisa Marie, whose opinions outweighed her vocabulary, called it stupid.

After Jinx moved out, Lisa Marie felt it was time to get a full-time job and not just the part-time, temporary gigs, like crossing guard and salesperson, that she previously had. Without much experience or education, her choices were limited, but she finally landed at a veterinarian's office.

"Helen will be delighted to hear that," Sloan said. "She volunteers at the animal hospital."

Alberta wasn't so impressed. "You never liked animals. You used to spray water at Riccotta all the time."

"Who's Riccotta?" Sloan asked.

"My cousin Vito's cat," Alberta replied. "All white, but not nearly the angel Lola is."

"Disciplining animals is key to controlling them," Lisa Marie claimed. "But you're right, I don't like animals, and I told Dr. Rivera that, which is why I got the job."

"A veterinarian hired someone who doesn't like animals?" Sloan asked incredulously.

"He said I'm the most efficient assistant he's ever had," Lisa Marie said. "I don't waste time playing with the animals. I stick to my job."

"He likes her so much, she had trouble taking some time off," Tommy said. "But she explained it was a family emergency."

Mention of the stress they were under brought about another uncomfortable pause that no amount of cheery holiday music could conceal. Alberta had learned that when faced with such a situation, it was often better to confront the source of awkwardness, not retreat from it. She hoped the rest of them would agree.

"Tell me more about my grandson," Alberta said. "What's he really like?"

Without much effort, Lisa Marie and Tommy's hands found each other on the table, Tommy's hand covering Lisa Marie's until they clasped. Alberta was comforted to know that she had been wrong about Tommy all along;

from what she could tell, he was a good man who loved his wife and family. He was a husband her daughter could count on, which was more than she got out of her own marriage.

"He was . . . *is* a good kid," Tommy said. "Decent grades, played soccer, he wasn't as focused on his education like Jinx was, so he went to a community college for a few years but never transferred to another school to finish out his degree."

"He was working with Tommy and seemed to take to electrician work," Lisa Marie said. "I guess after watching his father growing up, he knew so much about the business before he even started. The moment Natalie came into his life, though, everything was ruined."

"How did they meet?" Alberta asked. "Sergio and Natalie."

"It was all my fault," Tommy said.

"No, it wasn't," Lisa Marie protested.

"Was too," Tommy replied definitively. "I had this raging sinus headache and sent Sergio to the CVS to pick me up some medicine, Natalie was there getting some antihistamines for her allergies, they bumped into each other at the checkout, and the rest is history."

Alberta's cell phone vibrated on the table, and when she read the text Vinny sent her, she announced that their lunch was over.

"Looks like we're going to find out a bit more about Natalie's history," she said.

The second time they were seated in Vinny's office, Lisa Marie and Tommy were filled with more hope than dread. They knew he wasn't going to miraculously pull Sergio from out behind a secret door, but they were hopeful that whatever information he had found on Natalie would bring Sergio back to their doorstep. Having much more experience sitting in Vinny's office waiting for him to share his findings during a case, Alberta was less optimistic.

"Natalie Vespa is twenty-seven and a graduate of Rowan University," Vinny announced.

"Isn't that in Jersey?" Sloan asked.

"Glassboro," Vinny confirmed. "Less than an hour from Atlantic City."

"You've heard of it, Sloan?" Alberta asked.

"Yes, it's a good school," he replied. "Not really known for attracting out-of-state students, though, and Vinny already told us she was born in Pennsylvania."

"Emmaus, to be exact, which isn't far from the Jersey border," Vinny said.

"What was her major in college?" Alberta asked.

"Elementary education, with a minor in biology," Vinny said. "She taught for a few years at St. Ann's in Bethlehem."

"According to the background check Tambra did posing as a potential employer, Natalie was a respected teacher and St. Ann's was sad to see her leave," Vinny explained. "She doesn't have a criminal record and she's got a good credit report."

"Where does she work now?" Alberta asked.

"Nowhere," Vinny said. "She might be freelancing, but we can't find that she has a current employer."

"That was the whole reason she left for New York," Lisa Marie said. "For a new job."

"We're going to keep looking, but we did find that she worked for VitaGen, an online vitamin company, for two years," Vinny said. "The company's address is in Utah, so if she was living in Florida, she had to have worked remotely."

"What about her family?" Alberta asked.

"We haven't traced them yet, but Tambra's still working on that," Vinny said.

"That isn't much to go on," Lisa Marie said. "Some old jobs and where she was born. Where is she now, Vin? That's what we need to know."

"We're getting closer," Vinny said. "She's still using her cell phone—not a lot, which would indicate that she also has a burner phone that she uses. Her last known calls came from New Jersey and New York."

"That's terrific news," Alberta said. "At least we know she wasn't lying about her destination."

"She used to rent an apartment on East Tenth Street in the City, and she's made a few phone calls to a Rudy Lewendorf, who just happens to live on East Tenth Street," Vinny conveyed.

"Sergio never mentioned anybody named Rudy," Lisa Marie said.

"Natalie may not have shared that information with Sergio," Vinny said. "My guess is that Rudy and Natalie met in Florida, because Rudy went to the FORTIS Institute in Pensacola."

Lisa Marie shook her head with disbelief. "This is what you people call connecting the dots, right? I mean, I've watched my share of cop shows, but to see it unfold right in front of your face is a totally different thing."

"It's just the beginning," Alberta said. "We take it one step at a time, follow the clues, and they'll lead us straight to Sergio."

"I'll send a car over to question Rudy," Vinny said. "See what else he knows about Natalie and Sergio."

"Don't do that!" Tommy exclaimed.

"Why not?" Vinny asked. "We need to question Rudy; he's the only link we have at the moment to Natalie."

"I understand, but would it be all right if we talked to the guy first?" Tommy asked. "I know my son, and if he gets wind that the cops are looking for him and Natalie, he's going to get ticked off and hide even better than he is right now."

"Sergio has a problem with the cops?" Vinny asked.

"My son doesn't particularly like authority," Tommy said. "No offense."

"Why not?" Alberta asked. "You said he was never in trouble with the police. Why should he mistrust them?"

"Because of me," Tommy said. "I got in trouble with the police, and ever since then, Sergio's had a chip on his shoulder wherever the cops are concerned."

Tommy explained that he was working for a large utility company and was accused of stealing equipment. Unable to prove his innocence, he was fired. The Florida cops made him a scapegoat and it tarnished his reputation, making it impossible for him to get hired by another company. A month later there were more thefts, and lo and behold, the real culprit turned out to be one of Tommy's coworkers, who was revealed to be the brother of a local cop. Sergio was young and impressionable at the time and it was his first real, hands-on experience with the police. They treated his father horribly and he could never forgive them.

"*Dipende sempre dalla famiglia*," Alberta said.

"That it does," Sloan agreed.

Lisa Marie's jaw dropped this time. She couldn't believe what she had just heard come out of Sloan's mouth.

"Do not tell me that you speak Italian too?" she asked.

"Since I've gotten closer to your mother, I've been studying Italian," Sloan said.

"His accent is terrible, but he gets his point across," Alberta said. "What I said was, it always comes down to family."

"That it does," Tommy said.

"And speaking of family, let's go and share this news with everyone," Alberta said. "It's time for us to plan our next move."

CHAPTER 8

Due sono la compagnia, tre sono una folla.

"The Mistletoe Ball is going to be the death of me!" Jinx made that declaration the moment she threw open the door and stood in Alberta's kitchen. Her long black hair looked more wild than wavy and the 1980s houndstooth overcoat she was wearing, with full padded shoulders, gave her the silhouette of a football player, so to the untrained eye she looked slightly foreboding. The only ones who were startled by Jinx's outburst, however, were her parents. The rest of them had gotten so used to people showing up unexpectedly, making grand statements, and looking borderline homicidal, that such dramatic entrances were greeted, if not with applause, then with acceptance. They had become the norm. Lisa Marie and Tommy had obviously lived a quieter life in Florida.

"Does no one knock around here?" Lisa Marie asked.

"I swear to God, somebody's going to give me a heart attack."

"Sorry, Ma," Jinx said.

"And you're lucky you have a boyfriend," Lisa Marie said. "Walking around town looking like a refugee from the early days of MTV isn't going to get you a date. I mean, where on earth did you get that coat?"

"From Aunt Joyce," Jinx said.

Lisa Marie turned to face her aunt and smiled, as if she hadn't just insulted her. "I should've known."

"Why does the Ball have you in a tizzy, lovey?" Alberta asked.

"Because it's making Wyck even more frantic than usual," Jinx replied. "It's bad enough that the Ball is making a reappearance after thirtysomething years."

"Thirty-two," Joyce replied.

"The Ball is also a kickoff to celebrate St. Clare's because the hospital's been around for who knows how long," Jinx added.

"A hundred years," Sloan replied.

"Plus, it's the start of a series of fundraising events to raise money for a new wing at St. Clare's to treat some disease," Jinx finished.

"That disease would be breast cancer," Helen said.

"Honey, isn't a reporter supposed to be the person who knows the facts?" Tommy asked.

"I know all the facts, Daddy!" Jinx yelled. "I'm just annoyed that I have to work on all this stuff while Sergio is missing. I swear to God, when we find him, I'm gonna slap him so hard my fingerprints will be permanently tattooed on his face!"

Lola, who was a born pacifist unless someone ever tried to remove her food dish before she was finished eating, tried to put an end to the yelling by purring and prancing in between Jinx's legs. It worked. It was also the perfect stress reducer, and when Jinx picked Lola up, she could feel her blood pressure drop. However, her pulse started to race again when she focused on her surroundings and looked across the room.

Jinx was not accustomed to seeing her grandmother and her mother sitting side by side at the kitchen table and it was an image that filled her with equal parts happiness and fear, not to mention an accelerated heart rate. She was thrilled that they were speaking to each other again, but she was terrified that their next argument was one wrong word away. Hopefully, the search for her brother would take priority and the brutal confrontation between the two women that Jinx feared would take place could be avoided. For a while at least.

"Now that you're all here, sit down, because we have some news to share," Alberta announced.

"That might bring us closer to finding Sergio," Lisa Marie added.

Mother and daughter were actually working together, Jinx thought. Could this be the first in a string of miracles?

"Unfortunately, we still have no idea where Sergio is," Alberta said.

So much for that.

"We did locate a guy who used to be Natalie's roommate in New York," Lisa Marie added.

That sounded promising.

"We're going to pay him a visit tomorrow morning," Alberta announced.

That was frustrating.

"The Mistletoe Ball strikes again!" Jinx cried.

"What are you talking about, lovey?" Alberta asked.

"I have an editorial meeting tomorrow morning at eight o'clock so I can't go with you to New York," Jinx said. "Wyck is revamping the paper to cash in on the publicity of the Ball, which means we're adding new columns and features, and I get to write an in-depth series of articles about the history of the hospital decade by decade!"

"I can help you with that, Jinx," Sloan said. "I have lots of notes and files on the hospital that go back to the seventies from when I contributed to the special edition of *The Herald* celebrating Tranquility's one hundredth anniversary."

"You're a lifesaver, Sloan," Jinx said. "I'll stop by the library after my meeting."

"Don't worry, lovey, we'll fill you in on what we find out when we get back home," Alberta said. "Helen, I assume you'll be our chauffeur into the city."

"You would assume wrong, Berta," Helen said.

"What do you mean?" Alberta asked. "You're always our chauffeur when we have to drive somewhere to interview a person of interest while investigating a new case."

Lisa Marie turned to her husband and threw up her hands. "I cannot believe those words just came out of my mother's mouth."

"I hate to disappoint you, but I'll be with Jinx tomorrow morning," Helen said. "I have a meeting with Wyck at nine a.m. sharp."

"What does Wyck want to see you about, Helen?" Sloan asked.

"Something about the opportunity of a lifetime," Helen replied. "I know Wyck is prone to exaggeration, but I'm always willing to entertain new ideas."

"I have a Mistletoe Ball Committee meeting tomorrow morning," Sloan said. "I would try to reschedule, but Bambi is very strict."

"You're having a meeting with a Disney character?" Lisa Marie asked.

"No," Joyce said. "Bambi's the hospital administrator at St. Clare's."

"A grown woman named Bambi is running a hospital?" Lisa Marie commented.

"Her real name is Bambina DeBenedetto," Sloan explained. "Bambi is the lesser of two evils."

Lisa Marie once again looked at her husband with a bewildered expression. "I can't believe the things that come out of any of their mouths."

"Joyce, you're the head of that committee; does that mean you can't go tomorrow either?" Alberta asked.

"The meeting is for library and hospital personnel to discuss the making of the video that tells the history of St. Clare's," Joyce explained. "I'm off the hook and can join you."

"Gram, keep me posted on what you find out tomorrow," Jinx said. "And Ma, where are you and Daddy staying tonight?"

"We'll check back into the Tranquility Arms," Tommy suggested.

"Nonsense," Alberta said. "You'll stay with me."

Lisa Marie smiled at her mother, and although Alberta could tell it was genuine, she could also tell it was strategic. Her daughter was trying to shield her from inevitable heartache. Wasn't that supposed to be the other way around?

"I don't think that's such a smart idea, Ma," Lisa Marie said.

Even though Alberta knew her daughter was right, she couldn't stop herself from pursuing the matter. "Why not?" Alberta said. "The two of you already broke in here, why not stay the night?"

"Just to make it clear with everybody, the back door was unlocked, so, technically, we did not break in," Tommy said.

"You're still my daughter," Alberta said. "You're always welcome in my home."

"Ma, it's really nice to see you again—nicer than I ever could have imagined—but I think if Tommy and I stayed here that would be pushing things," Lisa Marie said. "Living under one roof didn't go so well for us the first time; I don't want history to repeat itself. I want this time to be different."

Alberta was taken aback by Lisa Marie's heartfelt words. Her maternal instinct fought against the implication that her home could be considered a war zone, but it wasn't a concept her logical brain could successfully debate. What filled Alberta with hope was that Lisa Marie was hopeful that they could have a future. That was worth not having them stay in her home.

"I guess what you're saying is, *Due sono la compagnia, tre sono una folla*," Alberta said.

"I have no idea what that means," Lisa Marie said. "But I can guarantee you that I didn't say it."

"Yes, you did," Helen said. "Two's company, three's a crowd."

"Oh, well, yeah, I guess I did say that," Lisa Marie. "I'm sorry, Ma."

"Don't be. I want this time to be different too," Alberta said. "But I hate to think of you staying at the Arms. A hotel is no place for family."

"I'd invite you to stay at my place," Jinx said. "But I have a roommate."

"I have a cot from when I did missionary work in Costa Rica that is surprisingly comfortable," Helen said.

"I'm sure it is, Helen, but I have the perfect solution," Joyce said. "Stay with me."

"That's a wonderful idea, Joyce," Alberta said. "Her guest room is much more comfortable than anything you'd find at the Arms and you'll be with family, the way it should be."

"Aunt Joyce, you really don't mind?" Lisa Marie asked.

"I'll be insulted if you pick a room at Sanjay's instead of staying with me," Joyce said. "Just don't expect me to cook."

"Then it's settled," Alberta said. "You two stay with Joyce tonight and in the morning come here and I'll have breakfast waiting."

"That sounds perfect, Ma," Lisa Marie said.

And it was. After a good night's sleep in Joyce's guest room, they returned to Alberta's house in the morning and were greeted by the smells of eggs, bacon, pancakes, and sausage. The food tasted better than it smelled, which, considering Alberta was the chef, wasn't a surprise, and by the time they got into Tommy's Subaru to drive to New York they were fortified and felt ready for the day's adventure.

Lisa Marie thought she was going to be the one to walk up to Rudy Lewendorf's front door and bombard him with questions about Sergio and Natalie, but Alberta pointed out, very diplomatically, that that wasn't the best way to yield results. First, no one in New York was going to open their front door to a stranger, and second, no one in New York had a front door like they did in the suburbs. They had doors to their buildings, and the only way to make contact with them was to talk through an intercom to be buzzed up. The only strangers certain to get buzzed up to a New Yorker's apartment were those delivering food. Which was why Alberta's bag was filled with a sausage, peppers, and onion hero and a container of rigatoni and broccoli. She needed an option if it turned out Rudy was a vegetarian.

Tommy found parking across from Rudy's building, and when they found themselves so close to the first break in their case, Lisa Marie wanted to break the rules.

"I'm going in with you," she declared.

"No, you're not," Alberta replied.

"Ma, Sergio's my son!" Lisa Marie exclaimed. "I have to help him."

"No, *I* have to help him; that's why you wrote to me in the first place," Alberta corrected. "If you come with us, you'll get all emotional and ruin any chance we have of finding out where Sergio is. This is what we do. We're far from experts, but we get results. I need you to trust me on that."

Lisa Marie let out a deep breath. "Then why are you sitting here? Go find out where my son is."

Joyce scanned the names next to the front door and found *Lewendorf*. Before she pressed the buzzer to apartment 3B, she faced Alberta. "You realize he might have already left for work."

"Then we'll stake out the building until a guy in his late twenties returns," Alberta said.

"That narrows down the male population in New York City considerably," Joyce commented sarcastically.

"Press the buzzer."

Joyce did as she was told, and to their delight, they heard a voice come through the intercom. The voice, however, didn't sound as delighted as the women felt.

"Who is it?" the voice bellowed.

"Food delivery," Joyce said.

"I didn't order anything," the voice replied. "You got the wrong apartment."

"It's from Natalie!" Alberta shouted.

The five seconds it took for the buzzer to ring felt like an eternity. Before they entered the building, Alberta turned to give Lisa Marie and Tommy the thumbs-up, a gesture that was greeted by matching stunned expressions. Alberta practically floated up the three flights of stairs, secure in the knowledge that she had once again impressed her daughter. She would have to work harder to get the same response from Rudy.

"Whoa!" Rudy shouted. "You two don't look like Natalie's friends."

"We're not exactly *friends*," Alberta confessed.

"More like business associates," Joyce said.

Rudy looked doubtful. "Guess it takes all kinds."

After a brief hesitation he let them inside, and Alberta and Joyce immediately had flashbacks of the apartments that dotted the buildings where they grew up. Small boxes with little light and less elbow room. To their immediate left was a galley kitchen and to the right was a refrigerator with alphabet letter magnets on the door that didn't spell out any words found in the English language and, next to it, a closet door. Straight ahead was a dual-purpose space serving as a dining area and living room. The door to the bathroom could be seen just off the hallway to the right that presumably led to the bedroom because the lounge chair in the main area didn't look like it would make a comfortable bed even for someone as wiry as Rudy.

It was a typical New York apartment for a young man just starting out in life. But even though Rudy was a few years from his thirtieth birthday, he had a world-weary look about him. Alberta assumed it was the hallmark of the busy New Yorker, who burned both ends of the candle. Or she misinterpreted his look, and he was just nervous about having two strangers in his home.

Rudy drummed his fingers on the kitchen table and his left hand was clenched in a fist and digging into his waist. Every few seconds his foot tapped on the hard wood floor; he was rhythm in motion. A forced smile was interrupted by a facial tic that made the left corner of his mouth twitch like he was hearing something funny that no one else in the room could hear. If it weren't for his mop of thick red hair, which was tucked behind his ears and fell to just underneath his jawline, he'd come off as scary. Instead, he looked like an adorable, overgrown country boy trying to make it in the big city.

"You two really don't look like the type of people Natalie works with," Rudy said.

"We're not," Alberta said.

"You lied to me," Rudy stated.

"You might already know us," Alberta said. "My name is Alberta Scaglione and this is my sister-in-law, Joyce Ferrara."

"How would I know you?" Rudy asked.

"We know Natalie through Alberta's grandson, Sergio Maldonado," Joyce explained. "Do you know him?"

"Does he work at the hospital?" Rudy asked.

"No, he's Natalie's boyfriend," Alberta said.

"Not possible," Rudy said. "Natalie doesn't have a boyfriend."

"She and Sergio have been dating for about six months," Alberta said.

"They have not," Rudy declared. "I saw Nat a few months ago in Florida and she didn't mention anything about a boyfriend or a Sergio."

"Maybe she didn't want to make you jealous," Joyce suggested.

The drumming stopped. "If anyone is jealous, it's Nat," Rudy said. "She doesn't exactly approve of J. J."

"Your new girlfriend?" Alberta asked.

"Yeah, they had what you could call a falling out," Rudy explained.

"I'm sorry to hear that," Alberta said. "I hope that hasn't had an impact on your relationship with Natalie."

"Nat can't be mad at me, I'm her tristate contact," Rudy said. "Just last month I introduced her to some new clients in Jersey."

"They must've been VIPs because Natalie wanted to express her thanks to you in an unorthodox way," Joyce said. "With some of Alberta's famous sausage and peppers."

Alberta took the food out of her bag and placed it on the counter. Rudy sniffed and appeared to salivate. Clearly the bachelor didn't get many home-cooked meals.

"Wow, that smells delicious," Rudy said.

"Giada De Laurentiis might be skinnier, but she's got nothing on Berta when it comes to cooking," Joyce said.

"You should invite Natalie and some friends over for a holiday party and I'll do all the cooking," Alberta said.

Rudy smiled a bit too wistfully and replied, "That would be nice, but there's no way Natalie would ever come back here."

"Why do you say that?" Alberta asked.

"Nat's one of those girls who never looks back, whether it's an apartment, a city, a guy, once she's done, she's done," Rudy said. "You should, you know, warn your grandson about that. Unless she's done a complete one-eighty, that relationship isn't going to last much longer."

"I thank you for your honesty, Rudy," Alberta said.

"Look, I'm not really sure what you ladies are doing here, but I can't help you," Rudy said. "I don't know your grandson and I haven't seen Natalie in a while."

"If you do speak with either of them or get a text or an e-mail, please get a message to Sergio and ask him to get in touch with his parents," Joyce said.

"Or his sister Jinx," Alberta added.

"I doubt that'll happen, but if it does, I'll pass on the message," Rudy said.

"I put my phone number in with the sausage and peppers too," Alberta said. "Feel free to drop me a line if you hear from Sergio or see him with or without Natalie."

For the first time Rudy stopped moving. He stopped tapping his fingers on his belt, he stopped scratching his calf with the tip of his shoe, and he just stared at Alberta as if he was seeing her for the first time.

"You're right to be worried about your grandson," Rudy stated.

Alberta did not like the seriousness of Rudy's tone;

she felt herself losing control of her emotions and acting exactly the way she told Lisa Marie would be inappropriate.

"Why would you say that?" she asked.

"Natalie isn't dangerous, not like J. J. can be," Rudy said. "But she's mixed up, you can't trust her, and your grandson would definitely be better off without her."

Suddenly the man standing before Alberta and Joyce no longer looked worldly and disengaged. He had transformed into a lost young man. Alberta knew there was a lot more he could tell them, but he had said all he was going to say.

"Now if you ladies would excuse me," Rudy said. "I have to get back to work."

Before Rudy could make a move, Alberta opened the closet door to her right as if she were attempting to leave the apartment.

"What are you doing?" Rudy asked.

"*Ah Madon!*" Alberta said. "I thought this was the front door. These New York apartments are so confusing."

The contents of the closets of those apartments were even more confusing. Alberta was able to get a quick glimpse of what was contained in Rudy's closet before he shut the door. She didn't know why a young man would need a stack of boxes with stickers in the shape of flowers on them. Unless, of course, he was a florist.

"I'm a pharmaceutical salesman," Rudy said.

Or a pharmaceutical salesman?

"How interesting," Alberta said. "My husband used to be on a blood pressure medicine, I can't remember which one, but it was helpful. What do you sell?"

"Their names are really long and they're just rolling onto the market, you wouldn't recognize them," Rudy said as he ushered the ladies to the real front door. "Thanks again for stopping by, and for the food. And please remember what I said about Natalie."

The fact that Sergio had put all his trust in a girl who couldn't be trusted? That was something they would never forget.

CHAPTER 9

Il riso fa buon sangue.

The Christmas decorations at the newspaper's offices made it look like *The Upper Sussex Herald* was published out of Santa's guest house. Wyck's unbridled enthusiasm for the holiday would easily earn him the title of number one elf. Unfortunately, Wyck's number one reporter wasn't sharing his enthusiasm for her latest assignment.

"You want me to make Bambi look like she literally stepped out of some enchanted forest?" Jinx asked.

"She did!" Wyck cried.

"Snow White lived in the enchanted forest, Bambi's forest burned to the ground," Calhoun said. "If it possessed any magical powers, a strong wind would've come along to take out the fire and prevent Bambi from becoming an orphan."

Sylvester Calhoun had been Wyck's number one reporter until Jinx started to prove herself capable of writing more than fluff pieces and features about local garden competitions. Now that Jinx was getting the plum jobs, Calhoun had become more of a rival than a colleague. They usually butted heads and disagreed on how to approach an article, but in this instance their opinion was shared.

"Bambi isn't perfect," Jinx said. "And neither is St. Clare's."

"Right on both counts, Jinxie," Wyck said.

"Then why are you telling me to write a puff piece about Bambi DeBenedetto?" she asked.

"Because Bambi DeBenedetto wrote a huge check to the paper in exchange for publicity, that's why!" Wyck cried.

"That's unethical," Jinx said.

"We'll label it a supplement and make it look like an advertorial," Wyck said. "This is a business, and we could use the influx of cash."

"If you'd been a reporter for more than half a minute, Jinx, you'd know this is how things get done," Calhoun said.

"Just because this is how things get done doesn't mean it's right," Jinx said.

"Then maybe I should tell Bambi that Freddy isn't worthy of receiving this year's award," Wyck announced.

"What are you talking about?" Jinx asked. "What award?"

"The Small Business Owner of the Year award," Wyck replied. "Freddy's on the short list of nominations."

"He is?" Jinx squealed.

"Yes, but it's a secret," Wyck said. "I told Bambi that nothing would make me happier than if Freddy won and

Bambi said that she knows just how to keep a man happy."

"Oh my God Wyck, Freddy would flip if he won that award!" Jinx cried.

"I know that! Why do you think I made a not-so-subtle suggestion?" Wyck asked. "So stop talking about unethical journalistic practices and just follow the Gram rule."

"What's the Gram rule?" Calhoun asked.

"If you'd be a reporter for more than half a minute instead of a guy hungry for a byline, you'd know what Wyck was talking about," Jinx said. "It's how my grandmother cooks. She follows the recipe ninety percent to the letter but sprinkles in ten percent of her own personal touch."

"Jinx will keep her articles ninety percent fluff, but if she finds anything that makes her investigative nose tingle, she'll throw it in and we'll see if we can keep it," Wyck explained.

"If not, we hold the unprinted ten percent for a separate article," Jinx said. "Capisce?"

"Of course Calhoun capisces. He might not be Italian, but he knows I'm the capo around here," Wyck said. "Bambi has given us full access to the hospital's archives so we can do stories on the founders and interview all the prominent doctors."

"Does that include access to the hospital's photo archives?" Benny asked.

"It sure does," Wyck said. "You can set up a time with Bambi's office to rummage through those photos and use whatever you'd like."

"Benny, let's connect once you choose your photos," Jinx said. "We can use the ones that'll best enhance the editorial."

"Sounds like a plan, Jinxie," Benny said.

"Don't call her Jinxie!" Wyck cried. "I'm the only one gets to call her that."

"Correction, mister! The only one who gets to call Jinxie Jinxie is me."

The staff turned to see Helen standing in the doorway. Wyck and Jinx were the only ones not confused as to why a short, gray-haired woman wearing a black parka, black rubber galoshes, and carrying a large black pocketbook that dangled from the crook of her elbow was admonishing them. It was an odd sight, indeed, even for hardened reporters who were trained not to be shocked by their surroundings. True to their professional heritage, they remained calm in Helen's presence. All except Benny.

"Helen! How wonderful to see you again!"

Benny had to be forgiven his outburst. He had recently performed on stage with Helen in the highest-grossing production in the history of the Tranquility Players and still was having trouble coming down from his actor's high. Seeing Helen again made him feel like he was standing in the glow of the footlights and not under the fluorescent lighting of the boardroom.

"Benny, it's wonderful to see you again too," Helen said. "But I'm here to see Wyck. We had an appointment at nine a.m. sharp and it's now three past nine."

"Meeting adjourned!" Wyck cried. "Remember, people, the Mistletoe Ball is right around the corner and we need to sprinkle the magic dust around to make it something this town will never forget!"

The staff filtered out of the room, and just as Jinx was about to wish her aunt good luck and leave with the rest of her coworkers, Wyck told her to stay. He wanted Jinx to hear what he had to say. So did Helen.

"Spill it, Wyck," Helen said. "I'm a busy lady and I don't have all day."

"That's why you're here!" Wyck cried. "That attitude, that knock-'em-between-the-eyes approach, you sound exactly like my big sister."

"You don't have a big sister, Wyck," Jinx corrected. "You're an only child."

"I'm not talking about my real family, I'm talking about my professional family!" Wyck shouted. "Helen, I want to hire you to be *The Herald*'s newest advice columnist. You'll be Tranquility's very own Dear Abby, otherwise known as Big Sister, because you used to be a Sister and you got a big mouth."

"Dearie me, Wyck," Helen scolded. "How's a girl supposed to handle such flattery?"

"By accepting my offer," he replied. "You know it's a perfect fit, Helen, what do you say? Will you make me the happiest editor alive and join our team?"

They assumed that Wyck was going to make Helen some kind of offer, maybe a one-off op-ed, but not such a high-profile role at the paper. Faced with such a proposal, Helen didn't blink, her expression didn't indicate excitement or disapproval, her body language didn't betray her emotions. Helen didn't have a poker face, she had a poker body.

Finally, she walked toward the conference room table and sat down. She put her pocketbook on her lap and folded her hands, placing them on the thick leather handle. She didn't say a word, but Jinx could tell her aunt was in complete control. If Wyck wanted to continue the conversation, Helen was silently forcing him to make the next move. Jinx was not at all surprised when Wyck sprang into action.

He ran around the other side of the table so he could sit across from Helen and face her directly. Jinx plopped into a seat next to Helen just as Wyck began the second phase of his pitch, sounding more like a junior reporter than an experienced editor.

"*The Herald* hasn't had an advice column for years," Wyck began. "It's high time the tradition is resurrected, and who better to lead the resurrection than a former nun?"

Jinx had learned firsthand that Helen didn't approve of using religion as a punch line. She may have left the convent, but she had not abandoned her faith. Jinx waited for her aunt to chastise Wyck for his unholy remark. She didn't have to wait long.

"One more religious pun and I'm out of here," Helen announced.

Wyck understood. "I apologize," he said. True to his word, he finished the rest of his pitch without one jab at the church's expense.

He explained that the advice column had a storied history at the paper dating back to the very first issue. The *Dear Tranquility* column was an immediate hit with readers, anonymously doling out candid but sincere advice to the not-so-tranquil searching for answers to problems they were too ashamed or too scared to share with family and friends. The column ran for decades until the family-run paper was sold to a corporation that underestimated the small-town appeal and thought it could turn *The Herald* into a weekly rag with a more sophisticated, big-city presence. It failed miserably. When the current owners bought the paper they returned it to its community-driven roots, but as of yet the advice column had not made its way back into print. Wyck wanted to change that.

"All kidding aside, Helen, you are a beacon of honesty, a respected member of this community, and a gal with a lot of wit," Wyck said. "I'd be honored to publish your words and our readers will be better off when they read them."

Jinx watched her aunt's face soften and she knew that she was touched by Wyck's words. She also knew that Helen wasn't about to share her feelings with a potential new employer.

"*Il riso fa buon sangue*," Helen said.

"Is that a yes?" Wyck inquired.

"I think so," Jinx replied. "It means 'laughter is the best medicine,' doesn't it?"

"Keep it up, Jinxie, and you'll be a native speaker in no time," Helen said. "We have to come to terms on my salary and I'm going to want carte blanche, editorially speaking."

"As long as you don't make our lawyers jittery about a lawsuit, you can have free reign," Wyck said. "It's only your opinion after all."

"I also demand anonymity and I don't want the public finding out I'm the new advice columnist in town," Helen said. "I cherish my privacy."

"It'll be our little secret," Wyck said.

"Then you, Mr. Editor in Chief," Helen replied, "have got yourself a Big Sister."

On the other side of town at Alberta's house, Helen's little sister had some advice of her own to share.

"This morning was a complete waste of time, Ma!" Lisa Marie shouted. "We didn't learn a thing."

"That's not true, honey, we learned quite a bit," Joyce said.

"Like what?" Lisa Marie challenged.

"To begin with, we learned that Rudy and Natalie share a romantic past, but he's now dating some girl named J. J.," Alberta said. "We also learned Rudy and Natalie are in business together, though we aren't sure exactly what that business is and, sadly, we learned that your instincts about Natalie were right on target: The girl is trouble and will probably wind up breaking Sergio's heart."

"I counted four new things they learned," Tommy said. "What about you, Lees?"

"We're still no closer to finding him than we were a month ago," she replied.

Lisa Marie sat with her arms resting on the kitchen table and shook her head, just barely. She had lost her fight and her anger and was left with her sorrow. The tears she'd been holding back since she returned to Alberta's life finally fell in long, uninterrupted streams down her cheeks. Her grief was almost unbearable to watch, but her words were even harder to hear.

"I give up," she said. "My son obviously doesn't want to be part of our family anymore and there's nothing I can do about it. Talk about karma." She started to laugh and looked up at the ceiling. "You can knock it off, God, you win, I've learned my lesson."

Alberta couldn't take any more of her daughter's self-pity. She understood it, she had lived it, but it was not going to help them find her grandson.

"You listen to me," Alberta said. "You do not give up hope, do you hear me? If you do that, you'll have no chance of finding Sergio. Never once did I give up hope that I'd see you again and look at us now."

Alberta felt the emotions race from the pit of her stomach into her throat, but she had to quell them for now; she had a job to do. She sat next to Lisa Marie and, without worrying about the consequences, she held her daughter's tearstained face in her hands. To her immense relief, Lisa Marie didn't pull away. She needed her mother's love as much as Alberta needed to give it to her.

"But if you find that you're starting to lose hope, you look to me," Alberta commanded. "We have had our differences, we have had our fights, but you are my life, and every ounce of my strength and my love and my hope is yours. Do you understand that?"

Lisa Marie remained silent. Alberta couldn't tell if she was overcome with emotion or if all the emotions she once had for her mother—the good and the bad—had disappeared as she once had. Alberta wasn't reluctant to push the moment, but she had to know. She had to know if she had any chance of reconciling with her daughter or if, despite her return, she was lost to her forever.

"Do you understand that?" Alberta repeated.

Lisa Marie's response was barely a whisper, "Yes, Ma, I do."

It was all Alberta needed to hear. It was enough of an invitation for Alberta to embrace her daughter with the certainty that Lisa Marie wouldn't struggle to escape. So that was what she did. The only one who was surprised that Lisa Marie didn't resist such intimate contact was Lisa Marie herself. She not only accepted her mother's hug but wrapped her arms around Alberta so tightly neither one of them let go until they heard Alberta's cell phone ping three times in a row.

J.D. Griffo

"Sounds like someone's eager to get in touch with you," Tommy said.

"Betcha it's that boyfriend of yours," Lisa Marie said. She got up to rip off a paper towel from the roll next to the sink to wipe her face. "He's crazy about you, he is."

Alberta looked at her phone and couldn't be happier that Lisa Marie was wrong. "It isn't Sloan. It's Rudy."

"Rudy!" the three other people in the room screamed.

"It's from an unidentified number," Alberta said. "Who else could it be?"

"What does he say?" Joyce asked.

"I'm not really sure," Alberta replied. "Trolloppe, Be, and Careful."

"You are many things, Ma, but trollop isn't one of them!" Lisa Marie cried.

Joyce took the phone from Alberta's hands so she could read the texts. "Rudy isn't calling Berta a Jezebel, he's giving her a clue."

"How do you know that?" Tommy asked.

"Because he spelled Trolloppe wrong. The word that Mr. Rick James once described as not the type of girl you'd bring home to mother is spelled t-r-o-l-l-o-p," Joyce explained. "This Trolloppe isn't a woman, it's the new cardiac wing at the Sussex County Medical Center in Newton, named after Alistair Trolloppe, who was a brilliant surgeon born in the area."

"You're almost as bad as Sloan," Alberta said. "The two of you are walking encyclopedias about all things Tranquility."

"With age can sometimes come wisdom," Joyce said.

"Now this text makes sense, especially if Rudy really is a pharmaceutical salesman," Alberta said. "Maybe

Natalie's new job is at this Trolloppe wing and Rudy is trying to lead us to it."

"Then let's go see this Trolloppe!" Lisa Marie cried.

"We can't just waltz into a place like that," Alberta said.

"That's true, we can't," Joyce agreed. "We'll need to make an appointment."

They stood in silence and listened as Joyce pulled some strings, thanks to her role as chairperson of the Mistletoe Ball Committee, board member of St. Clare's Hospital, two-time winner of the Sussex County Amateur Artist's Competition, and former Wall Street wizard who could talk her way into any situation to seal a deal, including a men's-only Turkish sauna in Brooklyn back in 1995. She ended the call and told them she had an appointment with the hospital administrator at the Medical Center in an hour. She hadn't even broken out into a sweat.

"If Mrs. Passanante lived in Tranquility her head would explode," Lisa Marie said. "She wouldn't be able to keep up with the action."

"Why do you think I started to jog in the park with Jinx?" Alberta said. "I needed to keep up my energy."

"My mother jogs?" Lisa Marie asked.

"See what you've missed moving down south," Joyce said. "Now hurry up, folks, we don't want to keep D. Edward Carmichael waiting."

Fifty minutes later, the Subaru was parked at the entrance of the Sussex County Medical Center. This time when Alberta suggested Lisa Marie and Tommy wait in the car while she and Joyce met with the administrator, no one put up a fuss. The mother-daughter dynamic had taken a turn for the good.

"Be careful," Lisa Marie said. "I don't trust this guy."

"Honey, a real detective gives their subject the benefit of the doubt before assigning guilt," Alberta said.

"I'm not a real detective, so I can assign all I want," Lisa Marie replied. "Anyone whose first name is just an initial is hiding something."

When Alberta and Joyce were standing outside Carmichael's office, they discovered Lisa Marie's intuition was right. Fortunately, he had left the door ajar, which made it easy for them to hear what he was trying to hide. His office was off the hall and while there were two chairs outside his door there was no reception area, which made it even easier for them to eavesdrop without worrying about getting caught.

"You know how sorry I am, but this isn't going to work out," Carmichael said.

"Give me another chance, please. I'll work the overnight shift, I'll clean bedpans, I need a job, Eddy."

They couldn't see into the room, but the woman's voice sounded young, and although it wasn't the stereotypical New Jersey accent, it did sound gruff. She could be making a sweeping generalization, but Alberta thought the woman sounded like she came from the wrong side of the tracks, closer to where she was raised, and not from the upper echelon of society. Regardless of where she came from, Carmichael wasn't happy that she was now in his office.

"You should be thanking me for not calling the police!" Carmichael shouted. "After everything I tried to do to help you, all you did was act like a noctor, zeroing in on the frequent flyers."

"Nothing can be proven, it's all hearsay," the woman replied.

"You did enough to get your nurse's license revoked!"

"Because of her and you know it!"

"The only thing I know is that I want you out of here . . . now!"

"You people seriously think you can get away with this, don't you?" the woman asked. "I'm warning you, Eddy, don't push me!"

They heard the woman coming toward them and had just enough time to stand against the wall and were hidden by the door when the woman pushed it open to leave. She didn't see Alberta and Joyce peeking out from behind the door, but they saw a woman with a mass of black, curly hair that fell past her shoulders stomp down the hallway and make a right toward the elevator bank.

Alberta was about to tell Joyce to follow the woman when Carmichael appeared in the doorway. He only saw Joyce at first, until he moved the door to reveal Alberta standing next to her. The women couldn't tell if he was alarmed to see them because they could scarcely see his face. He was wearing a Santa Claus outfit.

"Ho, ho, ho!" Carmichael bellowed. "Joyce, I thought you were coming over to discuss Mistletoe Ball business, not have me interrogated by Tranquility's own Trixie Belden."

"That's a name I haven't heard since I was in grade school," Alberta said.

"Alberta and I were in the middle of running errands, and with all the snow, I didn't want her waiting for me out in the car," Joyce fibbed.

"Of course not," Carmichael replied. "I wouldn't want anyone catching their death because of me. Come in."

"Thank you, Edward," Joyce said.

Carmichael stood to the side and with an elaborate wave of his arm gestured for the ladies to enter his office. They did and he followed up with another arm gesture, waving them over to a small settee that looked incredibly uncomfortable and terribly expensive. When the ladies sat down they felt as if they were sitting on an overpriced slab of concrete.

"Now, what exactly can I do for you?" Carmichael asked, sitting in a more comfortable-looking armchair opposite them.

"For starters, you could explain why you're dressed as Santa," Alberta said.

"Edward is already getting into character," Joyce said. "He'll be playing Santa at the Mistletoe Ball."

"I thought I'd give the outfit a test drive and visit some of the children in the pediatric ward," he explained. "It's hard to be a kid in a hospital any time of year, but it's especially difficult at Christmastime."

"*Che Dio li benedica tutti,*" Alberta said, more to herself than her host.

"That's my hope, Mrs. Scaglione," Carmichael said. "Every child deserves to be blessed by God."

"You speak Italian?" Alberta asked.

"Working at a hospital that serves such a diverse community, I've picked up phrases in many languages," he explained. "Joyce, I assume you're here to talk about the display the hospital is sponsoring at the Winter Wonderland."

"Yes," Joyce said. "Because it opens in Tranquility Park the day after the Ball, I wanted to make sure that you had all the support you needed. There won't be any time to solve problems in between the two events."

"Efficient as ever, you are," Carmichael replied. "We'd be completely on schedule if the mayor's office would cooperate."

"What seems to be the problem?" Joyce asked.

"We need a variance to allow an increase in electricity usage," Carmichael explained. "The light display we have planned exceeds the current available rate, and I think you can agree that if we don't go big, we might as well stay home, have some figgy pudding by the fire, and watch *It's a Wonderful Life* for the fortieth time."

"That would be cozy, but not at all the holiday spirit the town is craving for this year," Alberta said.

"I'll pay a visit to the mayor's office first thing in the morning to clear things up and get you what you need," Joyce said. "If the Winter Wonderland had a blackout, that would be a disaster."

"Thank you, Joyce, I can always count on you," Carmichael said. "Maybe you should run for mayor of Tranquility!"

"*Ah Madon*!" Alberta cried. "That's a brilliant idea!"

"I don't think I'm ready for political office," Joyce said. "But I'll do what I can to make sure the Wonderland is a priority with the mayor."

Carmichael clasped his hands together and smiled. "All of us here at the hospital thank you."

"I know that you have your hands full, what with the

new Trolloppe cardiac wing," Joyce said. "That must take up so much of your time."

"It's the pride of the hospital, actually both hospitals," Carmichael said as he tugged on his Santa beard. "For so many years we were rivals with St. Clare's, and then one day Bambi and I were talking things over and we realized we'd accomplish so much more if we worked together."

Alberta understood exactly what Carmichael was talking about. At first she and Jinx resisted working with Vinny and the police, until they realized they could both benefit from a partnership. Sounded like Carmichael and Bambi had the same kind of epiphany.

"It took many years to raise the funds, but we finally did it with the help of several shall we say *anonymous* donors and some . . . how should I put it? Out-of-the-box thinking when it came to fundraising efforts," Carmichael explained. "All the hard work was worth it when you consider all the lives we'll be able to save."

"The real Santa Claus couldn't have said it better himself," Alberta said.

"I do my best to keep things running smoothly," Carmichael said. "Even though there are some bumps in the way and some unexpected eruptions, I always make sure we get to the finish line."

"Like the small kerfuffle between you and your lady friend that we overheard while we were waiting for you," Alberta said.

Even hidden behind his Santa hat, wig, and beard, Alberta could see that she had said something that definitely put her on Santa's naughty list.

"Oh that . . . that . . ." Carmichael stuttered. He suddenly took off his hat and wig and pulled at his beard, as if it was suffocating him until he was freed of it. He was much older than Alberta thought. Early seventies at least, and he had a gaunt face that was lined in wrinkles, and his hair, although cut very short, was almost as white as his fake beard. For a moment Alberta thought he might be ill, but then realized he was nervous. "It's such a common occurrence I'd already forgotten about it."

He had also forgotten that he had taken off his Santa beard, because he started to pull at his chin as if it was full of whiskers.

"I think I'll remember it for quite a while," Alberta said. "I thought she was going to flatten us against the wall when she stormed out of your office."

"It was simply the result of one employee's greed and refusal to take responsibility for her own actions," Carmichael said. "You must understand that 'I'm sorry' doesn't cut it in the hospital business. We cannot afford errors here."

"That's what my grandson's college roommate was just telling me," Alberta said. "He's a pharmaceutical salesman, maybe you know him? His name is Rudy Lewendorf."

"No, that name doesn't ring a bell," Carmichael replied. "And I'm quite good with names."

"What about Natalie Vespa?" Joyce asked.

Carmichael got so jittery when he heard Natalie's name, he leaned back in his chair so far that he almost toppled over. Alberta and Joyce each had to grab his hands and pull him back or else he would've slammed his head into the bookshelf directly behind his desk. If the mere mention of Natalie's name could almost render a man unconscious, what damage could the real Natalie Vespa do?

CHAPTER 10

È meglio dare che ricevere.

The children's choir could have used more practice. Their rendition of "Away in a Manger" sounded as if they had snuck into Father Sal's liquor cabinet and spiked their hot chocolate. They sounded more like lowing cattle. As sweet as baby Jesus was, not even He could lay down His head with all the racket going on. Mercifully, Father Sal put the kibosh on any attempt of an encore.

"Thank you, children," Father Sal said. "I'm happy to report that next week's entertainment will be a performance of *The Gift of the Magi* . . . in mime."

Sitting in between Helen and Sloan in a pew in the middle of the church, Alberta stifled a laugh; she never knew if Sal was telling the truth or talking for effect. Whether the tales he told were based on fact or bits of fiction, they worked; St. Winifred's was packed. Of course, the church's population tripled around this time of year, but Sal's services were the most popular. Luckily, he loved the attention, otherwise he would have retired a few years ago and relocated to Puerto Vallarta, which was his original plan. Tranquility wouldn't be the same without the colorful cleric. Colorful and compassionate.

Sal concluded the service by lighting a second purple candle and then addressing the congregation with a very personal message.

"It's Christmastime, the most wonderful time of the year, if we're to believe Johnny Mathis and every storefront window in town," Sal said. "It also means that it's a time for us to step out of the darkness and into the light. A time for peace and renewal and miracles. Not God-size miracles, but ordinary ones, miracles that each one of us could perform.

"Medical breakthroughs are ordinary miracles created through your donations to events like the Mistletoe Ball, whose proceeds will help fund St. Clare's new breast cancer wing," Sal advised. "And miracles like returning a lost lamb to its flock.

"My dear friend's grandson, Sergio Maldonado, has been missing for several weeks and his family wants him to come home just as God awaits the arrival of His family every Sunday," Sal explained. "Please take a moment to pray for Sergio's safe return and look at his photo in the back of this week's bulletin. If by some miracle you see the boy, alert the police so they can reunite him with his family. We all know how much I love to receive a gift at any time of year, but during this holy month let's remember what the Bible tells us, it is truly better to give than to receive."

Sal had no idea that his words had just given Alberta an idea that might lead them to Sergio. If that happened, it could definitely be considered a miracle.

Another miracle was the fact that Lisa Marie and Tommy had just spent the past hour sitting in a pew. The last time they did that on a regular Sunday and not to attend a wedding or a funeral was twelve years ago, when Jinx received confirmation. Alberta hadn't expected them to come, but they were desperate and were willing to grasp at a spiritual straw if they thought it would lead them to Sergio. To cover all her bases, Lisa Marie lit candles at every saint's statue in St. Winifred's. She even threw three dollars and forty-six cents' worth of change into the Holy Well.

After mass Sal greeted parishioners at the back of the church. He stood in between two evergreen wreaths that were wrapped in gold ribbon. He wore his Kelly green vestments again, as he would throughout the month, which meant he was perfectly coordinated with his backdrop. Anyone who knew Sal wouldn't expect anything less.

Helen, however, was always surprised by how much more there was to Sal.

"You never cease to amaze me, Salvatore," Helen said. "One minute you're a jackass, the next you're Jesus's right-hand man."

"One's personality, like one's wardrobe, Helen, should be unpredictable," Sal said.

"She's right, Father," Lisa Marie said. "I'm not going to lie and say you turned me into a convert, but the sincerity of your words did make an impression."

"A spiritual journey is made by putting one foot in

front of the other," Father Sal said. "None of us can transform water into wine."

"Uncle Scotty could," Helen said. "But he was all thumbs with fishes and loaves."

The lights in the church flickered, and they wondered if the rectory forgot to pay the electric bill or if God was telling Helen to stop using His name in vain. Sal explained that they'd been having trouble with the lights lately and suspected it had something to do with the town grid, because Donna Russo, the principal of St. Winifred's Academy, also mentioned having trouble with the electricity at the school, but with all the upcoming festivities they hadn't had a chance to call in an electrician. Joyce told him he might be right because Carmichael had just told them he was concerned it was a town-wide issue. The flickering had stopped, but now a soft glow permeated the church. Gone was the bright aura; it was as if someone put the lights on a dimmer.

"I'm not sure if it qualifies for a miracle, but you're looking right at an electrician," Tommy said. "Would you like me to check it out?"

"That would be very kind if you did," Father Sal said. "Are you sure?"

"Of course," Tommy said. "Plus, I owe you for the nice things you said about my kid."

"Then follow me to the basement and show me the light," Father Sal said.

"I'll be right back," Tommy said, squeezing his wife's hand before leaving.

Alberta was about to usher the group outside to fill them in on her plan to locate Sergio when Vinny came rushing over, with Donna and Tambra right behind him, to fill them in on their first clue.

"I just received a text that there was activity on Sergio's ATM card," Vinny announced.

"Oh my God!" Lisa Marie cried. "Where?"

"Nearby," Vinny replied. "In Newton."

"We were just there yesterday," Alberta said.

"According to the bank records, Sergio withdrew five hundred dollars from his savings account," Vinny explained.

"Was there a surveillance video?" Alberta asked.

"Yes, it was definitely him," Vinny replied. "And he was accompanied by a woman matching Natalie's description."

"Did you see a car in the video?" Alberta asked. "This isn't New York, people don't walk around, everybody drives."

"You really do have a nose for sleuthing," Donna said. "That publisher was wrong."

"What publisher?" Sloan asked.

"The one who rejected Vinny's book," Donna replied. "He said no one will believe that an old Italian lady with no real detective skills has the wits to solve a murder faster than the police."

"I'm sure your book is a fun read, Vinny, but could we please get back to my brother?" Jinx asked.

"There's a reflection of a car in the video, but the Newton police are having a hard time reading the license plate," Vinny said. "Lisa, I gave them your cell phone number and instructed them to text you the moment they have any more information."

"Thank you, Vinny, I really appreciate that," Lisa Marie said. "I better make sure I charged my phone. My mind's been so scattered lately."

"Speaking of phones," Alberta said. "I have an idea that might lure Sergio out of hiding."

"What is it, Ma?" Lisa Marie asked.

Alberta's proposal was the classic twist on the old if-you-can't-beat-'em, join-'em philosophy. If Sergio and Natalie were primarily using their burner phones instead of their real cell phones to communicate, they should use burner phones as well. Instead of trying to connect with Sergio as members of his family, they would disguise themselves as people who had a better chance of ferreting him out into the open. Slowly, the lights in the church increased their intensity until they were back to their usual bright glimmer. Alberta wasn't sure if it meant God approved of her plan, but at least Sloan and the rest of the group did.

"That's a clever idea, Berta," Sloan said. "When did you come up with that?"

"During Father Sal's sermon," Alberta said. "He reminded me of something, *È meglio dare che ricevere*, it's better to give than to receive. If it works for gifts, it should work for cell phone calls."

"We give Sergio a call on his real cell phone instead of waiting to receive one from him," Helen said.

"As bait, we can use the information Joyce and I learned from Rudy," Alberta said. "Which should make him more agreeable to respond."

"What part of our conversation with Rudy do you plan to use?" Joyce asked.

"He said Natalie doesn't like his new girlfriend, J. J.," Alberta said. "What if we texted Sergio from a burner phone as J. J. and told him that she needs to get in touch with Natalie?"

"If Natalie doesn't like this J. J., wouldn't she just blow off the call?" Freddy asked.

"Not if we said it has to do with the business she's involved in with Rudy," Alberta said. "We need to make it sound as if J. J. is on the verge of jeopardizing Natalie's job."

"Whatever that job might be," Lisa Marie said.

"I think it's brilliant, Gram," Jinx said. "The only thing to add is that J. J. wants to meet Natalie at a particular place. Maybe Tranquility Park?"

"That's a good idea, Jinx," Joyce said. "It's a public space, so they won't feel like they're being trapped in a corner."

"We can have undercover cops on all the entrances in case they try to run once they know it's a setup," Vinny said.

"They'll be unarmed, right?" Lisa Marie asked. "My son may not be thrilled to see us, but he isn't a criminal."

"Yes, I'll instruct my team not to carry," Vinny said.

"Mrs. Scaglione?" Tambra said. "Are you certain Sergio is going to show up at all? If the request is to meet with Natalie, he might stay put, wherever he is."

"My grandson is in love with this girl," Alberta replied. "If Rudy wasn't exaggerating and this J. J. could be dangerous, Sergio will never let Natalie meet up with her alone."

"She's right," Lisa Marie said. "My son takes after his father, he's an old-fashioned gentleman."

"Sounds like a solid plan to me, Alfie," Vinny said. "Let's get the burner phones, make contact with Sergio, lure them to the park, and then reveal that we're the ones who sent the text and not J. J."

"Then I'll kill Natalie," Lisa Marie declared.

"Ma! You're not going to kill anyone," Jinx said.

"After what she's put us through, she's lucky if that's all I do to her," Lisa Marie said.

"You're not going to kill anyone, but Sergio might want to kill us," Helen said. "You know you run the risk of angering Sergio if you trick him."

"I do know that, but it's a chance we have to take," Alberta said. "Are we all ready to do this?"

"Do what?" Tommy asked as he rejoined the group.

"Get our son back," Lisa Marie declared.

Alberta had no idea burner phones were so readily available that they could be bought at corner bodegas or department stores like Walmart and Target. She, like many of the others, thought they were illegal or hard to find and would have to be bought in some complicated way that involved a cash-only transaction with a shady character wearing a trench coat on a shadowy street. Clearly, she had been watching too many noir films on TMC starring Humphrey Bogart and a string of femme fatales played by unknown MGM contract players. In the end it only took one trip to the Tranquility General Store to purchase the phone, along with several rolls of the Reed's Butterscotch hard candy Helen loved so much. The teenaged boy at the cash register was more surprised that someone purchased the candy than the phone.

Now that phase one of their plan was completed, it was on to phase two, which would be conducted at a booth at the Tranquility Diner. Kwon greeted them at the door and led them to a booth next to one of the windows. The place was packed with both the after-church and late-Sunday-morning-riser crowds, Dean Martin's mellow croon was circulating through the air commanding nature to let it snow, and from the kitchen could be heard the loud clanging of china plates, silverware, and metal trays as the waitresses and the two short-order cooks did their jobs. The joint was jumping in multiple directions and would distract anyone from thinking Alberta and company were doing anything more in their booth than having Sunday brunch.

It was a tight squeeze, but they all managed to fit into the large booth. Alberta, Sloan, and Helen on one side, Lisa Marie, Tommy, and Jinx on the other and Freddy and Joyce sitting on chairs Kwon brought over that were placed at the side of the booth. Vinny and Tambra had gone back to the police station and waited for the signal to assemble a team at the park's entrances and exits. They quickly ordered coffee and food for the table to thwart any suspicion that would be cast their way if they hogged up a table just to fiddle with a phone.

They engaged in innocuous conversation about the Mistletoe Ball and the weather while Alberta surreptitiously removed the burner phone from its plastic packaging. She finished just as Kwon reappeared with a tray of cups and a pot of coffee. He was so busy he didn't even notice.

"I see that business is booming, Kwon," Joyce said.

"You can say that again," he replied. "I'm the owner, one of the chefs, and now a part-time waitress. Not that I'm complaining, I'm living my dream."

Alberta raised her coffee cup in the air and the others joined in, "*Salud!*"

Snow was beginning to fall outside and the blinking lights on the window made it appear as if they were watching flames dance in a fireplace. They were comfy, cozy, and ready to connect with Lisa Marie's long-lost son. If only Alberta could find the words.

She had punched in Sergio's cell phone number, but when she went to type a message, she stalled. What should she say? Or rather, what would J. J. say?

"What would a possibly dangerous woman in her twenties text a young man as a warning to her rival?" Alberta asked.

Since the only woman in her twenties at the table was Jinx, she reached over to grab the phone from Alberta and started to compose a text.

"What're you saying to him, Jinxie?" Helen asked.

Jinx held up the phone, and they all squinted and huddled together to read the text. **Hey, it's JJ, she with you?**

"That's straight and to the point," Lisa Marie said.

"J. J. sounds like a woman who doesn't mince words," Jinx said.

"Neither does Sergio!" Alberta exclaimed. "He replied."

His one-word answer of **Yes** confirmed several things. He knew who J. J. was, he knew who J. J. was asking about, and *you know who* was very close by.

"Jinx, tell him J. J. needs to see Natalie ASAP," Lisa Marie said.

"I got it, Ma," Jinx replied as she typed another message.

She hit the Send button and read the message out loud. "I need to see her now."

"Nice going, dude," Freddy said. "She put the word *now* in all caps to make it sound urgent."

The phone pinged and the group let out a shriek. Their excitement waned a bit when they read Sergio's succinct response. **Why?**

Everyone started to offer suggestions on how to respond, knowing that the next text was crucial to the success of their plan. It had to be threatening, decisive, and, of course, it had to sound legitimate. It had to convince Natalie that her only choice would be to follow J. J.'s orders. Over the past few years Jinx had grown much more confident personally and professionally and she didn't have to work very hard to find the right words to instill a little panic in Sergio's paramour.

She sent three texts in quick succession: **She knows why. She screwed me. Tell her to meet me in an hour or else I talk.**

"Talk about what, lovey?" Alberta asked.

"I have no idea, Gram, but it sounds like a threat."

The burner phone pinged again. "Sounds like the threat worked," Sloan said.

"He's taking the bait!" Jinx screamed. "He wants to know where they should meet." She typed out the location. **Tranquility Park, under the entrance sign.**

Almost immediately, Sergio responded with a word that made them all cheer: **OK.**

Kwon stood at their table with a tray filled with their food and thought their cheers were meant for him. "This town has given me such a warm reception. It's like Christmas morning every day!"

An hour later it felt more like a Christmas morning where they were staring at unopened packages but had not yet been given the go-ahead to open them up. Vinny was sitting on a bench near the main entrance with Tambra stationed at the exit, while undercover cops were positioned at the two side entrances on the right that ran along Tranquility Boulevard. On the left side of the park was a fence that ran the entire length and was covered by clusters of bushes and trees. None of the officers were armed, but they were equipped with earbuds that were actually two-way radios so they could be in constant contact.

Alberta, Helen, Joyce, Lisa Marie, and Tommy were sitting in Joyce's Mercedes in a parking lot across the street because they didn't want to risk Sergio seeing them before he entered the park. Freddy and Sloan, neither of whom Sergio would recognize, were standing near the black metal archway that was the entrance to Tranquility Park and close to where Vinny was sitting. They were engaged in a faux conversation while Vinny was pretending to be engrossed in a paperback. The only wild card in the scenario was Jinx. Sergio would, of course, immediately recognize his sister, but Natalie thought she was meeting a young woman and Jinx was the only young woman in their group. The problem was, Jinx was supposed to be J. J. and they had no idea what J. J. looked like.

The only solution was to slightly change Jinx's appearance to make her appear like someone who was deliberately trying to look incognito in the hopes that it would fool Natalie and Sergio long enough for the others to gather around and prevent them from escaping. Jinx wore a pair of oversized sunglasses, one of Helen's black overcoats, and pinned her hair up to bob length instead of letting it fall down her back as she usually did. She topped off the look with a baseball cap that sported the logo of Freddy's Ski 'n Scuba Shoppe. When she used the mirror app on her phone to check herself out, she was pleased with what she saw. Her brother wouldn't immediately know it was the girl he grew up with, which would give them a chance to pry him away from the girl he had grown very close to.

Jinx entered the park, ignoring Freddy and Sloan to her right, and sat on the far end of the bench Vinny was occupying. The park was in the process of being turned into the Winter Wonderland in a few weeks, which meant the usual immense, flat landscape was filled with materials that would build stands and tents to transform the park into a holiday playground. Too anxious to remain seated, Jinx got up and immediately saw Sergio and a woman walking toward her from the opposite side of the park. She instinctively looked down at the ground to prevent Sergio from getting a clear view of her face until he got closer, but Natalie, acting her role as She Who Pulls the Strings, had other ideas.

"J. J., is that you?" Natalie called out.

Jinx hesitated for as long as she dared, hoping that Sergio and Natalie continued to walk closer to her during her silence, but the time had come for her to reveal herself. As convincing as she hoped her outfit might be, they saw right through it immediately.

"Jinx!" Sergio cried. "You set me up!"

Natalie didn't wait to hear another word; she didn't need an explanation, she knew exactly what was happening, and she wasn't going to stand around for the scene to play out around her. She was writing her own ending to this particular story, and it didn't involve meeting her boyfriend's family.

Like lightning, Natalie turned and ran back from where she came from. When she saw Vinny run toward her from the right, she ran through the bushes on her left, momentarily disappeared from view, only to appear again as she climbed the fence. Just as Vinny rammed his large frame through the bushes in pursuit, Natalie leaped over the top railing and raced toward freedom. Vinny jumped onto the fence but struggled to get a good enough foothold to hoist himself over with the same ease and agility Natalie displayed. Knowing when to accept defeat, he called Tambra on his radio.

"Natalie escaped over the fence," Vinny said. "She's on your right."

Tambra responded with only two words: "On it."

While Natalie was on the run, Sergio hadn't had a chance to move.

As quickly as Natalie fled, Jinx lunged forward and grabbed Sergio's arm, joined seconds later by Freddy, who threw his arms around him in a bear hug. It was not the way Jinx had hoped to introduce her brother to her boyfriend, but she was glad that Freddy was three inches taller and several inches wider than Sergio. Natalie may have given them the slip, but her brother wasn't going anywhere.

"Let go of me!" Sergio screamed, wiggling in Freddy's arms.

"Shut up, Serge!" Jinx screamed back. "That's my boyfriend and he does what I tell him to do!"

"That's right, dude," Freddy said. "My orders are not to let you go until you explain what you've gotten yourself in to."

"It's none of your business!" Sergio cried.

"Well, it sure as hell is *my* business!"

When Sergio saw his father standing in front of him, chest heaving, fists clenched, a mixture of fear and relief etched into his face, an inkling of what he had put his family through must have started to formulate in his mind because his body went limp in Freddy's arms.

"Sergio!" Lisa Marie screamed. "Thank God you're all right."

Alberta watched her daughter do what any mother in her position would have done. She ran up to her son and hugged him tighter than Freddy had. Her sobs could be heard, provoking curious stares from bystanders, but Alberta knew Lisa Marie didn't care. She had found her son and that was all that mattered.

Lisa Marie released her grip and allowed Tommy to embrace their son. From the way his shoulders were rising up and down, Alberta could tell he was crying too. It broke her heart to see such love in a family and still know that Sergio would make a youthful, dumb decision to throw it all away. He was getting ready to follow that up with another dumb decision.

When he saw Jinx move toward him, he backed away. "I can't believe you did this to me!"

"You didn't leave us any choice!" Jinx yelled.

"Don't you see you've ruined everything!" Sergio cried.

"Don't yell at your sister!" Tommy yelled. "We're trying to help you."

"I don't need your help!" Sergio screamed. "All I need is Natalie!"

"She's gone!" Lisa Marie cried. "Your family is right here."

"I don't want you, don't you get it? I want Natalie!"

Alberta kissed the gold crucifix that hung from her neck and made the sign of the cross. So much for thinking her plan was foolproof. Instead of reuniting her family like she had hoped, the plan she'd devised seemed to be doing just the opposite—it was tearing them apart all over again.

CHAPTER 11

Come figlia, come figlio.

Even though the wayward son had come home in time for Christmas, there wasn't much joy in the Ferraras' world. They had found Sergio, safe and unharmed, and that should have been reason enough to haul out the holly, fill up the stockings, and have a grand celebration. There was only one problem: Sergio hadn't wanted to be found.

After the incident in Tranquility Park, it took quite a bit of begging and pleading to prevent Sergio from hopping the fence to go running after Natalie. He wouldn't speak with Jinx or Lisa Marie and all he did when Alberta tried to talk to him was bad-mouth his family. It was only when Tommy had a private conversation with his son that Sergio agreed to come back to Alberta's house.

It was decided that only the immediate family would return to Alberta's, to allow the family some privacy while they sorted out their differences. Alberta told everyone that she'd call them when the coast was clear. However, for the moment, the air was filled with strife and Sergio's voice was filled with anger. As much as he loved his grandmother's food, he didn't want to be seated at her kitchen table, he wanted to be with Natalie, and he made that very clear.

"You know I'm just going to find out where Natalie is and go back to her," Sergio said, shoveling a forkful of Alberta's lasagna into his mouth. "If she'll have me after what you people did."

"We're not *people*, Serge, we're your *family*!" Jinx yelled.

Lisa Marie pressed her hand on Jinx's shoulder to get her to lean back in her chair and relax instead of looking like she was a tigress ready to strike.

"Honey, I know you're upset with us right now, but you forced us to take drastic action," Lisa Marie said. "Why couldn't you just call us? Tell us where you were? You made us sick with worry."

"I'm twenty-three-years old, Ma, I'm an adult!" Sergio said, slamming his fist on the table. "I don't need to explain myself to you or anyone else!"

Tommy leaned over the kitchen table and grabbed his son's arm before he could take another bite of food. It didn't look like he was exerting too much pressure, but from the grimace on Sergio's face it was obvious that Tommy's hold was not meant to be broken. When Tommy spoke he didn't raise his voice, but he commanded his son's attention.

"Don't you ever talk to your mother like that again," Tommy said. "Do I make myself clear?"

Sergio could only hold his father's gaze for a few seconds before staring at his plate. "Yes, sir."

"What have I always told you?" Tommy said. "Look me in the eye when you answer a question."

Sergio raised his head and his black eyes, now devoid of defiance, looked directly at his father. "Yes, sir."

"Finish your lasagna and then we'll talk," Tommy instructed.

Although Alberta was in the kitchen with the rest of them, she felt as if she was observing the scene from a greater distance. It had been so long since she had been in a room with her daughter's entire family that it was unsettling. She felt closer to them than ever before, but on the other hand, she felt like an outsider. She knew these people and yet she didn't know them. They were a family of strangers.

Over the years she had developed a deep relationship with Jinx, of course, based on mutual respect, but Alberta had never witnessed Jinx interacting with her family. There was only a four-year age difference between Jinx and Sergio and yet she acted more like his mother than his sister. Alberta surmised that it had to do with the fact that Jinx had grown up tremendously while living on her own, while her brother had almost regressed living under his parents' roof.

What surprised her was how disrespectful he was toward his mother and how angry that made Alberta. She loved her grandson unconditionally, no doubt about that, but because she only had a limited relationship with him, much more superficial than the one she had with Jinx, she could see him as a person and not merely as a grandson. She wasn't happy with what she had witnessed so far.

However, Alberta was relieved to see that Tommy took his role as father seriously, much more seriously than Sammy ever had. Tommy loved his son but wasn't afraid to remind him that he was still the parent. Alberta was forced to silently apologize for ever considering Tommy unworthy of her daughter's love. He had surpassed all her expectations.

Her relationship with Lisa Marie was still so new and raw that she didn't know what to think. Her daughter was loud, blunt to the point of being crass, but a loving mother. It was unfair to judge her based on the few days they had been back in each other's company because for all that time she had been worrying about the safety of her son. Now that her prayers had been answered and she was calmer, Alberta hoped the real Lisa Marie would emerge. She honestly didn't know who that woman would be, but she was curious to find out.

Despite all the friction and all the snippy comments, there was a lightness in her heart. They had come out of this nightmare with many questions, but relatively few scars. And while they waited for those scars to heal and those questions to be answered, at least they had food. Alberta smiled to herself; it really was good to be Italian.

"Did you leave room for dessert?" Alberta asked.

Sergio smiled and said, "I may have to wait a bit, Gram, I kind of scarfed that lasagna down."

"When you're ready I have a cherry pie I picked up at the bakery and there's some leftover tiramisu in the fridge," Alberta said. "Help yourself."

"Thanks, Gram, I will," Sergio said.

She took his plate from the table and couldn't resist planting a kiss on his forehead. Instead of recoiling from her touch like some grandsons might, thinking they were too old to be on the receiving end of a semipublic display of affection, Sergio closed his eyes and hugged Alberta. Jinx, however, was confused. One minute he's screaming at her mother, the next he's hugging his grandmother. Her brother might be grown up, but he was still the good little boy she remembered. Of course, even good little boys had secrets.

"What kind of trouble have you gotten yourself into, Serge?" Jinx asked.

Her parents were startled by Jinx's question, but Alberta had expected it. In fact, she was surprised it took so long for her investigative reporter skills to kick in. As much as Alberta wanted to know the truth about why Sergio ran away, she wanted to protect her grandson. She wasn't sure she was going to be able to do both.

"I'm not in trouble!" Sergio yelled.

"Then why didn't you tell anyone where you were going?" Jinx asked.

"I did!" Sergio replied. "I said I was going to New York."

"Which was a lie because you were found in New Jersey," Jinx said.

"It's the same thing," Sergio spat.

"Tell that to a New Yorker," Jinx quipped. "Why didn't you return any of our calls?"

"I told you, I'm an adult! I don't have to update everybody on my every move!" Sergio said. "Do you keep them posted on your whereabouts twenty-four-seven?"

"I don't live under their roof," Jinx replied. "But I do return phone calls. Do you want to know why? Because I'm an adult and that's what adults do."

Alberta could see the questioning was starting to derail so, like a good grandma, she swooped in to save her fam-

ily before the squabbling turned into all-out war. She sat
down next to Sergio and placed a hand on his arm. Based
on his erratic behavior, she wasn't sure if he was going to
yank it away this time or accept her touch as he had just
done. Thankfully, he remained as calm as Alberta sounded.

"Honey, this is about Natalie, isn't it?" Alberta said.

"No," he replied immediately. "Well . . . maybe."

"Sergio," Alberta said. "You are many things, but
you're not a liar. You're a good boy and you shouldn't
fight that."

But he was. Sergio shook his head frantically and got
up from the table so quickly his chair teetered back and
forth before finally settling. Lola was about to enter the
kitchen from the living room, where she had been nap-
ping, but when she saw Sergio pacing like a caged animal
preparing to battle a gladiator, she turned up her nose and
retreated back to the safety of the other room.

"That's what Natalie always said!" Sergio cried.
"You're a good boy, Serge, stay that way. Talking to me
like I was twelve or something!"

"If the shoe fits?" Jinx said.

"Shut up, Jinx!" Sergio cried.

"How are we supposed to treat you like an adult if you
can't even do the adult thing and call your parents back?"
Lisa Marie said.

Alberta bit her tongue so hard she thought she tasted
blood. She wanted to interject and tell her daughter to
stop yelling at Sergio; she wanted to remind them all that
despite his actions, he wasn't a child and they couldn't
keep him chained up, he was free to leave at any time.
Just as Lisa Marie was. But this wasn't her fight, and she
didn't feel comfortable to butt in. Instead, she played the
role of the stereotypical grandma.

"I think it is time for that cherry pie," Alberta announced.

By the time Sergio finished his second slice and washed it down with a large glass of eggnog, the Maldonados had grown tired of talking about the differences between Florida and New Jersey, the inordinate amount of snowfall they'd already had this year, the Mistletoe Ball, even Lola. They wanted more answers and they wanted them from Sergio.

"I really think it's time you told us everything you know about this Natalie," Lisa Marie said.

Alberta held her breath because she expected a repeat of Sergio's volatile reactions from earlier. Maybe it was because he had a full stomach, but this time when Lisa Marie asked her son to tell them about this new girl in his life, he complied.

"Natalie is the most amazing woman I've ever met," Sergio said. "If I didn't follow her to New York, I would've lost her forever."

"What do you mean, you followed her?" Tommy asked. "You said you went with her to New York."

"I lied," Sergio said.

Alberta clutched the gold crucifix around her neck because she felt as if Sergio's confession was more of a warning. *Come figlia, come figlio.* Like daughter, like son, and both of them liars.

"Natalie broke up with me right before she left for New York," Sergio explained. "I told her I'd go with her, but she said I'd get in the way."

"Get in the way of what?" Jinx asked.

"She had some things to take care of, I'm not really sure what they were," Sergio replied. "I still don't."

"How could you not know?" Lisa Marie asked. "You've been with her for months."

"If there's one thing about Natalie, she knows how to keep a secret," Sergio said. "I don't know if you'll get it, but I don't care about any of that, all I want is to be with her. That's why I didn't tell you I was following her and that's why I didn't return any of your calls, because I knew that if I told you the truth you would drag me back to Florida."

"Is that why you got a burner phone?" Alberta asked.

"You know what a burner phone is, Gram?" Sergio replied.

"Whose idea do you think it was to use a burner phone to lure you out of hiding?" Jinx said. She then quickly realized she had just outed her grandmother. "Sorry, Gram."

"That was your idea?" Sergio said. "That's kinda cool. How do you know about J. J.?"

"Your Aunt Joyce and I paid Rudy a visit trying to find you," Alberta said. "He mentioned Natalie didn't like his new girlfriend."

"You went all the way to New York to talk to Rudy?" Sergio said.

"I would've gone to Australia if that's where the clues led," Alberta said. "We found out that Natalie lived with Rudy for a while on East Tenth Street and we thought he might have some answers for us."

"Had you gone a few days earlier, we would've been there," Sergio said. "We stayed with him for a bit when we first got to the city."

"Which means Rudy lied to me, he said he didn't know you and hadn't seen Natalie in months," Alberta said. "Here, I thought he was such a nice boy."

"Just because people are nice to you, Gram, doesn't mean they're, you know, really nice," Sergio said.

"Where did you go after you left Rudy's?" Tommy asked.

"We couch surfed with some of Natalie's friends, and for the last few weeks we've been at an extended stay hotel in Newton because she had to meet with some woman who lives there," Sergio explained.

"I assume you don't know who this woman is," Jinx said. "Or if Natalie ever met this woman."

"I'm not sure who the woman is and I don't think they ever met," Sergio replied. "Nat kept getting angrier every time she left her a message. I think the woman was avoiding her."

"Do you really expect us to believe that after spending months with this girl, you still don't know where she works or what kind of business she needs to wrap up?" Lisa Marie asked.

"I don't care what you believe, Ma!" Sergio said. "All you need to know is that Natalie loves me!"

"Will you grow up!" Jinx cried. "Natalie doesn't love you! She's using you, Serge, she literally ran as far away from you as she could about two hours ago."

"Why would you say that?" Sergio asked. "She isn't using me. She ran away because you all freaked her out."

"Has this girl who loves you so much as tried to get in touch with you yet?" Jinx asked.

"Shut up!" Sergio yelled.

"Serge, I am not going to tell you again, watch your mouth," Tommy ordered.

"Answer me, Serge," Jinx said. "Has Natalie tried to contact you since this afternoon?"

The muscles in Sergio's face and neck started to twitch and his cheeks reddened. He attempted to answer Jinx's question, but the only thing that escaped his mouth was an angry breath. He tried again and nothing. On the third try he only managed one word. "No!"

"Of course she didn't, and she isn't going to," Jinx said. "Because that's what some girls do to good little boys."

"I swear to God, Jinx, if you say that again, I'll . . ." Sergio yelled, raising his fist.

Tommy ran around the table and came between Sergio and his sister. "You'll what?!"

Sergio clenched his fists and jabbed at the air, letting out a sound that was part growl and part cry. Alberta was shocked that he'd raised his hand to his sister. She didn't want to believe that he would actually hit Jinx, but she had seen the fury in his eyes. She didn't think he was angry at her, but rather at Natalie and the entire situation, but it didn't matter, he had not been able to control his emotions and he had almost gotten into a physical altercation with his own flesh and blood. Such action was unconscionable as far as Alberta was concerned. No matter how angry Sammy had gotten at her, the kids, the world, he never struck her or their children and, truth be told, Alberta was never concerned that he would. For all his faults, Sammy was a decent man, and hitting any woman or child was a line he would never cross. She felt her knees buckle slightly because after what she had just witnessed she couldn't say the same thing about her grandson.

"Are we going to go through this again?" Tommy asked. "I said it before and I'll say it one last time, this temper of yours is not acceptable, so it ends . . . now."

"I'm sorry if I'm not perfect like you, Dad!" Sergio yelled. "I'm sorry if I didn't get married right out of high school like you two did!"

"I don't understand any of this, Sergio," Lisa Marie said. "Can't you see that this Natalie has changed you? You never acted like this before, you were never so selfish and disrespectful."

"Like you should talk!" Sergio cried. "How much respect did you ever show Grandma? You never even talk about her, it's like you wished she was dead, and I'm sure the feeling is mutual!"

"*Basta*!" Alberta cried. "Your mother and I have had our differences, but we are family. *Family*, Sergio! Do you understand what that means? It means that no matter what happens, no matter what is said, no matter how much you hurt one another, you know in your heart that your family loves you. And you never, *ever* turn your back on your family when someone needs your help."

Alberta was shaking and had to grip the back of the chair to steady herself. When she was a little more in control of her body, she turned around and leaned onto the kitchen counter. She stared out the window and took in the view. Memory Lake had been a constant in her life for the past few years; it always looked the same—large, inviting, and mysterious—just like her family.

But her family had just changed before her eyes. The cracks were visible, and they could no longer hide. Alberta took a dish towel and wiped her hands; they weren't wet, she just needed something to do. When she was done she folded it neatly and placed it on the counter.

"It's been a long day," Alberta said, still looking out the window. "I'm going to go up and take a nap."

She left the room without saying another word, leaving her family behind in silence. Jinx could tell that her brother looked ashamed and regretted the things he said, but she didn't care. They had been worried sick about him for weeks and this was how he repaid them, with insults and outbursts and hurting one of the people on this earth who was closest to him. It had been a few years since she had lived with Sergio, but she knew he wasn't the same boy she grew up with, she knew that he had changed. The reason she was frightened was because she knew it was not a change for the better.

CHAPTER 12

Come il cacio sui maccheroni.

Jinx woke up and couldn't get the tune out of her head. "What Child Is This?"—the Vikki Carr version, which was her grandmother's favorite—had been playing on a loop inside her brain since the moment she opened her eyes. She would have liked to attribute the nonstop recording to the fact that Christmas was a few weeks away, but she knew that wasn't the reason. It was because she didn't know who her brother was. The childlike teenager she remembered before she left home was not the same young man who'd raised his fist to her last night. What had this child become?

Maybe an early morning jog would cleanse her mind of such unmerry thoughts? Nope. What about taking in the Christmas decorations on all the stores, or the plastic, life-size, Victorian-era carolers on the front lawn of the library? Definitely not. Could the giant gingerbread house that was the visual denouement of the Winter Wonderland being created in Tranquility Park do the trick? Not a chance. No amount of holiday magic could erase the uneasy thoughts that were squatting in Jinx's brain. She might as well get to work.

Today, work didn't mean going into the office at *The Herald*, it meant going to St. Clare's to interview the hospital administrator, Bambi DeBenedetto. While her mother still couldn't get over the fact that a grown woman chose to be called the same name as an anthropomorphic Disney character, Jinx was in no position to judge because she had disregarded her Christian name, Gina, in favor of the moniker she received moments after her birth. An elderly woman playing the slots at the casino when Jinx was born had said that she'd had nothing but bad luck ever since Lisa Marie had gone into labor and considered the newborn babe a jinx. Gina was history.

In the elevator on the way up to the third floor of St. Clare's, Jinx could still her hear brother's voice raging at her. He had never screamed at her with such anger. She knew his outburst was a reaction to his frustration over this Natalie person more than at what Jinx had said, but still, it greatly bothered her. She'd seen a side of her brother that she couldn't reconcile.

When the elevator door opened it took her a moment to reconcile what she was seeing. The east wing on the third floor of St. Clare's was currently under construction. To the right she saw the wooden frames of what would become the new cancer research center. Through the plastic sheets that were hung to contain the sawdust and noise, she saw several workers drilling, hammering, and using power tools Jinx didn't recognize to build the space into the most prestigious, cutting-edge research facility in the East. At least that was according to the most recent press release St. Clare's communications department had sent out.

To the left were the administrative offices, which had already been constructed and were being occupied. Human Resources, accounting, a large conference room, and the hospital administrator's office, which was where Jinx was headed. The walls were painted a light gray, the couch and chairs in the small waiting area outside Human Resources were in a fabric of the same shade, and the coffee table in the corner of the room was glass and chrome. The only splash of color came courtesy of the three imitation Christmas trees that stood on the coffee table. The coned structures varied in height and each was painted a different shade of pink. Jinx was a traditionalist when it came to Christmas, so she disapproved.

Not as much as she disapproved of Bambi's outfit.

Wyck had warned Jinx that Bambi was cartoonish, but she assumed he was making a bad pun. He wasn't. Bambi was a full-figured woman, with an ample bosom, curvy hips, and a round face. Her makeup choices were bold, her black hair was teased, and her accessories were chunky. It was a dramatic look that matched her fashion sense.

She was wearing a tight-fitting Diane von Furstenberg wraparound dress in fire engine red, which did score her some points because it was Jinx's favorite color. When Jinx spied the Cartier Panthère watch in yellow gold wrapped around Bambi's right wrist, she thought she was seeing things. The watch had a retail value of about ten thousand dollars.

But it was Bambi's shoes that made Jinx gasp out loud. She was wearing a vintage pair of Miss Wonderful's red patent leather Pilgrim pumps with a gold buckle and a chunky heel. Jinx couldn't contain herself.

"I absolutely love your shoes," Jinx squealed.

"Thank you," Bambi replied. "Life can be so boring most of the time, I like to spruce it up with my ward-robe."

"You sound like my Aunt Joyce," Jinx said.

"Joyce Ferrara?" Bambi asked.

"That's the one," Jinx replied.

"Who do you think I stole them from?" Bambi said.

Luckily, Jinx had acquired most of the answers to the questions she was asking in the first part of her interview because she kept mentally plotting ways she could return Bambi's shoes to Joyce's closet so she could have access to them. While one side of her brain was creating outfits to wear with the shoes she coveted, the other was listening to Bambi share facts about her life.

A recent widow, Bambi was fifty-seven years old and had held her current position for a little over six years. During her tenure she had spearheaded the hospital's efforts to become a big player in medical research and boasted to Jinx that it was her idea for St. Clare's to enter into a joint venture with the Sussex County Medical Center. The partnership allowed them to share costs, talent, and expertise. As a result, they would be doing clinical trials for two new cancer drugs in the upcoming year.

"That's quite a feat," Jinx said, pulling her thoughts away from her own feet. "Are you allowed to give me more information about the trials?"

"I can't disclose any facts until after the public announcement is made in January," Bambi said. "But you can definitely give your readers a tease of what's to come."

"Perfect," Jinx said. "I'd like to do a follow-up with you once it's okay to talk further. This is the kind of stuff I want to share with our readers and not just what you'll be wearing to the Mistletoe Ball."

Jinx hesitated a moment and then realized Bambi might be wearing something else that was stolen from Joyce's closet. "On second thought, what will you be wearing to the Ball?"

"I haven't bought a gown yet, but I'm doing that later today actually," Bambi said. "I think this event is a good enough reason to splurge on a new dress."

"Personally, I think any reason is good enough to splurge on a new dress," Jinx said.

Their laughter stopped short when they were interrupted.

"Bambi, have you heard from my . . ." The woman stopped abruptly when she saw Bambi had company. "I'm so sorry, I didn't know you had a meeting."

"Not to worry," Bambi said, all smiles. "I think the interview is wrapping up."

"Aren't you the doctor who treated my grandmother's boyfriend, Sloan McLelland?" Jinx asked. "He had a brain injury and you had to induce a coma."

The woman's stunning good looks and platinum blond hair didn't fit into the stereotypical look of a doctor, but that was her occupation.

"Yes, of course," the doctor said. "You're Alberta's granddaughter, Jinx."

"Dr. Kylie Manzini is one of our best," Bambi said.

"I'm going to see Sloan soon, he has his yearly follow-up," Kylie said. "I trust all is okay and he hasn't had any repercussions."

"He's perfectly healthy and still courting my Gram," Jinx said.

"I'm so glad to hear it," Kylie said. "Give my best to him and your grandmother. Bambi, I'll check in with you later."

After Kylie left the room Bambi leaned forward on her desk. "I didn't want to say anything while she was in the room because she's not one of those doctors who has a huge ego, but Kylie is going to lead our research team."

"I thought she was a surgeon," Jinx replied.

"She's career transitioning," Bambi said. "Her new focus will be managing the drug trials and making break-throughs to combat cancer."

"That sounds like incredibly important work," Jinx said.

"It is," Bambi agreed. "*Come il cacio sui macche-roni.*"

"Despite my heritage, my Italian isn't so good," Jinx said. "Did you just say, 'It's like cheese on macaroni?'"

"Your Italian is better than you think! That's exactly what I said!" Bambi squealed. "It's the literal translation, colloquially it means 'Just what the doctor ordered.' And confidentially speaking between the two of us style mavens, Dr. Manzini needs to carve out a better balance between work and family life."

"I don't think I could ever separate the two," Jinx said. "My family and work lives often merge into one."

"You're young," Bambi said. "Give it some time and you'll rearrange your priorities. I did."

Jinx knew that she could give it all the time in the world, she wouldn't want to have a life that wasn't chock-full of her relatives. She also knew that she had to get those shoes back if it was the last thing she did.

"Benny, my photographer, will be taking photos of you tomorrow, but could I get one with you now?" Jinx asked. "Your outfit is gorgeous and the red will really pop against the black curtains."

"I'd like to hem and haw about hating a photo shoot, but who am I kidding? I love being in the spotlight," Bambi confessed. "Should I touch up my makeup?"

Jinx didn't think it was possible to touch up her red matte lipstick, bronze eye shadow, and maroon rouge any further without making her look like a clown. "I wouldn't touch a thing."

Bambi stood against the black taffeta curtains that hung in front of the bay of windows on the left side of the office. As Jinx aimed her phone, she realized the curtains weren't concealing windows, but a sliding glass door that must lead to the outdoor patio. Bambi put both hands on her hips to create a powerful, Wonder Woman stance, and just as Jinx snapped the photo, someone out on the patio walked into the frame.

"Sorry, let me take one more shot," Jinx said. "Someone got in the photo."

Bambi's powerful expression faded for a moment. "It must have been one of the girls in accounting. Some of them still go out to the patio to smoke."

"At a cancer lab?" Jinx said.

"You'd be surprised by the things people get away with at work," Bambi said.

* * *

Now that Sergio had been found, his family was able to turn their attention to Christmas and the upcoming Mistletoe Ball, which promised to be the event of the season. A relic from Tranquility's past, the Ball was making a comeback after thirty-two years. And it was all thanks to Joyce.

In the beginning of its establishment, Tranquility was a vacation spot, a place where families from cities like Hoboken, Jersey City, and even New York, would come to spend a few weeks every summer by Memory Lake to escape the oppressive heat. In fact, before the town was officially declared a town it was simply known as Memory Lake because other than the lake and a few cottages, there was little else in the area. It wasn't until a few years later that Aldo Nunzicola, a butcher from Hoboken, christened the original three hundred acres Tranquility.

After a while some of the families spent the Christmas holiday here as a way to avoid the hustle and bustle of the city during what was supposed to be a reflective time of year. They would have sleigh rides through what is now Tranquility Park, sing Christmas carols on the land upon which St. Winifred's was built, and even skate on the frozen surface of Memory Lake. Despite its idyllic setting, most of the families came from good, blue-collar stock: small business owners, dock workers, manual laborers, and as far from high society as the sidewalk is from the top of the Empire State Building. They all came from similar backgrounds and they all understood the importance of family, both their own and the larger community.

What started out as simple pot-luck dinners held at a different family home each year evolved into a large celebration held at the biggest house in Tranquility, owned by Giuseppe Viccio, an ironworker from Guttenberg with seven kids, a wife, and two sets of in-laws. The party was held as soon as the families got to Tranquility as a way to start the holiday season and soon came to be known as the Viccio Ball. Since *vischio* is the Italian word for mistletoe, it was an easy metamorphosis for the annual gala to quickly find its more festive moniker, the Mistletoe Ball.

Each year the Ball got bigger as more families flocked to Tranquility to spend the Christmas season in more peaceful surroundings. At the same time, the town was beginning to transform into a year-round municipality and not just a vacation spot for two weeks out of the year. In quick succession mainstays were erected: Tranquility Arms, Tranquility Library, Tranquility Police Station, Tranquility Park, the original Tranquility Diner, St. Winifred's of the Holy Well, and, most important of all, St. Clare's Hospital.

After several decades excitement for the Mistletoe Ball turned into apathy, and what was once the premiere event in the town became another obligation. As the population grew and people became busier with their lives and commitments, interest in the Ball waned. Communities splintered into clusters of individual groups, and what had once been a can't-miss event was, until recently, a a very distant memory.

That was all about to change, thanks to Joyce's stroke of genius.

As a member of the Board of Trustees of St. Clare's Hospital, Joyce headed the committee in charge of commemorating its upcoming centennial anniversary, which would also serve as a fundraiser for the new research initiative. The hospital's birthday was December 10, so Joyce thought it would be fun to create a celebration that would also serve as a holiday kickoff, an event that would not only highlight the hospital as a Tranquility landmark but bring the people of the community together. What better way to do that than to connect Tranquility's past with its future? Resurrecting the Mistletoe Ball was the perfect way to honor the town's history and usher in a whole new era.

It would also mark a major change for the Ferrara family. Lisa Marie had agreed that since the event was next week, they would stay and attend. Alberta, ever the realist, didn't read too much into her daughter's decision because Sergio had made it clear that he wouldn't return to Florida without first reconnecting with Natalie, and Lisa Marie wasn't about to return home without her son in the back seat of her Subaru. No matter the reason, her daughter's decision to extend her visit made Alberta realize that this would be the first holiday season in more than a decade that she'd get to spend with her entire family. It was a time to celebrate.

The only issue that arose was when Lisa Marie found out the Mistletoe Ball was a black-tie affair. She told her mother that with her and Tommy away from work, they didn't have the extra money to buy fancy clothes to attend some Christmas party. As the matriarch of the family, Alberta said that she had an easy solution, she would pay for everyone's new outfits.

The clause in Carmela's will stipulating that Alberta couldn't bequeath her money or her house to anyone was almost over. The language in the will, however, never stated that Alberta couldn't shower her family with gifts. Which is why Sloan had taken Tommy to the Tranquility Tux Rental Company to get fitted for a tuxedo with Alberta's credit card. Being the natty gentleman he was, Sloan owned his own tux, and being the blue-collar guy Tommy was, he refused to allow Alberta to buy him a brand-new tux; a rental would suit his needs perfectly.

Meanwhile, Freddy and Sergio had gone to Wilhelm's, a trendy menswear boutique, where they could buy new tuxes and accessories for the Ball. Alberta had already made a visit and told Wilhelm himself to send her the bill directly. Although Sergio was being chaperoned, Lisa Marie and Tommy were still nervous about letting their wayward son out of their sight, so Jinx quelled their fears by instructing Freddy not to take his eyes off her brother or she would kill him. Freddy knew that his girlfriend wasn't exaggerating.

Just as she started her car in the hospital parking lot, Jinx got a text from Freddy. Actually, several texts. **Sergio's getting antsy. Keeps looking at his phone. I think he's gonna bolt.** Jinx texted back, **On my way**.

Most people didn't consider Jinx's Chevy Cruze a sportscar, but she would disagree. She made it to Wilhelm's in seven minutes when the trip should've taken fifteen. From her parking spot across the street she had a perfect view of the front door of the men's shop and she didn't have to wait long to see Sergio walk out of the shop by himself, quickly turn left, and run up the street. Slowly, Jinx pulled her car out onto the street to follow her brother. She didn't worry that he would see her because he didn't know what kind of car she drove, but even if he did, he appeared to be so focused he wouldn't have noticed her if she drove up beside him, beeped, and told him to hop in.

Her phone rang and it was Freddy. She put her boyfriend on speaker, and before he could speak, she cried, "I'm on his tail."

"You found him!" Freddy yelled.

"I got here just as he was leaving the store," Jinx said.

"Dude! You're amazing. I came out of the dressing room and the next thing I knew he'd given me the slip," Freddy explained.

"It's all right," Jinx said. "I'm not going to let him out of my sight."

"Did he hail a cab?" Freddy asked.

"No, he's on foot," Jinx said. "And I think I know exactly where he's going."

Jinx kept following Sergio, who had slowed down a bit to a jog but was still moving across town, away from the center to the more residential area. Right in between the two sections of town, however, was his destination. Jinx parked across the street from the Tranquility Arms and waited for her brother to do what she knew he would: enter one of the rooms.

Her heart beating a little faster than normal, Jinx walked over to the Arms, smashing the snowy ground with her boots, and when she was standing outside room 8, she banged on the door as loudly as she could. When she didn't get an answer she did her best to match the high pitch and high volume of the manager's voice.

"This is Sanjay!" Jinx bellowed. "I need you to open up this door right now. Open up, I say!"

When Sergio opened the door he was stunned to see his sister instead of the hotel manager. Jinx, however, was not at all surprised to see a young woman lounging on the bed behind him. She knew in her gut that the woman was none other than Natalie.

CHAPTER 13

Breve orazione penetra.

"You must be Natalie," Jinx said.

"And you must be this bad omen Sergio's told me so much about," Natalie replied.

"I could be *your* bad omen if you don't start explaining yourself," Jinx said. "What are you doing here and what do you want from my brother?"

In response, Natalie threw her head back on the pillow and laughed. Her throaty cackle filled up the room, a sound filled with ridicule, derision, and disrespect. She might be flat on her back, but Natalie was the type who looked down at the world from high atop her own self-made perch. Unfortunately, Jinx could tell she was also the type who made every man on the ground want to look up at her.

Natalie wasn't merely pretty, she was Hollywood starlet beautiful. Fresh face, perfect figure, and just the teensiest bit trashy. Jinx thought her father had described her quite accurately, though her long legs, currently stretched out on the bed, made her look taller than her five foot five height, at least when viewed horizontally. Jinx had learned it wasn't wise to judge someone by their appearance, but she made an exception this time. She grew up with a lot of Natalies in Florida, so without ever having met her before, Jinx knew exactly what this girl was like.

Natalie Vespa was a bad girl.

All throughout high school and college, Jinx had seen those girls in action. Making sure that even if they were wearing sweatpants and a T-shirt or running to cheerleader practice at the crack of dawn, they were impeccably groomed. Wearing just enough makeup to look natural, smelling like a spring breeze in a field of jasmine, and always showing just the right amount of flesh to ensure a stare and ignite a fantasy. It was a manufactured look that attracted a lot of potential buyers.

Once they lured in their catch, the bad girls went to work. They pouted until the guy pulled out his credit card to buy her the trinket she would die without. They applied more lip gloss until the guy ditched his friends to write her paper that was due the next day. They whispered insults until the guy changed his ways to make himself more worthy in her eyes. The bad girls manipulated, teased, and belittled in order to get a guy to obey her every command and fulfill her every wish. Jinx had seen it dozens of times, and even if her brother was blind to his girlfriend's machinations, she knew that was exactly the kind of hold Natalie had over Sergio.

It was time he learned the truth.

"I asked you a question," Jinx said. "What do you want from my brother?"

Sergio answered for her. "She doesn't want anything from me! She's my girlfriend!"

"A girlfriend doesn't tear her boyfriend away from his family, make him go on the run, and hide out in some hotel," Jinx replied. "She's using you and I want to know why."

"I love your brother."

Natalie's statement was offered quietly, but it resonated as if a bomb went off in the room. It was not the response Jinx was expecting. For a moment it threw her, but she quickly reminded herself that guys weren't the only ones who could succumb to the wiles of the bad girl—girls like Jinx were just as susceptible.

"Nice try, Nat," Jinx said. "But you wouldn't be interested in love if it was seventy percent off at Nordstrom. Girls like you don't do love, they do ownership."

"What do you think I am, Jinx?" Sergio asked. "Some kind of dog?"

"You don't make a move without asking Natalie which direction, you don't say a word unless Natalie has said you could speak," Jinx replied. "I know it sounds harsh, but yeah, she's turned you into her own trained poodle."

"I swear to God, Jinx, I could strangle you sometimes!" Sergio shouted.

He raised his hands and opened them up like he was going to wrap them around Jinx's neck. This was the second time in their lives that her brother had threatened her, both times when the subject they were discussing was Natalie. The first time it occurred Jinx was shocked, this time she was ticked off.

"If you're gonna hit me, Serge, do it and get it over with!" Jinx cried. "Because the next time you threaten me, you're going to be the one sprawled out on the floor!"

"Now I know where Sergio gets his temper from," Natalie said. "Looks like it runs in the family."

Sergio glared at Natalie, and Jinx could tell he wanted to direct his rage at her. But how could he do that? Natalie would leave him because that's what the bad girls did. They dangled the threat of a breakup if their boyfriend acted improperly and didn't follow the rules. To a guy in his twenties, who was head over heels in love, getting dumped was worse than death. Or hearing the truth.

"I know you're using my brother, but I want to know why," Jinx said. "What kind of trouble are you in, and why are you dragging my brother down with you?"

"Natalie isn't using me!" Sergio yelled. "Get out of here and leave us alone!"

"I'm not going anywhere without you," Jinx said.

"I'm not going anywhere without Natalie!" Sergio screamed.

Natalie knelt on the bed and grabbed Sergio's arm, more like a gentle touch really, but the way Sergio reacted, it was like he was stabbed with a red-hot poker.

"Easy, Serge," Natalie said. "Jinx is only doing what a big sister is supposed to do, taking care of her little brother. I can respect that."

"Don't flatter me, Vespa," Jinx said. "Talk."

And finally, Natalie did.

As Sergio sat on the floor in one corner of the room sulking, Jinx sat in the chair across from the bed and listened as Natalie, sitting on the edge of the bed, told her story. Or the highlights she chose to tell.

"I don't come from a good family like yours," Natalie

started. "When I first met Sergio, he talked about his family and how great they were, how supportive, and it sounded like a fairy tale that I wanted to be a part of."

"According to my parents, you didn't even try to have a relationship with them," Jinx said.

"I'm older than Serge and I do have a reputation—completely unwarranted, of course—but I knew your parents would never accept me, I'm not the type of girl parents would choose for their sons," Natalie replied. "That's why I broke up with Sergio."

"Knowing that my brother wouldn't take no for an answer," Jinx said.

"No matter how many times I told him to leave me alone, he kept telling me that he loved me and wanted to build a life with me," Natalie said. "No one had ever said anything like that to me before. Most guys didn't even want to tell me their last names and your brother wanted to give me his."

"Instead of marrying my brother, you left Florida for New York," Jinx said.

"It was time for me to go," Natalie said. "My business in Florida was done and an opportunity in New York came up, so I took it."

"With Rudy?" Jinx asked.

"I heard your family snooped into my past," Natalie said. "Rudy helped me network."

"What exactly do you do?" Jinx asked.

"Consulting," Natalie answered, and then quickly changed the subject. "I told your brother not to follow me, but he's a stubborn one and a few days later he was in New York. Do I think I'm the right girl for your brother? No. But for now there's nothing I'm going to do or say to convince him otherwise. And I do greatly enjoy his company."

"You still haven't answered my question," Jinx said. "What kind of trouble are you in?"

Natalie stared at Jinx for a moment, maybe trying to gauge how honest she should be, how much information she should share, Jinx couldn't tell. She got up and walked to the window and pulled the curtain away to look at the long patch of untouched snow in the back of the Arms and the small creek, its rushing water racing toward someplace better. She pulled her cardigan sweater tighter around her to ward off the draft that came through the window.

She turned to look at Sergio, and Jinx could see the tenderness in her profile. Maybe she really did love Sergio. But even if she did, she had no right to involve him in whatever mess she was trying to get out of.

"I got involved in a deal that turns out wasn't entirely on the up-and-up," Natalie said, still gazing out the window. "I'm working with the local authorities, but I need to lay low for a while until the trial. I told your brother to go back home where he belongs, but like a true gentleman he refused to leave my side. He wanted to protect all of you, which is why we hadn't responded to any of your family's calls or texts."

All the pieces of Natalie's story fit, they sounded plausible, and yet Jinx didn't think she was hearing the truth. "I'm not sure how much my brother has told you, but my family is pretty tight with the local authorities," Jinx said. "We work with them all the time, and my grandmother used to babysit the chief of police. What I'm trying to say is that we can help you."

Natalie turned to face Jinx, and it looked like she was going to accept Jinx's offer. She was wrong.

"This is local to New Jersey, but very high up, like Supreme Court high," Natalie said. "No offense to your grandmother and Vinny, but he's too low on the totem pole to help me."

"Tell me more about this business partner of yours," Jinx said. "I'm an investigative reporter, I dig for information, I get answers, it's kind of what I do."

Natalie smiled, but she wasn't happy. "It really does run in your family."

"What?" Jinx asked.

"Kindness," Natalie said.

Jinx had never thought of her family as being particularly kind because she assumed that was a trait all families possessed. It was a naïve thought, but after everything she had seen these past few years, Jinx liked to cling to her naivete whenever possible.

"You're both coming with me," Jinx announced.

"I'm not going to the police," Natalie said, just as firmly.

"We're not going to the police, we're going to my grandmother's," Jinx said. "You're staying with us until this thing blows over because, trust me, we can protect you better than anybody else in this town."

By the time they arrived at Alberta's the troops were there to greet them. It was a full-on family affair. The Maldonados and the Ferraras. Before she left the Arms with Natalie and Sergio, Jinx had texted Vinny to tell him that she'd found Natalie, but asked him to please stay away until they could find out more about what she was up to. Based on how she reacted in the park, Natalie, like Sergio, was clearly allergic to the police and would repeat her disappearing act if Vinny showed up on the scene. Vinny agreed and only asked that Jinx keep him posted if she learned more or if they tried to run again. In the past Jinx had been reluctant to cooperate with the police, but now she was convinced it was better to work with Vinny than against him.

When they arrived at Alberta's, however, Jinx was convinced that her family might elicit a worse reaction from Natalie and Sergio than the police would have.

One by one they bombarded Natalie with questions. Lisa Marie wanted to know if she had committed a crime, Tommy wanted to know why she was keeping Sergio from them, Joyce asked the name of her business contact, Helen asked if she worked in the medical industry, and Alberta wanted to know where her family was.

"Stop it!" Sergio cried. "You don't want to help Natalie, you want to crucify her! You're all mad at me, but you don't have the guts to say it, so you're taking it out on her. I'm telling you right here and now, if you want us to stick around you treat Natalie with the respect that she deserves. She is my girlfriend and I love her, and I will not allow any of you to treat her like she's some criminal!"

Sergio had done what he set out to do—he silenced his family. Although Alberta wasn't sure Natalie was a criminal, she suspected the girl was far from innocent. Still she was proud of her grandson for sticking up for his girlfriend. That was what a man was supposed to do for the woman he loved. Even if that love might be a tad misguided.

She saw that Natalie was equally moved by Sergio's words. The woman wiped the tears that fell from her eyes, and Alberta heard her words that were barely a whisper. *"Breve orazione penetra."*

"What did you say?" Alberta asked.

Startled, Natalie wasn't sure at first if Alberta was talking to her. She hadn't realized she had spoken out loud.

"Something my mother used to tell us," Natalie said. "Short prayers reach heaven."

"I know the phrase," Alberta said. "Pray for little things and they'll come true."

"Big prayers are for other people, she used to say," Natalie said. "The rest of us can only hope that heaven hears our smaller prayers."

"*È la verità*," Alberta said. "Your mother's a wise woman."

"Was," Natalie replied. "She's dead."

"*Dio mio*," Alberta said. "I'm so sorry to hear that."

"It was a long time ago," Natalie replied.

There was a respectful pause after Natalie's announcement. When Jinx thought it went on long enough, she turned the conversation back to more practical matters.

"Gram, I told Natalie that she could stay with you until the FBI sorts this all out," Jinx said.

"The FBI?" Lisa Marie exclaimed.

"Natalie is working with the authorities to help them bring some criminals to justice," Jinx said. "Until that happens, she needs a place to hide out."

"No better place than an old lady's guest room," Alberta said.

It was the first time Natalie had smiled since she entered the house.

"I'll stay with you," Helen said. "Two old ladies are better than one."

Tommy followed Natalie and Sergio out to Jinx's car

to get her luggage, which gave the ladies a few minutes to talk openly without being overheard.

"Do you believe Natalie is telling the truth?" Alberta asked.

"Not entirely," Jinx said. "That's why we need to keep an eye on her under your roof."

"Helen, you don't have to stay with me," Alberta said.

"We don't know what this Natalie is capable of," Helen replied. "I'm not leaving you and Lola alone with her."

"Thank you, Aunt Helen, I'll feel better if you're here," Lisa Marie said.

"Maybe you could tap into your old social worker tactics and get her to open up more," Jinx said.

"Also too, don't you have a column to write?" Joyce asked.

"How do you know about that?" Helen demanded. "That's supposed to be a secret."

"Nothing's a secret in this family," Joyce said. "We all know you're *The Herald's* new Big Sister."

"I'm so proud of you," Alberta said. "This town needs to hear what you have to say."

"If the amount of e-mails and letters I'm already receiving are any indication, they sure do," Helen said.

"A lot of people are searching for answers," Alberta said. "Especially at this time of year."

Instinctively, the women grabbed hands and formed a circle. Three generations of women, connected by blood and memory, acknowledging they were not alone, but part of something much greater.

Alberta turned to her daughter. "I know what brought you here wasn't a reason for celebration, but now that you're here I'm so happy you're going to stay for the Mistletoe Ball. It'll give us a chance to relax and take a breath."

Lisa Marie looked embarrassed, but equally thankful. "I'm looking forward to it."

"Speaking of the Ball, I have to run," Joyce said. "I'm meeting with Bambi to talk about the clinical trials they're starting on some new cancer drugs."

"Oh Gram, I forgot to tell you," Jinx said. "Sloan's doctor is in charge of the trials."

"Dr. Manzini?" Alberta said.

"Kylie's doing amazing work," Joyce said. "She lost her mother to breast cancer, so the research is personal for her."

"If she can save some poor women like she saved Sloan, the world will be a better place," Alberta said.

It took some convincing, but Sergio finally relented and agreed to stay at Joyce's with his parents. He didn't want to leave Natalie, but she told him it wouldn't be proper for them to stay together in his grandmother's house and he didn't need to sleep on a couch when Joyce had not one but two guest rooms at her home. After everyone had left the guest at Alberta's quickly made herself at home.

Sitting on the couch, Natalie cuddled Lola, who was delighted to have a new playmate. Watching them from the kitchen, Alberta and Helen weren't sure what to make of the scene. For all of her hard edges and brusque exterior, there was a softness to Natalie. It was like she was a child stuck in a grown-up's body. They knew they couldn't trust her entirely, they knew she wasn't telling them the full truth about her circumstances, but they couldn't help feeling that they needed to protect her. Just as Sergio did.

Alberta brought a tray of hot chocolate and some Zuccarini from Vitalano's Bakery. The rolled dough cookies with anisette frosting were Alberta's favorite. She placed the tray on the cocktail table and sat next to Natalie while Helen sat opposite them in the easy chair. Lola maintained her position in Natalie's lap.

The sisters kept the conversation light, discussing how nice it was to hear Christmas carols on the radio, how calming it was to stand still underneath the falling snow, and what they were going to wear to the Mistletoe Ball. Natalie said that she had heard about the event, and although it sounded like it would be a heavenly diversion from the reality of her life, she didn't think it would be wise to attend such a public outing. Alberta mentioned that the entire family would be there, along with half of the Tranquility Police department, so it couldn't be safer, but Natalie wasn't fully persuaded. She said she would have to sleep on it.

Slowly, Alberta moved away from small talk to ask more probing questions about Natalie's past. "After your mother died I assume it must've been hard on your father."

"I'm not sure he even noticed," Natalie replied.

There wasn't a trace of bitterness in her voice, but the harshness of her words couldn't be ignored.

"He must have," Alberta said. "I mean, she was his wife."

"In name only, there was no love between them," Natalie said. "I don't expect you to understand that."

Alberta did understand, only too well. "Marriages can

be . . . complicated, isn't that the word everyone likes to use when they don't want to admit the truth?" she asked.

"Then let's say my relationship with my entire family has always been complicated," Natalie replied.

"What do you mean?" Helen asked.

Natalie took a sip of hot chocolate and seemed to savor the rich flavor. She looked at the photos on the wall, and Alberta was almost embarrassed. She knew the large array of photos conveyed a story of a family's love, which filled her heart with joy. To someone like Natalie, however, who appeared to come from a less-than-loving family, that same story might instill jealousy, even sorrow.

"Your family looks happy," Natalie noted.

"For the most part we are," Alberta said. "Not all the time, hardly, but the only families that are always happy and never fight and never have any problems are created by people who know nothing about what family truly is."

"I might qualify to write one of those really bad stories," Natalie said.

"You seem like a realistic woman to me," Helen said. "I'm sure you know what a real family is."

Another wistful smile formed on Natalie's face. She took a sip of hot chocolate and licked a drop of whipped cream from her lips before she spoke.

"My father was demanding and expected perfection from all of us, including my mother," Natalie said. "Everyone seemed fully capable of ignoring him except me. I didn't want to look at him, but the harder I tried, the harder it was to look away. The main thing I remember from my childhood is being constantly afraid."

"*Poverino,*" Alberta said. "That's no way to grow up."

"What other way is there when you're constantly

afraid of disappointing your father?" Natalie asked. "I was afraid of saying the wrong word, doing the wrong thing, making a wrong move. He would always say, 'If you can't be perfect, it's better to be nothing.' I knew I would never be perfect, especially not in his eyes, so I chose to be nothing."

"That's no way to live," Helen said.

"Not trying was better than failing, at least that's how I felt," Natalie said. "Everyone else around me knew precisely what they wanted to do with their lives. They were focused, they were driven, they eventually succeeded. Me, I've never found my footing."

"You may not believe this, but I felt the same way for a very long time," Alberta said. "I had given up trying to make my life any different than what it was."

"How did you change things around?" Natalie asked.

"I started to believe that I could change," Alberta replied. "Granted, the universe gave me a push. I inherited this house, I moved to a new town, met new people, but change wouldn't have come if I didn't believe it was possible."

"Be careful what you say, Mrs. Scaglione," Natalie said. "Words like that could give a girl hope."

Alberta felt like she was looking at a younger version of herself. This girl that she hardly knew, the one Rudy had warned her about, was as frightened and broken as Alberta had once been. "Hope is the most beautiful gift in the world."

"Don't ever give up trying," Helen said. "Everyone makes mistakes. You can have a bright future ahead of you if you want it."

Natalie looked at the wall again and saw Sergio's high school graduation photo. It made her laugh out loud.

"That's what Sergio keeps talking about, our future," Natalie said. "Up until this moment I didn't think we could have a future together. I know that he's destined to have . . . all of this, but me . . . I never imagined something as good and as permanent as what your family has could ever be something that I could call my own."

Alberta and Helen didn't have to speak to know what they were each feeling. They weren't ignorant, they knew there were many people who moved through the world alone without the support of a family, whether that family was bound to them by blood or by choice. Hearing Natalie's words, and the resignation in her voice, was staggering. Alberta knew she had to throw Natalie an anchor.

"He's a good boy, my grandson," Alberta said.

"He really is a sweetheart," Natalie said. "I just don't want to screw up his life like I've screwed up mine."

During the pause in the conversation Lola decided it was a good time to flip over onto her feet and jump from Natalie's lap to the carpet. In doing so she bumped into the mug Natalie was holding, making its contents spill all over her cardigan sweater.

"I'm so sorry," Natalie cried.

"Lola! You're a bad girl," Alberta yelled.

"I hope I didn't get any on your couch," Natalie said.

"Don't worry about the couch," Alberta replied. "Let me help you take off this sweater before you burn your arm."

When Alberta pulled Natalie's sweater off she saw that Natalie hadn't been burned, but she had been hurt. She had a black-and-blue mark on her biceps that almost wrapped around her entire arm. Alberta looked at Helen and they both saw fear in each other's eyes.

"Who did this to you?" Alberta asked.

"It's nothing, really, Sergio was upset and . . ." Natalie replied.

"Sergio!" Alberta cried.

Out of the corner of her eye, Alberta saw Helen make the sign of the cross for both of them.

"My grandson did this to you?"

"He didn't mean it," Natalie said. "It was an accident."

All three women in the room knew that the bruise on Natalie's arm was not the result of an accident. But all three women in the room wished to God that it was.

"Promise me, Mrs. Scaglione, you won't say a word about this," Natalie begged. "It'll only get Sergio into trouble."

It didn't matter if she kept silent or shouted it throughout the town with a megaphone, Alberta knew her grandson was already in serious trouble.

CHAPTER 14

Venite tutti voi fedeli.

The most wonderful day of the year had finally arrived. It was time for the Mistletoe Ball. It was the event that filled the entire town with holiday spirit. Alberta and Helen would have been as excited as everyone else if they could only forget what they had learned last night.

The morning sun filled the kitchen, brightening the space, and Alberta let the light fall on her face. She greeted the sunlight as she did every morning, by silently reciting the Hail Mary. This morning she added an Our Father and a Glory Be. When she was finished she looked at Helen, who was sitting on the other side of the kitchen table, her eyes closed, her lips moving quickly. Alberta was sure Helen was praying with the same intention—to save Sergio's soul.

Save him from what exactly? Thus far the only thing

he was truly guilty of was leaving home without permission to follow Natalie to New York and not being in communication with his parents. Disrespectful and inconsiderate, but hardly criminal. If he did, in fact, cause Natalie's injury, there could be extenuating circumstances. They didn't feel it was likely, but they had learned many times before not to jump to conclusions.

As evasive as Natalie was acting, they couldn't pin a crime on her either. According to her version of the story, she'd tried to persuade Sergio not to follow her or even remain her boyfriend, but he didn't listen. She was also involved in a business venture that had gone south but had been cooperating with the authorities. So far, so good. Then why did Alberta and Helen feel worse than if they had stumbled upon a triple homicide? Because the cliché was right, this time it was personal.

"If this is true, Berta, Sergio is going to need counseling," Helen said. "It can't be ignored or swept under the rug, he has to own his anger and control it."

"I know, but for the life of me, I can't wrap my head around the fact that my grandson could've hurt a woman like that," Alberta said. "A woman he supposedly loves."

"You think domestic abuse takes place among strangers?" Helen asked. "We can't make up excuses for Sergio. I've seen this type of thing play out too many times before, we have to break the cycle before it breaks that boy."

"You constantly amaze me, Helen," Alberta said. "Everyone thinks a nun does nothing but sit around and pray while life passes them by. The things you've done to help people, the teaching, the counseling, the prayer work, you've done more in your lifetime than most of us could do in two."

"We all have our purpose, Berta," Helen said. "Yours is to be the matriarch of this family, mine is to boss everybody around."

The chief of police's purpose was to ruin their morning even further.

"She lied to us?" Alberta asked.

Vinny sat at the table, a fresh cup of coffee in front of him, Lola rubbing against his leg, and nodded. "Straight to your face. I spoke with several members of the FBI, not to mention staff at the governor's offices in both New Jersey and New York, and there is no investigation involving Natalie Vespa. She made the whole thing up."

"Why would she do such a thing?" Alberta asked.

"The main reason people lie is to cover up the really bad stuff they've done," Vinny said.

"Now we just have to figure out what really bad stuff Natalie has done," Helen said.

"And possibly Sergio too," Vinny added.

Alberta took a sip of coffee and wondered if she should share what they suspected about Sergio's behavior. She knew that in such matters Helen always followed her lead, so she wasn't worried that she would blurt out that Sergio may have hit Natalie. She also knew that the Ferraras and Vinny had entered into a pact not to hide information from one another while they were working on a case, but they weren't working on the case, so Alberta could remain silent about her suspicions and it couldn't be considered concealing information. She was simply keeping a family matter private. For now.

"I know it will be hard to accept, but Sergio might be more involved in whatever Natalie's involved in than he's admitted," Vinny said. "He might not be such an innocent kid after all."

Alberta sighed and nodded her head. "We understand and we'll cross that bridge when we come to it. For now, I think we should wake up Sleeping Beauty and find out if we've been harboring a criminal."

They went upstairs and stood outside the guest room. After a slight hesitation, Alberta knocked on the door. She waited a moment and then knocked again. When there was no response a second time Alberta looked at her watch.

"It's after nine o'clock," she said. "It isn't that early in the morning."

"Natalie!" Helen shouted. "Come out here. We need to talk to you."

This time the silence caused alarm in all three of them and they knew when they opened the door they would find no one inside. They were right.

"She must've left at the crack of dawn," Helen said. "We both got up around seven."

The room looked like no one had been there for months. The bed that Alberta had turned down last night had been remade so perfectly an Army vet would be proud, the pile of towels on the armchair in the corner of the room meant for Natalie's morning shower remained folded, and the small wastebasket next to the end table was empty. The only thing that gave any indication someone had been in the room was the note on the pillow. The paper was folded in half and Alberta's name was written on it. The letters large and circular, as if they were written by a teenage girl.

"Is it okay if I read it, Vinny?" Alberta asked.

"There's no mystery about who wrote it," Vinny said. "Only touch it by the corners in case we need to lift her prints from it."

Alberta gingerly lifted the note as Vinny instructed and began to read it out loud. She was thankful it was only a few lines.

"'Dear Mrs. Scaglione,'" Alberta began. "'Thank you for your kindness. I'll remember it wherever I wind up. Please tell Sergio he can do better. Natalie.'"

When she was finished, Alberta sat on the bed and tears welled in her eyes. She was heartbroken because she could hear the sadness and heartache in those few words that Natalie scribbled out before taking her few belongings and leaving in the middle of the night to parts unknown. She felt that the poor girl must've been at the end of her rope. Helen had a different take on the turn of events.

"She duped us," Helen said. "She played us all."

"Helen, what do you mean?" Alberta asked.

"The whole story about the FBI was a lie and so was the sob story she told us last night," Helen said.

"What sob story?" Vinny asked.

Helen relayed what Natalie had told them last night, that she lost her mother at a young age and her father led the family with a closed fist instead of an open heart. She presented a living portrait of a lonely girl trying to find her place in the world when, in truth, she was a lying woman who knew exactly what her place in the world was. One step ahead of getting caught.

"I don't know, Helen," Alberta said. "I mean, *Dio mio*, could she really have faked all that emotion last night?"

"Alfie, you know better than most how easily people will lie and conjure up emotions in order to get out of a jam or divert attention," Vinny said. "I know Christmas magic is in the air, but don't ever forget that no one can be trusted."

"*Per l'amor di Dio!*" Alberta cried. "Yes, I know that. I don't want to believe it, but I know that."

"How do we explain this to Sergio?" Helen asked.

An hour later Alberta and Helen still hadn't figured out a way to tell Sergio that Natalie had run off without knowing it would break his heart. Before he left, Vinny promised not to share the info, and the only solution they had was not to tell him until after the Ball.

"Don't you think Sergio is going to expect to talk to Natalie at some point today?" Helen said. "Even if she isn't going to the Ball, he's going to want to see her and show off his tux."

"Or convince her to change her mind and be his date," Alberta said.

"We could say that Natalie's sick and is taking a nap," Helen suggested.

"Or use the burner phone I bought to send Sergio a text saying it's from Natalie, telling him she has the stomach flu and needs to stay away because she's contagious."

"As Father Sal is fond of saying," Helen said, "*una piccola bugia bianca fa male solo un po.*"

"This little white lie might hurt Sergio a lot," Alberta said.

"I think it's a chance we have to take if we're going to salvage this night," Helen said. "Otherwise, you might as well replace all the mistletoe with poison ivy."

When Lisa Marie and Tommy burst into Alberta's kitchen a few minutes later it felt like that had just happened. Lisa Marie was frantically waving a note and Tommy looked like he wanted to punch the wall. She slammed the note on the kitchen table in front of Alberta, and for the second time that morning she read aloud someone's handwritten words.

"'Don't be angry, but I can't stay here any longer,'" Alberta recited. "'Natalie needs me and I have to be with her. I'll call you in a day or so. Love, Sergio.'"

"This doesn't make any sense," Helen said.

"Didn't you hear the note, Aunt Helen?" Lisa Marie asked. "Once again Sergio up and left because of that . . . *sciattona*!"

"You know about three words in Italian and that's one of them?" Alberta asked.

"What does it mean?" Tommy asked.

"Remember how much your wife hated Natalie before?" Helen asked. "Double it."

"What Helen means is that it doesn't make any sense that Sergio left to be with Natalie," Alberta said. "Because Natalie left us a note saying she was leaving town without Sergio."

"She dumped my son?" Lisa Marie asked.

"Isn't that what you wanted from the beginning?" Helen asked.

"Well, yes, but I never thought she'd actually do it," Lisa Marie said.

"Based on Sergio's note, I'm not sure if she actually did," Alberta said. "Maybe she lied to us again to make us think she left Sergio?"

"Either Natalie's lying or my son is," Tommy said. "Either way, I don't like it."

"Neither do I, Tommy," Alberta said. "But, unfortunately, there's nothing we can do about it."

"What do you mean, there's nothing we can do about it?" Lisa Marie said. "This is exactly what you do. You solve mysteries."

"Yes, Leese, we do," Alberta said. "But for now, we're

going to let the police handle this and we will begin our search tomorrow. Because if you haven't forgotten, we have a party to get ready for."

The Tranquility Manor had been the home of many festive occasions since it opened its doors in 1972. Countless wedding celebrations, St. Winifred's Academy's junior and senior proms, the annual conference of the Italian American Business Leaders of New Jersey, and a very successful fundraiser for the not-so-successful Walter Mondale/Geraldine Ferraro presidential campaign run of 1984 all took place at the one-hundred-square foot venue.

The banquet hall was built in the Greek architectural style. A strong rectangular foundation with a white façade and six Doric columns created a semicircle at the entrance, and a small dome topped the entranceway that served a dual purpose as a bell tower. Inside, the hall was divided into five rooms of various sizes named after precious stones. The Sapphire and Emerald rooms were the smallest and were used for Venetian hours and small business luncheons, the Ruby and Pearl rooms were used for proms, conferences, and reunions, and the largest of them, the Diamond room, was ideal for large weddings, the occasional bar mitzvah, and spectacular events like the Mistletoe Ball.

A festive event needed a festive locale, and the Diamond room was the perfect match. The floors were pink marble, red velvet wallpaper with a delicate floral inlay design lined the walls, on top of each table was a Swarovski vase filled with flowers that represented the event's theme, and four Empire-style crystal chandeliers hung from the four corners of the room with one larger, crystal Rain chandelier hanging from the center. It was New Jersey opulence at its best. Which is exactly what the Mistletoe Ball deserved.

Once the rest of Tranquility heard about the Ball's big comeback, enthusiasm had spread throughout the town like pixie dust. Even the Scroogiest adults were transformed into wide-eyed children looking up at the night sky in hopes of seeing the glimpse of a rotund man in a red suit driving a sleigh led by flying reindeer. Imaginations started to run wild.

Every Tranquilitarian wanted to be involved. *The Herald* started running a series of teaser articles that would culminate in Jinx's multipage homage to the histories of the Ball and St. Clare's, Vitalano's Bakery added the Mistletoe cookie to its menu, which was a cluster of red berries in the center of a pistachio cookie shaped like a leaf, and the Tranquility Library created a short video using archival footage to which Sloan added commentary as narrator that ran on a loop in their rotunda to serve as visual documentation of the Ball's history. Christmas had truly come early to this part of New Jersey.

The town leaders imagined that the Mistletoe Ball would serve the same purpose it always had, which was to act as the official kickoff to the holiday season. With that in mind, they worked with the mayor, the Department of Public Works, and Vinny as chief of police to turn Tranquility Park into a Winter Wonderland.

There would be pop-up stores selling everything from hot chocolate to homemade ornaments, a petting zoo complete with several nonflying reindeer, and a Christmas craft workshop where local artisans would teach kids how to make popcorn garland, Styrofoam snowmen, and licorice candy canes. Strolling carolers would conduct impromptu sing-alongs, Santa Claus would listen to children's wish lists, and an ice-skating rink would be constructed to let skaters show off their skills. The highlight of the Winter Wonderland would be the giant gingerbread house built by members of the community that would showcase a holiday concert performed by the St. Winifred's Academy school chorus on Christmas Eve. All of those festivities would give the town a chance to enjoy the playful spirit of the season, to have fun and frolic outdoors. The Mistletoe Ball, on the other hand, was a chance to revel in the elegance and glamor of Christmas Past.

The black-tie, adults only affair meant that the guests would be sporting their holiday best. Men in tuxes, women in gowns, waiters in white gloves, and decorations that were definitely not fashioned by a child's clumsy fingers. The Diamond room at the Tranquility Manor had been reimagined as the promised land for those who believed Christmas was best served in style.

Two silver aluminum Christmas trees complete with garland and ornaments all in red hung upside down from the ceiling, their illuminated red star toppers constantly rotating to sprinkle light onto the crowd below. Vases on every table were filled with red and white poinsettia plants with a cluster of mistletoe in the center, and the tablecloths alternated in color from silver to gold, but all were made of velvet.

The decorations were not only pleasing to the eye, but the nose as well. Natural pine wreaths decorated the walls and standeliers—standing candelabras that held ten to fifteen balsam-scented candles—were placed around the room. Their scents mixed and mingled to create a yuletide aroma.

As a way to camouflage the entrances to the kitchen and the utility room, a large tableau was built to depict a modern replica of the North Pole. A portion of a ski chalet could be seen peeking out from a bevy of pine trees, a life-size snowman and snowwoman were taking a stroll in the woods, and beautifully wrapped presents were piled in stacks in the fake snow. Every time a waiter exited or entered the kitchen, they looked like they were emerging or disappearing into a forest. Even the microphone stand that was placed next to the snow couple was wrapped in garland to ensure that it didn't look out of place. It was a true Christmas cornucopia.

If Joyce wouldn't take public credit for being the mastermind behind the entire event, she had no choice but to accept praise from her family.

"*Come un sogno che si avvera*," Alberta gushed, clutching Joyce's hands.

"It is like a dream come true, isn't it?" Joyce said.

"All thanks to you," Alberta said.

"It took a huge team effort to create all this magic," Joyce replied. "Your handsome beau did a lot of the heavy lifting."

"*Basta*! Stop being such a *testarda* like Helen," Alberta said. "None of this would have happened without you."

"Even a stubborn old mule like me can admit it," Helen said, joining the ladies. "*Ben fatto*, Joyce, well done."

Joyce grabbed Alberta and Joyce's hands and smiled. "What I'm most proud of is that we're all here together to share this moment. I know things haven't been easy lately, but it means everything to me that my family is here."

"We wouldn't have missed this for the world," Alberta said.

"Also too, when am I ever going to have another chance to wear a gown like this?" Helen asked, borrowing Joyce's catchphrase.

"I could say the same thing," Alberta said. "I know this is nothing new for you, Joyce, but I've never been so dressed up in my entire life."

"Look at the three of us," Joyce said. "We've come a long way from Hoboken, haven't we?"

Indeed, they had. All three women looked spectacular in their festive get-ups, as Alberta called them. Helen was wearing a baby-blue sequined gown with matching bolero jacket that Alberta bought for her at The Clothes Horse, with matching silver shoes and purse that Joyce found for her through a bridal store connection. The former nun's no-nonsense, short gray hair had been given a bit of a lift that morning by Adrianna from A Cut Above, nothing too drastic, but enough so she looked as chic above the neck as she did below.

Joyce was wearing a vintage Yves Saint Laurent gown she'd picked up on a shopping spree in Soho in 1992. She fell in love with the shimmery, emerald-green dorian caftan gown that spread out like angel's wings when she lifted her arms. It took her a few decades to attend an event glitzy enough to wear it, but it was worth the wait.

It took a while for Alberta to find a gown that she felt comfortable wearing. The only other time she had worn a gown was at her own wedding, having worn tea-length dresses to both her children's nuptials. Alberta knew that if Sloan was going to stand at her side in a tuxedo, she needed to submit to a makeover.

After much deliberation, Alberta chose the sixth gown she tried on. Not because the Carolina Herrera piece of couture fit the best, not because it was the most comfortable, but because she could never have envisioned herself wearing something like this before she moved to Tranquility. The gown represented the woman Alberta had become and not the woman she used to be. She would never admit it to anyone, except maybe Sloan after drinking a few glasses of Red Herring, but the gown also made her feel sexy.

The deep, V-neck top was made of embroidered lace and had a three-quarter sleeve that accentuated Alberta's bosom while smoothing her waistline. The bottom was pleated chiffon that flowed when she moved. What made the outfit so breathtaking was its color: eye-catching fuchsia. Alberta was making a statement, no one could not help but notice she was a forceful presence in the room, not even Alberta herself.

She had joined Helen at A Cut Above earlier and let Adrianna style her hair with a bit more pouf and height than normal. She even let her hairdresser apply makeup beyond the usual dash of lipstick she wore. Her gold crucifix, diamond studs, and the bracelet Sloan bought her for their anniversary were her only accessories. The dress made enough of a fuss, she thought, it didn't need any extra help.

Looking around the room, Alberta thought, *Venite tutti voi fedeli,* "O Come, All Ye Faithful," it was a who's who of Tranquility's finest. Everywhere they turned they saw someone they knew. Luke, the orderly from the morgue, was munching on hors d'oeuvres and chatting with Tambra, Vinny's second in command; Pedro Suarez, the medical examiner, was admiring the jewelry that Donna, St. Winifred's Academy's principal, wore; D. Edward Carmichael, dressed up as Santa Claus for the occasion, was listening intently to something Dr. Manzini was whispering in his ear; Sanjay was very animatedly telling a story that made Wyck and Benny from *The Herald* laugh hysterically; and Kwon, who had closed the diner early to attend, seemed to be flirting with Virginia, the organist at St. Winifred's.

The trio were so engrossed in their people watching, they didn't know they were being stared at until they were approached by another equally well-dressed trio.

Sloan, Father Sal, and Vinny all greeted the women with appropriate accolades, kisses, and surprised expressions. They had known the women for quite some time, in some cases decades, but they had never seen them dressed so formally before. Father Sal, not one for being subtle, bowed in front of Helen.

"Finally, your outside beauty has matched the beauty that emanates from within," Father Sal said.

"I see you've been nipping from the holy chalice already," Helen said. "You might want to pace yourself, Sal, it's going to be a long night."

"Now I understand why you wanted me to meet you here," Sloan said, holding Alberta's hand. "Had I seen you like this at home we may never have gotten out of the kitchen."

Alberta blushed and playfully slapped Sloan on the shoulder. "You look rather handsome yourself."

She was right, Sloan did look handsome, and so did Father Sal, in their simple tuxes. Despite how put together they looked, however, no man in the room could

hold a candle to Vinny. He was movie-star glamorous
from head to toe and cut the kind of powerful figure that
the camera, and every woman around him, adored.

Square jawed and standing at six foot four, Vinny wore
a single-breasted Armani tuxedo with satin lapels that fit
him so perfectly it reminded everyone he had the shoulders of a linebacker and the waist of a man half his age.
His black bow tie was oversize, his black onyx cuff links
were dazzling, his black socks had a bit of a shimmer to
them, and his black patent leather loafers in a wide-width
size thirteen all worked together to make quite a fashion
statement.

"Holy Marlon Brando!" Helen shrieked. "You missed
your calling, Vinny, you coulda been a contender."

"Never mind me," Vinny said. "You ladies look sensational!"

"Never mind us." Alberta gasped. "The lady entering
the ballroom right now is going to steal all our thunder."

Along with everyone else in the room, the group
turned to the front entrance, and for a few seconds the
only sound that could be heard was the instrumental version of "Do You Hear What I Hear?" that was flowing
from the speakers. If anyone could have spoken, they
would have said *Do you see what I see?* but the power of
speech was momentarily lost as Jinx, holding Freddy's
hand, entered the room. It was a sight to behold.

The bright red satin Versace dress was a marvel of
construction, loosely draped and body hugging at the
same time. The long sleeves were full, tapering to a three-
inch cuff at the wrist, the plunging neckline and bodice—
accented at the waist by a large flowing bow—was
formfitting, but it was the body of the gown that made
Jinx look like a model taking ownership of the runway.

The full skirt was a wraparound, which meant that every time Jinx took a step, her left leg emerged from within the undulating fabric and caused the material to ripple behind her like a satiny breeze. She wore her favorite Jimmy Choo cocktail sandals in sparkling silver with a three-inch heel that had thick straps across the bridge of her foot and around her ankle. She couldn't make a wrong move if she tried.

Jinx took advantage of the natural volume of her hair and had it styled so it was parted on one side, falling in massive waves on the right side of her face, while the left side was held back by a ruby-and-rhinestone hair clip. It was a dramatic look that was accentuated by her makeup: bronzed lips, defined cheekbones, and just a hint of burgundy eye shadow.

"Holy mackerel," Alberta said.

"Holy cow," Helen said.

"Also too, holy Gina Lollobrigida," Joyce added.

It may have appeared that Jinx was channeling Lola's namesake, but if you asked her, she paled in comparison to how Freddy looked. She knew the guests were making a fuss over her ensemble, but she took one look at Freddy, who was resplendent from the neck down in a perfectly tailored tuxedo, but from the neck up quite the opposite thanks to his trademark unmanageable mop of thick, brown hair and floppy ears, and Jinx thought he was the handsomest man in the world. By the way Freddy was grinning, she was confident he knew how she felt.

The luminous couple joined the rest of their family, and after several minutes of exchanging compliments and oohing and aahing over how sensational everyone looked, they realized the entire family wasn't present.

"Where are my parents?" Jinx asked.

"I thought they were coming with you, lovey," Alberta replied.

"No, my mother told me she was going to drive over with Aunt Joyce," Jinx said.

"I had to get here early to make sure everything was running smoothly," Joyce said. "Your mother told me she would come with you."

"Have you checked your phone?" Alberta said. "Maybe she texted to say she's running late."

"I left my phone in the car," Jinx said.

"I thought that thing was surgically attached to your hand," Helen said.

"I had no place to carry it," Jinx said. "I can barely fit my underwear underneath this dress."

"*Ah Madon!*" Alberta said. "I don't want to hear any-more."

"Never fear, it's the boyfriend to the rescue," Freddy said, pulling out Jinx's cell phone from his inside pocket. "I knew you weren't going to last five minutes without this thing."

"Thank you, Freddy," Jinx said. She took the phone from Freddy's hand and was relieved to see a text from her mother. "They're running late."

"I'm sure they'll be here soon," Alberta said.

"They better!" Jinx cried. "Otherwise they're going to miss seeing Freddy get his award."

"What award?" Freddy asked.

Jinx's eyes grew wide as she looked at her boyfriend and the rest of the group. They were all staring at her wearing confused expressions. Joyce and Sloan were the only ones who seemed to know what she was talking about—most likely because they were both privy to the night's scheduled festivities. Following the induction and before the first course, Bambi was going to announce the winner of this year's Small Business Owner of the Year award that thanks to Jinx's slip of the tongue everyone knew would be presented to Freddy as the owner of Freddy's Ski 'n Scuba Shoppe.

"Dude!" Freddy shouted. "Am I getting *the* award?"

"I'm so sorry," Jinx said. "Forget I said anything and just act surprised."

"If you'd like to get some practice, turn around," Sloan said. "Here comes Bambi."

"Would you get a load of those headlights?" Helen asked.

"Now I know what it must've been like to be Sophia Loren sitting next to Jayne Mansfield at that Hollywood dinner party," Father Sal said.

Indeed, Bambi was a sight to behold. Her plus-size frame was wrapped in a sleeveless, gold lamé corset dress with a mermaid skirt. She wore a gold mesh necklace, a gold snake bracelet, and gold drop earrings. It appeared that she had either spent time in a tanning booth or had lathered bronzer all over her body because she glimmered in the light, making her look like she could have starred in the James Bond film *Goldfinger.* Luckily, the woman didn't have to save the world or dodge an insane mastermind hell-bent on destroying it, she simply had to waddle a few steps to the microphone to make a speech.

Unfortunately, before she could say one word, Alberta noticed something odd about the life-size snowwoman. It was supposed to be standing next to the snowman, but instead it was starting to tilt to the other side. The other odd thing was that she was bleeding.

A thin stream of blood was running down the left side of the snowwoman's body. Alberta got up, but before she could move toward the tableau to investigate the scene further, the snowwoman fell onto her left shoulder and rolled onto her back. Bambi looked annoyed at being upstaged by an oversize Christmas decoration, but her attitude changed when the snowwoman's body cracked open at the seam to reveal what had been hidden inside. She stumbled backward at the sight, knocking over several trees in the process, until D. Edward Carmichael, still dressed as Santa Claus, came up behind her, grabbing her around the shoulders to keep her upright.

The rest of the guests reacted in the same way, screaming and holding on to one another, all except the people at Alberta's table. They were silent and couldn't move because they were terrified. Yes, they were stunned to see Natalie Vespa lying motionless in the shell of the snowwoman with blood covering her entire chest. What was more horrifying, however, was when they looked up and saw Sergio standing in the doorway of the ski chalet, an equally bloody knife dangling from his hand.

CHAPTER 15

Non così buon Natale.

Ounholy night.
　　The first words that appeared on Alberta's lips weren't meant for anyone else but God. The words themselves were barely a whisper, but the Lord's Prayer had never been spoken with more intensity and urgency. These words had to reach their receiver, these words had to make an impact, her grandson's life depended upon it.

There was chaos all around Alberta as she stood motionless, having her private, pivotal conversation with the Almighty. But she had learned some important lessons over the past few years, and one of them was that she always needed to be aware of her surroundings no matter how panicked she felt. Clues were always hiding in plain sight.

Unmoving, she watched as Pedro knelt next to Natalie's body holding her wrist, presumably searching for a pulse. His fool's errand was rewarded as expected and he shook his head. He informed everyone that the woman, as everyone in the ballroom suspected, was dead.

Alberta watched as Benny's professional instincts kicked in and he took photos of the dead body and the surrounding activity with his phone as Wyck, standing next to him, typed furiously on his. The Mistletoe Ball was going to make headlines in *The Herald* for all the wrong reasons. Dr. Manzini had joined Carmichael and Bambi at the microphone, and they were looking at Natalie's body with almost an air of curiosity. They were, after all, medical professionals and had seen their fair share of death, so that wasn't highly unusual and after a moment their more human instincts kicked in. Carmichael made the sign of the cross, Kylie wiped tears from her eyes, and Bambi gripped the microphone stand to steady herself. The rest of the attendees were either gasping in horror, whispering in shock, or navigating the crowd to get a closer look at the evening's surprise guest. Alberta had waited long enough; it was time for her to take action.

Jinx had the same thought, and without saying a word, she and Alberta clasped hands and walked toward the scene of the crime. They heard footsteps and commotion all around them, but they maintained their focus. They had one mission in mind and that was to get to Sergio. Vinny had other ideas.

"Alfie, stop," Vinny said.

Alberta and Jinx turned around to see Vinny and Tambra walking toward them. She could tell that Vinny had addressed her as the chief of police and not her longtime friend. She understood that he had a job to do, but he needed to understand that she had her own task to perform, and that was to make sure her grandson knew he wasn't alone. She trusted Vinny would respect that.

"I need to speak to Sergio," Alberta said.

"You can after I do," Vinny replied.

The words Vinny shared with Sergio were not nearly as comforting as the ones Alberta would have used, but given the circumstances, she knew that protocol took precedence over compassion. They listened in disbelief as Vinny read Sergio his Miranda warning, the young man not looking at the cops but straight ahead at his girlfriend's lifeless body less than twenty feet away. Alberta and Jinx, with their family and friends behind them, waited for Vinny to finish so they could wrap their arms around him. But Vinny wasn't done just yet.

He turned to face the crowd and raised his arms over his head to get their attention.

"No one is allowed to leave this room," Vinny shouted. "I need you all to please take your seats and sit quietly."

"What's going on, Vinny?" Wyck asked. "We have a right to know."

"No, you don't," Vinny said.

Alberta wasn't surprised by Vinny's tone and curtness. If he didn't take charge and show the guests who was in command, pandemonium would reign, which would have been almost as disastrous as what had already taken place: the reveal of a dead, clearly murdered body at what was supposed to be a joyous occasion. Alberta shook her head and thought, *Non così buon Natale.* It was definitely not a merry Christmas. Especially for Natalie.

She couldn't believe the young woman who last night sat in her living room sharing memories of her childhood was now dead and covered in blood. There was the possibility that the glimpses into her past that she spoke about were fabrications, but Alberta had believed her. She also believed in her grandson's innocence, though it appeared that not everyone shared her opinion.

Tambra crossed in front of Sergio, who would not take his eyes off Natalie's unmoving body, and approached a waiter coming out from in between two pine trees. The waiter looked terrified, her face pale, her eyes wide open and unblinking behind her thick glasses. With one hand she readjusted her glasses like Lisa Marie often did, and with her left she handed a plastic bag and some latex gloves to Tambra. The waiter stood still after Tambra thanked her, and for some reason Alberta was drawn to the woman. It might have been a trick of the light or because the woman's body was trembling, but it looked like her blond curls were bouncing. Out of the corner of her eye she saw that she wasn't the only one transfixed by this woman. Kylie, Bambi, and Carmichael were all staring at her as well. Though Alberta couldn't be sure if they were fixated on the woman or the transaction that had just taken place. The spell, however, was broken when Alberta saw what Tambra did next.

She had seen the young cop wriggle her fingers into blue latex gloves before, but now the action seemed surreal because the gloves clashed horribly with her strapless, canary yellow gown. With one hand Tambra held Sergio's wrist and with the other she grabbed the handle of the blade and inserted the knife into the plastic bag. She quickly sealed the bag and took a few steps back, allowing Vinny to take over.

"Sergio Maldonado," Vinny said. "You are under arrest for the murder of Natalie Vespa."

The crowd ignored Vinny's previous command to remain quiet and their loud voices, filled with shock, disbelief, and even excitement, grew into one cacophonous sound. Alberta and Jinx gripped their hands tighter and they couldn't believe what they were witnessing. How could Vinny do this? How could he arrest a member of their family? The answer was quite simple—their grandson and brother had been found holding a bloody knife near a bloodied dead body. Open-and-shut, case closed. Alberta and Jinx both knew that wasn't the end of the story.

"Sergio," Alberta said. "Look at me."

Slowly, the young man's eyes moved from Natalie's corpse to his grandmother's face. He looked heartbroken, as if he had just seen his future yanked from his clutches. The life he had dreamed of had been viciously ripped away. Would the couple have lasted more than a few more months? Would Sergio turn from Natalie once all her lies were exposed? None of that mattered. The only thing that mattered was what was in his heart.

"I didn't do this, Grandma," Sergio said. "I didn't kill Natalie."

"We know," Alberta said. "And we're going to set things straight."

"Sergio, what happened?" Jinx asked. "How did you get the knife?"

Jinx asked her questions with good intentions but failed to realize if Sergio answered them, there could be grave consequences.

"Don't say a word, Sergio," Sloan said.

He stood behind Alberta and whispered, "Sergio shouldn't answer any questions in front of the police, especially without a lawyer."

"*Ah Madon*," Alberta said. "You're right."

"He has to tell the truth and clear his name," Jinx said.

Freddy came behind Jinx and wrapped his arm around her waist. "He'll do that, but not here and not now."

Jinx nodded and held on to Freddy's hand. She had been thinking like a big sister and not the reporter she was. If Sergio spoke now, no matter what he said—truth, lies, some hybrid of the two—it would be used by the police against him. Or, eventually, by the legal team who would try to put her brother behind bars for the rest of his life. She closed her eyes tight and inhaled. She knew when she opened her eyes she would still be standing in the middle of a nightmare, but at least she would be equipped with a clearer head.

"Sloan's right, Sergio, don't say another word," she said.

"I have to explain!" Sergio protested. "I didn't do this."

"We know that, honey," Alberta said. "But you must keep quiet until we get you an attorney."

Alberta had been a witness to this scene many times before, she had known some of the people who had been arrested for murder, had personal connections to them, but never had someone in her own family been accused of such a vile crime. The Ferrara family tree was filled with its share of colorful characters, some possessing questionable morals, but no one—at least to Alberta's knowledge—had ever committed murder. She did not believe that had changed and she vowed to herself she would prove that.

"Sloan, please call Bruno," Alberta said. "I know he's out of town, but tell him we need him."

"I will," Sloan said.

"Joyce," Alberta said. "Call your bank and make sure

you have enough money for bail. I can pay you back, but you take care of these financial matters much quicker than I do."

"I can transfer funds on my phone," Joyce said. "And you most certainly will not pay me back."

"Freddy," Alberta said. "I need you to find my daughter and her husband."

"Already on it," Freddy replied. "I haven't reached them yet, but I won't stop until I do."

Freddy pulled Jinx's cell phone out of his pocket to check if she had any texts, but no one had reached out to her. He was about to give the phone to Jinx when he noticed she was staring off into space.

"Baby, are you all right?" Freddy asked.

Jinx grabbed her boyfriend's hand but didn't turn to look at him. "I'm surveying the area, trying to take a mental picture of the scene of the crime."

"Dude, why don't you just take pictures with your camera?" Freddy asked.

Suddenly, Jinx did turn around and looked into Freddy's eyes, light brown with the faintest flecks of gold, and felt a deep and profound love. Now was not the appropriate time to tell him how she felt—she would wait until the air around them was calmer and not thick with fear and anxiety—plus, her boyfriend had some work to do on her behalf.

"Start snapping," Jinx said. "Don't think, just click."

Freddy didn't take time to reply. He started taking photos of the entire ballroom with Jinx's phone as inconspicuously as possible. It helped that several other members of the police force and paramedics arrived to take the suspect and victim away, which created a diversion. It was also about to create even more chaos.

A cop Alberta didn't recognize walked up to Sergio and told him to put his hands behind his back. Sergio stared at the man as if he was speaking a different language. Alberta thought at first that her grandson was frozen with fear, but then she saw his fists clench and realized he was filled with rage.

"Berta, do something before things get worse," Helen said quietly so no one but her sister could hear.

"Do what the man says, Sergio," Alberta commanded. "Everything is going to be all right, but Grandma needs you to cooperate."

Sergio looked at Alberta, and the fury that consumed him only moments earlier seemed to rush out of his arms. His fingers uncurled and pointed straight to the floor, and after a second he placed his arms behind his back. Crisis averted.

"We'll meet you at the police station," Alberta said.

Vinny turned to face Alberta and the others, and he dropped his professional veneer so he could talk to his friends. "I hope you know I had no other choice."

Alberta was too emotional to speak. Instead, she nodded her head and clutched Vinny's hand. The others added their acknowledgment. They knew Vinny had been conflicted, but they also knew he had a job to do. Unfortunately, his job was not yet done.

The policeman who handcuffed Sergio gave him a little shove to get him to start walking. Sergio stumbled a bit, but corrected himself. He was only able to take a few steps when he stopped, right next to the gurney that held Natalie's body. He watched as an EMT covered his girlfriend's face with a white sheet, and it was more than he could stand. His body bent forward and he started to shake, his face contorted into a grotesque resemblance of its normal self, his mouth opened but producing no sound. Until he wailed.

His cry, raw and grotesque, filled the huge room and brought the chatter that had continued since Natalie's body was first revealed to an end. No one spoke, no one moved, except Alberta.

She grabbed her grandson by the shoulders, and the policeman holding Sergio attempted to keep her from making contact. Alberta was not going to let that happen but didn't need to make a move to thwart the cop's actions; Vinny did it for her. He held up his left hand, which was all the cop needed to see to let go of Sergio and back away.

Sergio's sobs continued, and the sounds coming from his body alternated between gruff moans and high-pitched screams. It was frightening to watch, and Jinx buried her face in her hands and leaned back to allow Freddy to support her weight. Father Sal put his hands over Helen's, her rosary beads rubbing against the many rings he wore, and together they prayed. Sloan pulled the white handkerchief from his breast pocket and gave it to Joyce to wipe away the tears that were streaming down her face. They were all taking care of one another as a family should, and then it was Alberta's turn.

She hugged Sergio tightly and rubbed his back the way she had when he was a baby and suffering from colic. Her hand wrapped around the nape of his neck and she felt his sweat and the heat emanating from his body. She leaned his head to the left so it rested against hers and she spoke words that could only be borne from a grandmother's love.

"I need you to be strong, Sergio, and I need you to trust me," Alberta said. "You have my word in front of God Himself that I will not rest until I prove your innocence. Because you are my flesh and my blood, and I know you are not capable of taking another's life. I need you to remember that you are loved. You have your family, and your family will never let you down."

Alberta's words acted as a salve, extinguishing the fire that was burning in Sergio's heart and calming the thunder that pulsed through his veins. He took a few deep breaths and stood with his back straight, still terrified but proud to be joined to a group of people who loved him and would do whatever they had to in order to protect him.

He looked at Alberta, his red eyes and cheeks still wet with tears, and made an attempt to smile. "Thank you, Grandma."

Alberta smiled and wiped the tears from Sergio's face as best she could. She then stepped back to join the rest of the group and watched as Vinny placed a hand on her grandson's shoulder and led him through the crowd of gawking onlookers. Some of them turned away as Sergio passed them, others gazed in fascination, some, like Benny, took a photo. *We all have jobs to do*, Alberta thought.

When Vinny and Sergio left the Diamond room, the EMTs, with Pedro by their side, wheeled out the gurney carrying Natalie's body. This generated another round of gasps and cries from the more sensitive members of the crowd, including, quite unexpectedly, Dr. Manzini and Sanjay. Death worked in mysterious ways.

The court system, however, had its own set of rules

that it didn't like to stray from. Even on a Saturday night during Christmastime.

"What do you mean, the district attorney won't let Sergio out on bail?" Alberta cried.

Vinny's office was crowded. Alberta, Jinx, Helen, Joyce, Sloan, Freddy, and Father Sal were standing on one side of his desk while Vinny and Tambra were on the other. They were all still dressed in their Mistletoe Ball finery, but now that they were situated in an environment that was far less grandiose than the Tranquility Manor, they looked woefully out of place. None of them cared about the optics, what they cared about was getting Sergio released on bail to prevent him from having to spend the night in jail, but the powers that be weren't cooperating.

"She knows that I'm a friend of the family and she doesn't want the public perception to be that she's giving Sergio special treatment," Vinny said.

"I'll take out an ad in *The Herald* claiming that the Ferraras hate your guts," Helen said.

"The DA is new at her job," Vinny explained. "She's being cautious, plus, she's well within her rights given the circumstances."

"What do you mean 'circumstances?'" Joyce asked.

"Sergio was found near Natalie's dead body with what is most likely the murder weapon," Vinny started. "He doesn't have an alibi and his history of running away makes him a flight risk. If it were up to me, of course I'd let Sergio out on bail, but this isn't my decision."

"Is there no way to change her mind?" Jinx asked.

"The DA sees this as a slam dunk, domestic violence gotten out of hand," Vinny explained. "She believes Sergio and Natalie had a fight, it got out of control, and Sergio killed Natalie, then panicked and tried to dispose of the body."

"Please dear God in heaven, Vinny, tell me you don't believe that too," Alberta said.

"Of course I don't," Vinny replied. "But this isn't the unofficial Ferrara Family Detective Agency, it's a real-life court of law, and we have rules that I took an oath to follow. Which doesn't mean I'm not going to continue with the investigation."

"Neither will we," Alberta said.

"That's what I'm counting on," Vinny replied. "If we work together, I know we can find out who really killed Natalie Vespa."

"We have to, Vin," Alberta replied. "My grandson's life depends on it."

CHAPTER 16

Il bacio mortale del vischio.

It felt as if Tranquility had been turned into Somber-town, the setting of the Rankin/Bass Christmas classic *Santa Claus Is Comin' to Town*. No joy, no happiness, only gloom.

Alberta was suddenly so exhausted she asked Sloan to drive her BMW back to her house. Helen, Father Sal, and Joyce were in the back seat. Karen Carpenter's aching alto played on the radio, promising to be home for Christmas. It was a pathetic excuse for a holiday carol. They all knew she was lying, she was only going to spend Christmas with her loved ones in her dreams. If things weren't bad enough already, Karen just made them worse.

"*Ah Madon!*" Alberta cried. "This night has been an unmitigated disaster. *Tale sventura.*"

"First, a dead woman pops out of a decoration," Joyce said.

"Then Sergio is standing there in a fake forest holding the murder weapon," Helen said.

"I kept looking around for falling locusts," Father Sal said. "Or an angry mob of frogs."

"Better chance of seeing them than watching Lisa Marie and Tommy make an entrance," Helen said.

"Berta, did they call you?" Joyce asked. "Do we have any idea where they are?"

"No," Alberta said. "They don't even know that Sergio has to spend the night in jail."

"I think they're about to find out," Sloan said.

He pulled the car into the spot in front of the house because the driveway was being taken up by Tommy's Subaru.

"I am sick and tired of my daughter's disappearing act!" Alberta screamed. "She writes me and doesn't show up! I call her, she doesn't respond! She tells us she and Tommy are going to meet us at the Ball, they go AWOL! *Lo giuro su Dio, su tutti gli angeli e sui santi!* I have had it!"

Furiously, Alberta unhooked her seat belt, but when she tried to open the car door, it was locked. She unlocked it, but by the time she pushed on the door to open it, it was locked again. Because Sloan had taken control of the locking mechanism from the driver's seat.

Alberta turned to look at Sloan. "*Dio mio!* What are you doing?"

"Passengers should remain seated until we pass through this turbulence," Sloan replied. "If you barge into your house to confront your daughter and her husband like some crazy Italian woman, you can kiss all the repair you've done to your relationship good-bye."

"Your boyfriend's right, Alberta," Sal said. "Better to

swallow your rage now than spit it out like machine gun bullets to an unsuspecting congregation on Spy Wednesday."

"I know I'm not a born Catholic, but I thought I was up on all the lingo," Joyce said. "What in the world is Spy Wednesday?"

"It's the day Judas betrayed Jesus," Father Sal explained. "Also known as Holy Wednesday, but to my ear Spy Wednesday has a much better ring to it."

"Sal's right, Berta," Helen said. "Calm yourself down before today becomes known as the day Alberta betrayed Lisa Marie."

"How am I going to betray my daughter?" Alberta said. "She's the one who's constantly lying to me."

"A mother is supposed to accept her child's failures, not flaunt them in their face," Helen said. "Plus, you need to be in the right frame of mind to tell her and Tommy what happened tonight."

Alberta threw back her head against the headrest and closed her eyes. She knew they were right, she knew that she was stressed and scared and if she went into her house now, she would take out her frustrations on her daughter. Not that Lisa Marie didn't deserve to be on the receiving end of Alberta's wrath, but no, it was Alberta who needed a time-out.

"Is there any good news at all that we can cling to?" Alberta asked.

"Bruno texted me, he's taking a red-eye home tonight and will be back in Tranquility tomorrow morning," Sloan said. "He's already reached out to the DA to try to get her to reverse her decision about bail."

"That's wonderful news," Joyce said.

Not entirely, Alberta thought.

Bruno bel Bruno was a public defender and a loyal friend to the Ferraras. He'd helped them on cases before, and Alberta was praying he'd not only get Sergio free on bail, but free from the charges against him. Part Sicilian and part Swedish, Bruno was tough, but fair. Unfortunately, he was also honest. If he felt they would need a miracle to win, he'd tell them that, and although she was a devout Catholic, Alberta didn't want to leave her grandson's fate solely in the hands of God.

She reached over and grabbed Sloan's arm, which was resting on the center console. She let out a sigh and shook her head. No more stalling.

"I think I'm ready to go inside," Alberta said.

"Are you sure?" Sloan asked.

"No, but I'm getting cold," Alberta replied.

"That's as good a reason as any," Sloan said.

When Alberta opened her front door, she saw Lisa Marie and Tommy seated at the kitchen table, their heads tilted toward each other, Tommy's hands clasped around Lisa Marie's. She didn't see rosary beads, but she knew they were praying. Keeping them company was Lola, who was sprawled out on the table even though she knew she was lying in the forbidden zone. When Lola noticed that there were others in the room she let out a loud meow.

Lisa Marie and Tommy looked up at the group huddled by the door still dressed in their fancy clothes and appeared embarrassed, as if they had been caught doing something wrong. Alberta was mortified that she was going to have to add to their sorrow.

"I thought the Ball was going to go well past midnight," Lisa Marie said. "What are you doing home so early?"

"I could ask you two the same thing," Alberta said. "Why didn't you show up like you said you would?"

"Where have you been all this time?" Helen asked.

"Also too, why aren't you at my place where you've been staying?" Joyce asked.

Lisa Marie watched as Alberta and the others took off their coats and gloves, placed their purses on the table, and pulled out chairs to sit. Alberta knew she was stalling but remembered what they had discussed in the car and didn't confront her daughter, instead, she went over to the sink and filled a teakettle with water. Lisa Marie wasn't the only one who could mark time.

"We weren't up for a night out," Lisa Marie said. "We came here to tell you, but you had already gone. I should've come clean and called you, but we knew that you and everybody else would try to convince us to go to the Ball. We chickened out and turned our phones off."

"Only for a bit, though," Tommy added. "We were afraid Sergio would call or text and we'd miss him."

"We've been so worried lately, staying up late, getting up early, that we both sat on the couch to relax for a bit and the next thing you know, we fell asleep," Lisa Marie explained.

"I only woke up because Lola kept whacking me with her paw because she was hungry," Tommy said. "Otherwise, we'd still be asleep."

"Sergio didn't reach out, if you're wondering," Lisa Marie said. "We still don't know where our son is."

"We do," Alberta said, turning the flame on to boil the water. "You need to prepare yourself because it isn't good."

After Alberta finished telling Lisa Marie and Tommy

what had transpired that evening, they looked as shocked as if they had witnessed it firsthand.

"Not good? Ma, this is the worst possible thing that could have happened!" Lisa Marie screamed. "We have to go see him."

"You can't," Sloan said.

"Don't you tell me what I can and can't do!" she screamed. "My mother might have to obey you, but I don't!"

"*Smettila*!" Alberta said. "Sloan doesn't give me orders and I wouldn't obey them if he did. But he's right, we were at the police station and they wouldn't let us see him."

"Why not?" Tommy asked.

"Because the DA is taking a hard line on the case," Joyce said. "For the moment she refuses to set bail and she won't let Sergio have any visitors until the morning."

"We need to find a lawyer," Tommy said. "I can call Elliott."

"He does personal injury cases, Tom, he helped you when you slipped on that jobsite," Lisa Marie said. "Natalie isn't injured, she's dead!"

"He's the only lawyer I know!" Tommy cried.

"I already took care of that," Alberta said. "Bruno's on a red-eye and he'll meet us at the police station in the morning."

"Is he good?" Lisa Marie asked.

"He's the best," Helen replied. "Even if he's only half Sicilian."

Lisa Marie abruptly rose from her chair and started to pace around the kitchen. Her fists were clenched and angrily shaking at the innocent air. "I should've been there for my son, what kind of mother am I?"

She finally stopped and stood in front of the kitchen sink, gripping the edge of it tightly. Without warning, she pounded her fists onto the counter several times, releasing a guttural cry with each blow. Tommy made it to Lisa Marie's side first and wrapped his arms around his wife, grabbing her wrists to stop her from hurting herself. He couldn't, however, stop her from sobbing or blaming herself.

"My son needed me and what was I doing?!" she exclaimed. "I was taking a nap!"

"There was no way we could've known," Tommy said.

"We're his parents! We should've known," Lisa Marie replied.

"Parents don't always do the right thing," Alberta said. "We both know that."

Lisa Marie's body went limp in Tommy's arms. An entire lifetime of pain and regret was etched into Alberta's face and she didn't try to hide any of it, not the mistakes she made, the fights she started, the silence she perpetuated, she owned all of it. Everyone in the room knew the truth; there was no way she was going to run from it, not when her daughter needed her so desperately.

"Ma, I'm sorry," Lisa Marie said. "I wasn't talking about you."

"I know you weren't," Alberta replied. "I was."

"I have to admit that I never really thought about how you must have felt for all those years," Lisa Marie said. "I assumed you were happy to be rid of me, but experiencing this pain, knowing that I wasn't able to comfort my child in his time of need, it's almost unbearable. How did you survive all this time not knowing what was going on in my life?"

Alberta swallowed hard and took her daughter's hands in her own. "Because I knew at some point this day would come and I would be able to make up for all the years I wasn't there for you."

"Guilt is a two-way street, Ma, remember that," Lisa Marie said.

"I'll tell you the same thing I told Sergio when the police took him away," Alberta said. "I will not rest until I find out who killed Natalie because that's what family does for one another. We make things right."

The Ferrara family set out to make things right a little differently than most other clans. The next day their to-do list started with a trip to the medical examiner's office.

Vinny was scheduled to have an early morning meeting with Roxanne Garcia, the DA, to discuss Sergio's case, leaving Tambra to meet Alberta and Jinx at St. Clare's. They had been to the basement of the hospital that housed the morgue and the medical examiner's office many times before, but the trip never got easier. The gray walls, the antiseptic smell, the idea that dead bodies were lying in drawers a few feet away, did not create an inviting atmosphere. The only saving grace was that they got to spend some time with Luke, the orderly who ran the morgue. Except when they entered the room someone else was sitting at Luke's desk. Whoever this person was, she was not nearly as friendly as Luke.

"Who are you?"

"We're here to meet Tambra Mitchell," Alberta said. "I'm Alberta Scaglione and this is my granddaughter, Jinx Maldonado. Who are you?"

"I'm the gal who gets to tell you that your name isn't on the list, which means you need to turn around and leave."

Jinx leaned over and read the woman's name from her badge. "Excuse me, Tilly, we're guests of the Tranquility Police Department and also friends of Pedro Suarez, your boss, so if I may make a suggestion, lose the bad attitude and find our names on that list pronto. Capisce?"

From the scowl on Tilly's face, it was obvious that she was going to keep her attitude intact. Luckily, Pedro came out of his office and greeted Alberta and Jinx warmly, dousing cheer on Tilly's surly nature.

"Alberta! Jinx!" Pedro exclaimed. "Lovely to see the two of you again."

"Hello, Pedro," Alberta said. "I'm sorry we didn't get a chance to speak last night."

"*Il bacio mortale del vischio,*" Pedro replied.

"I didn't know mistletoe was deadly," Alberta said. "It's supposed be an excuse to kiss."

"Kiss underneath it, for sure, but mistletoe is a semi-parasitic plant and, if ingested, it can cause blurred vision, vomiting, even seizures," Pedro explained. "It's definitely poisonous to animals, so keep it away from Lola."

"No wonder the night ended in tragedy," Alberta said.

"From what I hear there were two tragedies," Pedro said. "I'm sorry to hear about your grandson, but maybe I can help clear his name."

"Thank you, Pedro," Alberta said. "We can use all the help we can get."

"Looks like the cavalry has shown up right on time," Pedro said as Tambra rushed into the room.

"Sorry I'm late," Tambra said. "It's been a very hectic morning."

"Pedro," Tilly said. "None of these people are on the

list. You know the protocol, the names of all visitors must be on the list before they can be allowed entry."

"So put their names on the list," Pedro suggested. "Ladies, follow me."

Inside Pedro's office the women pulled up chairs and sat in front of his desk. They avoided small talk because they were all anxious to hear the results of the autopsy Pedro performed on Natalie's body last night. For a man who spent most of his days with only a corpse as a companion, Pedro was surprisingly astute when it came to reading body language. He could see the women wanted answers and that's what he gave them.

"Natalie Vespa was killed by a single knife wound to the heart," Pedro stated. "The knife that Sergio was holding when he was found was the murder weapon. From the angle of the wound whoever stabbed Natalie came from behind and was holding the knife in their left hand."

"My brother's right-handed," Jinx said.

"That's good," Tambra said. "But it isn't definitive proof that Sergio isn't the killer."

"She's right," Pedro said. "Just because someone is right-handed doesn't mean they don't do certain things with their left, it's not an exact science and, on its own, won't be much help."

"Did you find anything that will help us?" Alberta asked.

"We might have," Tambra said. "Forensics found two strands of blond hair inside the snowwoman's shell."

"That doesn't sound suspicious," Alberta said. "Natalie was a blonde."

"Two strands of *synthetic* hair," Tambra said. "The kind that wigs are made of."

"Now that does sound suspicious," Alberta replied.

"Although I'm sure you're going to tell us the strands could have gotten onto Natalie's body at any point during the day."

"A prosecutor would say that," Tambra agreed. "Again, it helps build a case that someone else could've attacked Natalie."

"There was also latex residue on Natalie's face, concentrated around her mouth," Pedro explained. "Meaning, whoever grabbed her from behind was wearing latex gloves."

"That waiter gave you a pair of latex gloves last night," Alberta said.

"The banquet hall's kitchen was stocked with latex gloves," Tambra replied. "I requested one of the waiters bring a pair out to me, along with a plastic Ziploc."

"Have they done a complete search of the entire Manor?" Jinx asked.

"Spent all night doing just that and came up empty," Tambra said. "They didn't find a wig, the used gloves, or any other hard evidence that could be used to point this murder to anyone except Sergio."

"*Per l'amor di Dio,*" Alberta muttered. "Then we keep looking. Anything else you can tell us, Pedro?"

"Natalie also had a bruise on her left shoulder, just above the biceps," Pedro said.

Alberta prayed no one saw the flicker of alarm that showed on her face. She forced herself to look surprised and ask, "From the attack?"

"I don't think so," Pedro said. "There was no trace of the latex residue on her arm and the bruise wasn't fresh, which leads me to believe that it wasn't caused during the altercation that led to her death."

"Could it be the result of the fall she took in the snow-woman shell?" Tambra asked.

"It wasn't postmortem," Pedro replied. "She definitely got the bruise when she was alive, but it had to have been a week or so ago because it was in the process of healing."

Alberta made sure she stared straight ahead and looked at Pedro, but from the corner of her eye she could see Tambra staring at her. An experienced cop's instinct was going to assume the bruise was the result of domestic violence and Alberta didn't want to give Tambra any more ammunition to believe her instinct was correct. She needed to introduce some new evidence.

"What about the toxicology report?" Alberta asked. "Is it much too soon for that?"

"Last year we received a grant and were able to beef up our toxicology lab, allowing us to run a bulk of the routine tests quicker and more efficiently," Pedro said. "I'm not going to have the full report for a few weeks, but I was able to detect traces of drugs in her system."

"Street drugs or prescription?" Tambra asked.

"It's hard to say at this point because, for the most part, Natalie was a healthy young woman and I didn't detect the kind of physical deterioration that's common among drug addicts," Pedro said.

"I don't think Natalie was addicted to drugs," Alberta said. "She spent the night at my house and we had a very rational conversation."

"She didn't exhibit any strange symptoms?" Pedro asked. "Sweating, being fidgety, dilated pupils, erratic behavior?"

"None of the above," Alberta said. "She was calm,

lucid, and talked openly about her life, though, sadly, she could've told us a nice piece of fiction."

"You think she lied to you about her history?" Tambra asked.

"At the time I believed every word she told us. That she didn't have a good family life and she was essentially on her own," Alberta said. "But Sergio told us that Natalie wanted the two of them to run away again, which contradicts the note she left for me, so I don't know what to believe."

"Natalie Vespa was definitely a complicated woman," Jinx said.

"I think it's time we started to uncomplicate her," Alberta said.

"How do we do that?" Jinx asked. "The only person who knew her is my brother and he's in jail, accused of killing her."

"He's not the only person," Alberta said. "I think it's time we went back to New York and paid Rudy a visit."

CHAPTER 17

Bussa, bussa. C'è nessuno in casa?

The drive to New York took a lot longer this time due to the heavy snow that was falling. Since Alberta's BMW and Jinx's Chevy Cruze weren't cars that were necessarily built for driving in a snowstorm, Freddy acted as chauffeur and drove them in his Ford Ranger. They didn't even have to worry that Helen would get angry that someone was taking over what had become her de facto role when they had to go out of town for an investigation; she was the one who suggested Freddy be her substitute. Helen was too busy doling out advice in her new role as The Herald's Big Sister and couldn't spare the time to trek to New York even if it meant following a lead in their case.

This time of year, the traffic into the City always increased. The Bridge and Tunnel Crowd, as New Jersey-ites were fondly dubbed by native New Yorkers, flooded the George Washington Bridge or the Holland and Lincoln Tunnels to come into New York on a quest to capture the type of holiday magic only a big city could offer. People would spend hours in traffic just to see the Christmas tree at Rockefeller Center and maybe spend some time attempting to remain vertical while skating at the adjacent rink. They navigated the busy crowds to ogle the store windows decorated by some of the most imaginative artists in the world. Out-of-town audiences flocked to the countless Broadway shows, concerts at Madison Square Garden, and the pinnacle of holiday entertainment, the *Christmas Spectacular* at Radio City Music Hall. It was an enchanted time of year, when New York City sparkled and was bursting with the spirt of the season. The effect was transformative, and even the most cynical New Yorker found they could believe anything was a possibility. Sitting in the back of Freddy's Ranger, the only thing Alberta could believe was how long it was taking them to get through the Lincoln Tunnel.

"*Che palle!*" Alberta exclaimed. "We've moved two feet in the past twenty minutes. My pet turtle, Alphonse, could've gotten us here quicker."

"You had a pet turtle, Gram?" Jinx asked.

"My grandfather found it on the docks and brought it home," Alberta said. "I think he wanted my grandmother to make soup, but we kids adopted it."

"Alphonse might be able to avoid the traffic, but could he bring you the smooth sound of Sinatra singing 'Silent Night'?" Freddy asked as he turned up the radio, filling up the car with the Hoboken-born crooner's voice.

"How many times do I have to tell you I hate Frank Sinatra?" Alberta barked.

"No one hates Frank Sinatra," Freddy said. "Especially no one from Jersey."

"Too skinny and too full of himself, that's what he was," Alberta said. "Then he got fat and smoked too much. When he sang he sounded worse than Jerry Vale."

"Now you don't like Jerry Vale?" Jinx asked.

"Don't even get me started on that one!" Alberta bellowed.

"Sounds like Aunt Helen came with us after all," Jinx said. "Seriously, Gram, you have to calm down. There's nothing you can do about tunnel traffic except go with the flow."

"I know, I know," Alberta said. "It just feels like we're wasting precious time to save your brother and every second counts."

"If anybody can prove Sergio's innocence, you and Jinx can, Mrs. Scaglione," Freddy said.

"I pray you're right, Freddy, the entire town already thinks the real murderer is behind bars," Alberta said. "I read that online article Calhoun wrote about the murder. It was a regular smear campaign and practically begged the court to lock Sergio up and throw away the key."

"I tried to stop it, Gram, but I couldn't," Jinx said. "Wyck told me that every word Calhoun wrote was true, and he was right. We all know Sergio's innocent, but the evidence against him is making it really hard to sway opinions."

"That's why it's so urgent we talk to Rudy," Alberta said. "He's the only other person who knew Natalie, he's got to be able to tell us something about the girl that will lead us to her real killer."

Finally, the cars in the tunnel began to move and Freddy was able to drive at a normal speed. "Looks like we're back on track," he said. "It won't be much longer now before we're at Rudy's."

They couldn't find a parking spot on Rudy's street, so Freddy would have to keep circling the block until he found one. He told Jinx to text him if they needed him to run a red light to get back to them in case they were in a jam. Jinx appreciated her boyfriend's willingness to get a moving violation but told him they would be fine. Alberta had already had one conversation with Rudy, what could go wrong during her second?

Everything.

Alberta rang Rudy's bell a third time and still there was no response. The wind had started to pick up and although the mounds of snow on the pavement were miraculously white and had not yet been topped with the layer of soot and dirt that made them look like unappealing chocolate snow cones, it felt more like they were being enveloped by an Arctic breeze and not a cozy wintry embrace. They weren't sure how much longer they'd be able to stand on the front steps in the cold waiting for Rudy before they had to call Freddy for an emergency rescue.

After the fourth attempt to reach Rudy, an older man, bundled up like Nanook of the North about to take a hike through the tundra, came out of the building. He nodded to Alberta, and as he walked down the steps, holding on to the railing to avoid a slip and fall, Jinx held the door open with her foot to make sure it didn't close behind him. They were able to slip into the building before the man stepped foot onto the sidewalk.

Once inside the ladies took a moment to thaw out and then climbed the stairs to Rudy's apartment. When they got to the third floor Jinx was thankful her grandmother stopped in front of 3B, she didn't relish the idea of climb-

ing another flight in her boots and marveled at the fact
that sometimes Alberta had more energy than she did.
She would have to remember to add another mile to her
early morning jogs.

Alberta was about to knock on the door when Jinx
stopped her. "Gram, what makes you think he's going to
be inside if he didn't answer the buzzer?"

"A million things," Alberta replied. "He could be taking a shower, taking a nap, taking a phone call that can't
be interrupted."

"I didn't take those things into consideration," Jinx
replied. "Okay, knock away."

Alberta did, three times.

"*Bussa, bussa. C'è nessuno in casa?*" Alberta asked.

"You can keep knocking, but it doesn't look like anybody's home," Jinx said, translating her grandmother's
remark.

Instinctively, Alberta gripped the doorknob and gave it
a twist. When she felt it turn in her hands she pushed and
opened the door. The ladies were shocked to discover
Rudy's apartment door was left unlocked; they weren't
city dwellers, but they knew such a finding was a rare occurrence. No one left their doors unlocked in Manhattan,
it was like inviting trouble into your own home and
telling it to take whatever it liked. It just wasn't done. For
some reason it had been done, and the ladies knew they
weren't leaving the building until they found out why.

"Rudy," Alberta said. "Are you home?"

No answer meant no one was forbidding them from
entering. They weren't sure if that logic would hold up in
a court of law, but they were willing to take the risk if it
meant they could rummage through Rudy's apartment to
find a clue that could save Sergio.

Alberta entered first and Jinx followed, closing and locking the door behind them. They stood in the kitchen and thought the first thing they should do was search the apartment to confirm that they were alone. Just because Rudy didn't answer didn't mean he wasn't there, and since the door had been unlocked it was possible someone else was there hiding in a closet or behind the shower curtain. Oddly, none of these thoughts made the women nervous enough to hightail it out of the apartment and back to the relative safety of the city street. On the contrary, it fueled them, it motivated them to make their good fortune of being able to get into Rudy's place pay off. Before they started their search, however, they did need to arm themselves just in case their good fortune turned bad.

A fire extinguisher that was lodged in between the garbage can and the kitchen cabinet and a golf club leaning against the pantry door would serve perfectly as weapons against the unknown. Alberta grabbed the extinguisher while Jinx picked up the golf club and, together, they walked through the apartment in search of uninvited guests. Technically, they were the uninvited guests in this scenario, but they conveniently ignored that fact.

By the time they returned to the living room area they were confident the apartment was empty. They put their impromptu weapons back where they found them and started to search for the evidence that could point the finger of accusation at someone else other than Sergio. But they felt like blind men in a maze and had no idea where to start looking.

"Jinx, you search in here and I'll take the bedroom," Alberta said. "I have no idea what we're looking for, but I guess we'll know when we find it."

"Roger that, Gram," Jinx said.

"Be careful not to make too much of a mess," Alberta said. "We don't want Rudy to know anyone has been here."

Jinx looked underneath couch cushions, opened the doors of the media cabinet, rifled through Rudy's small collection of vinyl records, and even lifted the threadbare rug in the middle of the room, but found nothing incriminating or slightly interesting. Until she knocked over a stack of magazines on the cocktail table.

She saw that they were mostly medical industry magazines with the occasional *Sports Illustrated* thrown in the mix, but when she bent down to pick them up, she noticed one of the magazines had flipped open to a page that had been dog-eared. The magazine was *New Jersey Pharma* and the article was about the Trolloppe cardiac wing at the Sussex County Medical Center. *Trolloppe* was the word that Rudy allegedly texted Alberta, and D. Edward Carmichael worked at the Medical Center. It was definitely more than a coincidence, it linked the two men, even though Carmichael had told Alberta and Joyce that he had never heard of Rudy.

"Gram, I think I may have found something," Jinx said.

Alberta rushed into the living room. "Good, because I didn't find a thing except a pile of laundry. I don't think Rudy's washed his clothes for over a week. It stinks to holy heaven in there."

"That's typical for a guy," Jinx said. "If I didn't remind Freddy, he might never do his laundry. Check this out."

"What is it?" Alberta asked.

"It might be our first real clue," Jinx said.

Alberta read the article and confirmed what Jinx already knew, that Carmichael most likely had lied to them.

The fact that Rudy marked an article about the Trolloppe wing by itself didn't definitively connect him to Carmichael, who was the center's hospital administrator. But add in the fact that Rudy knew Natalie, who had been in Newton the day before she was murdered, and it made a more persuasive argument that Rudy and Carmichael were somehow connected. But what was that connection? Enemies, friends, business associates, two men who teamed up to kill Natalie? They had no idea.

"Why don't you roll up that magazine and put it in your bag?" Alberta suggested. "It might come in handy later."

They quickly inspected the only other room in Rudy's apartment, his bathroom, and discovered that he was better at doing laundry than he was at keeping his bathroom clean.

"Let's get out of here before we catch something, Gram."

As they were heading toward the front door, Alberta remembered the stash of boxes Rudy kept in his pantry, the ones with the stickers of flowers on them. He had given them the impression that they were part of his job as a pharmaceutical salesman, filled with medical supplies. When Alberta opened the door, it appeared that Rudy may have gotten a new job; the pantry was empty.

"*È strano*," Alberta said.

"What's weird?"

"Last time I was here this pantry was stocked with boxes, now it's empty."

"Gram, is it possible that Rudy left town and took the boxes with him?"

"Possibly, lovey, but it doesn't look like he took anything else. His closet is filled with his clothes and there were a few prescriptions in his medicine cabinet that were more than halfway full and weren't expired."

"Which means that if he did leave town, he might not have left by his own choice."

Alberta pondered Jinx's comment and concluded that she could be right. They knew very little about Rudy and as much as Alberta did like him, she had to admit that he was a shady character. He'd appeared nervous when Alberta and Joyce met him, he was evasive about his relationship with Natalie, and he was probably the one who sent her the text about the Trolloppe wing. Rudy, unfortunately, could be the type who found himself in a situation that forced him to leave town without any notice or was dragged out of town against his will. Either scenario would explain why his door had been left unlocked.

It would not explain why someone was knocking on the door now.

Alberta and Jinx grabbed each other when they heard the sound. The only thing odder in New York City than leaving your front door unlocked was hearing a knock at the front door that hadn't been preceded by the ring of a buzzer. It was a fantasy to think that neighbors in New York City apartment buildings were friendly enough with one another that they knocked on their doors out of the blue to say hello or ask to borrow some sugar. There was an unspoken code of ethics among New Yorkers: Thou shall not disturb thy neighbor. Whoever was banging on Rudy's front door never got that memo.

"Rudy, let me in!"

The voice was immediately familiar, and Alberta knew that she had heard it before, but exactly where she couldn't recall.

"Do not play games with me, Rudy, I need you!"

Jinx turned to face Alberta and mouthed the words, *Who is that?* Alberta shook her head and put her finger up to her lips to prevent Jinx from adding a voice to her silent question.

"I know you're in there so open up!"

Such a long pause followed the woman's last words that they thought she had given up and left. They were reminded that they were not the only women in the world who were tenacious.

"Fine, then I'll use my key."

This time when Jinx turned to face Alberta, she looked at her with fear. They were trapped inside an apartment they had essentially broken in to and were about to be caught by a strange woman who was going to enter the apartment legally. They had to hide.

They heard the key enter the lock and Alberta grabbed Jinx by the arm, leading her into the bathroom. She pulled back the navy-blue shower curtain and she and Jinx got into the bathtub. Instead of fully closing the shower curtain, Alberta left it open about a foot, exposing the shower head in the hopes that if the woman checked the bathroom, she wouldn't think anyone was hiding behind the curtain because it was partially open. It was a gamble, but Alberta had learned enough about psychological tactics to bet that it would do the trick. Most of the time people only saw what they wanted to see, and if the woman saw part of an empty bathtub, she'd assume the entire tub was empty and wasn't being used as a hiding spot.

They heard the front door slam and they knew it was only a matter of seconds before the woman inspected the bathroom. Alberta prayed her strategy would work.

"Where are you, Rudy? I need you!"

They could hear the woman open up another door, presumably the pantry, and slam it shut. They heard her walk past the bathroom directly into the bedroom and slide open the closet doors, slamming them closed so hard Alberta and Jinx were surprised they didn't hear them fall off their sliding tracks. They didn't know who this woman was, but they were convinced she was convinced Rudy should be in his apartment and that she was in desperate need of his help.

"Don't you know what happened last night?! The entire operation is going to blow up in our faces!"

The woman's screams and curses were followed by some loud banging and crashes. Whoever the woman was, she didn't care if Rudy knew she had been in his apartment. In fact, by the sound of it, she wanted Rudy to know she had been there. When she was done ransacking his bedroom she bounded into the bathroom and must've flung open the medicine cabinet because they heard it crash onto the floor.

"Dammit!" the woman screamed. "Serves you right, Rudy!"

They heard her leave the bathroom, literally stomping her feet, until she must have reached the kitchen. There was a long pause and then they heard the sound of the door once more opening and slamming. Alberta and Jinx remained in their hiding place for several minutes before deciding it was safe to exit. When they saw the medicine cabinet door on the floor, its glass smashed into little pieces, they realized they had made the right decision to hide and not confront the woman. She was clearly dangerous.

Out of the utmost caution and not necessarily necessity, Alberta and Jinx tiptoed through the apartment until they got to the kitchen. They stopped when they saw the message that was left on the refrigerator. The woman must have rearranged the alphabet magnets on Rudy's fridge to leave him a warning. It wasn't grammatically correct, but it was legible: Dont push me. It was signed JJ.

"Gram, who's J. J.?"

"Rudy's girlfriend."

"This is amazing, Gram! Look how much we've learned from one visit to Rudy's apartment."

"We learned more than you realize."

"What do you mean?"

"Rudy didn't only tell us that J. J. was his girlfriend, he also told us that she was dangerous."

CHAPTER 18

La verità potrebbe rendere qualcuno libero, ma manda anche qualcuno in prigione.

The holding cell at the Tranquility Police Station was a far cry from a maximum security prison, and not nearly as heartbreaking as when Judy Garland sang "Have Yourself a Merry Little Christmas" to a sobbing Margaret O'Brien in *Meet Me in St. Louis,* and yet it still filled Alberta and Jinx with dread, knowing Sergio was inside the building behind bars. Worse, they knew if DA Garcia had her way, he'd never see the light of day again.

Freddy had dropped them off at the police station when they got back from New York so they could join Lisa Marie and Tommy for their meeting with Bruno and Sergio. Their first stop, however, was to pay a visit to Vinny's office to disclose what they'd discovered at Rudy's apartment. Before they could present their case to him, he presented them with a roadblock.

"I wish I had better news for you, Alfie, but Roxanne

isn't budging," Vinny said. "She refuses to entertain the idea of allowing Sergio to post bail."

"That isn't fair!" Alberta yelled.

"I agree and I've stated my opinion to her very clearly, but the DA is adamant," Vinny said. "In two days Sergio is going to be transferred to the Keogh-Dwyer Correctional Facility in Newton, where he'll stay to await his trial."

"What about the evidence from the autopsy report?" Jinx asked.

"It's helpful, and I think Bruno is going to be able to use it effectively to cast doubt on the charges, but it won't change the DA's mind," Vinny said. "There's no possibility of bail."

"Even if we have another suspect?" Alberta asked.

"What other suspect?" Vinny asked in response.

"J. J." Jinx replied.

"Who's J. J.?" Vinny asked.

"Rudy's girlfriend," Alberta said. "We think she could have killed Natalie."

Vinny slumped into his chair and shook his head. "I think you need to explain yourself."

Alberta quickly filled Vinny in on what had happened when they got to Rudy's apartment and what J. J. said when she thought Rudy was on the other side of his locked door. She needed his help because the operation was going to blow up in their faces. She referenced the fiasco that was supposed to be the festive Mistletoe Ball, which meant she had a link to Tranquility, or at least the area. Unfortunately, they couldn't describe the woman, they didn't know what her initials stood for, they didn't know what kind of operation she and Rudy were involved in, or what role Natalie played in their business. The only thing they knew was that they needed to find out more about this unknown woman because instinct told them she was the key to unraveling the mystery surrounding Natalie's murder.

"That's not a lot to go on, Alfie," Vinny said.

"I know," Alberta said. "Maybe we should've come out of hiding and confronted the woman."

"No, you did the right thing," Vinny said. "This woman sounds like a loose cannon."

"She practically banged the door down," Jinx said. "She ripped the medicine cabinet off its hinges."

"If she is involved in this murder and you two popped out from behind the shower curtain, she might have popped a few bullets into you," Vinny said. "Trust me, the first murder is hard, all the ones that come after are as easy as Sunday dinner."

"I like that, Vin," Alberta said. "You should put that in your book."

"It already is!" Vinny replied. "Alfie says it to Vance, the chief of police, on page seventy-four."

"With dialogue like that I can't believe no one wants to publish your story," Alberta said.

"Believe it," Vinny said. "I got four rejection letters to prove it."

"*Il mondo è pieno di persone stupide,*" Alberta said.

"You're right about that," Vinny replied. "But at least your world has at least one smart guy in it."

"You?" Jinx asked.

Vinny smiled and shook his head. "Not me, Bruno."

When Vinny brought Alberta and Jinx into the meeting room where a person in lockup could speak with their attorney, Bruno was so deep in conversation with Lisa Marie and Tommy that he jumped when the door opened.

"If we didn't know any better, Bruno, we'd think you were a jittery lawyer," Alberta said.

"Mrs. Scaglione, so good to see you," Bruno said. "Even under these terrible circumstances."

Bruno and Alberta hugged warmly. Despite the difference in their ages and backgrounds, over the years they had developed mutual respect and admiration. They trusted each other with their lives. Alberta trusted Bruno enough to put the fate of her grandson's life in his hands.

"Thank you for getting here so quickly," Alberta said. "I know we made a mess of your plans."

"You did me a favor," Bruno said. "I got to leave a family wedding early and avoid two more days of bonding with relatives I don't particularly like very much."

"If it's anything like our family weddings, you avoided a black eye, a fine, and a night in jail," Lisa Marie said.

"Ma!" Jinx shouted.

"If I don't make jokes about this situation, I'm going to have a heart attack and die at your feet," Lisa Marie said. "Make your choice."

"Leese, I really do know what you're going through, but may I share a piece of advice?" Vinny said.

"I'll take whatever I can get," Lisa Marie replied.

"Let Sergio lead the tone of the conversation," Vinny said. "The boy is frightened out of his wits and he's got a tough road ahead of him. He may not be in a joking mood right now."

Lisa Marie smiled. "My mother was right, you really are a straight shooter."

Vinny nodded solemnly and said, "An officer will be bringing Sergio in any minute."

Bruno waited until Vinny shut the door behind him to speak. "Vinny's right, we need to do everything we can to instill hope in Sergio, but he can't think we're taking this lightly. This is serious business."

"We know that," Tommy said. "We're just as frightened as our son is."

"We all are, Daddy," Jinx said.

"I know, sweetheart," Tommy said. "But we're a family and we're going to get through this together."

This time when the door opened Lisa Marie and Tommy were the ones who jumped up. They watched the officer uncuff their son and leave the room. Then they watched their son look at them like he did when he was little and had hurt himself in the backyard. He looked like a lost boy who needed his parents.

Lisa Marie and Tommy rushed to Sergio and threw their arms around him. Sergio hung on to their arms for dear life and gave the sobs that he'd been holding on to all night the freedom to escape. After a minute Lisa Marie brushed away her son's tears and held his hand tightly, while Jinx gave her brother a long hug. Jinx wanted to give in to her emotions and break down like her brother did, but she was the big sister, she needed to remain strong, and most of all, she needed to introduce Sergio to his counsel.

"Grandma got you the best lawyer in town," Jinx said. "Sergio Maldonado, meet Bruno bel Bruno."

"Hi," Sergio said, jutting out his hand to shake Bruno's. "Did my grandma hire you because you really are good or because you're Italian?"

"A little bit of both, my love," Alberta said.

She wrapped her arms around Sergio and kissed his cheek a few times. If only they could stay in this room forever, hide from reality and live out their lives away from the fear of imprisonment. That wasn't going to happen, but the next best thing was for Bruno to win this case, and Alberta thought it was time he got to work.

"Bruno," Alberta said, "the floor is all yours."

The room was sparse, and except for one rectangular wooden table and several armless chairs with the slimmest of cushions, there was nothing else in the room. Sergio sat across from Bruno, flanked on either side by Lisa Marie and Tommy, Jinx sat to Bruno's right, and Alberta sat at the end of the table next to Jinx. Bruno's open briefcase lay on the table to his left and he pulled out a file and a pad. He took a pen from the inside breast pocket of his sports jacket and smiled at Sergio.

"Why don't I set up the rules for you, Sergio, and tell you how this works," Bruno said. "I'm your lawyer, which means anything you say to me is confidential and I can't repeat it. The same is not true for anyone else in this room, which means if you want to share something with me that you don't want to or shouldn't share with anyone else, tell me and I'll ask everyone to leave the room."

Sergio was startled and looked at his family. "I don't have anything to hide from them."

"That's good," Bruno replied. "But remember, it is always an option."

Bruno opened the file and from what Jinx and Alberta could tell, it was the police report.

"We know that Natalie was murdered last night, and we know that you were found holding the murder weapon close by," Bruno said. "Why don't you tell us what happened earlier in the day and how you wound up at the Ball under those circumstances?"

Sergio let out a deep breath and folded his hands on

the table. "You want me to tell you everything that happened?"

"I want you to tell me the truth," Bruno said.

Alberta felt a twinge in her stomach as she remembered what her grandmother always said about the truth. *La verità potrebbe rendere qualcuno libero, ma manda anche qualcuno in prigione.* The truth might set someone free, but it sends someone else to jail. If her grandmother was right, it meant Sergio had a fifty-fifty chance to go free. Not the greatest of odds.

Sergio explained that he started the day by having breakfast with his parents and his aunt Joyce. It was the day of the Mistletoe Ball and everyone except him had errands to run. While they were out, he tried to get in touch with Natalie, but she never responded. Which is why he kind of freaked out.

"I can't explain it, I honestly don't know how she makes me get so crazy . . . used to, I mean, but I knew I couldn't spend one more second in that house or in this town without her," Sergio explained. "That's when I wrote that note to my parents."

Bruno sifted through some files in his briefcase and pulled out a piece of paper. He placed it on the table and slid it toward Sergio. "This one where you tell your parents Natalie needs you?"

"That's the one," Sergio confirmed.

"It also proves Natalie's letter to my mother was a lie," Lisa Marie said.

"Actually, it doesn't," Alberta corrected.

"What do you mean, Ma? Natalie wrote a Dear John letter to Sergio and here she's telling him she needs him," Lisa Marie said.

"I was wrong," Alberta admitted. "Sergio's note only says Natalie needs him, not that she asked for his help. Isn't that right, Sergio?"

"It is, Gram," Sergio replied. "Natalie didn't contact me until later in the day."

"When did she do that?" Tommy asked.

"Around five, she sent some texts to my cell phone," Sergio said.

"We'll get to that, but we need to go back first," Bruno said. "You're at your aunt Joyce's house, you're restless, you can't get Natalie out of your mind. What did you do next?"

"I went for a walk," Sergio replied. "I don't know the town very well, so I didn't have anyplace in mind. After a while I stumbled upon Tranquility Park and looked at all the stands and rides they set up, and then I wound up at the diner and had something to eat."

"Tranquility Diner?" Bruno asked.

"Yeah, that was the place," Sergio confirmed.

"Do you remember who waited on you?" Bruno asked.

"An Asian guy," Sergio said. "I didn't catch his name, but I think he was the owner because he said he was closing up early to go to the Ball."

"That was Kwon Lee, the owner," Bruno said. "Do you have any idea what time that was?"

"I guess it was around noon, I'm not sure," Sergio replied.

"That's okay, Kwon will have a record of it," Bruno said.

"Why is it important to know the time I stopped at the diner?" Sergio asked.

"It establishes a timeline of your activities for the

day," Bruno said. "To put it bluntly, I need to establish that you didn't spend the day plotting Natalie's murder."

"Of course I didn't do that!" Sergio yelled. "Because I didn't kill Natalie!"

"Easy, son," Tommy said. "He needs to establish your whereabouts to give you an alibi."

"I shouldn't need an alibi!" Sergio said. "I should just have to say I didn't do it and everybody should believe me."

"Stop talking like an idiot!" Jinx snapped. "You're not twelve, Sergio, you're an adult and you're going to be on trial for first degree murder. If you don't want to spend the rest of your life in jail, cooperate."

Jinx's blunt talk seemed to knock some sense into Sergio. When he continued telling Bruno how he spent the hours before the Mistletoe Ball, he filled in all the details. He stayed at the diner for as long as he could, but Kwon finally kicked all the customers out at three o'clock. He continued to walk aimlessly until he got a text from Natalie. She said she couldn't stay in town any longer, but she also couldn't live without Sergio, so the only viable solution was for them to leave town together.

"I asked Nat about the FBI because I was worried that they'd get ticked if they couldn't find her," Sergio said. "She said she'd handle that, all she cared about was being with me."

"She didn't care about the FBI because they're not involved," Alberta said.

"That isn't true," Sergio protested. "She has information they need."

"She lied to you," Lisa Marie said. "She's been lying since day one."

Bruno reached across the table and placed a hand on

Lisa Marie's arm to get her to stop talking. It worked but didn't prevent her from cursing Natalie under her breath.

"They're right, Sergio, there is no FBI investigation and they've never heard of Natalie Vespa," Bruno said. "She concocted that story to hide whatever business she was involved in."

Sergio was stunned. "I can't believe that."

"It's true, honey," Alberta said. "I have a question, though. How do you know the text came from Natalie? Did it come from her cell phone?"

"No, it came from her burner phone," Sergio replied.

"Why would Natalie use her burner phone to send a text to your cell phone when she knew it could be traced?" Alberta asked. "She should've sent it to your burner phone, right?"

"I guess that would make more sense to keep it totally untraceable," Sergio said.

"The only thing that makes sense is if someone else sent the texts," Alberta said. "They wouldn't know how to contact you on your burner phone, they'd have to use your cell phone."

"Do you have any idea who would have sent you those messages if it wasn't Natalie?" Bruno asked. "One of her friends or business associates?"

"She kept me in the dark about all that stuff," Sergio said. "I don't know anybody in her life."

"What about Rudy?" Jinx asked.

Recognition flashed across Sergio's face, but neither Jinx nor Alberta could determine if it was honest or manufactured. "Give me a break! Rudy wanted Natalie for himself, he wouldn't send me a text impersonating her."

"I thought Rudy was dating J. J.," Alberta said.

"Who's J. J.?" Sergio asked.

"You've never heard of her?" Jinx asked, her voice dripping with doubt.

"No," Sergio replied. "As far as I know, Rudy wanted to get back with Natalie. That's the real reason we left his apartment, the three of us couldn't live under the same roof."

"Okay, so back to the day of the Ball," Bruno said. "What did you do after you got the texts from Natalie?"

"She told me to meet her at the Tranquility Manor at seven o'clock," Sergio said.

"That was when the Ball started, right?" Bruno asked.

"Yes, she said she had to meet with someone before she left to settle a score, and once she did that we'd leave," Sergio explained. "I went to the Manor early. I think I got there around six thirty because I didn't want anyone in the family to see me. I went around the back and I saw Natalie talking to someone."

"Can you describe this person?" Bruno asked.

"Not really, they were wearing a red parka with the hood up and I only saw them from the back," Sergio said. "I'm pretty sure it was a woman because they were around Natalie's height and build, but Rudy's kind of skinny and only an inch or so taller than Nat, so it could've been him too."

"What happened next?" Bruno asked.

Sergio exhaled to gather his strength. When he started his story he spoke quickly, as if to get it over as quickly as possible.

"I hid behind some bushes and saw them go into the Manor through the back door entrance, but when I tried to follow them inside, the door was locked, so I couldn't get in," Sergio began. "I waited outside and after a while a waiter came out to have a cigarette. I acted like I was late for my shift and he let me in. I took the stairs and made my way up to the kitchen. Everybody was so busy, no one noticed me. I heard a lot of noise and followed the sound that led me into the ballroom. What I didn't realize was that they built that forest thing to camouflage the kitchen entrance, so with all the trees I thought I might be outside, but I knew that was impossible. I wound up in the ski chalet, which is where I found the knife. I picked it up and walked outside to find Natalie dead on the floor."

Sergio caught his breath and looked around at his family staring at him. "Do you think anyone's going to believe my story?" he asked.

Bruno tilted his head from side to side. "They might. There are a few things in the autopsy report that I think will help as well."

"Like what?" Lisa Marie asked.

"There's a good chance the murderer was left handed and Sergio isn't," Bruno said.

"What about the latex residue found around Natalie's mouth and the synthetic fibers?" Alberta asked.

"I see Pedro filled you in as well," Bruno said, smiling. "Sergio being in the kitchen gives him access to the gloves, and unless we can find where the synthetic fibers came from, they won't be much help. We won't get the full toxicology report for a while, so I don't want to speculate, but there was one other thing that came up in the report that seems odd."

Alberta touched the gold crucifix around her neck because she knew what Bruno was going to say. And she was afraid of how Sergio would respond.

"It seems Natalie had a bruise on her left arm, an earlier injury and not caused during the assault," Bruno said.

"Do you have any idea how that bruise got there, Sergio?"

Sergio's cheeks started to turn a bright shade of red and he leaned over the desk to get closer to Bruno. "You think I would hit Natalie?"

"It doesn't matter what I think," Bruno said. "I can't afford to be blindsided in the courtroom."

Sergio didn't wait to blindside Bruno in the courtroom, he did it right there during their meeting. Shocking everyone, Sergio hauled off and punched Bruno in the eye. The way the left side of Bruno's face started to swell and discolor, it was obvious this altercation was not going to remain part of their attorney-client privilege.

Lisa Marie had been wrong—Bruno's early exit from his family wedding didn't prevent him from getting a black eye. Alberta, however, had been right. She had been afraid and with good reason, because now everyone, including the DA, was going to know Sergio had a violent temper.

own eyes. Bruno asked a valid question and Sergio answered with a rapid punch.

Her grandson's actions weren't the only thing Alberta found disturbing. While Jinx was truly stunned by Sergio's outburst, Alberta had an inkling that things might get physical because she knew there was the possibility that he caused the bruise on Natalie's arm. She was bracing herself for an altercation, and she noticed Lisa Marie and Tommy were doing the same thing. They were eyeing Sergio nervously, as if they expected him to lash out at any moment. It was because they knew their son had a problem with anger management.

Alberta remembered that Tommy said Sergio threw a punch at him, Lisa Marie admitted that he had a temper, he even raised his hand to Jinx. She didn't want to give in to stereotypes, but Sicilians of both genders were known to have an aggressive streak, they were loud, confrontational, and some of them were violent. It was hardly a general characteristic, just a cliché, but her grandson did have a history of uncontrollable behavior. A background that would be brought up by the prosecutor at trial in order to paint a profile of Sergio's character as being unstable and prone to striking out at those he loved. In skilled hands a jury could be molded to think that her grandson had been a murderer waiting to find the perfect victim. Once they believed that, they wouldn't wait very long to return from deliberation with a guilty verdict.

Alberta looked at Lola, who was sitting on the window ledge over the sink gazing at the outside world. This had to be the worst Christmas season of her entire life, she thought. Even worse than the time both her kids had chicken pox and Sammy decided it was a good time to invite his sister and her family to visit. Alberta disliked her sister-in-law Edna almost as much as Edna disliked Alberta. They both rubbed each other the wrong way. Sammy could do no wrong in Edna's eyes and Alberta saw his faults very clearly. Had she only had a better relationship with Sergio, seen him more often, knew what he was really like as a person, Alberta might have known him as well as she knew Sammy. Despite his flaws, Alberta knew what her husband was capable of and how he'd react in any given situation, she couldn't say the same thing about her grandson.

Was it possible that he could have killed Natalie in a fit of rage? Could she have done or said something that would have gotten him so angry that he could take a knife and stab it through her heart? From everything she knew about their relationship, Natalie could ignite passion in her grandson, why not revulsion? The line separating love and hate was sometimes invisible. But the line separating innocence and guilt was much thicker.

Alberta saw firsthand how distraught Sergio had been when he saw Natalie's dead body. She'd held him as he sobbed. He wasn't crying for himself or for his role in what happened, he was crying because a woman he loved had been slain, her life struck down, left to lie on the ground at his feet. Even when he resorted to violence and punched Bruno, he was doing it because he was being accused of physically hurting Natalie, which was something he couldn't comprehend. He couldn't find the words to express himself, so he let his fists talk for him. It wasn't wise, it wasn't mature, but it wasn't the action of a guilty man. As Sergio's grandmother, Alberta was certain of his innocence, but she wasn't sure if twelve strangers on a jury would share her opinion.

She had wanted to take another trip to New York to see

if she could make contact with Rudy this time instead of roaming around his empty apartment, but Vinny informed her that he was working with the local police department to track Rudy down. The NYPD had been advised that Rudy Lewendorf was officially a person of interest in the murder of Natalie Vespa. Alberta was not happy to learn Vinny had to tell them he wanted help to find Rudy as a way to strengthen the state's case against Sergio, but he felt it would sound more legitimate. If Roxanne found out Vinny was trying to get another state's police force to hunt down a suspect when she believed the murderer was already behind bars, Sergio would ultimately suffer the consequences.

With a trip to the Empire State nixed, Alberta's backup plan was to question Carmichael again. The dog-eared magazine they found in Rudy's apartment linked the two men, and Alberta suspected the hospital administrator hadn't been fully honest the last time they spoke. She wanted to find out what his connection was to Rudy and if that connection extended to include Natalie and perhaps even J. J. She was all set to take a drive to Newton when Jinx told her to cancel her plans.

Since it would have been a blatant conflict of interest if Jinx wrote about the Vespa murder case, Wyck assigned her to cover the newfound partnership between St. Clare's Hospital and the Sussex County Medical Center. The institutions were former rivals and had been jockeying for position to be named the best hospital in New Jersey, St. Clare's through its cancer drug trials and Sussex County with its cardiac wing. Wyck figured there had to be something scandalous to make them want to exchange their rivalry for camaraderie.

It was a jaded approach, but he was hoping there

would be some juicy gossip, doctor bashing, and questionable ethical behavior among the professionals that
would bring even more eyes over to the pages of *The
Herald*. Jinx told Alberta that she already had appoint-
ments to meet with Carmichael and Bambi, and if Alberta
got to Carmichael first, he might clam up when Jinx interviewed him. Alberta had to agree that he'd be more comfortable talking to a journalist and not the grandmother of
a murder suspect. With Jinx, Carmichael might let down
his guard and unwittingly reveal a tidbit of information
they could use to help Sergio, but with Alberta he would
choose every word he spoke wisely, especially if he had
something to hide.

Without a Plan C, Sloan was able to convince Alberta
that she needed to take a break from all the stress she'd
been under these past few weeks, first with the search for
Lisa Marie and Tommy, then the search for Sergio and
Natalie, and now trying to find Natalie's real murderer to
spring Sergio from jail. Spending an hour or two being
Sloan's girlfriend and not an amateur detective would
help recharge her battery and lift her spirits. If that was
true, though, why did she feel like such a Grinch?

"Doesn't the town square look beautiful?" Sloan
asked. "The snow, the decorations, the Christmas joy."

"Bah, scempiaggini!" Alberta cried.

"That's enough out of you, Ebenezer," Sloan said.
"You promised you'd welcome the spirit of Christmas
into your heart this morning."

"I'm sorry," Alberta said. "My heart is heavy and my
mind is racing with thoughts of how to free Sergio. It's
hard to feel any joy at the moment."

"I know," Sloan replied. "And I'm not trying to make
you forget what's really happening, but I do think you

need a brief diversion to reclaim your strength. Things are going to get worse before they get better."

"How can things get any worse?" Alberta said. "You just spent ten dollars for two cups of coffee!"

"May I remind you that you ordered an eggnog latte?" Sloan said.

Against her will, a smile appeared on Alberta's face. She looked at Sloan and was once again reminded how handsome he was. The few lines around his mouth and across his forehead, the crow's feet around his sparkling blue eyes, only added to his good looks. When she took a moment like this to stop and let the world around her continue to move forward without her, she felt like a schoolgirl who saw her life as one filled with promise. It had been a long time since she held that feeling in her heart and she was delighted it had returned when she met Sloan. Sometimes she had no idea what she was doing, embarking on a relationship with a new man at her age, but at other times, at times like this, she knew one of the best decisions she had ever made was accepting Sloan into her life. Even on mornings like this, when she wanted to strangle him.

And yet she knew he was right. She knew she needed to step away from the turmoil and pain she was feeling watching her grandson face such devastating charges and do something normal for a little while. In the long run this respite might just prove beneficial.

"Let's buy Lola a treat," Alberta said. "I think my baby's getting jealous because I've been spending so much time with Lisa Marie."

"That cat has you wrapped around your little finger," Sloan said. "Which means Lola and I have something in common."

A full-on smile emerged on Alberta's face this time. She grabbed Sloan's hand and led him to the pet store.

"C'mon, signore, let's go shopping."

Thirty minutes later Sloan and Alberta were no longer holding hands because Sloan's hands were otherwise engaged, carrying two large shopping bags. One filled with toys and treats for Lola that Alberta planned to dispense on a daily basis from now until Christmas as sort of a living Advent calendar for her cat and the other filled with pastries from Vitalano's Bakery. Alberta thought it might lift everyone's spirits if they had some homemade baked goods the next time they met instead of their usual buffet of Entenmann's desserts. Everyone deserved an upgrade around the holidays.

Which is exactly what it looked like Bambi had given herself.

Alberta saw the woman crossing the street carrying four shopping bags from four different stores, the priciest shops in town, and wearing a full-length shearling coat and a brown suede fedora. The woman looked like she could give Joyce a run for her money in the fashionista department, but Alberta felt that Joyce's philosophy concerning her wardrobe was that she looked at well-made clothing as almost works of art that she, as a patron, needed to display. Joyce didn't go in for trendy items that she'd throw out at the end of the season, almost her entire wardrobe was filled with classic pieces from the last century. When she looked at Bambi, her chin held high with a bit of a smirk formed on her lips, Alberta got the impression that she wore expensive clothes to show off. Alberta decided to use that to her advantage because what show-off could resist an audience?

"Hi, Bambi!" Alberta yelled, waving her hand in her direction.

The woman proved Alberta's theory wrong. Upon seeing Alberta, Bambi immediately veered to the right to avoid walking toward her. She even quickened her pace and moved as quickly as the three-inch stiletto heels of her brown suede boots would allow.

"I don't think Bambi saw me," Alberta said.

"I don't think Bambi *wants* to see you," Sloan said.

"Why wouldn't she want to see me?"

"Because of the Mistletoe Catastra-Ball."

"Catastra-Ball? What's that?"

"It's what some people have dubbed the Mistletoe Ball since it was such a catastrophe."

"You think Bambi's avoiding me because I'm Sergio's grandmother and she blames him for ruining her event?"

"That's what I like about you, Berta, you catch on quick."

"Well, we better start jogging if we're going to catch up to Bambi."

Sloan watched as Alberta ran ahead, avoiding patches of snow that crept onto the sidewalk and holding her arm out to the side in an attempt not to spill her eggnog latte. Sloan shrugged his shoulders and did what every dutiful boyfriend has done since the beginning of time—he ran after his girlfriend.

"Bambi!" Alberta cried. "Wait up!"

Bambi didn't, but Alberta didn't give up. She convinced herself she was on an early morning jog with Jinx, wearing her sneakers, running gear, and sports bra, and increased her speed until she was alongside Bambi, panting but victorious.

"Oh hi Alberta!" Bambi cried. "I didn't even see you

there. Guess I'm having one of those mornings with my head in the clouds, all wrapped up in the joy of the season."

"I can see," Alberta said. "Are you Christmas shopping or doing some retail therapy?"

"A little bit of both," Bambi said.

Alberta's prayers were answered and Bambi finally stopped walking. She could see that the woman's heavy makeup couldn't hide the deep circles under her eyes and Alberta assumed Bambi had also lost a few nights' sleep. Bambi looked to the right, as if searching for an escape hatch, and when she came up empty she sighed and bowed her head.

"I'm sorry," Bambi said. "I shouldn't have tried to avoid you, but with everything going on . . . I just don't know what to say to you."

"I understand that, I really do," Alberta said. "You must know that we're on the same side."

"All I know is that the Mistletoe Ball was supposed to be the premiere event of the holiday—of the entire year, for God's sake—and it's turned into front page news and not the good kind," Bambi said. "As the person in charge of running St. Clare's and keeping it as far from scandal as possible, you can imagine this tragic turn of events has put me under a tremendous amount of stress."

"I do know what you're going through," Alberta said. "My world has been turned upside down as well."

"I'm sure it has," Bambi said. "Your grandson is responsible for destroying what was supposed to be the biggest publicity event in St. Clare's history."

Alberta suddenly realized she and Bambi might not be on the same side. "There is such a thing as innocent until proven guilty."

"There's also such a thing as cause and effect," Bambi replied. "What Sergio caused to happen at the Ball has had a profound effect on me and this entire community."

Alberta glanced at the shopping bags swinging from Bambi's agitated arms.

"I can see how upset you are," Alberta said.

"When I'm upset I shop," Bambi replied. "My late husband would always know something was wrong if I needed help carrying my purchases from the car."

"We all have our own ways of handling life's hardships," Alberta said, her tone undeniably sarcastic.

"I don't mean to be rude, but I'm meeting a friend for breakfast and I'm already running late," Bambi said. "I know that you and your family are dealing with an extraordinary crisis and personally my heart goes out to you, but speaking in my professional capacity, it would be better if our paths didn't cross again."

Sloan finally ambled up to the women, breathing heavily. "Hi, ladies, what have I missed?"

"Bambi was just giving me some professional advice," Alberta said. "Which has been duly noted."

"Excellent," Sloan said. "I hope you gave Berta a discount."

When Sloan's joke was met with silence he didn't act like a wise man and keep his mouth shut, he acted like the nervous man he was and kept rambling. "You know, because it's the holiday and there are sales all over and from the number of bags you're carrying, you cannot resist a sale. Plus, a discount would be a really nice Christmas gift because, you know, the two of you are . . . friends."

That was an overstatement. Alberta and Bambi were friendly, but any friendship they may have had had definitely become a thing of the past. There was someone, however, whose relationship with the hospital administrator was still going strong.

"Bambi, where've you been? I've been standing outside waiting for you."

When Bambi turned around Kylie Manzini was able to see who had been preventing her from keeping her scheduled breakfast date. Kylie's expression went from annoyed to shocked to uncomfortable in less than three seconds. Alberta was starting to feel like the town pariah.

"Dr. Manzini," Sloan said. "This is a nice surprise."

"Yes . . . yes, it . . . it most certainly is," the doctor stuttered.

From the look on Kylie's face, not to mention her difficulty speaking, the woman didn't agree; it was definitely a surprise, but not a nice one. Her face was almost as pale as her platinum blonde hair. Alberta remembered that the doctor had told her when they first met that her father was from Oslo, Norway, which explained her hair coloring. It didn't explain why her Scandinavian father had an Italian surname.

"Kylie, I've always meant to ask you," Alberta said. "How did your Norwegian father come to have an Italian last name?"

Now the doctor looked annoyed. Alberta assumed it was because doctors didn't like to be questioned by those outside the medical community. Or Kylie, like Bambi, wasn't happy to be in the company of the grandmother of a presumed murderer.

"I can't believe you remembered that," Kylie replied.

"She's got a mind like an elephant, Berta has," Sloan said. "I can't tell you how many times she'll ask me a question about something I said three months ago. Trust me, nothing escapes her."

Despite being compared to an elephant, Alberta smiled. She thought it was nice to be complimented by her boyfriend when two women she hardly knew were glaring at her simply because they thought her grandson ruined their holiday charity event. It suddenly struck Alberta that the women—well, at least Bambi—seemed more concerned that the Mistletoe Ball had been cut short than the fact that a woman had been murdered.

"Was your father's mother a native Norwegian?" Alberta asked. "That would explain your fair coloring."

"What?" Kylie asked, obviously forgetting Alberta's original question. "Oh yes, his mother, Olga, was from Oslo, which is where she met my grandfather, Pasquale, who was born in Sorrento."

"*Santo Cielo!*" Alberta cried. "How did a fella from Sorrento get to meet a gal from Oslo?"

"Research," Kylie replied. "My grandfather was part of one of the first research teams trying to find a polio vaccine. They weren't successful, of course, but some of their discoveries helped lay the groundwork for the vaccine that Jonas Salk eventually invented."

"That's fascinating," Sloan said.

"I'm very proud of my grandfather," Kylie said.

"I see his legacy continues," Alberta said. "Now that you're going to head the cancer research lab at St. Clare's."

"You'll read all about it in our press releases," Bambi said. She then turned to Kylie and ordered, "We should be going."

Not just yet, Alberta thought. For whatever reason she was interested in hearing more about Kylie's background. There was something about her actions lately, her state of mind, that seemed off. Yes, there was a lot of change and turmoil going on around her, but she was a doctor, for God's sake, wasn't that what they trained them for? To be the calm in the storm.

"You come from a family of doctors, then?" Alberta asked.

"Yes . . . well, most of us," Kylie replied. "My father instilled in us a strong work ethic and the personal belief that one can always do better. Some of us have been able to live up to his expectations."

"Not everyone in your family has?" Alberta asked.

"Alberta, you should know better than anyone that there's always one bad apple hanging from every family's tree," Bambi said.

It was Alberta's turn to glare at Bambi. All the feelings she had been trying to suppress about the woman came to the surface. She didn't like her attitude, she didn't like her comments, and she most certainly didn't like her fashion sense. Bambi was what Alberta's mother, Elena, would call *farsi bella,* a girl who had to doll herself up to capture a man's eye. That type of girl had to dazzle a man with her physical attributes to keep him from noticing she was empty inside, that she lacked compassion and didn't possess typical feminine traits. Admittedly, it was part of an old-fashioned commentary on how a woman should present herself, but Alberta felt it was an appropriate critique of the woman who had just become her enemy.

"I'm sure you know better than anyone, Bambi, that there's always another way to examine a situation," Alberta said. "When I prove my grandson's innocence you'll see him in a different light. Like what it must be like to look at yourself in the mirror before you apply all that makeup."

Bambi's eyes grew so wide she did almost resemble a

cartoon character. Before steam started to magically pour out of her eyes, Sloan started to cough. He wasn't choking, it was a diversionary tactic that proved to be successful.

"Are you all right, Sloan?" Kylie asked.

Swallowing hard to make it look like he was trying to suppress his coughing fit, Sloan replied, "You can confirm that next week at my checkup."

"Yes, Jinx mentioned you were coming in for your last follow-up exam," Kylie said.

"I was planning on thanking you properly at the Ball," Sloan said. "But the evening had plans of its own."

"I'm still trying to wrap my head around the whole thing," Kylie said. "We had all worked so hard and the hospital was really counting on the silent auction to bring in a hefty amount to enhance our fundraising efforts. The lab can only reach its potential if it has the money to keep running."

"I must say that this persiflage has been delightful, but we really must go," Bambi said, lifting her right arm to check the time on her watch. "As much as we'd like to rewrite history, I think we can all agree that the Mistletoe Ball is something we need to put behind us."

If only it were that easy.

After their run-in with Bambi and Kylie, even Sloan's holiday spirit withered away like a dry, brown poinsettia leaf in February. They decided to call it quits on their attempt to capture Christmas magic and went back to Joyce's house to see how Lisa Marie and Tommy were doing. When they heard their raised voices, they knew they were having an even worse morning.

"What's wrong?" Alberta asked, entering Joyce's house.

Lisa Marie was leaning against the living room wall

with her arms crossed in front of her and Tommy was pacing the floor, talking on his cell phone.

"Can't you leave the job early to get back to Crystal Lake?"

Alberta looked at Lisa Marie as if to say, *What's going on?* but her daughter put up her hand to prevent her mother from distracting her. She didn't want to miss a word of the one-sided conversation.

"I know it's a big job, Hector, but so's the job in Crystal Lake, and that one's more important," Tommy said. "The property management company who handles that complex is my biggest client."

Whatever Hector was saying on the other end of the line was not at all what Tommy wanted to hear. He covered his forehead with the palm of his hand and started to massage his temples with his thumb and forefinger. "It's just that I have a lot going on right now and I don't think I can get back home."

He dropped his hand to his side in defeat. "I understand. Good-bye."

"It doesn't sound like Hector is acting very saintly," Sloan said.

"There's a power outage at the Crystal Lake condo complex and I don't have anyone down there to fix it because I had to lay off all my employees last year when things got tough," Tommy explained. "Hector was my only hope and he's down in Coral Gables, working for his brother."

Lisa Marie took a deep breath and exhaled. "I'll book you a flight."

"I can't go and leave you alone to deal with all of this," Tommy protested.

"I'm not alone," Lisa Marie said. "I have my mother. Sergio and I are in good hands."

"Are you sure, Leese?" Tommy asked. "I mean, Sergio's in jail."

"Which is where he's going to stay," Lisa Marie said. "You heard Bruno and Vinny, the DA isn't going to let him out, so there's absolutely nothing you can do for him here."

"I could help find out who really killed Natalie," Tommy said.

Lisa Marie smiled and grabbed her husband by the shoulders. "I think you should leave that to the professionals, like my mother and our daughter."

"Don't forget Helen and Joyce," Alberta said.

"Or the rest of us," Sloan added. "We're all going to do everything we can to prove Sergio's innocence, you can count on that."

Tommy scrunched up his face to fight back his tears and nodded his head several times. "Fine, I'll go!" He then pointed his finger at his wife. "You keep me posted every step of the way and I'll be back as soon as I can."

"Focus on saving your business," Lisa Marie said. "My paltry salary from the vet's office isn't going to keep us living in the grand style we've become accustomed to."

Tommy hugged his wife and said, "Make sure you tell Sergio that I love him."

"He already knows that, but I'll remind him," Lisa Marie said.

Within fifteen minutes Lisa Marie had booked Tommy on the next flight to Florida, he had flung some clothes and toiletries in a duffel bag, and Sloan was warming up the car to drive him to Newark Airport. Alberta suggested the men drive on their own as a way to decompress; it was also a subtle ploy that allowed her to be alone with her daughter for the first time since she had arrived. She would wind up regretting the decision.

The moment they watched Sloan drive down the street, Lisa Marie's calm demeanor changed. She became antsy, distracted, and more like the churlish daughter Alberta remembered. Perhaps because it was the two of them and Lisa Marie no longer had to wear a disguise, didn't have to play the role of the optimistic mother of a jailbird or the supportive wife, she only had to be herself. Or it could be that Lisa Marie still hated to be in her mother's company and, try as she might to control her emotions, she was rebelling from being in such close proximity to her mother without another relative around to serve as a buffer. Either way, Alberta needed to know the truth.

"Do you dislike me that much, Lisa Marie?" Alberta asked.

Lisa Marie had been gathering up the clothes that wouldn't fit into Tommy's bag but stopped in her tracks upon hearing her mother's remark.

"What are you talking about, Ma? I thought we'd gotten past that."

"I hoped we had, but we haven't talked about anything, not really. We've acted as if this visit is normal, something you do all the time and not once every fourteen years."

"There hasn't been the time to delve into our whole backstory."

"It's only the two of us now and whatever you say to me stays between us. Good or bad."

Tommy's wrinkled T-shirt hung in Lisa Marie's hands. "I didn't leave for any one reason, you know that. I left to

save what remained of us. It wasn't all your fault, I think
we both can agree that I'm not the nicest person, never
have been. That's one thing I always resented about you."

"That I'm nice?"

"And it's one thing I didn't inherit. It skipped a gener-
ation."

"Lisa, you shouldn't say things like that about yourself."

"Honesty, Ma, c'mon, if we're not honest about ourselves, we don't have anything. Look, I don't dislike you,
Ma. I don't hate you. And I don't resent you. Can you say
the same thing about me?"

"How could you even ask me that question? I'm your
mother."

"I'm your daughter and you had no problem asking me."

Alberta tilted her head to the side, her daughter did
have a point. "For the record, I love you, I always have,
and that will never change. Over these past few days,
however, I've come to like you very much. You're different than you were."

"Not nearly as different as you, Ma. You're like a completely new person. What's the phrase everybody uses?
You've reinvented yourself. You're stronger, more decisive, and the things that you, Jinx, and the others do, I
honestly don't know where you get the guts to run around
like some troupe of lady spies."

Alberta howled at Lisa Marie's description of her new
vocation. It fit.

"There's a lot of the old Lisa Marie in you still, but
you've changed too," Alberta said. "Despite the circumstances, you're patient, you listen, you and Tommy obviously have a wonderful marriage."

Lisa Marie smiled. "We've had our ups and downs, but I love my husband and I know he loves me. Plus, where else are we going? We're stuck with each other."

"It's obvious how strong your marriage is. I was wrong about Tommy, he's a good husband. Most important, you're a good mother."

"Then why do I feel like a complete failure?"

"Do you think good mothers walk around telling themselves how good they are? They're the ones blaming themselves for their kids' shortcomings or the problems their kids might have even though they're not to blame."

"Those are all nice words, Ma, but it doesn't change the fact that I'm scared. It's as simple as that. In my heart I know Sergio is innocent, there's no way he could've done something that vicious. But in my head I think, is it possible? Could he have snapped? You read about things like that in the papers all the time, but you never think it could be your kid. My kid would never commit a crime, my kid would never commit murder, but now that it's happening to me, I have to wonder if Sergio could have done this horrible thing. Those aren't the thoughts of a good mother, trust me."

"I had the same thoughts myself."

Lisa Marie looked at Alberta with surprise that she would admit such a thing, but her expression quickly gave way to one of relief. "Do you still feel that way?"

"No, I know Sergio is innocent, but it's human to question the extent of someone's capabilities. You can't give into it, though, you can't let those thoughts take over what's in your heart. Because a mother's heart always knows best."

Alberta gave in to her instinct and walked up to her

daughter. She didn't hesitate, she didn't ask permission, she just hugged her. To Alberta's sheer delight, Lisa Marie hugged her back.

It was a truly blissful moment, only spoiled when Alberta looked over Lisa Marie's shoulder and saw Tommy's tuxedo shirt lying on the floor. On the front was a stain that looked an awful lot like blood.

CHAPTER 20

Dannato se lo fai e dannato se non lo fai.

Alberta was as dizzy as an elf without a shelf.

She didn't know what to do. Should she stay quiet and not ask Lisa Marie why there was blood on Tommy's shirt? Or should she ask her and risk finding out that her daughter had been hiding the fact that her husband killed Natalie and not her son like the rest of the town suspected? She could hear her father's voice in her head, *Dannato se lo fai e dannato se non lo fai.* It was what he always said when faced with a dilemma, damned if you do and damned if you don't. She wasn't proud, but she made the cowardly choice to remain silent. At least for now.

By the time she got home she knew she needed company or else she was going to wrestle with the thoughts that were eating away at her. She knew that if this were another case she was trying to solve the choice would've been simple, she would've picked up the shirt and demanded an explanation. She would've brought the shirt to Vinny to be analyzed and determined if the blood on the shirt belonged to Natalie. She wouldn't have stopped until she got an answer. But this case was different and she didn't want an answer. What she wanted was her big sister.

"Helen," Alberta shouted into her cell phone. "I need you to come over."

"I'm working on a deadline," Helen replied.

"This is important."

"Is it about the case against Sergio?"

"Yes."

"Is it good news or bad news?"

"I don't know."

"How can you not know?"

"Because I only have part of the news and I need you to help me figure out if I want to find out the rest!"

There was a long silence before Helen replied. "I'll be right over."

There was another long silence after Alberta explained to Helen what she saw at Joyce's house. They were sitting at the kitchen table, untouched cups of coffee in front of them both, the chirping from a very chatty bevy of sparrows penetrating the quiet, causing Lola to squirm in Alberta's lap. It looked like Helen was staring at the Tranquility Library calendar that hung on the far wall, but Alberta knew that she wasn't gazing at anything that could be seen with her eyes, she was looking internally, contemplating the information she had just been given by contemplating the contents of her soul.

Alberta knew her sister better than almost anyone on earth. Still, Helen was not the easiest person to read. She turned left when it was almost certain she'd turn right. She'd laugh when you thought she'd scold. She'd up and quit the convent after doing God's work for forty years when you thought she'd spend the rest of her life as a nun. Which meant Alberta had no idea what kind of advice her big sister was going to give her now. Neither did Helen.

"This is a tough one, Berta," Helen said.

"I know," Alberta agreed. "That's why I called you over. I need your input."

"You remember what Daddy used to say, don't you?"

"Yes, I've already heard his voice in my head, but it still didn't help me make a decision."

"I'm going to say to you what I would tell someone who wrote into *The Herald*—you only have one choice."

"And what is that?"

"You have to let Lisa Marie explain herself. There's a chance she doesn't even know there's blood on Tommy's shirt. Didn't you say you saw it lying in a heap of clothes?"

"On the side of the couch, the clothes Tommy wasn't taking back home with him."

"Who did the packing?"

"Tommy mainly, but Lisa Marie helped."

"Then there's a fifty-fifty chance that she knows about the bloodstained shirt, and if she does, there's another fifty-fifty chance she knows how the blood got there."

"That's too much math for me, Helen, could you please just do what you always do and get straight to the point?"

"The only way you're going to rest is if you talk to your daughter."

"I think I want a second opinion," Alberta said.

Joyce sat at the kitchen table warming her hands around a mug of hot chocolate. She had just finished with a board meeting at St. Clare's when she got Alberta's phone call telling her there was an emergency and she had to come straight to her house. She listened to Alberta describe her predicament, then she listened to Helen's suggestion on how to resolve the problem, and then she watched both women stare at her waiting for her to either agree with Helen or offer an alternative.

"This reminds me of a time back in 1986 when I was working on Wall Street," Joyce said.

"Is this trip down memory lane going to be worth it?" Helen asked.

"Yes, just listen," Joyce replied. "I had a client who was skittish about investing in the market aggressively—he always wanted to play it safe—and I finally convinced him to buy stock in a new technology company. And I mean a lot of stock. At first things were moving slowly, daily moderate increases, and then on Friday the market took a turn and the price of stock fell not just through the floor, but to the subbasement. I knew if I told my client he had lost an incredible amount of money that he had only invested based on my urging he was going to have a stroke, but I also knew he was on a fishing trip with his sons, which meant he probably wouldn't hear about the stock plummeting until Monday. I had to make a choice. I could wait it out over the weekend and pray that the stock would start to go on the uptick or I could call him and let him know the truth."

Joyce paused for dramatic effect, but the drama was too much for Alberta. She needed to know what Joyce did and she needed to know immediately.

"Don't leave us hanging, Joyce, what did you do?!" Alberta yelled.

"I called him and told him the truth," Joyce replied. "I caught him just as he was about to leave for his lake house."

"Did he bail on the fishing trip and try to hunt you down?" Helen asked.

"He acted like it was no big deal," Joyce said. "As if I told him we ran out of mozzarella and only had provolone."

"Clearly your client was an Irishman," Helen said.

"Funny enough, he was, and he remained my client until the day I retired," Joyce said. "It didn't hurt that on Monday the stock did rise and hasn't stopped rising since then, but the point of the story is that my being honest gained his trust. That's what you need to do with Lisa Marie."

"You know how much it pains me to agree with Joyce, but you're right," Helen said. "There's been too much *rancore,* the both of you are too *coccciuto,* the two of you seem to be in a good place now, you don't want to ruin it."

"That's why I'm afraid to say anything to her," Alberta said. "I don't know what I'd do if I found out that she knew about this and kept silent while her son's in jail."

"Berta, you can't believe she'd actually do that, do you?" Joyce asked.

"Think about it," Alberta said. "Lisa's convinced that we're going to be able to prove Sergio's innocence. The whole reason she reached out to me is because she's been tracking our achievements, which are reported in *The Herald*, so she knows we have a darn good track record. But what if the reason she's convinced we'll be able to prove Sergio didn't kill Natalie is because she knows Sergio isn't the murderer, but Tommy is?"

"Which means if she keeps evidence against Tommy hidden and the charges are dropped against Sergio, both her husband and her son will stay out of jail," Helen explained.

"*Il paradiso abbi pietà della mia anima*," Alberta said.

"Why do you need heaven to have mercy on your soul?" Joyce asked.

"Because I can't believe I'm thinking something so terrible about my own daughter," Alberta replied. "I have to be the worst mother on the planet."

"I don't know about the worst," Joyce said.

"But definitely in the top ten," Helen added.

"Let's go!" Alberta announced.

"Where are we going?" Helen asked.

"Into the lion's den," Alberta said.

When they arrived at the den and Alberta explained why they were there, the lioness was not happy.

"You think I'd conceal evidence that could help my son go free?!" Lisa Marie shrieked. "I said I wasn't nice, Ma, I didn't say I was evil!"

"I never said you were evil!" Alberta cried.

"I thought we were making progress! I thought we were getting closer and bridging this huge gap between us!" Lisa Marie yelled. "Who's the *stunod* now?"

"That's why I'm here, to bridge the gap, to make sure that there are no secrets between us," Alberta said.

"Like my husband's bloodied shirt!"

"Well, now that you've mentioned it," Helen said.

"If you could explain how blood got onto the tuxedo shirt Tommy was going to wear to the Mistletoe Ball, it really would clear everything up," Joyce added.

"Is that what I need to do, Ma, to get you off my back?" Lisa Marie asked.

Alberta let out a deep sigh. "Yes, I need to know the truth."

"It's because I accidentally cut myself making Tommy a snack while we were getting ready to go!" Lisa Marie explained. "I was slicing some tomatoes, I got distracted, I nicked my finger, I turned around and bumped into Tommy, my hand pressed against his chest, and blood got all over his shirt. It was then that we pretty much decided we were in no mood to go to some ridiculous Christmas party and make small talk while our son was still missing."

Lisa Marie paced back and forth a few times, shaking her head and exhaling like she was doing bench presses with a three-hundred-pound weight. A few times she waved her finger at Alberta but bit her lip before speaking. Finally, she stopped and faced her mother.

"What's the verdict, Ma?" Lisa Marie asked. "Does that pass the Alberta Ferrara Scaglione smell test?"

"Is there a reason you're not wearing a Band-Aid?" Alberta asked.

"Oh my God! It's high school all over again and I'm living under a magnifying glass!" Lisa Marie screamed.

"Answer the question," Helen demanded.

"I couldn't find a bandage and then the bleeding stopped so I didn't need one," Lisa Marie said.

She held her finger in front of Alberta's face so she could get a close-up look at her cut. "Satisfied!"

"If you would've just explained yourself in the first place, I wouldn't have suspected anything," Alberta said.

"You didn't give me the chance, Ma!" Lisa Marie screamed. "You saw the shirt and hightailed it out of here. The only reason you came back is because Aunt Helen convinced you it was the right thing to do!"

"I appreciate the compliment, Leese, but Joyce is the one who convinced your mother to have an open dialogue with you," Helen said.

"Seriously?" Lisa Marie asked.

"Why do you sound so surprised?" Joyce asked.

"I didn't think my mother listened to anyone except Aunt Helen," Lisa Marie said. "Things really have changed around here."

"Another thing that's changed is that I can apologize when I know I'm wrong," Alberta said. "I'm very sorry for suspecting you. I should've had enough trust in us to ask you about the shirt when I first saw it. I should've known better."

Lisa Marie shook her head, but this time it seemed that she was trying to clear it from the anger she had been feeling and not because she wanted to pulverize her mother. "It's all right, Ma, and I'm not just handing you a line to make you feel better," Lisa Marie said. "I can understand how it looked, especially to someone who's always looking for clues around every hidden corner. I need you to promise me something, though."

"What's that?" Alberta asked.

"From now on, no more secrets, no more lies, if you

want to ask me something, ask it, if you want to say something to me, say it," Lisa Marie said. "Capisce?"

"*Capisco,*" Alberta said.

"Now, could you please make us some food? I am starving," Lisa Marie said.

"Let me take care of it, I'll make us dinner," Joyce said.

"Seriously?" Lisa Marie asked.

"Again with the seriously?" Joyce asked.

"Sorry, Aunt Joyce, but you said you don't cook," Lisa Marie said.

"I don't," Joyce replied. "I'm ordering takeout."

An hour later they were all sitting around Joyce's living room finishing up their Chinese food. Empty China Chef cartons were lying on their sides on the cocktail table next to unopened soy sauce packets and used chopsticks. The ladies were sitting on the couch and the floor to allow their stomachs to settle until it was time to eat the frozen chocolate cheesecake that was defrosting on the kitchen counter. It felt like a normal night and they reveled in it, all the while knowing it was nothing more than a pause before the madness roared again.

Tomorrow Lisa Marie would have to go to the police station to say good-bye to her son, who was being sent to the correctional facility until the start of his trial, and inform him that his father had had to go back to Florida and wouldn't be able to say good-bye in person. They were all worried that Bruno would stop representing Sergio after getting punched in the eye for simply doing his job. Up until now he said he had no intention of quitting, but everyone knew he was remaining Sergio's lawyer out of respect for Alberta. It had nothing to do with his desire to be the boy's counsel. Knowing tomorrow was going to bring more stress and anxiety, they decided they might as well enjoy the night. And maybe even some holiday cheer.

The balsam candle was lit, making the living room smell like they were in the woods, the lights on Joyce's small artificial tree were twinkling, and a CD of golden age crooners singing holiday classics played on the stereo. Perry Como was currently singing "We Wish You a Merry Christmas," which the women all secretly hoped was a foretelling of their future. But if Mr. C. truly had an uncanny knack for both singing number one hits and prophesizing, proof of that would have to unfold on its own. For right now the women just wanted to unwind.

"Aunt Helen," Lisa Marie said. "Make me laugh."

"Who am I, Bozo the Clown?" Helen asked.

"The two of you do always wear the same outfit all the time," Lisa Marie observed.

"It's a holdover from my old profession," Helen said. "After forty years you get used to wearing a uniform."

"Tell us about your new job," Lisa Marie said.

"Are the letters already starting to pile in?" Alberta asked.

"Also too, what's your catchphrase?" Joyce asked.

"Wyck and I haven't made a final decision on how I'm going to sign off the column just yet, but we've narrowed it down to two choices," Helen said. "'Peace be with you' or 'See ya, see ya, wouldn't want to be ya.'"

"Let me guess," Alberta said. "Wyck came up with the second one."

"He did, he thinks it captures my humor," Helen said. "Which it does, but I told him that I didn't want this to be a joke column, and I'm not going to poke fun at people who are looking for answers to their problems."

"Has he accepted that?" Joyce said.

"He has to," Helen replied. "I told him that if he edits my columns to make them sassier or more sarcastic, I'd sue him for every penny he has."

"As much as I hate that Wyck, I'm happy for you," Lisa Marie said.

"Why do you hate Wyck?" Helen asked.

"Because that traitor in chief has plastered my son's name across *The Herald*'s headlines for days but hasn't once mentioned the name of the tramp who got Sergio's name put there in the first place!" Lisa Marie explained.

"By tramp, you mean Natalie, right?" Joyce asked.

"Is there another tramp in Tranquility?" Lisa Marie questioned.

"According to the letters I've received there are at least seven," Helen replied.

Once again Helen had been able to diffuse the situation, and Lisa Marie's groaning quickly turned to giggling.

"Thanks, Aunt Helen, I needed that," she said. "Seriously, I think it's wonderful that you're embarking on such a different career from what you had previously been doing."

"Being an advice columnist is a lot like being a nun," Helen said. "I listen to people's problems and try to get them to face their truth by showing them they have choices. Take Mike DeDordo, for instance."

"Is he one of our cousins on Mommy's side?" Alberta asked.

"Oddly enough, he's not a relative, he's one of my readers," Helen said. "He wrote in just today asking for relationship advice."

"Is he having an affair, Aunt Helen?" Lisa Marie asked. "Please tell me he's having an affair even if he isn't, I just need to hear it."

"He is having an affair," Helen said.

"*Dio mio!*" Alberta said. "Really? A man wrote in to you and told you he's having an affair?"

"Not the kind you think, it isn't a physical relationship but an emotional one," Helen said.

"Oftentimes that can be worse," Joyce said. "A man sleeps with another woman and it could be blamed on lust, which is no excuse or justification for cheating, but if he confides in another woman, shares an emotional connection with her, that means their marriage is broken at its core."

"That's so sad," Alberta said.

"It's true," Helen replied. "He didn't tell me his age, but I assume he's an older man because he said the woman that he's having a relationship with is much younger and he said his wife is infirm. Not sick, but in-firm."

"That's definitely an old person word," Lisa Marie said. "Not that I would use that word to describe any of you."

"Thank God for small blessings," Alberta said.

"This man broke it off with the woman not because he didn't want to start a new life with her, but because he couldn't leave his wife," Helen said.

"What kind of advice does he want from you?" Joyce said.

"How to rid the woman from his mind," Helen said. "Despite their age difference and some problems that she caused with his job that he didn't get in to, he loves this woman, but I think it's more like a father loves a daughter than a man would love a mistress."

"What do you mean, Aunt Helen?" Lisa Marie asked.

"He said he wants to protect her, shield her from her enemies, and give her the kind of life she deserves and the kind of love her family never gave her," Helen said.

"He sounds like one complicated man," Joyce said.

"What did you tell him?" Alberta asked.

"I told him that he tried to have his cake and eat it too and now he has to suffer indigestion," Helen said. "He's not going to be able to care for his wife in the way that she needs and deserves to be cared for by her husband if his mind is always thinking about how to care for someone else. He made a vow to his wife to be at her side in sickness and in health. God doesn't take those vows lightly and neither should he."

"Remind me never to write you for advice, Aunt Helen," Lisa Marie said. "I don't think I could handle the tough love."

"Don't underestimate yourself," Alberta said. "You could handle anything thrown your way."

"Sometimes people just need a reminder that they can do the right thing," Helen said. "That's what this Big Sister is here for."

Alberta raised her cup. "I'd like to make a toast," she said. "To my Big Sister, long may she reign!"

The evening was everything they needed. Simple, normal, filled with silly stories, funny comments, and the comfort that only the company of family can provide. Unfortunately, the outside world could only be held at bay for so long. At some point the safety net had to be cut down, the barrier to reality had to be removed, and the peace of mind that was so hard to find had to be disturbed. That point came when Vinny called.

"Vinny, *Madon*, it's so late," Alberta said. "What's wrong?"

"We found another dead body."

And with that they kissed their normal night good-bye.

CHAPTER 21

Anche il male ride.

It was a silent night, it was a deadly night.

The setting was ironic. Looking around, it appeared as if the pages of a classic holiday story had come to life. Christmas decorations filled every shop window in the Tranquility town square, the large pine trees that dotted the street were brightly lit, the gazebo in the center of the square was filled with a life-size nativity waiting for the miracle child to be born, and from the hidden speakers that played nonstop day and night came the sultry sound of smoky-voiced Peggy Lee singing "It's Christmas Time Again" to caress the cold night air. Looking down at the dead body lying in the gutter told a different tale. This holiday season had not offered the townsfolk much to celebrate. It had offered the Ferraras even less.

Alberta, Helen, Joyce, and Lisa Marie had left their relaxing evening behind to join Vinny at the town square after they received his disturbing phone call. It was after midnight, and although all the stores were closed, the Christmas lights in their windows were kept on to create a serene glow throughout the square for any late-night strollers. When the soft blue lights of the Tranquility Book Store illuminated the young man's dead body, the image was eerier than ethereal.

"*Per l'amor del cielo!*" Alberta cried. "It's Rudy!"

"Rudy Lewendorf?" Vinny asked. "Natalie's old roommate?"

"One and the same," Alberta said. "This is horrible."

"The only person we know of who knew Natalie is dead," Lisa Marie said.

"This is linked to the man you found about a week ago in Newton," Alberta stated.

"Yes, Rudy's the fourth overdose in the area this month," Vinny replied. "How are you certain these deaths are connected?"

"Rudy's neck is swollen like the other man's and they both seem to have burn marks at the corners of their mouths," Alberta replied.

"My God, Ma, I can't see without my glasses and you can zero in on details like that," Lisa Marie said.

"Your mother's got a detective's eye," Vinny commented. "She's right, it looks like they both OD'd from the same drug."

"I can't believe Rudy was a drug addict," Joyce said. "He tried to help us, Berta, he even told us to warn Sergio about Natalie."

"Even good boys can become drug addicts," Helen said. "For some all it takes is one experiment with a drug and they find themselves hooked."

"Alfie, did you notice any signs when you spoke with Rudy that might indicate he was using?" Vinny said.

"I think I told you he was fidgety and anxious, but I attributed his behavior to the fact that he had two strange women in his apartment asking cryptic questions and pulling out food from their bags," Alberta said. "I'd be nervous too."

"Do you know what he OD'd from?" Helen asked.

"Not yet," Vinny replied. "Looks like there's a new street drug making itself known and taking no prisoners. We have an undercover team working on finding the source, but we don't have any leads yet. All we know so far is that it's cheap and it's deadly, which is not a good combination."

"Have you done any outreach to local addicts?" Helen asked. "Maybe someone at the methadone clinic, or that rehab center in Hamburg?"

"How do you know about this stuff, Aunt Helen?" Lisa Marie asked.

"Your aunt is more than just a former nun, honey," Joyce said. "She has degrees in social work and education, plus decades of experience working in both fields."

"Here I thought you got the job being an advice columnist simply because you have a big mouth and you're opinionated," Lisa Marie said.

"Those were the primary reasons Wyck offered me the gig," Helen said. "But I do have what the kids call street cred."

"That you do, Helen," Vinny said. "To answer your question, we have spoken to our contacts in the clinics and homeless shelters and they all confirmed that a new, highly addictive drug is making its way through this part of Jersey."

"Is it odd for a drug to be isolated in one geographical area?" Alberta asked.

"Not at first," Vinny replied. "Drug dealing is like any other business: You give out samples of your product to get people hooked, then you let the word out and suddenly business is booming."

"I don't think this is the kind of word-of-mouth that increases a product's demand," Joyce said.

They all looked at Rudy's motionless body lying at their feet.

"Sadly, this isn't going to deter anyone from trying the drug for themselves," Vinny said. "When you get to the point where you're addicted to drugs, you're no longer choosy. In fact, your ability to make any kind of rational choice is gone."

"All you want is your next fix, consequences be damned," Helen said.

"Vinny, could we have a moment?" Alberta asked. "I'd like to say a prayer for Rudy."

"I'll give you some privacy," Vinny said. "I see Pedro over there. I asked him to come and look at the body."

While Vinny went off to confer with the medical examiner, Alberta led the ladies in a series of prayers. Lisa Marie was astonished to see that all three women carried rosary beads with them. She, like the rest of her family and everyone else she knew growing up in Hoboken, had been raised Catholic, but as she got older, she left the old traditions behind. Until now she hadn't questioned her decision.

At first, the chaos of daily life had gotten in the way of maintaining any kind of religious order, and later the not-so-saintly revelations of the Catholic Church made her distrust the institution. Lisa Marie had raised her children Catholic out of habit, not due to any sense of belief in the religion's sacraments. She remembered Alberta telling her that the building might be corrupt, but the ideals that built its foundation were pure. Lisa Marie didn't want to hear that kind of rationalization and proudly considered herself a lapsed Catholic.

Now, watching her mother and her aunts joined in prayer, asking God to have mercy on the soul of this young man they barely knew, made her realize her mother may have had a point. Having spiritual beliefs, loving mankind, and embracing all of the teachings of Christianity did not bind a person to a building. Spirituality was not only available to those who worshipped in a church on Sunday mornings, it lived within every one of God's children and could be practiced independently. By the time the women said "Amen," Lisa Marie had lent her voice to the group.

When Pedro addressed the women his tone was much more somber than the last time he met Alberta. He might be a man whose colleague was Death, but he was a man who also understood his colleague could often be cruel. Taking the life of a young man before he could truly live was devastating. It was also happening much too frequently these days.

Pedro skipped the formalities and dove right into explaining what kind of foe they were facing.

"From the burn marks on the corners of his lips and his swollen neck, I can tell you that he died from an overdose of Flower," Pedro said.

"Flour?" Alberta repeated. "He didn't die from too much cake, he died from too many drugs."

Pedro allowed himself a smile. "Not the flour that you cook with, Alberta, flower like a rose. That's the name of the drug."

"How'd such a deadly drug get such a pretty name?" Joyce asked.

"The components that make up the drug give off a foul odor during the chemical process," Pedro explained. "The heinous among us do have a sense of humor, so they called it Flower."

"*Anche il male ride*," Alberta said.

"Very true, Alberta," Pedro said. "Evil does like to laugh, and make a mockery of what we hold most dear, which is life."

"Wherever this Flower comes from, it's more powerful than Molly, which, before you ask, is another street drug, and it's just as addictive as meth," Vinny said. "To sum it all up, nothing about this new killer is good."

"Pedro, you said that there were traces of a drug in Natalie's body," Alberta said. "Do you think it'll turn out to be Flower?"

"That's my assumption," Pedro said.

"Even though Natalie didn't have the same burn marks and swollen neck?" Alberta asked.

"She probably died from the stab wound before the drug could take any real effect," Pedro said. "Whoever's making Flower is tweaking it almost on a daily basis, causing the physical side effects to vary slightly from person to person."

"Or in this case corpse to corpse," Joyce said. "What a tragedy."

"It's like that Whac-A-Mole game," Vinny said. "The minute we think we have one drug under control another one pops up, it's a never-ending cycle."

"An indiscriminate one too," Helen said. "It doesn't matter how old you are, how rich, how poor, how successful, you can get addicted to drugs no matter what walk of life you come from."

"The only thing all those people have in common is that they all seem to end up the same way," Alberta said. "Dead."

The evening had put things into perspective and the next morning, when Lisa Marie with Alberta and Jinx by her side went to see Sergio off to the Keogh-Dwyer Correctional Facility, the women were much calmer, optimistic even. They might be saying good-bye to their son, grandson, and brother, but they weren't saying prayers over his dead body. Hope was not yet lost.

Neither was the impact that family could have.

Lisa Marie was sitting in the meeting room waiting for Sergio to be brought in, Alberta and Jinx on either side of her. Someone had put an old-fashioned Christmas decoration on the otherwise bare walls, a 3D poster of Santa Claus smiling and holding a bottle of Coca-Cola. Instead of making the room look cheerier, it had the opposite effect. Good ole Kriss Kringle couldn't make the bleak room appear any less dreary. By the confident smile on Lisa Marie's lips, however, it looked like she wasn't going to give in to her surroundings.

"Thank you," Lisa Marie said.

"Thank you for what, honey?" Alberta asked.

"For being here," she replied.

"Where else would we be?" Jinx asked.

Lisa Marie smiled wearily. "A thousand miles away."

Alberta understood what her daughter was trying to say. For the past fourteen years whenever Lisa Marie had faced a crisis, she only had Tommy by her side. If Tommy had been the one in danger, she faced it alone. After handling one emergency after another with Tommy as her only support system, Alberta knew that Lisa Marie must be greatly relieved to be surrounded by family. It made dealing with emotionally draining situations less exhausting because the pain and stress could be shared. Alberta smiled, knowing that despite all the turmoil and separation, she had definitely raised a practical child.

When Tambra brought Sergio into the room he looked like he did back home in Florida, bright-eyed, smiling, his curly hair unkempt, the only difference was that he was wearing an orange jumpsuit and handcuffs instead of jeans and a T-shirt. Nothing was perfect.

Tambra unlocked the handcuffs and removed them from Sergio's wrists. They dangled from her hands and clanged together as she addressed the women.

"Bruno will be here in a minute, but take as long as you need," she said. "I'm going to be the one to transport Sergio to Keogh-Dwyer and I'm not in any rush to go out in that cold."

They understood Tambra was extending them this favor not out of professional courtesy, but because they were friends. Alberta didn't know if Tambra believed in Sergio's innocence or not, but she did know that the cop believed in fair treatment and helping out a friend whenever she could. If she ever got around to Christmas shopping again, Alberta would have to remember to find something special for Tambra.

"You look good, honey," Lisa Marie said. "Did you sleep well?"

"Like a baby," Sergio replied. "I guess I was exhausted from everything that happened and, you know, fighting back every step of the way."

"I assume you mean punching Bruno in the face," Alberta said.

"Not something I'm proud of," Sergio admitted.

"You should be ashamed, honey," Alberta said, not mincing words. "Bruno is a good man, and he hasn't stopped fighting for you even though you've given him every reason to walk away and let you be someone else's problem."

Sergio nodded his head and spent a few seconds examining the table. "I was a jerk and I've learned my lesson. Bruno and I had what Dad likes to call a man-to-man chat and straightened everything out."

"I'm glad to hear that," Lisa Marie said.

"Where is he, by the way?" Sergio asked. "Is Dad talking to Bruno?"

Alberta was about to speak but bit her tongue. She knew if Sergio needed to hear bad news, it should come from his mother. Lisa Marie grabbed her son's hands, and when she spoke it was evident that she was working hard to make her voice sound light and matter-of-fact.

"There was an emergency with the Crystal Lake job, your father's biggest account, and he tried to get someone down there to fix it, but Hector is out in Coral Gables handling another problem and he couldn't find anyone else," Lisa Marie said.

"Dad went down there to solve the problem himself," Sergio said, finishing her sentence.

"Yes," Lisa Marie confirmed. "He had to hop on the next flight."

"Sloan had to speed the whole way to the airport to get him there on time," Alberta said.

"He wanted to say good-bye, but there just wasn't

time," Lisa Marie said. "He did want me to tell you that he'll be back as soon as he can and that he loves you."

Sergio beamed. "Like I don't already know that."

"If there was any way to avoid going, he would have, but you know how important the Crystal Lake account is," Lisa Marie said.

"I get it, really I do, and I'm not upset," Sergio said. "There's nothing Dad could do here for me anyway except worry, and you're doing enough of that for everybody, Mom."

"We're all worried," Jinx said.

"I know you are, but there's really nothing to worry about," Sergio said. "I'm in good hands."

As if he had been waiting for the perfect entrance line, Bruno opened the door and walked into the room. Despite it being a snowy day in mid-December and his being indoors, Bruno was sporting a pair of dark-lensed sunglasses. When he took them off his Scandinavian good looks were only slightly marred by the black-and-blue shiner he was sporting.

"Ouch!" Alberta cried. "*Madona mia*! Does it hurt as bad as it looks?"

"It's fine," Bruno said. "On-the-job hazard."

"I'm so sorry, Bruno," Lisa Marie said. "I can't thank you enough for not bailing on us."

"Sergio and I had a heart-to-heart, and he now understands that his emotions are the enemy and not me," Bruno explained. "He also realizes that anger management therapy will be part of his future as well."

"I'm glad to hear that," Alberta said. "The only way to fight your demons is to own them."

"I know that now, Gram," Sergio said. "I wish I had figured that out before I whacked my lawyer."

"How are you going to explain that shiner when you stand in front of a judge?" Jinx asked.

"That's also something else Sergio and I discussed," Bruno said. "If I'm asked, I'm going to have to tell the truth because I will not lie in a court of law."

"But it won't look very good for Sergio if you explain that your client answered a difficult question by punching you in the face," Alberta said.

"That would be like admitting to the judge Sergio is violent," Jinx added.

"I volunteered to step away and have my assistant handle all court proceedings, but Sergio refused that strategy," Bruno explained. "He wants me to be in the courtroom with him."

"Then what're you going to do?" Lisa Marie asked. "Get a makeover to hide the evidence?"

"Present it in a different light," Bruno said. "The black eye is a result of Sergio passionately defending the honor of the woman he loved. He believes in her good character so deeply that words failed him, and he protected her the way he wished he could have protected her when she was attacked."

"That's a bit of a stretch, isn't it?" Alberta asked.

"It will present Sergio as a man who is in emotional turmoil because of the murder of his girlfriend and, hopefully, cast enough doubt that such a man, with no documented history of violence, would be able to brutally kill someone he loved," Bruno said.

"Won't they just say it was a crime of passion?" Jinx asked. "Sergio flipped out, grabbed a knife, and stabbed Natalie."

"Most crimes of passion happen face-to-face," Bruno said. "Natalie was stabbed from behind, which is unusual, because there are no indications that there was a struggle. If Sergio did kill her, there most likely would have been a fight preceding the murder, then Natalie got turned around, and Sergio killed her from behind, but there's no forensic evidence to support that theory and it doesn't fit with the profile."

"By the time you have to present your case we'll hopefully have more evidence you can use," Alberta said.

"If I know you, Mrs. Scaglione, you'll have tons," Bruno said. "First, we need to deal with what's going to happen today."

Bruno explained that Sergio would be transported to the Keogh-Dwyer Correctional Facility in Newton in a van with two other prisoners. He would go through all the typical procedures of admittance, be given a brief introduction to the rules of the institution, and be assigned his own cell. At some point after that was completed, he'd be able to meet with Bruno to discuss the pretrial hearing.

The women had no idea what to say because they couldn't find any reassuring words to give what Bruno had just described an optimistic spin. Luckily, they didn't have to because Sergio spoke for them.

"I know that all sounds really bad and trust me, I am freaked out and scared," Sergio admitted. "But if I'm going to survive this, I can't let my emotions get the best of me. Like Dad always says, it's time for me to man up."

"You will get through this, honey, and when you get out of that place, you'll be tougher and stronger than before," Lisa Marie said.

"Ma, I need you to understand that there's a chance I may not get out," Sergio said.

"Don't think like that, Bruno has never lost a case," Alberta said.

"There's always a first time," Sergio replied.

"For what it's worth, I don't plan on breaking my winning streak," Bruno said. "My hope is that Sergio's stay at Keogh-Dwyer will be a short one."

"I checked it out, Serge, and it isn't that bad," Jinx said. "Your cell has a window and you'll have access to television, a library, the bathrooms aren't private, but . . ."

"It is jail after all," Sergio said, finishing Jinx's sentence for her.

"As far as prisons go, you could do a lot worse," Lisa Marie said.

"It could be like the one on Rikers Island," Alberta said. "*Ah Madon*! Now that's a prison."

"You've been to Rikers Island?" Sergio asked.

"Only once to, you know, pay someone a visit," Alberta said.

"I was there too," Jinx added. "Believe me, the facility they're putting you in is like Disney World in comparison."

"Is this when I can finally admit I never liked Disney World?" Sergio said.

"Sergio Samuel Maldonado, that is a lie!" Lisa Marie cried. "You loved going to Disney World and you know it."

"I only loved it because it made you and Dad so happy," Sergio confessed. "The rides always made me a little sick. I don't have a strong stomach like you do and especially not Gram."

"My stomach's no stronger than anyone else's," Alberta said.

"Yeah right! You need an iron stomach to be a badass lady detective," Sergio said. "I think the word in Italian is *cazzuto,* isn't it, Gram?"

"Between you and your mother, you've chosen some

very special Italian words to add to your vocabulary," Alberta said.

"If anyone is going to get me out of here and find Natalie's real killer, it's you and your posse, Gram," Sergio said.

"We are making some headway," Alberta said.

"I have complete faith in you," Sergio said. "You too Jinx."

"What about me?" Lisa Marie said. "Am I chopped liver?"

"You're my mom," Sergio said. "You don't have to do anything else but that."

Lisa Marie didn't try to hide her emotions, she couldn't if she wanted to, and why should you try to hide your emotions from your family anyway? She reached out to hold her son's hand and cried.

"I'm so relieved to see you calmer today, Sergio, more at ease," Lisa Marie said.

"It isn't the way I want to spend the holidays, but I need to stop being my own worst enemy," Sergio said. "Had I only trusted you from the beginning, I might not be here. From now on I've decided to knock it off and be the good boy everybody says I am. Whatever is thrown my way, I'll cooperate."

Alberta thought it might be wise to challenge her grandson's sudden change of heart. She might not get a chance to speak with him again without guards listening in to their conversation and other inmates causing a distraction. Tambra had given them the gift of time, Alberta thought, she should take advantage of it.

"Did Natalie ever wear a wig?" Alberta asked.

"That's like a super random question, Gram," Sergio replied.

"Not random at all," Jinx said. "Strands of blond hair were found on Natalie's body, but not of the natural variety, synthetic, from a wig."

"Why would Natalie wear a wig, she has beautiful hair," Sergio said. He then corrected himself. "Had."

"What about what Bruno asked you about before, did Natalie ever do drugs?" Alberta asked.

"No, Gram, at least not that I know of," Sergio replied.

"Think hard, Serge," Jinx said. "Did she smoke pot, take pills, anything?"

"Nat wasn't like that," Sergio said. "She worked around hospitals and she went to that school in Pensacola for a while to study to be a lab technician."

"The FORTIS Institute?" Alberta asked.

"That's the one," Sergio said.

"Which is where she met Rudy," Alberta added.

"That's what they told me," Sergio said.

"Did Rudy do drugs?" Jinx asked.

"Not in front of me, but if he did, I'd be surprised if Natalie would stand for it," Sergio said. "She knew about the dangers of drugs, she mentioned it a few times, how friends of hers got hooked. I don't think she would ever put herself in a position to wind up the same way."

There was a pause after Sergio finished. None of the women spoke, but Sergio could tell their minds were racing. He wanted to know why. "What's with all the questions about drugs?" he asked.

"The medical examiner found traces of some kind of drug in Natalie's system," Lisa Marie explained.

"I was with her almost twenty-four-seven before she died and I didn't notice any change in her behavior that would've been caused by drugs," Sergio said.

"Did Natalie ever mention the word *Flower* to you?" Alberta said.

"Like a *bouquet* of flowers?" Sergio asked. "I'm sure she did, but I don't get the connection between flowers and drugs."

"There's a new illegal drug with the street name of Flower that's been killing people," Alberta said. "We don't have the toxicology report back, but I'm guessing that drug is going to be found in Natalie's system."

"It isn't what killed her, but if it's true, it's a link," Jinx said. "She may have been using and you didn't know it."

Sergio looked stunned. It was as if a veil had been lifted and he was able to see his girlfriend in her true form for the first time. He shook his head and instead of getting angry, which was what Jinx feared he would do, instead of getting defensive, which was how Alberta thought he'd respond, he apologized.

"I'm so sorry, Ma," Sergio said.

"For what?" Lisa Marie asked.

"For not trusting you enough when you told me I was making the biggest mistake of my life choosing Natalie over my family," Sergio said. "Don't get me wrong, I loved her, I still do, but sitting here with a murder charge on my head, I'd be a complete idiot if I didn't admit that I got played."

"Sergio, honey, we don't know anything for certain just yet," Alberta said.

"Not the whole picture, but I know enough that Natalie lied to me," Sergio said. "How much of our relationship was a lie I don't know, but there's so much I don't know about her background, her business connections, now she might be involved in using drugs. It doesn't change my feelings for her, and I wish to God she wasn't dead, but the fact is I didn't know Natalie at all."

"Don't be so hard on yourself, honey," Lisa Marie said. "A lot of people get fooled when they're too scared to face the truth."

Sergio started to laugh. "Now you sound like Natalie."

"Why would you say that?" Lisa Marie asked.

"Because she always told me I had a scared look in my eyes," Sergio said. "That I always looked like a deer in the headlights."

No one laughed along with Sergio because what they were thinking wasn't funny. It was frightening. The most famous deer in the world just happened to be working at St. Clare's Hospital and was two feet away when Natalie's dead body was discovered.

Thanks to Natalie's message from beyond the grave, Bambi DeBenedetto just became their prime suspect.

CHAPTER 22

Un nome è solo l'inizio di una persona.

If any night ever called for a smorgasbord of Entenmann's samplings and pitchers filled with Red Herrings, it was tonight. The Ferraras had had a few difficult days and they needed to regroup and refocus their efforts. They had acquired a lot of information that, when examined individually, didn't seem to mean very much, but when compiled, those unconnected scraps of knowledge could quite possibly form evidence that could be strong enough to prove Sergio wasn't Natalie's killer. They had done it before, there was no reason to think they couldn't do it again. Unfortunately, they had two big strikes against them.

First, Sergio's story, while plausible, was filled with holes. No one else but Kwon could vouch for Sergio's whereabouts the day of the Ball, and that was only for a few hours in the middle of the day. Vinny had told them that he interviewed Kwon and took his statement, but the only reason Kwon remembered Sergio had been in the Tranquility Diner was because he threw a cup of coffee against the wall. It had been an element of Sergio's alibi that he didn't disclose but, unfortunately, further proof that the young man had an anger management issue. It was hardly the type of revelation a murder suspect wanted exposed at their trial.

Then there was the fact that Sergio was found at the scene of the crime literally holding the murder weapon in his hands. It was feasible that his depressed and angry emotional state caused him to truly not know that he was walking into the Ball from the kitchen. Vinny had been able to track down the banquet hall employee who held open the back door for Sergio while taking a cigarette break, but the employee couldn't identify Sergio, nor had he seen Natalie and her companion enter the building. The story when taken in its entirety could be twisted by a prosecutor to make it appear that Sergio hadn't followed his girlfriend per her instructions, but rather stalked Natalie to the Ball intent on killing her.

The second obstacle was the DA. Roxanne Garcia grew up in poverty, spent time in the foster care system, earned full scholarships to both Rutgers University and Brooklyn Law School, and was the youngest person to become the DA in New Jersey history. She was determined, tough, and once she made a decision she would not bend.

For whatever reason she had chosen to make an example of Sergio. Perhaps it was because she felt—incorrectly—that he was one of those spoiled kids who never had to work a day in his life. Perhaps it was because she had read about how the Ferraras had been instrumental in solving several other murders in the area and considered their help to be interference. Or perhaps it was because she was simply convinced of his guilt. It didn't matter. The only thing that mattered was that she was going to exert every ounce of pressure and her considerable power as top legal dog in the state on the prosecuting team to make Sergio out to be the heartless, soulless, premeditated murderer she believed him to be. If the Ferraras were going to solve this case in time to prevent Sergio from going to trial, they needed to get their facts straight and sort out their clues.

Before they did anything, however, they needed to convince Lola to take her nap somewhere other than the kitchen table.

"Lola!" Alberta shouted. "Scoot."

Lola didn't move. She was lying on her back, her front paws raised and framing her face, her back paws stretched and pointing outward. Her position was as unladylike as a lady cat could possibly get.

"Lo-la," Jinx sang. "We need to use the ta-ble."

The only thing Jinx's singing did was act as a lullaby to put Lola to sleep. She yawned, stretched, and rolled onto her side. Her new tartan plaid holiday collar with the jangly bell jingled only once and then remained silent as Lola dozed off. As usual, Alberta's cat wasn't going to let the drama around her interfere with her nap.

"Do what we always do and arrange the food around her," Helen said.

As they were placing the boxes of Entenmann's on the table around the edges of Lola's body, the cat meowed and rolled over onto its stomach. Jinx poured Red Herrings into everyone's glasses and they filled their plates with several pieces of pastry before sitting down and calling to order this official meeting of their unofficial detective agency. As their designated leader, Alberta began the proceedings by shoving a piece of cheese danish in her mouth and saying the one thing that had been on everyone's mind.

"What do we really know about Bambi DeBenedetto?"

"She's got a stupid name," Lisa Marie said.

"Ma!" Jinx cried. "You seriously have to stop mocking people for no reason."

"I'm sorry, I'm one of those people who judges a book by its cover," Lisa Marie replied. "And I don't like her cover."

"*Un nome è solo l'inizio di una persona*," Alberta said.

"If you're going to yell at me, Ma, you have to do it in English," Lisa Marie said. "I know about five words in Italian and only four of them are appropriate to say in mixed company."

"What mixed company?" Helen asked. "We're all family here."

"I was referring to Lola," Lisa Marie said.

"What I said is that a name is just the start of someone," Alberta explained. "There's a lot more to Bambi that we need to figure out."

"She's the hospital administrator at St. Clare's," Jinx said.

"Which means she has an impressive position and probably makes a good salary," Alberta added.

"She doesn't make as much as you think," Joyce said. "The average salary is about one hundred twenty thousand dollars a year, and it could be less than that."

"That sounds like a pretty good salary to me," Lisa Marie said.

"Not for a widow whose husband left her a mountain of debt," Joyce said.

"Do you know about everyone's financial background?" Helen asked.

"No, but I know where to look," Joyce said. "I did some digging into Ms. DeBenedetto after I saw her at a Mistletoe Ball meeting the other day."

"The Mistletoe Ball crashed and burned already," Alberta said. "Were you having another meeting to dwell on what went wrong?"

"To figure out how to salvage the wreck," Joyce said. "The Ball was supposed to ring in the season, but it was also supposed to act as a fundraising event for the hospital. It's been decided that the Ball will be resurrected yet again in another week."

"Are you serious, Aunt Joyce?" Jinx asked. "I hadn't heard anything about it at the paper."

"It took a lot of persuasion and I had to use every negotiating tactic in my toolbox, but we just got confirmation from the Manor this morning that they would give us the Diamond room and we'd only have to cover the cost of food and drink," Joyce explained. "The announcement will be made tomorrow."

"Freddy will be so excited," Jinx said. "He'll finally be able to get his award."

"Unless something happens that makes the second Mistletoe Ball more of a disaster than the first," Alberta said.

"Ma! How could it possibly be worse?" Lisa Marie asked. "A woman was murdered and my son was carted off to jail."

"Hang around in this town long enough, honey, and you'll never ask that question again," Helen said.

"Joyce, tell us more about Bambi," Alberta said, getting the conversation back on track. "What made you want to dig up information on her?"

"At the meeting I noticed she was wearing a Cartier Panthère watch," Joyce said.

"I noticed that too when I interviewed her," Jinx said. "It costs thousands."

"Depending upon the exact style, it could go up to twenty thousand," Joyce replied. "Which is a lot of money to spend on a watch for anyone, but especially a woman who, financially speaking, is in the same boat as a waitress working for tips at a diner."

"I didn't notice her watch when I bumped into her the other day," Alberta said. "I did notice she was carrying shopping bags filled with purchases from the most expensive stores in town."

"She's definitely a clotheshorse," Jinx said. "Thanks to the crash course in fashion I've received from Aunt Joyce, I can confirm that Bambi's wardrobe is expensive."

"When emotions are tied to financial well-being, people act irrationally," Joyce said. "I don't know Bambi very well, but it's common for people, women mostly, to overspend when they're broke. The rush they get from buying an expensive item tricks them into thinking they're actually well-off."

Lisa Marie raised her hand. "Guilty!"

"All of us at this table except for Lola and Helen have done the same thing at one point in our lives," Joyce said.

"How do you know Bambi's expenses are considerable?" Lisa Marie asked.

"When it comes to money Joyce is an expert," Helen said.

"I worked hard for my money, but also too, I worked hard to make my money work smart," Joyce said. "I invested wisely, and unlike Bambi I never lived beyond my means, especially when it came to real estate."

"What did you find out?" Alberta asked.

"Her husband, Walt, was a dentist, but he drove his practice into the ground because he preferred to spend more time at the track betting on the horses than in his office working on his patients," Joyce explained.

"Hold on for just one God forsaken second!" Lisa Marie yelled. "Bambi's husband's name was Walt as in Walt Disney?"

"No, Walt as in Walter DeBenedetto," Joyce said. "But you're right, I never made that connection before."

"Isn't that something, Walt and Bambi," Alberta said. "I wonder if that's what brought the two of them together."

"I always thought Bambi was Tony Bennett's distant relative," Helen said. "His real name is Anthony Dominick Benedetto."

"She's a distant relative of Mickey Mouse!" Lisa Marie shrieked. "And you people call yourselves detectives?"

"When it's a detail that doesn't help us in any way, Ma, we just gloss over it," Jinx said.

"Speaking of details, Joyce, what were you saying about Bambi living beyond her means?" Alberta asked.

"When I saw the kind of watch she was wearing and Alberta told me her suspicions, I thought I'd be proactive and dig around a bit to find out her net worth and what kind of a mortgage she has," Joyce said. "Let's just say she's no Ebenezer Scrooge. Her money doesn't stay in one place long enough to get dusty."

"How much debt does she have?" Helen asked.

"She's had a mortgage on her home in Newton for seventeen years and still owes seven hundred fifty thousand dollars on it," Joyce conveyed.

"She lives in Newton?" Alberta asked.

"Forever," Joyce replied. "First in a condo by herself and then in this house. Why?"

"Well, Sergio said Natalie had a meeting with a woman in Newton," Alberta explained.

"You think Natalie was supposed to have a meeting with Bambi?" Jinx asked.

"It's possible," Alberta said. "What else did you find, Joyce?"

"Her stock portfolio, which is very small, hasn't shown a gain of more than three percent in ten years, and she owes over thirty thousand in credit card debit and another twenty-five to the IRS," Joyce explained.

"*Santo Cielo!*" Alberta cried. "What's her credit score?"

"Does she even have one?" Helen asked.

"Around four hundred, which is considered very poor," Joyce said. "Or as we used to say on Wall Street, 'Next!'"

"How can Bambi afford all the stuff she's been buying if she has to pay off such a huge sum with the IRS?" Lisa Marie asked. "Tommy and I had a bit of a tax issue a couple of years back and I will say the IRS worked with us to come up with a repayment schedule, but they were relentless until it was paid off."

"She steals things," Jinx announced.

"Lovey, do you have proof of that?" Alberta asked.

"As a matter of fact, I do," Jinx replied.

Jinx took out her cell phone and scrolled through some

photos until she came to the one that captured the incriminating evidence.

"Voila!" Jinx exclaimed. "Proof that Bambi is more like Ursula."

"Who's Ursula?" Lisa Marie asked.

"The octopus who stole Ariel's voice in *The Little Mermaid*," Helen replied. "You have to brush up on the classics Lisa Marie."

"Bambi is a thief!" Joyce cried. "Those are my shoes."

They examined the photo more closely, and Jinx explained that she took the picture in Bambi's office because the vintage red patent leather pumps she was wearing were Joyce's. Bambi admitted that she took them from Joyce's closet years ago and had no intention of returning them. That in itself was proof of thievery, but Alberta thought there was something else interesting in the photo.

"What's that in her closet?" she asked.

"Looks like a clump of yellow material," Lisa Marie replied.

"Did she steal my yellow cashmere sweater, too?" Joyce asked. "For the life of me I can't find that thing."

"I don't think it's a sweater," Alberta said. "I can't be positive, but it looks like a wig."

"Gram you might be right!" Jinx cried. "And there were strands of synthetic yellow hair found on Natalie's body."

"That's proof that Bambi killed Natalie!" Lisa Marie exclaimed.

"Not necessarily," Alberta said. "Even if it is a wig, it might not be the same one and Bambi does have an airtight alibi since she was at the Ball when the murder took place."

"Maybe the killer hid it there thinking it would be safe among the rest of Bambi's stolen goods," Helen said.

"*Dio mio*! I remembered something else about Bambi's watch!" Alberta cried.

"We're back to the watch?" Lisa Marie asked. "I feel like I'm down in Boca watching some retirees play tennis."

"What about the watch, Berta?" Joyce asked.

"Like I said, I didn't notice what kind of watch it was, but I did notice that it was on Bambi's right wrist," she replied. "Which would suggest that she's left-handed, just like Pedro thinks the killer might be."

"Maybe the southpaw is the murderer," Helen said.

"Natalie could have gone to meet with her to blackmail her and expose her part in whatever scheme she was really up to," Alberta said. "It's a long shot I know. I mean, if Bambi is the murderer and she's involved in something illegal and is in debt up to her eyeballs, how does she run around town like she doesn't have a care in the world?"

"Because she's figured out a way to make some money on the side," Jinx said.

"By doing what, lovey?" Alberta asked.

"Selling drugs on the street."

Jinx's pronouncement silenced everyone for a moment until they began to digest the accusation and reexamine their clues one by one. Once they discovered Natalie had lived with Rudy, they visited him, and he told them he was a pharmaceutical salesman who introduced Natalie to business contacts in New Jersey. Natalie was found in Newton, New Jersey, which was the location of the Trolloppe cardiac wing, and the only reason they knew about the place was because Rudy texted them the clue. D. Edward Carmichael was the hospital administrator of the institution, which was also highlighted in an article that Rudy had dog-eared in *New Jersey Pharma* magazine. The trail so far was one straight line that logically explained why the murder victim had traveled from Florida to New York to New Jersey. It was an even shorter line to explain why both Natalie and Rudy wound up dead in Tranquility.

The Sussex County Medical Center had entered into a joint venture with St. Clare's Hospital, causing Carmichael to work in tandem with the St. Clare's hospital administrator, who was none other than Bambi DeBenedetto. They had clearly established a link connecting Natalie to Bambi, but how could they persuade anyone to believe that Bambi was a drug dealer?

"We need more proof before we can throw around an accusation like that," Alberta said.

"Berta's right," Helen said. "Bambi and Carmichael are highly respected people in this community."

"We've known some highly respected people who committed some terrible crimes, Aunt Helen," Jinx said.

"That's true, but if we want the allegation to stick, we need tangible proof," Helen said. "We need a smoking gun to show that Bambi DeBenedetto or D. Edward Carmichael have gotten their hands dirty."

"I need to take another pause here," Lisa Marie said. "What in the world does the D stand for?"

Everyone looked at Joyce, who they suspected would have an answer.

"I have no idea," Joyce said. "For as long as I've known him, I've called him Carmichael."

"It's dumb for a grown man to have an initial for a first

name," Lisa Marie said. "That's proof enough for me that he's hiding something."

"You might be right, Leese," Alberta said. "The first time we went to see him we overheard him having a fight with a former employee who stormed out of his office, and the woman called him Eddy."

"Sounds like they may have had a personal relationship too," Jinx commented, "if she addressed him so informally."

"My thought exactly," Alberta said. "Carmichael also claimed not to know Rudy or Natalie, but there was something in his eyes that told me he was lying. Though it was hard to tell because he was dressed like Santa Claus."

"Another reason not to trust him," Lisa Marie said. "Grown men don't dress up in costumes."

"He said he was going to entertain kids in the pediatric cancer ward," Joyce said.

"A likely excuse!" Lisa Marie shouted.

"I have to agree with my mother," Jinx said. "I don't trust the guy. He's shifty and his behavior is odd."

"You know who else falls into that category?" Alberta asked, then answered her own question. "Dr. Kylie Manzini."

"How so?" Helen asked.

"At the Mistletoe Ball she was quite upset by Natalie's death," Alberta said.

"We were all shocked, Berta," Joyce said.

"It was more than shock," Alberta said. "At first she was fine and then she was crying like something about her murder clicked, and Carmichael has holding her by the arm."

"Maybe she realized Bambi was the murderer," Helen said.

"She's also heading the new research lab. Maybe she's planning on doing more in that lab than look for a cure for cancer," Alberta proposed. "It's outlandish, I know, but it isn't out of the realm of possibility."

Lisa Marie shook her head. "I don't like any of this. I mean, I never liked Natalie and I'm not going soft just because she was murdered brutally and shoved unceremoniously inside some life-size Christmas decoration, which I know makes me sound as cold-blooded as the snowwoman Natalie burst out of, but this whole drug dealing thing frightens me. Had Natalie not been killed who knows what would've become of Sergio? He might have gotten caught up in the whole thing all because he loved the wrong woman."

"Like Mike DeDordo, who wrote in to me," Helen said.

"That name doesn't sound right," Lisa Marie said.

"Knock it off with the names, Ma," Jinx said.

"No, she's right," Joyce added. "It is odd."

"Because it isn't his real name!" Alberta shouted. "*Dio mio*! Break it down. Mike for Michael, then D, and Edordo is Edward."

"It's Santa Claus!" Lisa Marie screamed.

"D. Edward Carmichael is Mike DeDordo," Alberta said.

"Berta, that's brilliant!" Joyce cried.

"Maybe he was writing to me about Natalie," Helen suggested.

"It would fit if Natalie was telling us the truth about

her bad family life," Joyce said. "He was trying to protect her like a father should."

"Joyce, remember he told us that the new wing was built thanks to anonymous donors?" Alberta asked. "Maybe 'anonymous donors' is synonymous with drug money."

Alberta closed her eyes and conjured up all the key players in her mind—Rudy, Natalie, Bambi, Carmichael, even Kylie—and tried to remember how they appeared the first time she saw them. How were they acting? What did they look like? Was there something they were hiding? She opened her eyes because she remembered seeing something Rudy didn't want her to see.

"*Per l'amor el cielo*!" Alberta cried. "They're definitely part of this whole drug dealing thing."

"What did you figure out now, Gram?" Jinx asked.

"The boxes I saw in Rudy's closet had stickers on them in the shape of a flower!" Alberta cried. "It didn't make sense so it slipped my mind, but it couldn't be any clearer: The Flower drug was in those boxes."

"Oh my God, Gram! That's proof that they're all somehow involved in selling this new drug," Jinx claimed.

"Then we need to take a closer look at Bambi, Carmichael, and Kylie," Jinx said. "I've rescheduled my interview with Carmichael because he bailed on me the last time."

"I'm going with Sloan to his checkup with Kylie," Alberta said.

"I can make some excuse to meet with Bambi," Joyce said.

"That leaves me to try to track down J. J.," Lisa Marie said.

"I guess that means we're making you an honorary member of the team," Jinx said. "Welcome aboard, Ma!"

"Let's raise a glass to the newest addition to the unofficial Ferrara Family Detective Agency," Alberta said.

All the ladies raised their glasses of Red Herring, but before they took a sip, Lisa Marie added, "Let's hope I don't live to regret it."

CHAPTER 23

Nessuno parla inglese?

Before Lisa Marie could express any further misgivings about her new unpaid and potentially unhealthy position within the family business, some other honorary members barged into the house. Lola woke from her nap, hissing loudly, as she watched Sloan, Freddy, and Father Sal struggling not to drop the six-foot Douglas fir they were carrying. Alberta's house would not be the only one in Tranquility without a Christmas tree.

"What are you doing?" Alberta asked. "I told you I wasn't putting up any decorations this year."

"I know that's what you said, but I know that's not what you meant," Sloan said.

"Do not argue with us, Alberta, we are three wise men bearing gifts," Father Sal said. "Frankincense and myrrh are so first century, but I have brought with me Barbra Streisand's Christmas album, which is certified gold."

"Where should we put this baby, Mrs. Scaglione?" Freddy said. "Please don't tell us there's no room at the inn because we'll collapse if we have to carry this back out to my truck."

Feeling like the one tone-deaf citizen of Whoville, Alberta knew she was outnumbered and didn't attempt to argue with the boys. Instead, she instructed them to put the tree in the corner of her living room. Jinx and Joyce helped move the floor lamp and the console table that usually lived in that area and placed those pieces in different parts of the living room. Then the ladies watched the men get to work putting the tree in its stand, making sure the trunk was held in tightly, and cutting the protective netting so the branches could stretch and come to life. Despite her protestations, it brought a smile to Alberta's face. The tree was exactly what had been missing from her home.

Christmas Day was rapidly approaching and even though the family was hoping for a Christmas miracle, their decorations remained in storage. The men completely understood the reasons why they were lacking holiday spirit, but they also understood that nothing would energize them more than if they took a break to decorate a tree. If Lola, whose hissing had turned into rapturous purrs, was any indication, the ladies would soon be humming carols and stringing lights on the tree. Which was exactly what happened.

"I know I shouldn't be enjoying myself with my husband trying to salvage his business and my son, God help him, in jail," Lisa Marie said. "But I am."

"Neither one of them would blame you," Alberta said. "These things take time, but we're getting closer to the truth."

"In the meantime, I have a box of ornaments that I've had stashed in my attic for years," Sloan said. "It's time we put them to good use."

"I bought some new decorations too, Mrs. Scaglione," Freddy said. "I hope I didn't overstep."

"You couldn't if you tried, Freddy," Alberta said. "Go get them so we can turn this place into our own little winter wonderland."

Alberta stared at Lisa Marie and her heart fluttered because she hadn't seen that expression for decades. Her daughter's smirk, combined with one raised eyebrow that lifted her birthmark an inch, could only mean one thing: She wholeheartedly approved of both Sloan and Freddy. Of course there was no reason not to approve of the men as they were kind, considerate, loyal, funny, and handsome.

"You and my daughter have snagged yourselves two fine men, I must say," Lisa Marie said. "I have a feeling I'm going to have to make the trip back up here for a wedding . . . or two."

"*Silenzio!*" Alberta shouted.

"If my gambling days weren't over, I'd bet my house that the Ferraras are going to have a wedding within the year," Lisa Marie said.

Alberta shook her head and laughed. She couldn't fully describe what it felt like to be standing so close to her daughter having a silly conversation with her, but part of her wanted to break down and cry and the other part wanted to hug her and not let her go. Both reactions might result in Lisa Marie packing up the Subaru and camping outside the correctional facility where Sergio was being held, so Alberta chose to keep her thoughts and arms to herself. Her opinions about decorating, those she shared openly.

"Freddy, what are those things you're putting on the tree?" Alberta asked.

"They're ornaments made to look like iconic Italian foods," Freddy explained. He then lifted the ornaments one by one from the box. "This one's a slice of pizza, here's a piece of lasagna, spaghetti and meatballs, ravioli, a little chicken parm, and, for dessert, a nice hunk of tiramisu."

"Jinx if you don't marry this fella, I will!" Lisa Marie exclaimed.

"Ma!" Jinx exclaimed loudly. "Ignore her, Freddy."

"Dude, competition is healthy," Freddy joked.

"The ornaments are beautiful, Freddy, thank you," Alberta said. "Where'd Sloan get to with his ornaments?"

"I don't know," Freddy said. "He was right behind me."

When Sloan walked through the kitchen door carrying a large box of ornaments, he looked nervous because he brought with him uninvited company. Jinx looked even more frightened because she knew her personal and professional lives were about to collide head-on. Lisa Marie just looked furious.

"Is that your double-crossing, two-timing boss?!" Lisa Marie screamed.

"I have been called that on one or two occasions," Wyck replied.

Lisa Marie ran into the kitchen and was only prevented from making contact with Wyck because Jinx and Alberta each grabbed an arm and held her back. No one put a hand over her mouth so they couldn't stop her from threatening to kill Wyck.

"You better get out of this house now!" Lisa Marie

screamed. "Or I swear on my mother's life you're gonna be front-page news as Tranquility's next murder victim!"

"Please, I'm not here to cause trouble," Wyck said. "I come bearing gifts."

He lifted his arms to show that he was holding a bag in each hand, the contents of which were presumably some kind of peace offering.

"We already used that line, Wyck," Father Sal said. "You'll have to come up with something more original."

"How about *I'm sorry*?" Wyck said.

"Sorry for what?" Lisa Marie asked. "For plastering my son's face all over your two-bit paper?"

"Hey, I work there, Ma!" Jinx shouted.

"Except for the articles Jinx writes," Lisa Marie added. "The rest of *The Herald* isn't worth using for toilet paper."

"Mrs. Maldonado, I understand why you're angry and that's why I felt it important that I try to explain my position," Wyck said.

"The only position I want to see you in is horizontal with your arms folded across your chest!" Lisa Marie screamed, breaking free of Alberta and Jinx's hold.

"Ma! Enough!" Jinx shouted. "Wyck has a job to do, he runs a newspaper, and like it or not, Sergio is news. Wyck could've turned the whole thing into a sensationalistic nightmare, but he hasn't. He's bent over backward to ensure that Sergio gets treated fairly in every article that's written about the murder."

"That's right, Lees," Alberta said. "He left out Natalie's name because Vinny asked him to until they can reach her next of kin."

"I consider Jinx the daughter I never had, all of us at the paper consider her to be family, except maybe Calhoun," Wyck admitted. "They have what could be described as a professional rivalry that pushes them to produce good journalism, but doesn't always evoke compassion."

Sloan leaned closer to Wyck and whispered, "Stay on track."

"What I'm trying to say is that I'm not only an editor in chief, I'm a father too, and I understand your pain," Wyck said. "I'm trying my best to make sure we don't make matters worse and I wanted you to know that."

Everyone stared at Lisa Marie to see how she would respond, but she kept her gaze fixed on Wyck, her arms crossed in front of her chest and her lips etched into what seemed like a permanent snarl.

"What do you say, Ma?" Jinx asked.

"How about some squid pro quo?" she asked.

"I think you mean *quid* pro quo," Joyce corrected.

"We say things differently in Florida!" Lisa Marie said.

"What do you have in mind?" Wyck asked.

"In exchange for me not ripping every fake strand of red hair out of your head," Lisa Marie started. "You let Jinx write an exposé on this new street drug called Flower."

"First, I'm a natural ginger," Wyck said. "And second, that's an excellent idea."

"It is, Ma!" Jinx cried. "It gives me a credible reason to interview Carmichael and Bambi again and even pay a visit to Kylie's lab."

"The apple really doesn't fall very far from the tree," Helen said. "Even if that apple rolled all the way down the hill and didn't stop until it landed in Florida."

"If you do anything to cross me, Red, I meant what I said, I'll kill you," Lisa Marie stated.

"I'll print whatever Jinx writes," Wyck said.

"Then you shall live," Lisa Marie said. "For now."

"Ever since I've been spending more time with this family, I really do feel that in a past life I hobnobbed with the Inquisition," Sal said.

"Dude, Catholics don't believe in reincarnation," Freddy said.

"I've always been a rebel, Frederick," Sal replied.

"Now that it's been decided the kitchen won't see any bloodshed," Helen said. "Why don't you hand out your gifts, Wyck?"

"I know you're the best cook in all of Tranquility, Alberta, but not such a great baker," Wyck said.

"That's the understatement of the century," Alberta said.

"I thought you'd all like a taste of my homeland, some Irish trifle," Wyck said.

Jinx's eyes lit up. "Is it Mrs. Wycknowski's personal recipe?"

"She'd divorce me if I ate any other kind," Wyck said.

"This is going to be a special treat, people, this trifle is almost as good as Gram's lasagna," Jinx said.

"And what's in the other bag?" Sloan asked.

"Evidence of Helen's success." Wyck beamed. "This week's Big Sister letters."

"*Sul serio*?" Alberta asked. "That whole bag of letters in just one week."

"Yup," Wyck said. "And every one of them is for Helen."

"I didn't think people wrote letters anymore," Jinx commented.

"They do if they want to preserve some kind of anonymity," Wyck explained. "We've received a slew of e-mails too, but they can be easily traced. Big Sister's the biggest hit *The Herald*'s had in years and it's all thanks to Helen's tough love approach."

"Just remember that it runs in the family," Lisa Marie said. "Now, why don't you leave your gifts and go?"

"Ma, stop being so rude," Jinx begged.

"Your boss is still standing, isn't he?" Lisa Marie asked.

"Thanks, Wyck, but you should probably go," Helen said. "I've got some letters to read and we may need to tranquilize my niece."

After Wyck escaped without enduring bodily harm, Alberta turned to her daughter to ask why she wished harm on her.

"Why'd you swear on my life, Leese?" Alberta asked. "I'm not dead."

"When did I do that?" Lisa Marie asked.

"When you threatened to kill Wyck," Alberta replied.

"Which time?" Father Sal asked.

"The first time," Alberta clarified. "You said 'I swear on my mother's life' that he'd be the next murder victim in town."

"Don't nitpick, Ma!" Lisa Marie cried. "Be grateful that in my moment of distress you're the first person I thought of."

It had been such a miserable December, Alberta decided to take any bit of holiday cheer that came her way.

An hour later the holiday cheer had multiplied tenfold.

The first floor of Alberta's home had been transformed into what could've been the centerfold spread of the holiday issue of *New Jersey Homes* magazine. The tree was fully decorated with ornaments, old and new, twinkling lights, silver garland, and the gold star topper Alberta's grandmother had given her so many decades ago. It was the same one that had been tossed to the wayside when Lisa Marie decided she wanted an all silver and white color scheme for her last Christmas with her parents. Alberta couldn't bring herself to use the topper to decorate her tree because it only conjured up bad memories, so it had been in a storage box all this time waiting for the perfect time to make its comeback.

Lisa Marie's humbled expression let Alberta know that her daughter immediately recognized the topper when Freddy placed it on the tree, and she understood its significance. "Looks like your grandmother's topper is back where it belongs," Lisa Marie said.

Alberta smiled and whispered in Lisa Marie's ear, "Just like my daughter."

The nativity was placed on the media center next to some elves taking a ride on a supersized candy cane, and the porcelain baby Jesus in a cradle of hay was placed on one of the end tables next to a gold crucifix candle. Tradition called for the cradle to remain empty until Christmas Eve, at which time the baby Jesus would be placed on the hay, symbolizing his birth. Like Father Sal, however, Alberta rebelled against the accepted ritual because seeing the baby on a daily basis filled her with joy. And that's what Christmas was all about.

It was also about food.

The group gathered around the table and devoured Wyck's trifle as Barbra continued to sing about the delights of the season. Alberta even gave Lola a little taste that quickly led to the cat sauntering into the living room to take up residence near the baby Jesus and lapse into a sugar-induced nap. Energized by the dessert, the rest of them decided to open Wyck's other gift, the letters to Helen seeking advice.

Helen read the signature of one of the letters and was confused. "What's an OG?"

"Original gangsta," Freddy explained.

"I'm giving advice to hardened criminals?" Helen asked.

"No, it comes from the hip-hop world," Freddy said.

"What about GOAT in all caps?" Helen asked.

"That's Greatest Of All Time," Joyce explained.

"Hmm, of course you'd know that one," Helen snapped.

"*Ah Madon*!" Alberta cried. "*Nessuno parla inglese*?"

"This is new English, Berta," Sloan said. "We're a bit too old to speak it fluently."

"What about Noctor J?" Helen asked. "Is that a new English phrase?"

Finally, the group was stumped. Maybe it was someone who was nocturnal and preferred to stay up all night. Or someone who fancied themselves another Doctor J, the nickname given to the great basketball player Julius Irving. Or it was a Tony Orlando and Dawn superfan who liked to knock three times.

"Maybe the letter itself will give a clue," Alberta suggested. "Read it to us."

"'Dear Big Sister, I'm in trouble,'" Helen started. "'I got involved with a woman who double crossed me and now I've lost my career and can't find a job. I sold her pink footballs and Goodfellas and China girls and I've got absolutely nothing to show for it! They took everything from me. I want my life back or I swear I'm going to take hers because she's the real reason I'm in this mess. Big Sister, help me before I do something we'll both regret.' And it's signed Noctor J."

"This Noctor person threatened a woman's life," Lisa Marie said.

"Is there a postage mark on the envelope?" Alberta asked.

"Yes," Helen said. "It was mailed in town the day before the Mistletoe Ball."

"You mean the day before Natalie was killed," Lisa Marie said, getting more excited.

"Let's not get ahead of ourselves," Alberta said. "There's a lot about this letter that doesn't make any sense."

"It makes a lot of sense, Gram," Jinx said.

"What do you mean, lovey?" Alberta asked.

"I didn't want to burst my mother's bubble before, but I've already been planning on writing about the string of overdoses from this new Flower drug that's been making people OD," Jinx explained. "I've been doing some research and all those things mentioned in that letter are street drugs."

"You mean *Goodfellas* isn't the movie that won Joe Pesci an Oscar?" Alberta asked.

"'China Girl' isn't a nod to one of David Bowie's biggest hits?" Helen asked.

"Also too, pink footballs isn't part of some new Lady NFL?" Joyce added.

"That's a *no* to all of the above, but extra points to Aunt Helen for knowing David Bowie's back catalog," Jinx said.

"What are they, then?" Alberta asked.

"They're all names for illegal drugs sold on the black market," Jinx conveyed.

"Oh my God!" Lisa Marie cried. "You were right, Ma! This fits perfectly in to what you were saying before, that Tranquility is the center of some new drug ring."

"Then you think this Noctor J is a drug dealer?" Sloan asked.

"It's very possible," Alberta said. "We looked at our clues and they all seem to point in the same direction, that someone in town is a drug kingpin."

"Berta, you're going to think I'm crazy, but I've heard this name before," Joyce said. "I think it was when I was with you."

"You and I went to Rudy's apartment, but I don't remember him saying anything about a noctor," Alberta said.

"But then the two of us paid Carmichael a visit and that woman ran out of his office," Joyce explained.

"That's right!" Alberta screamed. "He was yelling at her and he called her a noctor. We had no idea what it meant at the time, but it was definitely an insult."

"Maybe this woman was a bad doctor," Father Sal suggested.

"I don't think so, Sal," Joyce replied. "The woman was looking for a job and said she'd clean bedpans, that's more of what a nurse does."

"That's it!" Alberta cried. "Carmichael told the woman that whatever she did was bad enough to get her nurse's license revoked. A nurse impersonating a doctor fits the bill, so a noctor must be a nurse who thinks she's a doctor."

"Oh my God!" Jinx exclaimed. "This means that Noctor J is the woman Mike DeDordo is in love with."

"Dude, who's Mike DeDordo?" Freddy asked.

"D. Edward Carmichael," Lisa Marie replied. "Keep up, will ya."

"She must've done something huge to get fired and blackballed from ever working as a nurse in a hospital again," Jinx said.

"And want to get revenge on the person she blames for destroying her career," Joyce added.

"It sounds more and more like that person was Natalie Vespa and this Noctor J killed her as payback for destroying her life," Alberta said. "Lovey, I think it's time you paid Carmichael a visit to find out exactly who he fired."

"We can go tomorrow," Jinx said. "I've already e-mailed him asking to set up another time for an interview since he canceled on me the last time. We'll just show up and not leave until he sees us."

"I'd love to, but I'm going with Sloan to see Dr. Manzini for his checkup," Alberta said.

"You don't have to come with me," Sloan said. "I'm sure it's just routine anyway."

"I want to be there in case the results, God forbid, aren't good, so don't argue with me," Alberta said.

Sloan smiled and even blushed a little. "I wouldn't dare."

"I can go with you, Jinx," Joyce said. "I need to talk to him now that the Mistletoe Ball has been rescheduled."

"That's perfect," Alberta said. "Don't let Carmichael off the hook until he gives you that woman's name. I have a strong feeling that she's our Noctor J."

If the women didn't have to interrogate a hospital administrator who they suspected of somehow being involved with a drug dealer who may have also ventured into the world of homicide, it really would have been a very lovely morning. There was fluffy, new-fallen snow on the ground, the sun was glistening on the icicles that had formed on bare branches, and birds were whistling a tune that sounded like a higher-pitched version of the deep-voiced Bing Crosby's classic rendition of "White Christmas." But Jinx and Joyce had a job to do and they couldn't be distracted no matter how holiday perfect their surroundings looked. They were, after all, semiprofessionals.

Standing outside Carmichael's office, they got the feeling that he was not quite professional either. For the second time in a row he was involved in a screaming match with an unidentified woman. His door was closed this time, but they could still hear him yelling with someone and dismissing any attempt at maintaining professional decorum.

"Don't you dare threaten me!" he shouted. "After all this time have I said anything? Have I done anything wrong?!"

"It better stay that way or else!" the woman yelled.

"Or else what?! What exactly are you trying to say?"

"You know what I'm trying to say, and you know that I'm not afraid to back up my words with actions."

"You listen to me . . ."

"I don't listen to anybody, haven't you figured that out by now? I have not gotten where I am by following the orders of weak-willed, lovesick fools like you and I'll be damned if I'm going to let you or anyone else take me down because they don't have the guts to follow through!"

"You've changed, do you know that? You're out of control and I want no part of this anymore."

"It's too late to back out now, buster! You're in this until the day you die, remember that!"

The women had just enough time to jump away from the door and back into the seats outside Carmichael's office before the door burst open.

"Bambi," Joyce said. "I thought I recognized your voice."

They didn't recognize Carmichael at first, however, because he was once again dressed up in costume, this time as a nutcracker. Had the situation been less serious it would've been comical. A woman resembling a plus-size Barbie doll standing next to a man who looked like he belonged in a sugarplum fairy tale. But no one was laughing. In fact, Bambi looked like she wanted to kill Joyce. It took the woman a moment to transform her expression into something more appropriate when unexpectedly bumping into an acquaintance.

"Joyce!" Bambi squealed. "How lovely to see you. I was just telling Carmichael how excited I am now that the Mistletoe Ball is back on the calendar."

"It sounded more like you were yelling," Jinx said.

Daggers flew out of Bambi's eyes and directly into Jinx's throat. "What the French call a passionate *bataille d'esprit,* a tête à tête . . ."

"A rip-roaring brawl," Jinx said, finishing Bambi's sentence.

"First Santa Claus, now a nutcracker, are all your suits at the dry cleaner?" Joyce asked.

A raucous laugh emerged from Carmichael's belly that could only be described as fake. "Joyce, you are a wit, I've always said that about you," he said. "I'm the master of ceremonies at tonight's lighting ceremony for the Winter Wonderland at Tranquility Park."

"Let's hope the ceremony doesn't end in tragedy like the first Mistletoe Ball," Bambi said. "Jinx, dear, like I was telling your grandmother, I'm so sorry to hear that your brother has been arrested for Natalie's murder. I'm sure it's a complete misunderstanding."

Bambi had no idea she had misunderstood Jinx's ability to zero in on the most important facts of a conversation no matter how personal that conversation may have been.

"I didn't realize you knew Natalie," Jinx said.

Again, a pall took hold of Bambi's face and any trace of politeness, friendliness, or humanity disappeared, leaving only the unmistakable mask of hatred. It didn't go away even when she spoke.

"I must have read it in the papers," Bambi said.

"The police haven't released her name yet because they haven't been able to contact her family," Jinx said. "Vinny did mention her name when he arrested my brother, but the way you said it just now, it was like she was a friend of yours."

"Me? Friends with a murder victim? That's absurd," Bambi said. "Which is what I told Vinny just this morning when he came to search my office."

Jinx couldn't believe that Bambi was speaking so openly about having her office searched by the police. They had advised Vinny about the wig they thought Bambi was hiding in her closet, but they didn't know he was going to jump on that clue so quickly. Though in retrospect, Jinx realized, that's exactly what cops do—follow up on clues. Since Vinny hadn't contacted them, she assumed the police must've come up empty and whatever they saw in the photo was nothing that could link Bambi to Natalie's murder.

"I told the police to search to their heart's content and they did," Bambi said. "And then they apologized for disrupting my day."

"The police are only doing their job and as an investigative reporter I completely understand the need to be tenacious and follow every possible lead," Jinx said. "So I'll ask you again, how do you know Natalie?"

Bambi's eyes flitted about the room and her hand fluttered underneath her double chin. She raised a chubby finger and nodded her head several times. "I know what it must have been, Luke told me her name, he still has ties to the morgue, and you know how that boy loves to gossip."

Jinx did know Luke, and she knew that when it came to hospital matters his lips couldn't be tighter if they were sewn together.

"That must be it," Jinx said. "I have to remember not to tell Luke a secret because it'll spread all over the hospital faster than one of those airborne viruses that refuse to stay put in the jungle."

"Yes, well, if you'll excuse me, I have to get back to St. Clare's," Bambi said. She started to march away and then abruptly turned around. "I almost forget the reason I came here in the first place. After the . . . incident at the Ball we beefed up security, so you'll need this new badge to gain access to both buildings."

She pulled out a laminated badge from her cleavage and handed it to Carmichael. Luckily, he was wearing white gloves.

"Thank you, Bambi," Carmichael said, holding the badge gingerly.

"Joyce, I have one for you too," Bambi said. "It's only

temporary and will expire at the end of the month. You can pick it up from my assistant."

"Thank you," Joyce said. "That will definitely come in handy."

"Toodles!" Bambi said. "There's really no rest for the weary."

Jinx was going to point out that the original biblical expression was "No rest for the wicked," but she didn't want to point out the obvious. She also didn't want to appear too obvious with Carmichael and start interrogating him, so she let Joyce control the course of the conversation. At least for a while.

Joyce had begun the discussion by asking him how they should handle the silent auction at the rescheduled Mistletoe Ball. She then moved the conversation to a topic that had broader medical implications and wanted to know what the hospital was doing in light of the new street drug Flower that had been introduced into town. Carmichael started to fidget in his chair, and he pulled off his white beard and top hat to reveal a face moist with sweat. He was nervous, and if Bambi's perception of him was correct and he was weak, Jinx felt it was time to use both those traits to her advantage. Her brother's life was on the line and she needed to be the tough big sister. It was time to channel her Aunt Helen.

"Could we please cut to the chase?" Jinx asked. "We know you're involved in something dubious and possibly illegal with Bambi."

"That is slander!" Carmichael cried. "I have done nothing wrong."

"That might be true, but from what we overheard, it sounds as if you know about something that's not on the up-and-up," Joyce said.

"Right now we're willing to let that slide," Jinx said. "All we want to know is the name of the woman you threw out of your office, the woman who wanted a job and you refused to give her one."

"I . . . I . . . don't know what you're talking about," Carmichael stuttered.

"The woman you called a noctor," Joyce added.

"That . . . that information is confidential," Carmichael said.

"You can tell us now or you can tell the police when Vinny slaps you with a subpoena to turn over your records," Jinx said.

"Medical records are legally protected," Carmichael said.

"Employment records aren't," Jinx said. "Give us the name and we'll leave."

"I'm not giving you anything and I'll ask you to leave right now."

Carmichael stood up, and although he was trying to look commanding and intimidating, the nutcracker ensemble he was sporting just made him look foolish. He must have understood what he looked like, or he was simply tired of playing a charade. He slumped back into his chair and, with an air of resignation, began to talk.

"She used to be a nurse and worked here and at St. Clare's," Carmichael said.

"She worked at both hospitals?" Joyce asked.

"Many nurses do that to make more money, like a freelancer," Carmichael said. "But Janine didn't just want more money, she wanted . . . more of everything, more status, more power. I tried to make her see she was only going to make things worse for herself, but she wouldn't listen to me. I really did try."

Whoever Janine was, Jinx thought, she was more than just a former nurse. She was someone Carmichael had tried to help, someone he was emotionally connected to. She'd figure that out later, right now she needed to know her last name.

"What's Janine's last name?" Jinx asked.

Ignoring her, Carmichael continued. "She overstepped and did things we couldn't ignore. You have to understand that Janine burned all her bridges, she wouldn't listen to any of us, that's why I had to let her go. Please understand, I can't say any more."

"Tell us her name and we'll leave you alone," Jinx said. "Otherwise I'm calling the police, and I think you know that the chief is a family friend."

Carmichael looked at both women. There was true fear in his eyes, but he didn't appear to be frightened by them, it looked like he was frightened of something far more dangerous. Jinx thought it could be Bambi, but she got the sense that it went deeper than that. She got the feeling that he was afraid of himself.

She remembered what Alberta once told her: Everyone had to take responsibility for their own actions. What had he done that would prevent him from uttering a woman's last name? What made him so terrified that he felt he couldn't trust anyone?

"You must understand, I'm an old man," Carmichael said. "My wife is infirm, and I was trying to protect this woman, be a father figure to her."

Don't fall for his sob story, Jinx told herself. And yet it was hard to ignore the sincerity in his voice mixed with something else. Shame? Humiliation?

"If you give us Janine's last name, I promise that we'll help you in any way we can," Jinx said.

A flicker of hope appeared in Carmichael's eyes. It was the lifeline he needed, to know that someone might be on the other side of whatever he did who would help him. He closed his eyes and breathed slowly and when he opened them he gave them the information they requested.

"Janniken," Carmichael said. "The woman I fired was Janine Janniken."

They realized Carmichael had given them more than they ever expected. He'd just told them who J. J. was.

CHAPTER 24

Una situación de ganar-ganar.

On the other side of town another mystery was unfolding.

Alberta and Sloan were sitting in the waiting room outside Dr. Manzini's makeshift office at St. Clare's Hospital. She was ending her traditional practice and transitioning into a research position, so she had given up her office in the main portion of the hospital and was working out of her new office on the research floor. Since she would be spending most of her time in the lab, it made sense that her office be located close by to prevent multiple rides up and down the elevator each day. Bambi's office was down the hall, and beyond that was the research lab, which was still under construction. It made for a noisy wait.

It was Sloan's final routine follow-up appointment after he was involved in an altercation a while ago that left him in a medically induced coma. He was incredibly lucky that his injuries hadn't triggered any long-range side effects, but medical protocol dictated that he check in with his doctor to make sure no unexpected complications arose. Thus far, Sloan had no strange symptoms that concerned him or could be traced back to the incident, but it was always better to be safe than sorry. Or as Alberta put it, *È meglio prevenire che curare.* Different language, same message.

Alberta also wanted to make sure that Sloan got the message that she was not going to let him deal with this alone. She didn't always know how to act like a girlfriend, but she knew how to act like a woman, and if a man went to see a doctor, his woman went with him. And Alberta was definitely Sloan's woman.

"You know you're not going to be able to come in with me to the examination room," Sloan said.

"I'll wait right out here," Alberta replied. "If there's an emergency, no one will go crazy trying to track me down."

"That's logical," Sloan said. "But there's not going to be an emergency, nothing's going to go wrong."

"Famous last words," Alberta said.

"I'm sure someone in your family went in for a routine doctor visit and wound up being rushed into surgery," Sloan said.

"You wouldn't act so smug if you knew what happened to my Uncle Leo," Alberta said.

"Are you going to make me guess?" Sloan asked.

"All you need to know is that it involved a four-hour operation, a three-week convalescence, and a very long catheter," Alberta said.

Sloan scrunched up his face and crossed his legs. He'd had to ask.

A buzzer on the receptionist's phone console rang and she picked up the receiver. She nodded twice, then put the phone back in its cradle. She looked in Sloan's direction and said, "The doctor will see you now."

"Thank you," Sloan replied. He gave Alberta a quick peck on the cheek and said, "I'll be out in a jiffy and don't you dare say a rosary while I'm gone."

Alberta smiled and playfully slapped Sloan on the shoulder. When he opened the door to the doctor's office, Alberta could hear Kylie greet Sloan, and it sounded as if she was genuinely happy to see him. Alberta was conflicted. She had nothing but respect for the doctor because as far as she was concerned, Kylie was the main reason Sloan was alive and had had no repercussions. However, she knew in her gut that Kylie was involved in Natalie's death. She didn't know how, but she vowed to find out. She touched the gold crucifix around her neck and made the sign of the cross, asking for guidance and forgiveness on the off chance she was wrong about Kylie. God wasn't the only one who noticed her actions.

"Spanish or Italian?" the receptionist asked.

"Me?" Alberta replied. "Italian."

"I'm Spanish, and the only people who make the sign of the cross in a doctor's waiting room are either Spanish or Italian," she said. "Filipinos too; they're very Christian, but you don't look like your people come from there."

"No, we're from Sicily," Alberta said. "And you?"

"Both my parents are from Madrid," she said. "I'm Maria, by the way."

"I'm Alberta."

"Don't worry, your husband is in good hands."

"Thank you, but Sloan's not my husband. He's, well, I

guess he's my boyfriend. I'm still not used to saying that."

"Oooh, *mírate*! I always say that love is in the air this time of year."

"That must be why there's no one waiting to see the doctor. Everyone's too happy to spend time in a hospital."

"Dr. Manzini is slowly handing her patients off to other doctors because she's going to head the lab. It should be a very exciting time for all of us."

"Will you be working with the doctor in the new lab?"

"On the administrative side. I'll be the doctor's executive assistant."

"Congratulations, that sounds wonderful."

Before Maria could respond the phone rang and she had to get to work.

Alberta sat back in her chair as Maria spoke to a patient on the phone, and she suddenly felt ashamed. What could Kylie possibly have to do with drug dealers or anything involving illegal activity? She was a celebrated surgeon, she was about to start a whole new career to find a cure for cancer. Alberta didn't know much more about the doctor other than that she had a sterling reputation and had never worked anywhere other than St. Clare's. Bambi and Carmichael, they were suspicious and were definitely hiding something, but not Kylie. The more Alberta thought about it, the more she realized she was letting her imagination grow wild, a common by-product of being an amateur detective, and it was ridiculous to think that the doctor was part of whatever evil scheme the others were up to.

Alberta was suddenly parched from her rambling internal monologue and searched her pocketbook for a mint or one of those butterscotch candies. She popped one in her mouth just as Maria started talking on the phone. Whoever was on the other end of the call was long-winded because all Maria said was "Yes, sir" every few seconds. She finally hung up and finished copying down the information on a telephone notepad.

"*Dios mio*," Maria said.

"I know that phrase in any language," Alberta commented.

Exasperated, Maria shook her head. "I don't know how the doctor does it. With everything going on at work, seeing patients, jumping every time Bambi barks, she also has to deal with her family."

Alberta nodded. "Family is the one thing you're forced to deal with no matter how hard life gets."

"I have my own crazy family and I don't have nearly the stress the doctor does, but even if I did, at least I know my family loves and supports me."

"You don't think Dr. Manzini gets the same love and support from her family?"

Alberta could tell from the way Maria was hesitating, she was reluctant to share too much information about Kylie's personal life. But Alberta recognized a talker when she met one, and she knew Maria just needed a little gentle prodding to spill Kylie's family secrets. Alberta didn't speak fluent Spanish, but it was a romance language like Italian, which meant there were many similarities that would help break down cultural barriers.

"Spaniards and Italians, we appreciate family, we understand no one is an individual," Alberta said. "Scandinavians, like Dr. Manzini's father, aren't like us."

Maria's eyes lit up and Alberta could tell that she understood. When she started to reveal more of Kylie's history, she knew she had made a confidante. Alberta was hoping Maria would provide some tidbit that she could use to lead her to who really killed Natalie.

"No, they aren't," Maria said. "I know that Mr. Manzini is a widower, which can change some men, like my Tito Ricardo. He lost his wife shortly after the birth of their third child and he was never the same. *El pobre hombre!* Ricardo was loving and gentle, but after Graciela passed, he was bitter and angry, a completely different man."

"Is that what Dr. Manzini's father is like?"

"He's not angry like a Spanish or Italian man gets angry, he doesn't yell, he doesn't raise his voice at all, but you can hear the disapproval and the—*¿cómo se dice?* The disgust in his voice. It's as if nothing the doctor can do is ever good enough."

"*Ah Madon!* What more could she do? She's one of the best surgeons in the state."

"I know! But if you think it's bad for her, it's worse for her sister. She's not nearly as successful as the doctor, so she gets it worse. The things he's said to me about her, *Dios mio!* I can only imagine what he's said to her face."

"A father should never speak to his child with anything but love."

"*Es verdad, pero* . . . He said once that he used to tell his children, 'If you can't be perfect, it's better to be nothing.'"

Alberta almost choked on her butterscotch candy. Her heart skipped a beat, and for a moment she thought she might have to barge into Kylie's office and have her resuscitate her. She wasn't having a hard time breathing because she thought what Kylie's father said was a horrible thing for a parent to say to a child, which it was; she was reacting so strongly because this was not the first time that she had heard that phrase. Natalie told her that her fa-

ther said the same exact thing to her the night before she
was murdered. Maria didn't realize it, but she just told
Alberta that Kylie Manzini and Natalie Vespa were sisters.

Just as Alberta was going to ask Maria to confirm the
name of Kylie's sister, the door to the doctor's office
opened and Sloan exited, followed closely by Kylie.

"Mrs. Scaglione," Kylie said. "We meet again."

"How's our patient?" Alberta said, too nervous to
make small talk.

"Sloan's doing great," Kylie replied. "I don't see any
reason for another follow-up; just make sure you don't
skip your yearly physical."

"Berta wouldn't let me if I tried," Sloan said. "Thanks
again, Doctor, and Merry Christmas if I don't see you
again."

"Thank you," Kylie replied. "Merry Christmas, to you
too, Mrs. Scaglione."

Alberta turned to face Kylie, and it was as if she was
seeing her for the first time. "Merry Christmas," Alberta
said.

She threw on her coat and slipped her arm through
Sloan's. She needed the extra support as she walked to
the hallway. From what she had just learned she felt light-
headed. But she was also bursting at the seams because
she couldn't wait to tell the others what she'd found out.
There was no way they could ever top this.

When they got in Sloan's Land Rover he turned to Alberta before he started the engine. "Are you going to tell
me what you found out while I was being poked and
prodded?"

"How do you know I found out something?" Alberta
asked.

"I've spent enough time around you that I can recognize how you look when you've uncovered a clue," Sloan replied.

"It's a whopper, but I want you to be surprised with everybody else," Alberta said.

She was about to send a group text to the gang to tell them to meet her at her house when she received a group text from Jinx telling her to do the same. Jinx said she and Joyce had incredible news to share that no one would ever be able to top. Alberta knew they were all working toward achieving the same goal, which was to set Sergio free, but she wasn't one to back down from a challenge.

"We'll see about that," she said. "Sloan, take me home!"

When she and Sloan entered her kitchen she was chomping at the bit to share her news and prove that what she had uncovered was untoppable. Helen and Lisa Marie were sitting at the table with Lola sparring with an imaginary fly in between them, while Jinx and Joyce stood on the opposite side of the kitchen, looking very excited to share whatever news they had discovered. Let the games begin.

"Gram, thank God you're here!" Jinx exclaimed. "You are not going to believe what Aunt Joyce and I found out at Carmichael's office."

"Sorry, lovey," Alberta said. "You are not going to believe what I found out at Dr. Manzini's office."

"Berta, I hate to burst your bubble, but there is no way you're going to top our news," Joyce said.

"I'm sure whatever little thing you and Jinx found out will be helpful," Alberta said. "But with all due respect, I hit the mother lode."

"We hit the trifecta, Gram!" Jinx cried.

"I'm gonna hit you both across the side of your head

with my pocketbook if you don't tell us what you found out and right now!" Helen barked.

"I think I'm going to sit down while they duke it out," Sloan said, sitting in the chair next to Lisa Marie.

"All right, lovey, you go first," Alberta said.

"Nice try, Gram. If your news is so special, you go first."

"That wouldn't be fair," Alberta said. "If I go first, whatever you say is going to pale in comparison to my earth-shattering news."

Helen picked up her pocketbook from the floor and placed it on the kitchen table with a loud thud, momentarily interrupting Lola's brawl. "I'm warning you girls, if one of you doesn't start talking in three seconds, I start swinging."

"Fine! I'll go first!" Alberta cried. "Dr. Kylie Manzini is Natalie's sister."

The screams from the group, including Sloan, were as loud as Alberta had expected and enough to make Lola throw in the towel and scamper to the safety of the living room. Alberta waited until the screams subsided and conveyed how she found out the doctor was the dead Natalie's big sister.

"That explains why Kylie was so emotional at the Mistletoe Ball after Natalie's body fell out of the snow-woman," Jinx said.

"It doesn't explain why Vinny can't find Natalie's next of kin if she's living right here in Tranquility," Lisa Marie said.

"It does if Vespa isn't Natalie's real last name," Alberta said.

"You think she's even lying about her name?" Joyce asked.

"I've always thought that Vespa sounded fake," Alberta said. "Now we know it probably is."

"Vinny's been wasting his time looking for Natalie Vespa's next living relative when he should've been searching for Natalie Manzini's nearest family member," Lisa Marie deduced.

"That still doesn't explain why Kylie kept quiet about their family connection," Helen said. "She was standing a few feet from her sister's murdered body and she didn't say a word."

"I hate to say it, but the good doctor must not be so good," Alberta said. "She must have something to hide and it must have something to do with drugs."

"I don't mean to be biased, but I don't see how you two can top Berta's discovery," Sloan said.

"Sorry, honey, but I have to agree. Your grandmother came up with a humdinger," Lisa Marie said. "Let's hear what you and Aunt Joyce found out and then Aunt Helen, Smarty Pants, and I will judge who's the winner."

"It's going to be close," Jinx said. "Aunt Joyce and I found out who J. J. is."

"You did!" Alberta screamed.

"Refresh my memory, I cannot keep up with you people," Lisa Marie said. "Who's J. J.?"

"J. J. is Rudy's girlfriend," Jinx said.

"The angry woman who got into Rudy's apartment while Jinx and I were there," Alberta added.

"Also too, she's the nurse who used to work at both St. Clare's and the Sussex Medical Center who Carmichael fired," Joyce explained.

"They're all the same person," Jinx said. "Janine Janniken, J. J. for short."

"I'm man enough to admit it, ladies," Helen said. "That was quite a buildup, but you didn't let us down."

"I think we have to call this one a tie!" Lisa Marie exclaimed.

"This is what they call *Una situación de ganar-ganar*," Alberta said.

"Yes, Gram, this is definitely a win-win situation," Jinx said.

"What do we do with all this information now?" Lisa Marie asked. "Do we share it with Vinny?"

"Not just yet," Sloan said.

"Why not?" Alberta asked. "We made a pact with him to share what we uncover because working as a team with the police only strengthens our case."

"That's what I want to do, strengthen our case," Sloan said. "I don't mean to point out a flaw, Berta, but Dr. Manzini's assistant only said she had a sister, she never said her name was Natalie."

"I thought you were smart?" Lisa Marie asked. "Of course they're sisters, the names Kylie and Natalie even sound alike."

"And what about the phrase Maria told me Kylie's father used?" Alberta asked. "It's the same phrase Natalie told me her father used to say—verbatim."

"The police are going to want more proof than that, especially if they haven't been able to make this connection themselves, and if we expect them to question Dr. Manzini about this, we can't go to Vinny with an anecdote, we need quantitative proof that Kylie is Natalie's big sister, so the DA won't be able to doubt the facts," Sloan explained.

"I swear to God, sometimes I hate you," Lisa Marie said.

"*O mio Dio!*" Alberta cried. "Leese, don't talk like that, Sloan is only trying to help."

"I don't hate him for that," Lisa Marie said. "I hate him because he's always right. Where the hell did you find him, Ma? The Land of the Silver Foxes?"

"We met at the library," Alberta said. "I went in to do some research on a case and, well, the rest, as they say, is history."

"It was one of the luckiest days of my life," Sloan said.

"Let's see if your luck holds," Lisa Marie said. "Do you happen to have a plan to convince the DA that Kylie and Natalie are sisters?"

Sloan smiled smugly, folded his hands, and placed them on the table. He didn't have to say a word for all the women to gather around and lean into him. He had a captive audience.

"What are you ladies doing tomorrow night?"

CHAPTER 25

Cammina con attenzione sul ghiaccio sottile.

Mistletoe Ball, take two.

Ever since the first Mistletoe Ball became a tragedy instead of a triumph, the board of directors at St. Clare's Hospital had been hoping for a do-over. They wanted the Ball to be remembered as a joyful event in Tranquility's history and not the horrific moment in time it had become. It had taken a lot of bargaining and begging and a small bribe from Joyce to get the manager of the Tranquility Manor to allow them to rebook the Diamond room to restage the Mistletoe Ball. The only night available was a Wednesday, but beggars never got to choose, so Joyce and the rest of the board gladly accepted the weeknight slot. Not everyone got a second chance to make a comeback and they weren't going to waste the opportunity.

A small army of volunteers put back all the decorations to make the ballroom look exactly the way it had been originally decorated. The wreaths, the upside-down Christmas trees, the lights, even the winter woods display, complete with the ski chalet and Santa and his reindeer were taken out of temporary storage to turn the ballroom into a holiday landscape. However, out of a sense of decorum, the snowman was now a bachelor.

Redoing the fundraising event would also give everyone a chance to wear their gowns and tuxedos again. Part of the festivity was to not only transform the venue, but to transform the VIPS as well. Top-shelf Tranquilitarians would get another chance to play dress-up. As Joyce often said, "When you look good, you feel good, and when you feel good, you're much more likely to donate money." She always had her eye on the prize.

And so did Sloan.

He figured if the entire town and especially most of the medical community were going to be at the Mistletoe Ball redux, it would be the perfect opportunity for him to break into the new research lab to find proof that Kylie was Natalie's sister. Sloan's hope was that the lab would be empty of all personnel, and if there was a security guard patrolling the area, he wouldn't be there all the time. All he needed to do was sneak in, hack into the HR computer, and search for Kylie Manzini's records to see if there was any mention of Natalie.

If Alberta was right and Kylie was indeed Natalie's big sister, then Sloan had a hunch that Kylie would have chosen Natalie to be her beneficiary. Most employees receive life insurance through their company as part of their benefits package and they have to choose someone to be their beneficiary in case they die while employed. Since Kylie wasn't married, her parents were presumably wealthy, and she didn't have any children, the logical choice would be Natalie. Who else would a big sister choose to leave her money to than her little sister?

They knew that Kylie and Bambi would be at the Ball, and Carmichael was playing Santa Claus at the Winter Wonderland, so there was no risk in one of them catching Sloan in action. Joyce, of course, had to attend the Ball at the Manor because she was on the hospital board, and Jinx had to be there because Freddy was finally going to get his award from the Tranquility Business Association. Vinny would be there as a representative of the police force and Helen and Father Sal really wanted to go because they were dying to taste the peppermint chocolate mousse that was on the dessert menu. They convinced Lisa Marie that she should attend instead of spending the evening alone, worrying about Sergio, and she reluctantly agreed.

The only ones left on the guest list were Alberta and Sloan. It was decided that they would make an appearance at the Ball and then drive to St. Clare's, use Joyce's temporary badge to enter through the back entrance, and take the service elevator up to the third floor, where the lab was being built. If they couldn't find what they were looking for in an hour, they'd return to the Ball, tell Vinny everything they knew, and let the police take over the investigation.

Everyone was in full support of the idea, and they knew that over the years Sloan's hacking skills had improved tremendously, giving him the expertise needed to acquire the information they sought. Lisa Marie lived up to her role as the outlier in the group and was the only one who was skeptical. It wasn't that she hadn't come to trust Sloan's motives or understand the gentleman possessed some ungentlemanly skills, she just didn't understand why there wasn't an easier way to determine if the women were truly sisters.

"How hard can it be to disassociate yourself from your family?" Lisa Marie said.

Everyone thought she was asking a rhetorical question. The person doing the asking was the same person who had packed up her family and moved a thousand miles away to do just that, disassociate herself from her family. Despite the blatant irony, she did have a point. In this age of rampant technology, where no data point, no matter how important or inconsequential, couldn't remain hidden for very long, how was it possible that the police couldn't find Natalie's family?

"There are lots of ways to scrub your identity from the Internet," Sloan said. "There are services that will use advanced software to expunge a particular incriminating photo or embarrassing video from the Internet."

"But can they delete an entire family?" Lisa Marie asked.

"Why not?" Sloan replied. "If Natalie or Kylie didn't want the world to know they were sisters, they could get some company to erase any and all ties from the Internet."

"The two women would both exist, it would just appear as if they existed independent of each other and not as part of the same family," Jinx said.

"That seems pretty drastic," Lisa Marie said. "I mean, how much do you have to hate your family to make them invisible?"

"Maybe hate wasn't the motivation, but fear," Alberta suggested.

"What do you mean, Berta?" Helen asked.

"Natalie told me that she felt like an outsider in her own home and insinuated that the rest of her family was grounded, but she was never able to find her footing," Alberta explained. "She blamed that on her father not being a very good man."

"You think she was afraid of her father?" Joyce asked.

"Yes, but that's not what I mean," Alberta replied. "I don't think her father physically abused her, but he definitely caused emotional damage. If this environment led Natalie to make some dubious life choices, like ultimately choosing to become a drug dealer, it could make her big sister very afraid. How could you focus on your career as a doctor if you were always waiting for your sister's criminal activity to be revealed? Maybe Kylie decided to eliminate that possibility."

"By eliminating the fact that she had a sister," Lisa Marie added.

"Which is exactly what I think Kylie did," Sloan said. "My hope is that there might be some remnant of the truth buried in her HR records."

"If there is, I know you'll find it," Alberta said.

Less than twenty-four hours later, Sloan's plan was in motion and his skills would soon be tested. But first there was a Ball to attend.

A searing sense of déjà vu took hold of everyone as they walked into the Diamond room at the Tranquility Manor. The décor looked exactly the same as it had the night of the first Mistletoe Ball, except for the now taboo snowwoman, and they all prayed that the evening's denouement wouldn't be another bloodstained corpse. The night, however, had only just begun.

The group gathered once again wearing their finest fashions, and to the rest of the attendees it appeared as if the Ferraras were having a fun family outing, not plotting to uncover evidence that would further cast doubt on Sergio's guilt, if not free him entirely. Jinx still looked like the belle of the Ball in her exquisite fire-engine-red Versace gown, Alberta felt like a queen in her fuchsia Carolina Herrera, Helen's sequined baby-blue ensemble was still a revelation, and Joyce's emerald-green Yves Saint Laurent number didn't fail to create some drama. This time even Lisa Marie got in on the fun.

Her heart really wasn't into attending the first Ball, so Lisa Marie picked out a simple A-line gown in navy satin. It was tasteful, but in comparison to the outfits worn by the rest of the women in her family, it was boring. She was lucky that all she did while wearing it was take a nap. This time, Lisa Marie decided to choose the gown of her dreams.

Having been a teenager in the late '80s, she had a fondness for padded shoulders, big hair, and leather. Realizing this was the only time she was going to get to indulge in such a fantasy—Jinx would never allow her to wear something as outlandish as the mother of the bride whenever that day might come—Lisa Marie embraced the opportunity to don the kind of gown she'd secretly wanted to wear to her senior prom at Immaculate Conception High School. Something Pat Benatar might wear in a video about teenage rebellion.

Adrianna teased Lisa Marie's hair into a poufy masterpiece and Joyce looked deep into the dark shadows of her closet to find a royal-blue strapless leather gown by North Beach Leather that had a matching bolero jacket with padded shoulders any quarterback would envy. Her accessories were minimal but chosen for maximum effort. A not-so-delicate streak of light blue eyeshadow, dark blue matte lipstick, and sapphire and rhinestone climber earrings that ran up the edge of her ears all combined to create a look that perfectly captured Lisa Marie's personality. Hard-edged, in your face, and fun.

When Tommy had seen what she looked like he'd thought she had lost her mind.

"What are you doing in that get-up?" Tommy asked.

Lisa Marie smiled into her camera while FaceTiming her husband and said, "My mother dragged me out to celebrate."

"Did they drop the charges against Sergio?"

"Not yet, but if this night goes as planned, we'll be one step closer to making that happen."

"I've been praying every spare second that you'll find the real killer."

"If there's one thing I've learned being back here, it's that when you have your family around you anything is possible."

"Are they there with you?"

Lisa Marie positioned the phone so Tommy could see the entire entourage. His shriek of surprise was louder than the collective greeting they all gave him.

"Holy moly! Y'all clean up pretty darn good, but Jinx, baby, you take the cake."

"Thanks, Daddy," Jinx said. "When can you get back up here?"

"In another day or so," Tommy replied. "I'm about to finish up this job and should get back in time for Christmas, and maybe in time to see Sergio get his freedom back."

"Keep the faith, Tommy," Alberta said. "We will."

"I hate to interrupt," Sloan said. "But I think it's time we got to work."

"I'll keep you posted, honey," Lisa Marie said. "Love you."

"Love you too."

The screen went black and the plan went into motion.

Alberta excused herself and said she was going to the ladies' room. Less than a minute later Sloan said he'd left his glasses in the car and wanted to retrieve them so he wouldn't miss any of the ceremony. As part of the planning committee, Joyce had made sure Vinny and Tambra were seated at a separate table, their backs to the Ferraras, allowing Alberta and Sloan to leave unnoticed by either law enforcement officer. It would prevent the cops from getting suspicious at their elongated absence.

Bambi stepped up to the microphone, once again swathed in gold lamé, her bosom working very hard to take the focus from her speech. She spoke about St. Clare's history, its achievements, its future goals, its partnership with the Sussex Medical Center, it seemed like she would ramble on forever, but after a few minutes Bambi finally got to the point of her monologue.

"Every year the Tranquility Business Association picks one very special Tranquilitarian as the Small Business Owner of the Year," Bambi said. "This year I'm proud to announce that the award goes to Freddy Frangelico, owner of Freddy's Ski 'n Scuba Shoppe."

The crowd roared and one particular table jumped to its feet. Proud, yet a little embarrassed by all the attention, Freddy hugged Jinx tightly. "I couldn't have done this without you." Jinx refused to cry in Freddy's presence—she didn't want to look like an overemotional girlfriend—and she'd be damned if she was going to ruin the fabulous makeup job she'd paid for.

At the mike, Freddy accepted the award from Bambi

and, with less enthusiasm, accepted her bear hug. When he was finally able to release himself, he smiled at the audience. Laid-back as ever, Freddy hadn't prepared a speech even though he knew in advance he was going to take home the prize, but he somehow managed to find the right words to express exactly how he felt.

"Dude, this is way cool!"

He held the Lucite award that bore his name high over his head. He had always maintained that he bought the business from his boss and expanded its services as a way to prove to Jinx that he was ambitious and the kind of guy worthy of her love. By the look of admiration in her eyes, it was clear that he had more than met that challenge.

About a mile away, Sloan was about to find out if he would be equally as successful.

As expected, most of the hospital staff was either at the Mistletoe Ball or away for the holiday, giving Alberta and Sloan easy access to the hospital. When they got to the third floor Sloan slowly opened up the service door and was relieved to see an empty workspace. Alberta pointed to the door marked Human Resources, and behind that door was where their search would take place.

Alberta waited outside as Sloan sat behind the desk and turned on the computer. The moment it booted up he used his well-honed skills to bypass the password so he could access the computer as an administrator. A few seconds later he was in, and from there he searched the employment records until he found Kylie's name.

"I'm almost there, Berta," Sloan said, unable to conceal the excitement in his voice.

"Hurry up," Alberta replied. "I think I heard a noise."

Sloan looked through the documents in her online

folder, but only found her W-9, a copy of her passport, and confirmation that she had participated in St. Clare's mandatory sexual harassment seminar. There was nothing in her folder that contained insurance beneficiary information or even who to contact in case of an emergency. He was about to pound the desk in frustration when he saw a file labeled Old Documents. He opened it up just as Alberta saw an old friend coming down the hallway. She pulled the office door closed behind her and walked as calmly as possible—without giving away the fact that her knees were shaking—toward the young man.

"Luke," Alberta said, loud enough so Sloan could hear. "What are you doing here?"

Luke stared at Alberta and his trademark smile disappeared from his face. "I think I'm the one who should be asking you that, Mrs. Scaglione."

Alberta had known Luke for years. As the orderly assigned to the morgue, he was one of the first people she had met when she and her family started their exploration of the investigative arts. It might have been that they both shared a respect for the dead, but Luke and Alberta had immediately bonded. She had encouraged him to look for a more important position at the hospital and he had supported her sleuthing, often providing her with tips that helped them solve their cases. Alberta was about to put their friendship to the test.

She remembered an old saying Italian mothers would tell their children. *Cammina con attenzione sul ghiaccio sottile.* Walk carefully on thin ice. She kept that in mind as she took her first tentative step toward talking herself out of this jam.

"Do you trust me, Luke?"

"Without question."

"Then you must know that I'm here for a very important reason."

"Can you tell me that reason?"

"The less you know, the better off it would be for you."

"Does it have to do with Dr. Manzini?"

Alberta realized Luke might already suspect there was trouble.

"Yes, it does. We're trying to find the proof before we go to Vinny."

"This has to do with your grandson and the murder of that girl, doesn't it?"

Alberta nodded. "I know that I'm putting you in a terrible position, Luke, and I understand if you feel the need to call security."

"I think I need to go to the bathroom."

"Excuse me?"

"The nearest men's room is down the hall behind me. It'll probably take me fifteen minutes before I come back here. If the coast is clear by then, I'll have no need to call security."

Alberta wanted to throw her arms around Luke and kiss his cheek, but she restrained herself. "Thank you."

She watched Luke turn around and walk down the hall just as he said he would. Alberta walked backward, not taking her eyes off Luke until he disappeared into the men's room, and then she entered the HR office. Sloan was staring at the computer screen in awe.

"Sloan, what's wrong? What did you find?"

"You are not going to believe it."

* * *

After everyone had congratulated Freddy, praised his business acumen and the astute vision of the Tranquility Business Association for thrusting the annual accolade on him, it seemed like their plan might be thwarted. Alberta and Sloan were conspicuously absent.

"Where's Alfie?" Vinny asked.

"She wasn't feeling well," Jinx said.

"She had too many Yule-tinis," Helen said.

"Also too, Sloan drove her home so she could rest," Joyce added.

Vinny looked circumspect but didn't try to poke holes in their statements. He did ask them to convey a message to her when they saw her.

"Pedro texted me to confirm that he found traces of Flower in both Natalie and Rudy," Vinny said.

"There *is* some kind of drug ring in this quiet little town after all," Lisa Marie said.

"I don't know if it's based here," Vinny said. "But it definitely has made an impact on our community."

It was frightening to think that even a small town like Tranquility could harbor such deadly secrets. Jinx shook her head and couldn't believe that her brother could've gotten himself mixed up with such people, even unwittingly. She made the sign of the cross and thanked God that she had surrounded herself with family and friends who were good people and would never do harm to another soul. She knew addiction was a disease and many people were predisposed to becoming victims, or were given prescription drugs by their doctors for an ailment and quickly found themselves hooked. It was the people who willingly sold drugs and pushed them into a community knowing the death and destruction that would rip through a town like a ripple of water in a breeze who she despised. She didn't know how those people could live with themselves.

Jinx shook her head. Those were important issues to contemplate, but for now she had a more immediate concern.

"I need to use the ladies' room, and in this outfit, it's going to take me a while."

"I'll join you," Helen said. "I may need help wrestling out of this thing."

"I heard one of the waiters say that this bathroom is out of order," Lisa Marie said. "You have to use the one by the Sapphire room, wherever that is."

"Follow me, Aunt Helen, I know the way," Jinx said. "Freddy, could I have my phone? I want to check my messages."

Helen finished first and, after washing her hands at the sink while humming along to Nat King Cole singing about roasting chestnuts, she started to reapply her lipstick. Jinx was finishing up and humming along as well as she heard someone talking to Helen. She peeked through the gap in between the door and the wall of the stall and, noticing the woman's white shirt and black pants, assumed she wasn't on the guest list.

"That's a beautiful dress."

"Thank you, dear," Helen said. "Are you part of the waitstaff?"

"No, I'm sort of crashing the party. I needed to see someone to tie up some proverbial loose ends."

"I see."

Jinx could detect some apprehension in Helen's voice; her aunt didn't sound scared, more like concerned.

"The truth is, girls like me don't usually get invited to fancy balls."

"I never got invited to any either, in fact, this is the first gown I've ever worn in my life."

"Because you used to be a nun."

When Helen spoke again Jinx did notice a slight tinge of fear.

"How do you know that?"

"Big Sister isn't the most subtle of sobriquets."

"Now that's a fancy word, I'll have to remember to use it in my column. Have you written me for advice?"

"Yes, and I wanted to thank you."

Jinx was trying to put herself together as quietly as possible so she could exit the stall and find out who was talking to her aunt, but her gown was making it difficult. She peeked through the crack again, but the way the woman was positioned, she could only see her black hair and a bit of her profile. From her viewpoint, the woman was unrecognizable.

"Did my words help you?"

"Yes and no. It was refreshing to know that someone cared enough to respond to me and try to help, but how's that old song go? A day late and a dollar short. I had already done the thing I was worried that I would do and now that I've done it, well, there's no going back."

There was a pause before Helen spoke, and Jinx imagined she was searching for the right way to find out what the woman was talking about. "How can I help you? Would you like to talk to a priest? The police?"

The woman started to laugh. "You're sweet. A tad naïve, but sweet. A priest wouldn't know what to do with a sinner like me and the police would only want to throw the book at me. After everything I've done, I'm beyond help."

"You listen to me, no one is beyond help. Now, what's your name?"

Jinx finally opened the stall as the woman answered Helen's question. "You can call me Noctor J."

When Bambi walked into the bathroom she called the woman by another name.

"Janine! What the hell are you doing here?"

CHAPTER 26

Non risolvere il puzzle finché i pezzi non si incastrano.

Usually there was a line of women waiting to get into the restroom. Inside the ladies' lavatory near the Sapphire room there were four women frantically trying to get out.

Bambi stood next to the door. Her initial shock at seeing Janine had turned to hatred. On the other side of the room was Jinx, who still couldn't believe she had finally come face-to-face with J. J. aka Noctor J aka Janine Janniken. In the middle were Helen and Janine, both wearing expressions that concealed their true emotions.

Jinx knew her Aunt Helen had been in dicey situations before as a nun, counseling members of marginalized communities and helping inmates get their lives on track, as well as working with the rest of the Ferrara ladies to solve murders. However, Jinx also knew that Helen took her social work very seriously, and while she hardly had a strong relationship with Janine, the girl needed help and it was Helen's nature to lend a hand to those in need. Unfortunately, from the way Janine was standing, she didn't appear to want any help.

Janine was petite. No more than five foot two, maybe one hundred pounds, but with the lean muscle of an athlete. She stood slightly bent forward with her arms a few inches from her side, like a wrestler ready to pounce. In a straight-up brawl based on physical stats only, Jinx would have to put her money on Bambi, who was twice Janine's size. But the underdog was in total control of her body, whereas Bambi's face was contorted in fury, her cheeks red and her chest heaving. As small as Janine was, Jinx knew she had the upper hand.

"I told you to get out of town and never come back," Bambi said.

"Kylie disagreed and wanted me to stick around," Janine replied.

"Because she thinks she can get you to confess," Bambi countered.

Jinx remembered something Alberta once told her when they were working on a case. *Non risolvere il puzzle finché i pezzi non si incastrano.* Don't solve the puzzle until all the pieces fit. Her spine tingled because she felt like she had all the pieces and could finally put them together to finish the puzzle that would set her brother free.

Jinx watched a trickle of sweat start to run down the side of Bambi's face. Why was the woman nervous if she thought Janine had to confess something? The most obvious confession would be that she killed Natalie. What if Kylie wanted Janine to confess something that would implicate Bambi? That would definitely make the woman sweat.

Jinx remembered what Joyce told her about Bambi's financial status and how desperate she had to be to make money to pay off her substantial debts. If she had been working with Natalie to sell drugs on the street, that could be a lucrative, albeit illegal, way of earning a side income. Where there's money, there's greed, and someone always wants more than their share.

When Jinx was investigating a crime for an article she was writing she would always follow the money. It might take her to unexpected places, but in the end it would always lead her to ground zero. She needed to replicate the same theory, but this time she had to follow the drugs.

As the hospital administrator of St. Clare's, Bambi had access to all kinds of drugs. However, she wouldn't be able to get her hands on them because she didn't have access to the dispensary and couldn't write prescriptions, which meant she would need help from someone who had daily hands-on access to the drugs, someone like a nurse. And that was where Janine came in.

Carmichael told them that he had to fire Janine because she got greedy, that she wanted to do more, that she did things that couldn't be ignored. Stealing drugs from a hospital was not something that could be ignored. Not by the hospital or by the person who got fired. The hospital might want to wipe the problem under the rug to avoid any bad publicity, but someone who got ousted from their job and their access to their side hustle might certainly want revenge.

Standing there watching Bambi and Janine face off, it all became clear to Jinx. Her brother had been carted off to jail and the real criminals were free. It all fit, but how to prove it? If she was going to make anything stick in court, Jinx had to get Bambi and Janine to confess to their part in Natalie's killing. She felt the blood pump through her veins, felt herself start to lose control of her emotions. No! She couldn't do that, she couldn't resort to hotheaded Jinx, she needed to think like her grandmother did in situations like this, even-keeled and levelheaded. Come to think of it, she needed to be calm and in control, more like Janine.

It was a good idea, but in order to be more like Janine, Jinx would have to be armed.

In one fluid move Janine bent down, lifted her trouser leg, revealed a pistol that was jutting out of an ankle holster, removed the pistol, and aimed it at Bambi. It was action-hero slick, but definitely executed by the movie's villain. As Bambi recoiled in horror, Janine grabbed Helen's arm and pulled her in front of her, the gun barrel inches from Helen's head.

"Janine, no!" Jinx cried.

"Didn't I tell you not to push me, Bambi," Janine said. "You think you run everything."

"Because I do, you *stunod*!" Bambi exclaimed.

"Your reign is about to end," Janine said.

"Put the gun down," Bambi said, wiping away a droplet of sweat that had dripped into her eye. "The chief of police is in the next room, you are not going to get out of here."

"If I get caught, I'll have a fantastic and detailed tale to tell the chief about you and your friends," Janine replied.

"You should've left town when I told you, you could've gotten away," Bambi said. "Why do you always have to push things? Why aren't you ever satisfied?"

"Shut up!" Janine cried. "I don't want to hurt Big Sister here, but I will if I have to."

"Janine, you don't have to do this," Helen said. "No one is going to hurt you."

"You're not a very good liar," Janine said. "I really do like you and it would upset me greatly if I had to hurt you."

"Hurt me, then," Jinx said. "Let me switch places with my aunt."

"Jinx, stop talking right now," Helen said.

"If you have any chance of getting out of here, you have to let me take my aunt's place," Jinx said. "She's old and she can't run in that dress, she's only going to slow you down."

"Jinx, what are you doing?" Helen asked.

"She's doing what a big sister is supposed to do," Janine said.

Jinx watched as Janine's features softened. She didn't loosen her grip on Helen, she didn't lower her gun, but all the anger in her face gave way to an aching sadness.

"She's trying to protect her little brother," Janine said. "If all big sisters were like you, Jinx, Natalie wouldn't be dead right now."

"I don't understand what you mean," Jinx said.

"It doesn't matter," Janine replied. "All that matters is that Natalie is dead and there is nothing anyone can do to change that. Like there's nothing anyone can do to bring back all the people who have died because of Bambi."

Janine swung around and pointed the gun at Bambi. She didn't shoot, but Bambi reacted as if Janine really did pull the trigger. She staggered and had to grab onto the top of the stall next to her to steady herself. Beads of sweat appeared on her chest and slid down her cleavage.

Jinx didn't know if she was having a heart attack or an attack of conscience.

"I have never killed anyone," Bambi declared. "Which is not something you can say."

"If that's what you need to tell yourself to sleep at night or look at yourself in the mirror, go right ahead, but we both know it's a lie," Janine said. "You have so much blood on your hands you'll never be able to get rid of the stains."

If Bambi was part of some drug cartel, Janine was right. The death of every person who died of an overdose from taking Flower could be traced back to Bambi and the rest of her partners. By the look of terror that gripped Bambi's face, Jinx could tell the woman agreed. But now was not the time for reflection, now was the time for escape.

"C'mon, Janine, you know if you want to get out of here without being arrested, I'm your golden ticket," Jinx said.

Janine's lips formed a snarl, and it looked as if she was going to growl, but instead she pushed Helen away and stood behind Jinx. She pointed the gun directly into the small of her back, right above the red satin ribbon of her couture gown. It wasn't the kind of accessory Jinx thought looked appropriate with her outfit, but she was relieved the gun was pointed at her and no longer at Helen.

"Make one false move and you're dead," Janine said. "You two count to a hundred before you leave this room. If I see you coming after me, I will start shooting."

Janine shoved Jinx forward and she started to walk toward the door. Jinx forced herself to smile and wink at

Helen. The last thing she saw before she left the ladies' room was her aunt making the sign of the cross.

They walked through the large foyer that separated the bathrooms from the banquet halls, and Jinx looked into the Diamond room. She could see Freddy talking to Father Sal, Joyce laughing with Donna and her mother, and Jinx desperately wanted to scream, but she was terrified. She wasn't certain that Janine had killed Natalie, but she was certain that Janine didn't possess a moral compass. She was also convinced that if she attempted to escape, Janine wouldn't think twice before shooting her. Jinx had to manage her fears and trust that she could outsmart her kidnapper.

With the metal barrel pressing against her, Jinx felt Janine silently guide her away from the one valet driver talking to an inebriated couple and toward the parking lot on the side of the Manor. When they got to a brown Toyota Corolla that looked like it had seen better days, Jinx heard Janine fumble with some keys and open the front door of the car. She told Jinx to sit in the driver's seat and closed the door. Instead of walking around the front of the car to the passenger side, Janine opened the rear door and sat in the back seat behind Jinx. Before the door slammed shut, Jinx felt the gun pressing into the back of her head.

Leaning forward, Janine dropped the car keys in Jinx's lap and said, "Drive."

As the car pulled out of the parking lot, Sloan's Land Rover pulled in. Instinctively, Jinx beeped, causing Sloan to turn his head to the left. Janine slapped Jinx on the shoulder with the gun and told her to step on the gas.

"I think that was Jinx," Sloan said.

Alberta turned to the right and saw the Corolla speed up as it ran through the yellow light. "It couldn't have been. Jinx came in Freddy's truck, must've been someone who looked like her."

Sloan gave the key to the valet and they walked into the Manor toward the Diamond room. They had decided they were done with heroics and would pass the baton to Vinny to inform him of the startling news they had learned. He and the police could take over the investigation that Alberta was confident would cast enough doubt on Sergio's guilt that the DA, despite her conviction and public declarations of her grandson's guilt, would have no choice but to set him free. When Helen came running out of the ladies' room, her gown hiked up to her knees, Alberta knew her plans for the rest of the evening had drastically changed.

"Berta!" Helen screamed.

"Helen what's wrong?" Alberta asked.

Even though Mariah Carey was belting out the one thing she wanted for Christmas and the attendees of the second and only slightly more successful Mistletoe Ball were chattering and participating in a silent auction, Helen's voice cut through the din. Ms. Carey had finally met her vocal match.

"Jinx has been kidnapped!" Helen yelled.

"Kidnapped?!" Alberta cried. "What are you talking about?"

"What happened to Jinx?!" Freddy screamed, racing over to Helen.

"Where's my daughter?!" Lisa Marie yelled, chasing right after Freddy.

"We were in the bathroom and this woman came up to

me, it was Janine, the J. J. we've been trying to find, and she pulled a gun on me," Helen said.

"*O dio mio!*" Alberta cried.

"Jinx convinced her to let her switch places with me and I couldn't stop her," Helen said. She grabbed Lisa Marie's hand. "I'm sorry, I tried, but she wouldn't listen to me."

"Of course she wouldn't," Lisa Marie said. "I would've done the same thing."

"Oh my God, that *was* Jinx in the car!" Alberta screamed.

"What car?" Vinny asked.

"Sloan thought he saw Jinx making a left out of the parking lot and driving a brown car," Alberta said.

"A Corolla," Sloan added.

"I didn't think it was her, she came in your car, Freddy," Alberta said. "We didn't even try to stop them, we let them drive away."

"Did you get a license plate?" Vinny asked.

"No, but it was orange, part of it anyway," Alberta said.

"Florida license plates have oranges on them," Lisa Marie said.

"Tambra!" Vinny shouted.

"On it," she replied.

They overheard Tambra putting an all-points bulletin out on a brown Toyota Corolla with Florida plates headed south.

"Janine is armed and she's dangerous," Helen said. "She's despondent and afraid, she feels like she has nothing to lose."

"Did she say anything that might be a clue as to where she would take Jinx?" Vinny asked.

"Nothing that I can recall, but maybe Bambi picked up on something," Helen said.

"Was Bambi in the ladies' room with you too?" Alberta asked.

"Yes, she came in and immediately knew it was Janine," Helen said.

"Where is she?" Lisa Marie asked.

"Where's who?" Father Sal said, walking toward them from the front entrance.

"Bambi De son of a . . . !" Lisa Marie cried.

"She flew out of here a few minutes ago with Dr. Manzini and was quite harsh with the poor valet," Sal said. "She was jabbering on and on about having to take care of an emergency, as if that's an excuse for rude behavior."

"Did Bambi say where she was going?" Vinny asked.

Father Sal shook his head. "No, but I assumed the crisis had something to do with the hospital."

"We just came from there and everything seemed fine," Alberta said. "There didn't seem to be any unusual activity."

"Were you feeling that ill that Sloan had to take you to the hospital?" Vinny asked.

"Don't ply me with a lot of questions, but we found proof that Kylie is involved in Natalie's murder," Alberta said.

"How did you find that out?" Vinny asked.

"You can prove that Kylie is Natalie's sister?" Lisa Marie asked.

"No," Alberta replied.

"What?" Lisa Marie cried.

"We can prove that Kylie is Janine's sister," Alberta said.

"What?!" Helen cried.

"How can you prove that?" Joyce asked.

"Sloan was able to hack into the Human Resource files at St. Clare's and found Kylie's original employment papers, and she named her sister her beneficiary," Alberta explained. "Janine Janniken Manzini."

"Janniken isn't a surname like we thought," Sloan said. "It's a popular girl's name. Berta looked it up on her phone on the drive over."

"Popular? In what country?" Lisa Marie asked.

"Norway!" Alberta said. "Which is where their father is from."

"Excellent work, Alfie," Vinny said. "Even if I have to feign amnesia from hearing about Sloan hacking into some computer files."

"That's what Janine meant when she said Natalie would be alive if big sisters were more like Jinx," Helen said. "She didn't mean Natalie's big sister, she meant her own."

"Vinny, they're all connected," Alberta said. "Natalie, Rudy, Janine, Kylie, Bambi, and even Carmichael. Our Sergio had nothing to do with any of it and he didn't murder Natalie."

"I believe you, Alfie," Vinny said. "We have to bring them all in for questioning and prove to Roxanne that she's made a huge mistake."

"This is all great information, but we're wasting time!" Freddy yelled. "We have to find Jinx."

"Does she have her cell phone on her?" Lisa Marie asked.

"Yes, but if she's got a gun to her head, she's not going to be able to take my call," Freddy said.

"Can you track her phone?" Vinny asked.

"Yes!" Joyce squealed. "I put the Find My Friend app on all our phones, remember?"

"That's right!" Alberta screamed.

"Freddy, you're quicker than I am," Joyce said. "Find Jinx!"

Freddy took the phone and his fingers immediately got to work, scrolling and tapping, until he found what he was looking for. "C'mon, c'mon, show me where Jinx is!"

They all crowded around the phone and watched a light blink on a map. It wasn't moving, which indicated that wherever Jinx's phone was it was stationary. Freddy enlarged the map once, then twice, and he did not like what he was seeing. He did not like it at all.

"No!" Freddy screamed. "No, no, no!!! Move, c'mon, move!"

"Freddy, what's wrong?" Alberta cried. "Where's Jinx?"

"According to this map, Jinx is right in the middle of Memory Lake."

CHAPTER 27

Non scherzare con una pazza signora italiana.

On the twenty-third day of Christmas, Jinx's true love gave to the town of Tranquility a high-speed car chase.

The second incarnation of the Mistletoe Ball was another unmitigated disaster. It paled in comparison to the first only because no one was murdered the second time around. However, one person had been kidnapped by another person, who was one of the suspects in the murder that had taken place at the first Ball and the other two suspects had fled the scene and were missing. By the time two waiters wheeled in the six-foot Christmas tree cake that was filled with the peppermint chocolate mousse Helen and Father Sal had been so anxious to taste, hardly anyone was left at the Ball. They had all fled to Memory Lake to save Jinx.

Freddy drove Helen and Joyce in his Ranger, Sloan

drove Alberta and Lisa Marie in his Land Rover, and Father Sal and Wyck rode in the back seat of Vinny's cop car with Tambra riding shotgun. Halfway to Memory Lake, Tambra called Alberta to tell her that Janine's Corolla was spotted near the town square driving east. Alberta realized that if Janine wanted to get lost in the crowd, east was the direction to go because that led right to Tranquility Park. In its temporary incarnation as the Winter Wonderland, it was filled with crowds, it was loud, and it was chock-full of distractions. It was the perfect place to hide in plain sight.

"Tell Freddy to head on to Memory Lake just in case Jinx is there," Alberta said, her voice emanating from Tambra's phone, which was on speaker and filling up the squad car. "We got stopped at a light so we're going to make a U-turn and head over to the park."

"That sounds good, Alfie," Vinny said. "I'm going to head to the lake because we're close, but I'm calling in backup to scour the park for Jinx and Janine."

"They should also be on the lookout for Bambi and Kylie," Sloan added.

"Roger that, Sloan," Tambra said.

"Will Helen's description of Janine be enough to find her?" Alberta asked.

"As long as she hasn't changed her appearance, we'll be able to find her," Vinny said.

When Janine walked into Tranquility Park a step behind Jinx, she looked completely different.

In the back seat of her car, she had altered her appearance while Jinx drove. She donned a blond wig that had been styled the way Natalie used to wear her hair, feathery and long, and instead of a white dress shirt and black pants she now wore a red hooded parka and jeans. Her look was typical suburban twentysomething and guaranteed she wouldn't stand out in a crowd.

Jinx, however, was still dressed in her red gown and rhinestone heels, not the best outfit to wear on a snowy night in December or to remain inconspicuous, which was why Janine had pulled out a long tweed overcoat from her trunk and made Jinx wear it. The coat was too big on Jinx, but it kept most of her gown hidden from view. The costume change did the trick, and when they walked through the park nobody noticed them. Everyone was too busy singing along with the strolling carolers, playing games of chance, eating and drinking, buying Christmas presents, and reveling in the few remaining days before Christmas was upon them.

Janine and Jinx had almost made it undetected to the giant gingerbread house when they bumped into the one person no one could hide from: Santa Claus.

"Janine," Santa said.

A man in a full Santa Claus outfit was standing to the left, and Jinx knew that he must have a perfect view of the gun Janine was pointing into her back. It took Jinx a moment to realize the man in the suit was Carmichael. Janine seemed to know it was him instantly because she pointed her gun at him but still kept her hand squeezed tightly around Jinx's arm to prevent her from running away.

When Carmichael spoke his voice sounded weary, as if he had run a marathon or was simply tired of living. "Janine, let's put an end to this once and for all."

"We both know it's too late for that," Janine replied.

"Haven't I always done my best to protect you?" Carmichael asked. "Haven't I always tried to help you the way that your father never did?"

Jinx could feel Janine pressing her arm tighter, though she couldn't tell if Carmichael was making Janine angrier or if his words were giving her pause and making her hold on tighter to her conviction.

"I'm grateful for everything you've tried to do for me," Janine said. "It's more than that horror of a father ever did."

"Then let me help you," Carmichael continued. "We've all made mistakes."

"Not as big as mine and you know it," Janine said. "I think it's time you started acting more like my father and realized, once and for all, that I'm beyond help?"

Carmichael looked like his heart had just broken. He really did love this girl as if she were his own daughter and like any father, he couldn't accept the fact that he had failed to protect his own child. He opened his mouth to respond, but before he could speak there was a loud buzzing sound, like a swarm of bees had descended upon the park. Just when the sound was almost too much to bear, it disappeared. Along with all the lights.

The wiring problems Carmichael had worried about proved to be cause for real concern. A blackout engulfed the entire park and left the hundreds of patrons, who had just been singing and reveling in Christmas joy, screaming in panic. Jinx thought she heard a gunshot blend in with the cacophony of sound all around her, but she couldn't be sure. If Janine had fired her gun, Jinx prayed the darkness caused her to miss her target. There was no way for Jinx to investigate because she was standing in almost total darkness and Janine was pushing her to move forward toward the huge structure that loomed in the distance.

The gingerbread house was built at the far end of the park and was only going to be used on Christmas Eve, tomorrow night, when there would be a candlelight concert. Now the building, like the rest of the park, was dark, but hardly desolate.

As they got closer to the house, Jinx's eyes started to acclimate to the darkness. It was a clear night and the moonlight, mixed in with the few stars in the night sky, created enough illumination so Jinx could see her surroundings. When Janine opened the door to the gingerbread house and pushed her inside, Jinx wished the moon and the stars would take a hike and return the area to blackout conditions. That way she wouldn't see the two other people occupying the cavernous space.

Bambi and Kylie were huddled together on the other side of the house. They looked like they were hiding from someone, but Jinx knew they had been waiting for their arrival. Jinx didn't acquire her knowledge because she had some kind of intuition, the gun in Bambi's hand gave it away. As did the deadly tone of her voice.

"Janine, why don't you tell me again that I'm not in complete control?"

Alberta and Lisa Marie held on to each other as they walked through Tranquility Park. They had split up with Sloan, who was searching the right side of the park as they were walking on the left-hand side toward the gingerbread house. Just as they hit a clearing that separated the main space of the Winter Wonderland and the house itself, the lights went out.

For a few seconds they just continued to hold on to each other and didn't move. Alberta heard a sound that she thought was a firecracker, but the screams and yells all around them escalated to a volume that made pinpointing one noise in the roar impossible. She couldn't do anything about the sound, but she could do something about the lights.

Alberta pulled out her cell phone and tapped and swiped the thing several times.

"What are you doing?" Lisa Marie asked.

"I'm trying to turn on the flashlight thingamajig on my phone," Alberta replied.

"You know how to do that?"

"Not really, but I know it's possible."

"Do you want me to try?"

"That'll be like the blind leading the blind."

"I think you have to swipe all the way up from the bottom."

"Like this?"

Whatever Alberta did, it worked, and finally the area they were standing in was brightly lit so they could see in front of them. Unfortunately, what they saw in front of them was Santa Claus lying on his back on the ground.

"Just what we need, a drunk Santa," Lisa Marie said.

"He's not drunk, he's been shot," Alberta corrected her.

Alberta ran to the man's side and let out a shriek when she pulled off his hat and beard. "Carmichael!"

"Oh my God!" Lisa Marie screamed. "Did Janine do this?"

Carmichael was gasping for breath, but he had something to say. After a few attempts he was able to speak. "She's the Flower."

Alberta wanted to continue the conversation, but she knew that Carmichael needed immediate medical attention. She called Vinny, explained what had happened, and told him that he needed to send an ambulance to the west side of the park. Vinny said he would also have one of the cops get to Carmichael to wait with him until the medics arrived.

Knowing that Jinx was nearby and at the mercy of a very dangerous woman, Alberta was forced to make a very hard decision. She put her cell phone in Carmichael's left hand and told him to hold it with the light pointing outward so the police and medics could find him. She took his right hand, placed it firmly on the spot where blood was pouring from his side, and told him to keep pressure on the wound.

Carmichael no longer had the strength to speak and could only nod his head. Alberta touched the gold crucifix and made the sign of the cross, hoping she had done enough to save the man's life and wasn't too late to save her granddaughter's. She grabbed Lisa Marie's hand and together they walked, huddled together, toward the gingerbread house.

"We almost found out what the D in D. Edward Carmichael stands for," Lisa Marie said.

"What's that?"

"Dead."

"Leese!" Alberta cried. "The poor man may not make it."

"You know something, Ma?" Lisa Marie said, her voice calm and resolved. "My daughter's been kidnapped and my son is in jail, so forgive me if I don't have time to feel sorry for a man who was probably going to get a stocking full of coal for Christmas anyway for being involved with drug dealers."

"*Ah Madonna mia!*" Alberta cried. "Now I have to say an extra Hail Mary for your soul too."

"Don't worry about me, focus on finding Jinx."

"If I'm right, she's in that gingerbread house, right up there."

"Then that's where I'm going!"

Lisa Marie broke free from Alberta and started to sprint toward the house. Alberta grabbed the flowing material of her gown and let out a curse just before she started to run after her daughter.

Seeing Bambi with a gun and Kylie lurking nearby preoccupied Janine enough that Jinx was able to slowly walk in a circle to the left. She was moving an inch or two at a time with the goal of getting near one of the huge candy canes that were positioned around the room. No one seemed to notice Jinx as they were too engrossed in their own conversation.

"If you think I'm going to let a no good *nothing* like you destroy everything I've built, you are sorely mistaken," Bambi said. "This is the end of the line for you, Janine."

"If I go down, the two of you are going down with me," Janine said.

"Will you stop this!" Kylie screamed. "This has gone too far."

"All because of you!" Janine screamed.

"How is any of this my fault?" Kylie asked.

"Because you're the big sister!" Lisa Marie screamed.

She flung open the door with such force that it slammed against the wall. She didn't have a gun, she didn't have any weapon, she was just a mother out to protect her daughter. What she did have was a reinforcement.

"Jinx, are you in here?" Alberta asked, running into the room and standing next to Lisa Marie.

"I'm over here, Gram," Jinx cried.

All heads turned in the direction of Jinx's voice, but no one could see her because she was standing behind the candy cane. When Alberta saw how well she was hidden, and saw that both Bambi and Janine were armed, she grabbed Lisa Marie and dragged her so they could stand behind the candy cane on the right side of the house.

"Lovey, we thought you were in Memory Lake," Alberta said.

"Janine made me drop my phone in there as a diversion," Jinx explained.

"Didn't do you much good, did it, Janine?" Lisa Marie said.

Frustrated, Janine aimed the gun in their direction and pulled the trigger, then once more, each time only managing to shatter the glass windows behind them.

"Looks like you're losing your touch, Janine," Bambi said. "You might need some more practice."

"Go ask your friend Carmichael if I'm a bad shot," Janine said. "Though I'm not sure he'll be able to answer you."

"You killed Carmichael?" Kylie said.

"Just like I'm going to kill the two of you," Janine cried. "And then *I'll* be the Flower."

Alberta's ears perked up, there it was again, the Flower. Carmichael had said, "She's the Flower," and now Janine claimed she's going to be the Flower. *They want to be a drug?* Alberta thought. That didn't make any sense. Not to her maybe, but to Lisa Marie it finally made perfect sense.

"Oh my God! Bambi is the Flower!" she screamed.

"No, Leese, the Flower is the name of the drug," Alberta said.

"It's named after her," Lisa Marie said. "Pedro said the drug stinks like holy heaven when it's being manufactured."

"Bambi wears a lot of perfume, but she doesn't stink," Alberta said.

"Not her, the skunk in the *Bambi* movie is named Flower!" Lisa Marie cried. "Bambi's the drug king, or queen, or whatever the hell you call it, she's the head of it all!"

"*Ah Madon!*" Alberta cried. "Lisa, that's brilliant."

"Thank you," Bambi said. "I thought it was a fun play on words. Name the whole operation after me without anybody knowing it."

"Why?" Alberta asked. "Why would you do such a terrible thing? Bring drugs into this town and get people addicted? You led innocent people to their deaths."

"I did no such thing!" Bambi shouted. "After my idiot of a husband left me with mountains of debt, I tried to get help, but I found out a hard truth—if you want help you have to help yourself. That's what I did. I saw an opportunity and I took it."

"And all the innocent people who died, they're just collateral damage?" Jinx asked.

"Nobody's innocent!" Bambi replied. "Everybody has to take responsibility for their own lives and for every choice they make."

"Well the choice you made is about to blow up in your face," Jinx said. "Now that everybody knows about what you've done you can kiss your drug empire good-bye."

"We might be interrupted for a while, but not for long," Bambi said. "I need to get rid of Janine, which will be deemed self-defense of course, since she's brandishing a gun at me. Kylie will never say a word because Kylie wants everyone to think she's beyond reproach. Rudy and Natalie are long gone and Carmichael's dead."

"I'm sorry to disappoint you, but Carmichael is going to live," Alberta said. "He's on his way to the emergency room right now."

"That's impossible!" Janine shouted. "I shot him!"

"Can't you do anything right?" Bambi shrieked.

"Maybe you should've snuck up behind him and plunged a knife in his heart like you did Natalie," Alberta said.

"You can't prove Janine killed Natalie," Kylie said.

"Yes, I can," Alberta replied. "She's wearing the same red parka Sergio said the person who met Natalie at the back entrance of the Manor was wearing the night of the Mistletoe Ball. That wig she's sporting will match the strands of synthetic hair they found on Natalie's body. And the way she's holding the gun proves she's left handed. Add all of that evidence to Carmichael's testimony that he will undoubtedly give and Janine will take my grandson's place in jail."

"Why did you have to kill her, Janine?" Kylie asked.

"Because she deserved to die," Janine replied.

"No, she didn't!" Kylie screamed.

"You're wrong, Doctor, Natalie most definitely had to die. Isn't that right, Janine?" Alberta asked. "After all, Natalie took everything away from you: your job, your standing in your drug cartel, you knew she could have Rudy any time she wanted, she even took your memories."

"Gram, I followed you up to that last point," Jinx said. "What do you mean, she stole Janine's memories?"

"The sob story that Natalie told me the night before she died was all made up," Alberta said. "It wasn't Natalie's past, it was Janine's."

"How did you figure that out, Ma?" Lisa Marie asked.

"'If you can't be perfect, it's better to be nothing,'" Alberta said. "Isn't that what Daddy Manzini used to say to his little girls?"

"He was right!" Kylie screamed. "If Janine had just tried to do something with her life other than steal and sell drugs, none of this would've happened."

"If you would have done your job as a big sister and protected me, none of this would have happened!" Janine cried.

"You can't blame this on me," Kylie said.

"If you had only stood up to Daddy when he treated me like garbage or intervened on my behalf when Carmichael fired me and Bambi tried to run me out of town, I wouldn't have had to kill Natalie!" Janine cried. "You left me no choice."

"But you had a choice, Kylie, and you chose to ignore it," Alberta said. "You knew your sister had killed Natalie and yet you kept quiet while my grandson was carted off to jail. Were you going to let him go to prison for life simply to avoid a scandal?"

"What would you have done, Mrs. Scaglione, had the tables been turned?" Kylie asked. "Would you turn in your own flesh and blood to save someone else's life?"

"Before tonight I might have given you a different answer, but after seeing my grandson being taken away in handcuffs, taken to jail possibly for the rest of his life, I would have told the truth," Alberta said. "As difficult as it would be, I could not allow another human being to take the blame for something they didn't do."

"Then you're a better woman than I am," Kylie said. "I'm sorry I kept quiet and didn't tell the police that my sister killed Natalie, but you need to understand that for most of my sister's life I had kept quiet. I let my father abuse her with his words, I let her spiral out of control and I didn't say a word to prevent it. I know you won't believe me, but even though I haven't acted like it, I do love my sister."

"I believe you."

Lisa Marie stepped out from behind the candy cane to face Kylie.

"I did the same thing to my mother," Lisa Marie said. "I turned my back on her and stayed away for fourteen years."

"Lisa, don't," Alberta said.

"It's true, Ma, it's what I did, but that doesn't mean I ever stopped loving you, and I hope you know that."

"I do," Alberta said. "Because I never stopped loving you, even though I didn't lift a finger to call you or write you a letter. I don't know why I never did, but I didn't. I always made some kind of excuse, that you wouldn't want to hear from me, or it would only make things worse. I let my ego and my fear get the better of me and I left it alone."

"That's how it was for me," Kylie said. "I had built a life for myself and there was no room in it for Janine. I convinced myself that we were both better off living separate lives, even when I knew she was going down a horrible path."

"And when I reached out to you, you told me to get lost!" Janine screamed.

"Because by that time you were so deep into selling drugs that's all you wanted to do," Kylie said. "You didn't want my help to save you, you wanted my help to get you more drugs."

"The one thing I don't understand, Kylie," Jinx said, "is why you kept quiet about Bambi?"

"She had to," Alberta said. "By the time she found out Bambi was in charge of the whole operation, it was too late."

"That's right," Kylie replied. "As much as what Bambi and Carmichael were doing disgusted me, I was forced to keep quiet."

"If you exposed Bambi, you'd expose your sister too, and you couldn't handle the shame or the scandal because no one would believe you were innocent, you were too close to all the major players," Alberta explained.

"Sounds like you understand me quite well, Mrs. Scaglione?" Kylie asked. "Do you also understand that I can no longer handle the guilt?"

Thankfully, Alberta did. She also knew what Kylie was going to do a second before Kylie did. She pushed the candy cane at Kylie just as the doctor yanked Bambi's gun out of her hand. When she pulled the trigger, instead of shooting herself the bullet was lodged in the ceiling.

Alberta ran for the gun at the same time Bambi did, and Jinx pushed her candy cane toward Janine at the same time Janine pointed her gun at Alberta. Jinx lunged at Janine, landing on top of her and preventing her from raising her hand to shoot. Jinx grabbed Janine's wrist and slammed it onto the floor several times until the gun went free. Lisa Marie ran over and picked up the gun and, for good measure, stomped her foot onto Janine's hand.

Alberta wrapped her fingers around Bambi's gun as Bambi's fingers wrapped around Alberta's throat. The women fell backward, Alberta on top of Bambi and Alberta unknowingly mimicked Jinx's actions and slammed Bambi's arm onto the ground until the gun was released from her grip and fell to the ground. Before Bambi could get up, Lisa Marie ran and picked up the second gun. She stood in the center of the four fallen women and held the guns out to her side.

Lisa Marie looked around the room and smiled.

"Here's a piece of advice my father-in-law used to say," she said. "*Non scherzare con una pazza signora italiana.*"

Alberta started to laugh. "That's right, don't mess with the crazy Italian lady."

"Especially when there are three of them," Jinx said.

Lisa Marie stood in the middle and wrapped one arm around Alberta and the other around Jinx, the guns still in her hands. They were exhausted, they were exhilarated, they were excited. They had done what they set out to do: prove Sergio's innocence and bring him home for Christmas. And they did it with a day to spare.

All three women were thinking the same thing. It had been a long road to get to this point, to be able to stand side by side by side, three generations of Italian women working together and not against one another. It felt good because it felt like family.

The only thing that made them feel better was when the rest of their family, those bound to them by blood and

EPILOGUE

Avremo anche noi un piccolo e felice Natale.

Christmas in an Italian family was always a day of major celebration. But this Christmas the holiday for the Ferraras was even more joyous, more meaningful, and more filled with family and friends than ever before. It would be a holiday to be remembered for decades to come.

Once Janine confessed to killing Natalie and shooting Carmichael, who would make a full recovery, the DA had no choice but to set Sergio free on Christmas Eve. Vinny forced Roxanne to make a public apology to Sergio and his family for the undue stress they were put under due to the state's rash rush to judgment. Sergio accepted her mea culpa with grace because how could he really fault her? Roxanne was as blind to Sergio's innocence as he had been to Natalie's guilt. He knew he needed to contemplate long and hard how he could have allowed one woman with such a questionable past lead him not only astray, but away from his family.

In an attempt to lessen her sentence, Janine cooperated with the authorities and told them all about the drug dealing operation and how Bambi was the mastermind behind getting Flower onto the streets. Bambi wouldn't spend as many years behind bars as Janine, but it would be a long time before she'd be able to buy designer clothes again. No criminal charges were brought against Kylie, but she also suffered. St. Clare's Hospital immediately revoked her position as head of the new research lab and put her on unpaid administrative leave subject to further inquiry into her role in the drug scandal. She had always thought it would be her sister who would cause her public humiliation and, in the end, she took care of that all by herself.

Tommy arrived from Florida just in time to join the rest of his family as Bruno and Vinny ushered Sergio out of the correctional facility and into his family's loving arms.

Through tears, Tommy told his son, "*Avremo anche noi un piccolo e felice Natale.*" They were going to have a very Merry Christmas indeed.

From the correctional facility they drove directly to St. Winifred's Church to hear Father Sal say Christmas Eve mass and were not surprised when Sal led the entire congregation in a standing ovation to acknowledge Sergio's freedom. The homily was filled with the importance of having faith not only during Christmas but all year long.

That night everyone gathered at Joyce's house for a catered spread of the seven fishes. Shrimp, clams casino, grilled octopus, stuffed calamari in tomato sauce, bac-cala—a fancy word for salted cod fish—marinated eel, and whole lobsters with drawn butter. Everyone agreed that Joyce served a delicious meal, because every item on the menu had been catered.

Christmas Day was like watching a classic holiday movie.

Snow was softly falling outside, not enough to make driving treacherous, but enough to make Memory Lake look as if it belonged in the Swiss Alps and not northern New Jersey. Inside Alberta's house, family and friends gathered for a feast that started with cold and hot appetiz-ers, antipasto, charcuterie, shrimp cocktail, and salad, then moved on to the pastas, which included lasagna, ravioli, and gluten-free macaroni to satisfy Jinx's per-snickety dietary needs, and finally the main course of roasted chicken, sausage and cranberry stuffing, roasted vegetables, lemon pepper brussels sprouts, and candied yams.

In keeping with the Ferrara tradition, dessert was an assortment of Entenmann's cakes and some pitchers of Red Herring with a little more prosecco than usual. It was a holiday after all.

As the day ticked on, it was obvious that the family was more aware than ever how lucky they were. They re-alized they had so much to celebrate, big and small. Vinny couldn't wait very long to tell them that a pub-lisher had finally shown interest in his book and he would receive a contract in the new year. *What's Murder All About, Alfie?* was finally going to be published. Helen's Big Sister column was a roaring success, especially after it was revealed that the letters she had received from Noctor J and Mike DeDordo helped bring Natalie justice.

The biggest surprise came during dessert, when Freddy got down on one knee in the middle of Alberta's living room and proposed to Jinx. Through tears of joy, she accepted his hand in marriage and was delighted that the diamond and ruby engagement ring he bought for her fight perfectly on her finger. Freddy said that he was going to ask Jinx privately the night of the Mistletoe Ball, but realized he wasn't just marrying Jinx, but her entire family. The proposal felt more appropriate with an audience.

Having witnessed firsthand how deep Freddy's feelings were for their daughter, Tommy and Lisa Marie gave their wholehearted support to the couple. After screaming, crying, and carrying on for a full ten minutes, Alberta, Joyce, and Helen informed the engaged couple that their wedding would take place in Alberta's backyard in June. Jinx and Freddy didn't even attempt to argue with them.

Alberta looked at Sloan, sitting on the couch with Lola in his arms, and couldn't believe how happy she was in her relationship with him. She smiled at him, and Lola, thinking the smile was for her, meowed back. Sloan wasn't jealous since he knew the majority of Alberta's smiles were only meant for him.

After all the dishes were loaded into the dishwasher and the Tupperware was filled with food that everyone would take home with them, Alberta saw that Lisa Marie had gone outside and was standing in the backyard. Alberta took her mother's quilt from the recliner in the living room and brought it outside.

"You'll catch cold out here," Alberta said.

"I forgot how much I missed this weather," Lisa Marie said.

Alberta threw the quilt around Lisa Marie's shoulders, stretching it to make it long enough so the other end wrapped around Alberta's.

Lisa Marie kept her eyes on Memory Lake when she spoke. "And I forgot how much I missed you, Ma."

Alberta held her daughter a little closer. "I can't tell you how many nights I prayed this day would come. My mother was right, if you pray long enough your prayers really do get answered."

Lisa Marie turned her gaze from Memory Lake, and when she looked at her mother, Alberta saw that she had been crying. Lisa Marie was an adult, a grown woman, and yet she was still Alberta's own, complicated little girl. She opened her mouth to speak, but Alberta stopped her.

"Don't say 'I'm sorry.'"

"But I am."

"You have nothing to be sorry about and neither do I."

"How can you say that? We've wasted so much time."

"No, we haven't, we were just waiting for the right time to come back into each other's lives."

Alberta looked at the snow falling on Memory Lake and felt Lisa Marie lean her head against her shoulder. She tightened the quilt around them and accepted the moment for what it was. A very merry Christmas.

Recipes from the
Ferrara Family Kitchen

ALBERTA'S STUFFED CALAMARI

It looks like it takes forever, but trust me, you can make it under an hour.

Ingredients:

12 calamari tubes—*My mother cut her own calamari and it took forever!*
2 green onions, finely chopped
8 cloves of garlic, minced and divided
½ pound chopped cooked shrimp
½ pound cooked crabmeat, diced
1 tbs lemon juice
¾ cup butter
12 oz. cream cheese, cut into cubes
3 cups milk—*Do not use non-dairy milk no matter what Jinx says!*
10 oz. grated Parmesan and 3/4 cup grated Romano—*I think you know by now you should only use fresh grated cheese!*
1 pinch black pepper
1 (8 oz.) package linguine—*Only use gluten free pasta if you absolutely must!*
24 large toothpicks

Directions:

Preheat the oven to 350 degrees.
Rinse the calamari tubes and pat dry.
In a large bowl, stir onions, 6 cloves garlic, shrimp, crabmeat, and lemon juice.

Spoon some of the mixture into each calamari tube—*Don't overstuff!*

Seal the ends of the tubes by sewing with large tooth-picks—*Some tubes only have one open end*

Arrange in a single layer in a 9x13-inch baking dish

Melt the butter in a saucepan over medium heat; stir in cream cheese and 2 cloves garlic

Gradually whisk in the milk and cook until heated

Remove from heat and stir in Parmesan and pepper

Pour over all of the calamari tubes

Sprinkle 2 tbs. of Romano over each one

Bake uncovered for 20 minutes

While calamari is baking, boil lightly salted water and cook linguine until al dente, approximately 8 minutes

Place linguine on plate, top with stuffed calamari, and pour the sauce over everything

FATHER SAL'S MARINATED ANCHOVIES

Ingredients

2½ lbs. small to medium fresh anchovies—*If you're like
  Alberta you will clean and scale them on your own—
  if you're smart, you'll have your fishmonger do it for
  you!*
The juice of 4 lemons
2 tbs. extra virgin olive oil
4-5 fresh basil leaves
Sea salt, fine

Directions:

Remove the heads from the anchovies—*Do it quickly
and it isn't so bad.*

Rinse and transfer to container.

Season generously with salt—*If you're on a low
sodium diet, eat these on a cheat day or avoid them alto-
gether.*

Pour lemon juice over the anchovies juice.

Cover and refrigerate for 5–6 hours. *You can keep
them in the fridge for a few days, but the longer you keep
them, the more acidic they'll become.*

To serve, remove the anchovies from the lemon juice
and transfer to a tray.

Drizzle on the olive oil and place basil leaves over the
fish.

JINX'S GLUTEN FREE STRUFFOLI

Ingredients:

3 eggs
2 cups all purpose gluten-free flour
$\frac{1}{4}$ tsp. pink Himalayan salt
1 cup almonds, finely chopped
1 cup raw honey
$\frac{1}{4}$ cup coconut oil
Liquid vanilla Stevia or regular sugar
Gluten free vanilla extract
$\frac{1}{2}$ tsp. cinnamon powder
Cooking oil—*keep it Italian and use olive oil*
Sprinkles

Directions:

For the Dough:
Heat about 3-4 inches of cooking oil on medium-low heat in an 8 oz quart pot

While oil is heating, sift flour and place in large glass bowl

Beat 3 eggs and mix with flour—*If the dough is sticky, add another egg*

Knead dough and let it rest for 5-10 minutes

Take small pieces of dough and roll into small balls the size of malt balls

Deep fry in oil until lightly golden brown and drain well

For the Topping:

In the same pot mix the honey, oil, liquid sugar, almonds, cinnamon on low heat to simmer

Turn off heat and let mixture thicken

Don't wait too long to pour in the fried dough pieces and mix together

Pour the honey balls into small bowl and sprinkle with Sprinkles!

VINNY'S CHOCOLATE PANFORTE

Ingredients:

½ cup all-purpose flour—*You can probably use gluten-free flour like Jinx would, but I don't know how that'll affect the recipe. Sorry!*

½ cup honey

½ cup of each of the following: walnuts, hazelnuts, almonds

½ cup of each of the following: dark chocolate, candied lemons, candied oranges, candied cherries, candied figs

1 pinch of each of the following: cinnamon, pepper, cloves, nutmeg

1 sheet rice paper wrapper—*You have to use edible paper otherwise the recipe won't be . . . edible.*

220 g, icing sugar

Directions:

Toast and chop the nuts

Mince the figs and candied fruit

In a large bowl, combine nuts, candied fruit, cinnamon, pepper, cloves, nutmeg, ginger, flour

Cut chocolate into bits and add to mixture

Heat icing sugar, honey, and ½ oz. water in small pan to boil

Remove from heat and add in mixture of fruit, spices, and chocolate

Cover the bottom of a cake pan with edible rice paper and pour in the mixture.

Coat your hands with the flour and spread the mixture on the paper

Preheat oven to 300 degrees, cook for an hour

Remove and cool, then sprinkle with the icing sugar

Connect with

Us

Visit us online at
KensingtonBooks.com
to read more from your favorite authors, see books
by series, view reading group guides, and more.

for sneak peeks, chances to win books and prize packs,
and to share your thoughts with other readers.

facebook.com/kensingtonpublishing
twitter.com/kensingtonbooks

Tell us what you think!

To share your thoughts, submit a review,
or sign up for our eNewsletters, please visit:
KensingtonBooks.com/TellUs.

Grab These Cozy Mysteries
from
Kensington Books